Renaissance Calling

Renaissance Calling

Michael Bernabo

This book is a work of fiction. Names, characters, places, and incidents either are products of the author's imagination or are used fictitiously.

Second Printing, 2017

ISBN-10:	Hard Cover	0-9986993-1-4
	Paper Back	0-9986993-0-6
	MOBI	0-9986993-3-0
	ePub	0-9986993-2-2
ISB-13:	Hard Cover	978-0-9986993-1-8
	Paper Back	978-0-9986993-0-1
	MOBI	978-0-9986993-3-2
	ePub	978-0-9986993-2-5

Impending Imagination, LLC
St. Paul, Minnesota

www.michaelbernabo.com

Dedicated to:

My parents, who not only let me raid their libraries but encouraged me to, and made me read the book before I could see the movie.

My friends, who invite me to role-playing games, exchange stories with me, and spend countless hours talking about being creative.

And everyone who heard me say 'I'm a writer' and smiled.

Acknowledgements

Thank you to Brittany, my editor, who has helped me sharpen my writing voice.

Thank you to Courtney, who took a few ideas for a cover design and ran with it.

Thank you to the friends and family members who critiqued the scenes I was worried about.

Chapter 1

Fox approached slowly, his rifle at the ready, choosing his path through the snow carefully. Something was wrong.

He crept along the shore of a lake somewhere in Walker County. He did not know the name of the lake, nor did he care. Minnesota had too many lakes, and most lakes were too common to hold his attention. This one would have passed into memory and been forgotten if not for the dwelling he had almost missed.

It was not a proper house, standing upright, but a dugout, sunk into the ground, the top of the roof maybe five feet above the snow. It was not uncommon for individuals to build such things, tiny holes where one might scratch out a living while avoiding the tax collectors. But this was a good sized building, large enough for a family.

That alone had piqued Fox's curiosity. Fox moved in closer and his stomach tightened. It was a cold March, and the sun was not high enough to warm the dwelling, yet there was no smoke coming from the poorly disguised chimney. There was a small pen, for goats or pigs, but it was empty, and a sack of feed lay scattered about. And all around the muddy ground were the tracks of horses, many horses.

County yeomen, Fox thought.

The tracks were not fresh. At least one day old, given that they had frozen again in the night. Fox scanned the woods anyway, and saw nothing. He approached the entrance to the dugout. The door was splintered and broken, hanging off one hinge. Fox checked the surrounding once more, then slung his rifle over his shoulder, drew his pistol, and ducked inside.

He understood right away why this dugout looked so peculiar. The walls were concrete, not some poorly built wooden wall or assembly of stones and mortar, but actual concrete. There were cracks and some discoloration from water, but the occupants had worked hard to clean it up and make it presentable. This work was centuries old; only the nobility, or the King himself, could afford something like this now.

This had once been a basement to a cabin or house, built more than four hundred years ago. The house had rotted or burned but the basement had remained. Someone had found it, built a small roof over it, and moved into it. It must have been the luckiest find of the man's life. If it was, his luck had run out. Three bodies lay on the floor. An older man, his hands bound behind him, executed by a bullet to the back of his head, sat crumpled against the wall. A woman, either his younger wife or possibly his daughter, lay on a bed, her throat cut, her dress ripped and exposing her body. And a child, a boy of eight or nine years, sprawled across the floor, his body shredded by a shotgun blast. The rest of the single room was ransacked. Anything that could be was broken, ripped or shattered, and lay strewn about the floor.

Bastards, he thought to himself. Count Walker used yeomen to intimidate his subjects. They were brutal men, who, in a civilized nation, would have been executed for their crimes. But Count Walker and his king wanted cowed subjects, and permitted such excesses.

Fox felt the pit of his stomach drop further when he noticed four beds. Four beds and three bodies. He could search the wreckage for some indication of who was missing, hoping to see one hidden in the wreckage, but he felt that he already knew what had happened. Yeomen had a taste for women, especially young and pretty girls, to do their cooking and laundry and warm their beds at night. Few went willingly. Now they had one more.

Fox left the dugout with a heavy cloak of guilt on his shoulders. He made his way back through the forest.

It's not your fault, he said to himself. He said it over and over as he marched through the snow. *It's not your fault. You didn't make the yeomen attack these people. The guilt is theirs and theirs alone.*

The yeomen attacked these people because they're scared and angry, the voice in his head said, *and you helped with that, didn't you?*

Fox forced himself to continue through the woods. The guilt still followed him.

Fox was more than six feet tall. He was slender – built of straw, some people said – but he was not weak. His black hair hung past his shoulders, and he had trimmed his beard down to a thin line along his chin and lips. His eyes had the glare of someone who spent most of his life out in the wild. He wore traveling clothes, not uncommon in these parts. Indeed, he would have looked like a common, traveling peasant, looking for work, if it were not for his weapons.

The long knife he might have been able to explain away. The pistol was an automatic death sentence, unless he could prove he was a county yeoman or an officer in the Royal Army, neither of which were a possibility for him. And the rifle was not the rifled-musket of a peasant hunter, used for shooting wolves. It was a long, ornate, precision weapon of a Verendrye woodsman.

Verendrye Woodsmen were considered ignorant savages by the peasants; barbarians who could not build houses and ate raw meat and killed with hand-crafted rifles they loved more than women. And if any peasants saw him, they would run for their lives and claim whatever horrors struck their fancy.

Fox was far from ignorant. He had attended school. And not some school of letters for sons of wealthy men. He had attended the Hilltop Archive in Duluth, one of the institutions of ancient knowledge that survived into this Dark Age, guarding itself for the future. One had to prove their intelligence to be accepted to an Archive. Fox was that intelligent, so he knew why the county yeomen were getting aggressive.

Count Walker was scared. He had started the year with fifty-three yeomen. He was down by twenty now. Fox and his friends had killed or wounded them, but only in the eastern half of Walker County. Count Walker was now worried that he would lose the western half, which included the highway and most of the population. He was scared of losing the revenue from the tolls and the taxes of the population, so he was tightening his grip.

Count Walker's yeomen were brutes, bullies in flashy uniforms. They had no skills in a forest, and normally stuck to the roads. That was why so many small families could live in the woods unmolested under normal circumstances. But the yeomen were forced to range further from the highway, looking for observation posts, or signs that someone was looking to haunt the highway. And a family could only get so far away from the roads.

The yeomen had come and found a family hiding in the woods. One that had not shown on their tax census. A family with a small herd of goats and an attractive daughter. Found by yeomen who had lost friends and taken fire. Yeomen were not supposed to die; they were supposed to do the killing. And if they could not find the men killing them, they would avenge themselves upon a poor family in the woods.

Fox forced himself to stop and glanced at the sun. It was getting close to noon. He looked around and realized he had lost track of where he was. He was supposed to be heading south. 'Idiot,' he said out loud. 'Pay attention!'

He looked around and saw a tall tree on a low hill, tall enough for him to see a fair distance. He had a precision scope for his rifle, and a pair of field glasses, so he climbed the tree, pulled out the glasses and looked around.

He had strayed too far west. He could see the highway, a largely mud track through the woods. It was not more than three miles to the west, much closer than he had wanted to be. He spied a town, slightly to his south on the highway. Three or four houses, only one with two stories, surrounded by a score of small dugouts. Smoke drifted from chimneys, and there was some sort of wooden post in the center of town.

Fox frowned to himself. He had walked along the highway between Bemidji and Park Rapids once or twice. One town had a wooden statue, withered into a formless post. He could not remember the name of the town, only that the statue was supposed to have been the woman who founded the town, and that no one had cared for the statue in some time.

He heard something: A cracking of a branch. Fox felt throat suddenly dry. *Please tell me I didn't screw up again!* The last thing he needed was to be captured by Count Walker's yeomen. He doubted any of them would recognize him, but they were too excited right now to be expected to show any leniency to a man marching through their county with a long rifle and a pistol.

Fox slid down into the tree's branches. If they were yeomen, they might not be looking up, and he could hide until they passed, then make his way east away from the highway. He shoved his field glasses into their case and held his rifle in his hands.

He heard the snap again.

Fox saw a figure duck from behind a tree. It was not a man in Walker County's green tunic. It was a boy, eight or nine years old, wearing black clothes. He was rushing his way across the forest, stopping behind trees and looking around. He looked like prey trying to escape a hunter.

Another snap. The boy started, turning around to search the forest.

He saw something and started running flat out. There were more figures in the woods, three of them, chasing the boy through the woods. The boy was running towards his tree. *Bullies*, Fox thought.

The boy tripped over a downed branch. The bullies circled the boy, taunting him.

'Come on, Alice! Stand up!' one of the boys jeered.

Alice?

Fox understood the black clothes now. The boy was an Alvanist, a sect of Christians who lived in small communities across most of the Great Lakes. They believed in hard work, little comfort, and were committed pacifists. Some called male Alvanists 'Alice', a boy being called a girl's name, as an insult. And some targeted them for bullying, for Alvanists would not fight back.

5

The boy reached the trunk of a tree nearby and turned, his back to the wood. The three boys circled him. They were not ten yards away from Fox's tree. None of them knew he was there.

'Oh, Alice,' the leader bully said, 'why did you run? That makes you tired! You don't squeal as much when you're tired. And we want you to squeal.'

'You can't!' the boy cried.

'I can!' the lead bully said, slapping the young child.

'God doesn't want us to fight,' the child sobbed. 'He wants peace.'

The bullies laughed. 'No he don't!' the lead bully slapped the boy again. 'God don't want peace. He wants strength. That's why we have nobles…they's stronger. They answer to the king, because he's stronger. And the king answers to the Great Emperor, because he's strongest of all!'

'So, Alice, if I'm strong, I get to do whatever I want. And I want to hear you cry!' he slapped the boy a third time. Fox noticed the bully simply slapped the boy. He did not punch, did not try to draw blood. He wanted the boy crying and afraid, not hurt.

Fox hated watching. He hated bullies, but the boy had obviously been through this before, and if Fox intervened, the bullies would simply come back later and they might punish the boy for being saved. Not to mention an intervention would alert the locals to his presence. He had to stay silent.

Fox kept his body still and he slowly moved his head and his eyes around to survey the forest. Villages often had extra fields planted within several miles of its location where they might be missed by the assessor, and if a nearby field had adults who heard the children, he might be discovered. He could also avoid watching the bullies attack the boy, and ignore the growing desire to intervene.

'Gah!' the head bully cried out. Fox snapped his head around. Someone else had intervened, but it was not an adult. It was another Alvanist.

Fox saw the largest bully go down as a large branch struck his head. It was an old branch, dead and rotten, and it shattered in an explosion of wood and moss. The bully dropped the boy and fell to the ground. The head bully fell backwards.

The third bully charged the new arrival. Fox knew there was not enough time to swing the branch again, but so did the newcomer. He spun the remnant of the branch and thrust forward like a spear, catching the next bully in the gut.

The newcomer stood over the crying boy the remains of the branch still presented as a sword. 'Leave him alone, Samuel Cartier!'

Fox's eyes widened. *It's a woman!*

A girl would be more appropriate. Sixteen years, maybe more, but not by many. She was a few inches short of six feet, and her hair was long and unbound, most likely unwedded, which was odd for a girl of her age in the countryside. And she was wearing the heavy black dress of an Alvanist. She did not look much like a pacifist, though, standing with a weapon in hand.

'Go home, Samuel,' she said. 'This is wrong.'

'Wrong?' Samuel laughed. The other bullies were standing up now, surrounding the young woman. 'The only thing wrong here, Sasha, is you! Women don't fight, especially not Alvanist women!'

'As long as you try to hurt my brother, I'll fight you,' Sasha said. She glanced to the two bullies at her sides, but she could not move from her position if her brother would not move, and he was curled into a ball, crying. She whispered something to the boy, but he remained where he was. She said something again, still he would not move.

She's going to lose because he won't move. And she won't leave him.

The three bullies charged.

Sasha attacked.

She rushed the bully to her left, the smallest of the three. She swung the small remnant of her branch at his head, knocking him down again but destroying what was left of the branch.

The large bully grabbed her, pinning her arms to her body. She kicked out with her legs, but he held her up so she could not find a target. Samuel rushed up and punched her hard in the stomach; she groaned and ceased struggling. The other bully, standing up again and bleeding from his lip, grabbed the young boy and stood him up as well.

Sasha said something, and Samuel laughed.

'No. Why would I let him go? You two need to learn a lesson. You're weak. You're women and pacifists. The world belongs to the strong! I am stronger than you, so I can do what I want!' Samuel punctuated his point by slapping Sasha. Blood dripped off her lip.

'You can't,' she said.

'Yes,' he slapped her.

'I,' he slapped her again.

'CAN!' he punched her hard, rocking her head back. The bully holding her laughed.

Samuel took a step back to look at his two captives. The boy was crying, staring at the ground, whispering prayers under his breath. Sasha was bleeding, but her breathing was deep, and she glared at Samuel.

'You will not get away with this,' she said.

Samuel turned to Sasha, and strutted over to her again.

'Sasha, you ain't listening. I can get away with this. My father is the Mayor! And he's stronger than your father. The yeomen like him. And who will they listen to?' He laughed. 'You know, I thought it was a shame when you left to be married last year. I had hoped I might get to show you your proper place. But God favors the strong, and he brought you back here, rejected by those Alvanists as too violent. I get to tame you, Sasha Small.'

8

Samuel stood close, still speaking, his voice lower now. Fox could not hear him anymore. He glanced about, and did not see anyone else coming.

When Fox looked back, one of the bullies had a wicked grin on his face; the other looked very nervous. Sasha was struggling and Samuel was reaching for the strings on Sasha's dress.

Four beds, three bodies.

Fox was already out the tree before he realized he jumped.

Everyone flinched as Fox landed. He strode over the roots and mud, raising his rifle to his shoulder, muzzle only inches from Samuel's head.

Everyone was still, frozen by his sudden appearance.

'The world belongs to the strong,' Fox said, 'and I claim the girl. Leave!'

No one moved. The other two bullies looked at Samuel, who was staring straight down the barrel of Fox's rifle, his eyes wide in fear.

'NOW!' Fox yelled. The bullies dropped their captives and ran off into the woods. The boy was again curled into a ball in the mud. The girl stayed on her feet, turning to watch the bullies run off, then back to face Fox. Her eyes ran over his weapons and his clothing; then she took a deep breath, clenched her fists and scowled at him.

'You can claim me, but I'll fight you anyway!'

'NO!' the boy screamed. 'No fighting!'

'Thomas,' Sasha started, but the boy had found his voice.

'Fighting goes against God! Father says so! He says that if you fight, you'll go to hell! You shouldn't fight!' the boy turned and looked at Fox as well. 'NO FIGHTING!' he said, then ran off himself, leaving Sasha and Fox alone.

Sasha glared defiantly at Fox, drawing herself up to her full height and clenching her fists. Her wild hair and bloody lip accentuated her scowl, and her deep breathing was almost a growl.

She was not an intimidating girl, though by no means small. She had common brown hair, and common brown eyes that burned with a righteous fury.

'There's no cause for alarm, Sasha,' Fox said as he slung his rifle over his shoulder. 'I have no intention of harming you.'

'How do you know my name?' she asked.

'I watched for some time before I intervened. You were having a good fight,' he smiled at her.

'There's no such thing as a good fight,' Sasha said quietly, looking at the ground.

'Bullshit,' Fox snapped at her. Her eyes darted to his. 'Your words lack conviction, Sasha. You know it was a good fight! Standing up, outnumbered, defending your family against attackers. That is a good fight.'

Sasha looked at him. He saw confusion in her eyes, and a realization dawned in his head.

'Of course,' he said, 'you're an Alvanist. Fighting is against your religion.' He chuckled. 'No one has ever complimented you on a fight before.'

Sasha shook her head. 'No. They have always been angry at me. My father believes fighting is a mortal sin. And the bullies don't think I should be fighting them.'

'Not surprising,' Fox said. 'If you fight them, you make their oppression harder, and bullies by definition do not like working for what they believed they deserve. And your father - and please do not take offense - but he is a fool, and a small man.'

Sasha smiled chuckled. 'Our family name is Small, woodsman. He is by his name a small man.'

'But you, Sasha Small, are not a small woman. Not if you stand up and fight whenever necessary.' He stopped for a moment and looked at the young woman - he could not consider her a girl - and thought for a moment.

He had a mission, true, and one that would take him far from here. But he could not simply leave this woman. He was supposed to keep an eye out for capable people, who might be useful to the cause.

Sasha Small had courage, enough to face three bullies at once, which was no small feat for a woman raised by pacifists in a world where her likelihood of making it to her wedding night with her virtue intact was slight. And she has moral fortitude; she did the right thing knowing she would be punished. *Maybe . . . .*

'Tell me, Sasha Small, when you fight, what goes through your head?' He saw Sasha hesitate. 'I won't judge. I am just curious.'

Sasha took a deep breath. 'I think that I am better than a dog.'

Fox blinked in surprise. 'I don't understand.'

'When I was younger, a dog bit me. My father said that an animal will bite to protect itself when it feels threatened. But when I first fought off Samuel and his friends, my father said I should not protect myself. A dog can protect itself; I cannot.'

She shook her head. 'My father believed that our superior reasoning means we should not act like animals. I agree. But I don't think I am acting like an animal for defending myself or my brother; I think they are acting like animals for attacking. And when I fight them, I cannot help but feel that I am in the right, despite what my father says.'

Fox smiled at her. He had not expected such an answer. He thought she would say she was angry, or scared, or that she did not know what she was thinking. Peasants were not known for thinking much beyond their farms and their Bibles, but Sasha's response showed she was capable of considering what she was being told. It was the response Fox had dared to hope for.

'Sasha Small,' he said, 'I know several women who think along similar lines. Many of them would have fought the bullies just as you did.'

'And the rest?' Sasha asked.

'The rest would have killed them,' Fox said. Sasha's face paled. 'Oh, I don't believe you would kill those bullies, Sasha Small, but when the yeomen take a notice to you, they won't be scared off by a dead branch and a mean scowl. It'll take blood to remove them, and if you're not ready to spill it in defense of yourself, the yeomen will take you, and your worst dreams will come true.'

Sasha swallowed and nodded. 'I . . . ,' She paused. 'I understand what you're saying. And I believe you.'

'That is wise,' Fox said, and smiled again. Sasha managed a meager chuckle, and watched as Fox dug into his satchel and pulled out a scroll case. It was a small thing, four inches long, dark brown leather with silver embroidery. He held it out to Sasha.

'For you, Sasha Small.'

'What is it?' she took the scroll from his hands.

'It is called the Declaration of Independence. Have you ever heard of it?' She shook her head. 'I am not surprised. The wealth of knowledge lost when the Before Time died is staggering. This document is almost seven hundred years old. It was once revered. Now, it is all but forgotten. I give it to you, Sasha Small, because I believe you will find it a profound document, and I think you will find your situation changing very soon.'

She began to ask a question, but he cut her off.

'Sasha, by now your friends have reached their parents, and they will worry that you are being held in the woods by a savage woodsman. I should be on my way.'

'I don't even know your name,' she said.

'Good,' he smiled. 'I will tell my friends about you, Sasha Small. All I ask in return is you read that, consider its words, and, when asked, tell everyone I headed north.'

Sasha nodded, and Fox smiled. His doubts eased, he turned south, continuing on his way.

Chapter 2

Sasha watched the strange man disappear into the forest. She wanted to follow him – she almost did – but she knew she could not. He saved her. He complimented her, on a fight no less. And he had given her a message that things were changing. But he had not invited her, and she could not ignore that.

I don't even know your name, she thought again. But it was too late.

She looked at the document in her hands. She could not read it now. Samuel and his friends would be back to town soon, and the townsfolk would not respond well to the word of an armed man in the forest. She had to get back. She rolled the scroll up and put it back into its case, then she opened her bodice and slid the small case between her breasts. She glanced around, saw no one, and began to walk home.

Sasha's mind raced as she walked. It was a good fight, he had said.

No one had ever said that to her before. He had smiled at her. He had given her hope. Vague hope, but hope nonetheless.

Her thoughts were interrupted by men moving noisily through the woods. Mayor Cartier was leading a dozen men. Most were armed with pitchforks or scythes. Old Man Sanchez carted his musket; the only firearm Penelope's Haven was allowed to have, to fend off wolves, though Sanchez was all but blind. All wore their mud stained leather pants and woolen sweaters. They stopped as Sasha approached them.

'Sasha!' Mayor Cartier said. 'Samuel said a man attacked you in the forest.'

'The man did not attack me,' Sasha said, but Mayor Cartier talked over her.

'I'm glad to see you got away. Where did he go?'

Sasha paused. 'North. He went north.'

13

'A brigand?' he asked.

'Yes, I think so.' she said.

Mayor Cartier motioned for the men to follow him, then turned to Sasha. 'Go home. Your father will want to have words with you.' He grimaced at her, and then led the men further out into the forest.

Sasha turned west, heading for Penelope's Haven. A bandit? HA! Sasha's father preached about the evils of knowing too much, that knowledge would replace faith. It was a rule Sasha broke whenever possible. And she knew enough to know that the man was not a bandit. Bandits did not roam alone. Bandits did not carry weapons as ornate as the ones she saw. And bandits could not slink through the woods the way he had.

He had to be one of the Northern Woodsmen, the Verendrye. She had heard stories; they were born under trees and died under trees. Their weapons were old, but well cared for and decorated, passed down from generation to generation. They had nobles, but their nobles were too scared to collect more than token taxes or conscripts, and their yeomen never touched the women, for Woodsmen were expert shots at hundreds of yards.

At least she was told. She only had second-hand knowledge, but she was sure she was right. She also knew she had to be quiet about it. Woodsmen were feared by peasants, who considered them to be unwashed barbarians who lived in trees. Knowing one was around might cause more of a scare than bandits. Silence would be better.

Penelope's Haven was surrounded by fields. Once the snow had melted and the fields could be cleaned up, they would alternate between fields for grazing the goats and the town's milk cow, and fields for their crops. Other smaller fields dotted the woods, but the important ones surrounded the town, leaving a wide open space between buildings and forest. Paths had been worn through the snow over the winter, and Sasha followed one around the southern edge of the town, able to see and be seen by the townsfolk.

Sasha trudged along the southern side of the town, approaching the center. The highway did not just cut through Penelope's Haven; it divided the town. The Lutherans lived on the eastern side, more than one hundred of them. The Alvanists, less than fifty souls, populated the western portion. At the center of town was the wooden statue of Penelope, long ago worn into a misshapen log. The only proper buildings of the town surrounded the statue: the mayor's residence, the barn, the meeting hall, and the Small family residence. Everyone else lived in rough shacks or dugouts.

Sasha saw no one outside as she approached her home.

'You're in trouble!' a voice taunted Sasha. Her brother had seen her coming and hidden around the corner, stepping out as she approached the door. 'Father knows you fought. I told him! And I told him that I didn't fight. He's angry with you now. And he's happy with me!' His smile broadened with the joy of a younger sibling who had convinced himself he was superior to his elder.

Sasha saw the smile, and the joy behind it. She also saw the bruises on his face. She wanted to scream at him, to demand why he was happy she was in trouble for standing up for him.

Instead, she said, 'Samuel and his friends should not have fought either.'

Thomas shook his head. 'No one should fight. But I'm the only one who didn't. So I'm the best!' He smiled again and disappeared behind the corner.

Sasha sighed and climbed the short steps to the door.

Though a proper house, it was not much better than the other dwellings in Penelope's Haven. It was one room, with a stone and mortar fireplace on one wall. Dressers and chests, holding the family's clothes and tools, were pushed against the wall and a single table sat in the middle. Two beds, one for her parents and one for her older sister, were pushed off to the side of the room until nightfall. Two sets of rungs built into the wall rose up to the small alcoves where Sasha and Thomas slept, each in their own space across the house from each other.

15

Her mother and older sister were not in the house. Her father was, sitting in his chair by the fireplace. The family Bible was open in his lap. He looked at Sasha as she came in. Sasha closed the door and took several steps towards her father.

'Sasha Evelyn Small,' he said, his voice stern and grave, 'you have been fighting.'

'Yes, Father.'

Alexander Small stood and looked down on his daughter. He was a tall, thin man, with a sharp chin and a sharp nose. His hair was graying, and a thin pair of spectacles perched at the end of his nose. His black Alvanist clothes were fitted to his thin body. He touched her bruised lip and frowned.

'There is no cause for fighting, Sasha,' he said. 'Fighting destroys the soul....'

'They attacked Thomas,' Sasha blurted out, 'and I did not have time to find an adult....'

'Sasha!' he said sharply. Sasha fell quiet. 'We do not fight. Fighting destroys the SOUL! It breeds ill will between men and sows discord within the town. A soul darkened by fighting cannot be ascended to heaven, Sasha. You should know this by now.'

'Yes, Father,' she said.

It was a good fight, the stranger had said.

He father sighed. 'You would be married by now, if you could control your temper. Young Christian Proctor had no complaint about you until you picked a fight with that drunkard.'

'I did not pick a fight, Father! He tried to steal my necklace.' Sasha and her Father had this argument often in the half-year since the cancelled wedding.

'And you fought back, Sasha. No man would want a woman who fights when she should accept the world around her and the sins that exist in it. Such women will spend their lives alone and miserable.'

He said he knew many women who would fight, and some who would kill, Sasha thought, but kept her mouth shut and looked to the ground.

Her father stepped towards her and put his hands on her shoulders. 'God gave me a willful child, Sasha. I love you, and I will pray with you that you learn to live in God's love, and to love all his children, no matter their corruption. But you have sinned today, and I cannot allow that to go unpunished. You are forbidden food until dawn, and you will spend the rest of the day reading in your alcove.' He gave her the Bible. 'May God grant you the wisdom to win your heart from your sinful ways.'

Sasha turned to climb to her alcove, and then turned.

'Father, I know I sinned, but I did what I thought was right. I am sorry.'

Alexander Small simply nodded.

With the Bible in hand, Sasha climbed to her alcove. It was a platform, six feet by four feet, built into the roof, with a small window overlooking the courtyard. Sasha used to share it with her older sister, but now she had it all to herself, and enjoyed the privacy. She closed the curtain, laid on the mattress, and stared out the window.

Sasha studied Penelope's Haven. She did not remember the last time any of the houses had been painted, and the only color some houses had was from new boards used to replace damage from the winter. The mud was everywhere. It had snowed last night, and already the highway and the town square was trampled to mud. There was even some mud on Sasha's window. It covered the ground, the people, and the houses. Sasha hated mud.

Sasha put the Bible down in front of the window and reached into her bodice, pulling out the scroll case. She paused and listened for any sound of someone climbing up to her alcove, but all she heard was her father rocking back and forth in his chair.

Sasha opened the scroll case and pulled out the scroll.

17

The scroll was already like nothing she had ever seen before. The letters were so small, but she could still read them. The ink had not run at all when it was printed. It was also encased in some sort of wax. She ran her fingernails over it, but nothing peeled off. She thought she might be able to cut it out with a knife, but she decided against trying. She did not want to destroy it. She read through the document. Very slowly. She did not understand the full meaning of every word. She whispered some of the words to herself, sounding out unfamiliar vocabulary. She had not yet figured out why the strange man would give this to her.

'Sasha?' someone whispered. She heard the steps creaking as someone crawled up. Sasha quickly hid the document and the scroll case under her mattress.

'Come up,' she said.

Sasha's elder sister, Michelle, slid the curtain aside and heaved her pregnant belly into Sasha's alcove. She stopped and took several deep breaths. 'I forgot how hard that is.' She pulled the curtain back and produced a small bread roll. 'From Mother.'

Sasha took the roll. It had been broken in half and sealed back together with honey. 'Thank you.'

Michelle smiled. 'You're welcome. Now eat, and I'll just take a nap for the next three weeks.' She closed her eyes. 'Thomas told me what happened.'

Sasha sighed. 'I didn't know what else to do. We were too far away to get help, and I had to act . . . .'

'I know, I know,' Michelle said. 'And I know what Father said, and I know that Thomas takes after him. I know many things are unfair and that they all make life harder. That is the one fact of life we are all aware of. I think it is unfair that my husband shared my bed for but one year before he was conscripted. You think it is unfair that you are punished harder for protecting Thomas than Samuel Cartier is for bullying him. That is life.' Michelle stretched her back. 'So is this.'

'What did Mother say?'

'She blames Mayor Cartier for not giving Samuel enough work to keep him busy. But she agrees you need guidance. She did want you to be safely married in Duluth by now.'

'Right,' Sasha said. The Proctors had brought Alvanism to Minnesota decades ago, and her father had arranged the marriage through correspondence. Her mother wanted her out of the countryside and into the city, where the Alvanists were more accepted. One encounter with a drunkard, however, and her planned future had been destroyed. Father had been angry; Mother had been disappointed; Sasha was disappointed to return to Penelope's Haven, but relieved that she would not have to marry a man she had met only a few days before.

'I can't imagine I would be happy living with Christian Proctor,' Sasha said. 'He would have me fat and pregnant by now.' She paused and looked at her sister in embarrassment.

Michelle Small was five years older than Sasha, but looked to be Sasha's twin, except for Michelle's pregnancy. But where Sasha could get riled up by bullies, Michelle was never flustered by anything. Even the insult Sasha had inadvertently thrown her way was forgotten as soon as it was heard.

Michelle just smiled instead. 'You'll find your way somehow, Sasha. God knows what that is,' she looked at Sasha, whose face turned red in response. Her smile flattened out. 'I do pray that you will learn to accept yourself, Sasha. There is too much to enjoy in the world to waste it as an old spinster watching over other's children. And I can't imagine you'd be happy wasting away in a factory.'

'I'll not whore myself, in any way,' Sasha growled.

'I know.' Michelle watched Sasha finish off the last of the roll. 'I was washing with some of the other women, including Mrs. Cartier, and it was brought up that Mayor Cartier and Father have had a discussion regarding you . . . and Samuel.'

Sasha frowned at Michelle for a few seconds before the words connected. 'No,' she sat up. 'NO! How could Father even think

19

that?' She dropped her voice to a whisper. 'Father wants me to join with the boy I fight with?'

'Father seems to think that if you and Samuel were to be married, you both would be forced to discard your childish conflict and grow up.'

'I can't believe Mayor Cartier would allow his son to marry an Alvanist!'

Michelle shrugged. 'Not that anything is written yet. God may have plans for you, and Father certainly won't stop until you're placed.' Michelle shrugged. She scooted over to the ladder down to the floor, looking at Sasha once she had her feet placed.

'If you're going to pray, Sasha, pray for acceptance. Father is right; you cannot change the world, and you should learn to accept what is before you.' She disappeared, hauling herself down the ladder.

Sasha watched her go, then closed the curtain behind her sister. Her father often preached the virtue of accepting the world and the sinful people in it. He had preached it when her oldest brother, Charles, had been conscripted into the King's Army four years ago. He had preached it when her brother-in-law had been conscripted last year. Whatever ill tiding threatened them, her father preached acceptance. And he was wrong.

Sasha could not explain why she felt that way, only that she always had. She often felt guilty that she did not follow in her family's path, but she did not accept the world. There was too much wrong with it. And the more people who tried to convince her to accept the world, either for moral reasons like her Father, or so they can victimize her like the Cartiers, the more she wanted to challenge the world.

And only one man had ever commended her. She felt under her mattress for the scroll and pulled it out. The world is changing, he had said. The man she wanted to follow told her to read this. This was important.

Sasha rolled over and started to read again. *What do you want me to know?*

♦♦♦

Mayor Cartier sent young Jim Webber north to Walker Estate to warn of possible bandits. The town had several horses, mostly draft animals for plowing, but one was a riding horse for just such an occasion, and Jim Webber was the smallest, best rider they had. But the best riding horse in a place like Penelope's Haven was still a broken down old horse that made the trip of fifteen miles in just over three hours, and the short day had all but ended by the time he reached Walker.

No one expected anything until late the next day. The yeomen of Walker County were nothing if not apathetic to the plight of the peasants they were nominally in charge of protecting. The past three emergency rides to Walker had resulted in Jim Webber walking his horse home the next day with word that the report had been acknowledged. But the next morning, not an hour past dawn, the town was shaken by the thunder of hooves.

More than a dozen yeomen rode into town. They wore brown leather riding pants, pine green jackets with yellow facing, and black tricorn hats. The leader wore broad shoulder boards and gold braids. All were armed with swords and a mixture of guns, mostly shotguns and carbines, though one had a wicked looking automatic with a large drum clipped to the bottom.

At the first sign of the yeomen, the peasants of Penelope's Haven moved into action. The yeomanry had expectations for hospitality, and in the fifteen years since the king and his nobility ascended in Minnesota, the peasants had learned how to placate them. Stores of wine and food, saved just for yeomen, were broken out; yeomen did not eat normal peasant gruel, but expected better sustenance, bacon and sweet breads, freshly warmed and served hot. Chairs and tables were brought out into the courtyard. The town's teenage girls, Sasha included, were assigned the duties of serving food and drink to the yeomen, while anyone who could not be busy elsewhere stood in a group around the statue, quiet and submissive. The officer in charge of the yeomen, with the shoulder

21

boards and the braids, disappeared into the Mayor's residence with Mayor Cartier and Alexander Small.

Sasha carried a water jug, filling cups as requested. In some ways, it was a typical yeomen visit. The yeomen were boisterous and crass, comparing the girls serving them in ways that made the peasants blush. Two of the girls responded positively, seeking the attention of the yeomen by smiling and unbuttoning the tops of their blouses, but most kept their eyes down and their minds on their duties. Yeomen were known for wandering hands, and Sasha felt a few hands caress her legs through her dress or pinch her bottom as she filled water cups. The yeomen demanded that the abuses be accepted as their 'due hospitality', to further remind the peasants of their place.

As Sasha suffered through service and hands, she noticed subtle differences. There were six more yeomen than normal, two of whom always watched the crowd of peasants. Two others were walking around the town with their weapons in hand, surveying the surroundings. Everyone had their weapons within reach, either on their shoulder or laying on the table. The yeomen were on guard. Did the man with the rifle worry them that much?

Someone grabbed Sasha's elbow. Sasha jumped, but her father's voice hissed through gritted teeth. 'You are needed, Sasha,' he said, pulling her away. She passed her jug on to another girl and followed her father to the Mayor's House. Samuel was being escorted from the house by his own mother. He glanced at Sasha as he left, but made no effort to talk to her.

Sasha remained quiet as they entered the Cartier residence. Mayor Cartier kept the largest house in Penelope's Haven, with a separate kitchen and two bedrooms, one for him and his wife, another for his children. The central room was used as the official place of work for Mayor Cartier. A wooden table was varnished to a dull shine and surrounded by a handful of wooden chairs with cushions on the seats. Where most houses had tools and shelves on the walls, Mayor Cartier has his adorned with papers, including a small painting of King Xavier, King of North Mississippi, and Great Emperor Tiheam the Great, Lord of the Imperial Commonwealth.

Mayor Cartier sat in his chair on one side of the table. Across from him sat the yeomen officer. Both looked at Sasha as she came in.

'Yeoman-Lieutenant Marks, this is my daughter, Sasha Small,' Alexander said. Sasha curtsied and glanced at the Yeomen-Lieutenant.

Yeoman-Lieutenant Marks was not a kind-looking man. His nose had been broken sometime in the past and never healed correctly. Instead of Alexander Small's skinny frame or Mayor Cartier's hefty bulk, Marks was muscular. Sasha saw his eyes gaze up and down her body; she could not decide if he wanted to rape her or eat her.

'You were attacked in the woods,' he said. Sasha nodded. 'Describe the man.'

Sasha was tempted to describe Samuel, but no one would care. She also wanted to lie about what she had seen, but Samuel had already given his description. She told the truth.

'You said he went north. Did you see him go that direction?' Sasha nodded. 'How did you know it was north? Why not south?'

'I know the hills around this town, sir,' she said, 'and I know he went north.'

'Ha!' Mayor Cartier slapped the table. 'The bastard's heading for those brigands to the east.'

Yeoman-Lieutenant Marks said nothing. 'What did you and the man talk about?'

Sasha turned red. 'He . . . ,' she stopped. She did not know what to say. She could not tell him about his praise, or the document he had given her. She looked at her shoes and tried to think.

Alexander spoke up. 'He made some advances on my daughter's virtue, to be sure, as any base animal would.'

'It is good that I moved fast to clear him out of the woods,' Mayor Cartier said, 'lest young Sasha lose her maidenhood to a bandit.'

Sasha could not imagine Mayor Cartier moving fast for anything, and Yeoman-Lieutenant Marks scoffed. He looked back at Sasha. 'Is that correct, Sasha?' he asked.

Sasha nodded. She hated to make the man in the forest a villain, but she saw no other choice. 'He had claimed me, he said, but I ran. He chased me for a little while, but gave up and hiked north.'

'We did protect her maidenhood!' Mayor Cartier cackled as he picked up a wine glass. Yeoman-Lieutenant Marks looked at Sasha. Sasha cringed slightly. There was something about the look he gave her that frightened her.

'I'm glad for it,' she said to Mayor Cartier. 'I have no wish to go soiled to my husband's bedchamber.'

'Are you spoken for?' Yeoman-Lieutenant Marks asked.

'I have heard tell that I'm promised to Mayor Cartier's son, sir,' she said, glancing at the Mayor before staring at her feet.

Sasha could not see her father's reaction, as he stood behind her, but he made surprised 'harrumph.' Mayor Cartier choked on a mouthful of wine but did not spit it out. Yeoman-Lieutenant Marks made no reaction.

'Very well then,' he said. He did not sound like he believed Sasha, and that worried her, but he made no effort to expose any of her lies and gestured to Alexander to escort her out.

'Where did you hear that?' Alexander asked once they were outside, turning on his daughter and speaking in a hushed tone.

'I hear things,' Sasha said, not wanting to give her sister up. 'Do you really imagine me and Samuel Cartier, Father?'

Alexander looked down on his daughter. 'Two masters cannot share a house, Sasha. One must bow to the other, and the supremacy of the masculine over the feminine is well established. If married, you must bow to Samuel, and find yourself welcome in the roles of wifedom and motherhood.'

Sasha often quarreled with her father, but rarely had she felt such a need to strike at him. Instead she nodded, turned and walked back to her duties with the yeomen. In fact, she was not surprised.

Her father's view of the world made him seek out challenges to endure, and he was proud that he endured them. For him to choose the worst possible option for her, to force her to endure her own challenges, was exactly what he would do. He expected she would accept his view of the world through such endeavors. She did not like that idea at all.

A yeoman pulled her into his lap and pawed at her breasts. Sasha fought her way clear and made her way to refill the water jug, as her attacker endured the jeers of his colleagues. It was the yeomen or Samuel, and neither option appealed to her.

I have to make my own option, she realized. *One for me.*

Chapter 3

'Stop fussing!' Abigail Small said. Thomas froze so his mother could wipe dirt off his cheeks. 'There. Sasha, are you ready?'

'Yes, Mother,' Sasha replied. She was up in her alcove, reading the document again. She was reading it every chance she could. She had taken to carrying it in her bodice so she had it with her at all times. She hid it again as her mother fussed about below. Sasha was pleased, for once, that she was large enough to hide the scroll casing. No one ever suspected.

'Are we all ready to go?' Michelle asked. No one said no, so she led them out.

It was warm, as the March thaw removed traces of winter. The family could walk to the town hall without heavy coats and hats. Thomas eyed the mud with a fondness he would indulge in if his mother had not been standing there. Sasha held Michelle's arm as they navigated a larger puddle.

Thomas stopped before an intersection of muddy paths and turned to his family. 'Sasha, you are not going to heaven!' he declared. 'You fight! No one who fights goes to heaven. Jesus won't let you! It will be the rest of the family, on a cloud, forever, without you!'

Abigail turned her stern gaze on Thomas. Michelle's jaw dropped. 'Thomas!' she said.

Sasha just shook her head. 'You want me to be punished, Thomas. That is judging me, not accepting me. Father says that is a form of violence, and that means you won't go to heaven.'

That was not really something their father had said, but Thomas was too young to know that. Instead, his face turned to horror. 'Mom,' he whined, 'tell Sasha I am too going to heaven!'

Abigail looked at her youngest children. 'I pray that all my children go to heaven,' she said, shooing Thomas towards the hall.

Michelle chuckled at her sister and the two continued on.

♦♦♦

Penelope's Haven had three large buildings; the mayoral family residence, the barn, and the town hall.

The town hall was a simple building, one large room with a storage shed attached. Benches and tables were either set out or pushed to the side. On Sundays it doubled as the town church, hosting the Alvanist mass at eight and the Lutheran mass at ten. There was no functional difference between the two services. Both Alexander Small and the Lutheran mass leader, an elder woman named Teresa who did nothing in the village but read the Bible and yell at the children, stood on a table at the front of their congregation, leading the mass from their elevated position.

Alexander stood at the door, welcoming each member of his community to the hall. He had been the leader of the Alvanist community in Penelope's Haven for more than ten years. In most communities, there would be a series of leaders, each leading from one Easter to the next. Penelope's Haven was too small, and too few members could read well enough. Alexander was allowed to remain the leader, and he took no small pride in that fact, when he allowed himself to.

Alexander was a good leader for the Alvanists. Every week, he had a different member help with the mass, reading scripture and leading songs. Alvanist mass and their lives in general were oriented towards group participation, and Alexander worked hard to make every member of the group welcome. Today, it was Mrs. Neilson, who led the first song and read the first scripture: a reading from Isaiah, Chapter 11.

Alexander knew Sasha had heard this before, but she made no face at the word. She may have flinched at Mrs. Neilson's harsh voice, but she was not the only one. The Alvanist faith was one of community. An individual was important, but their faith was as part of the group. Sasha was not expected to overcome her faults by herself, but by working within the community.

Everyone was expected to help her, and Alexander would guide this process. Alexander loved all of his children: one son, and a son-in-law, conscripted and serving in the King's army, in the wagon trains; a pregnant daughter, another headstrong; and a young son who looked to God for his future. All had their own challenges. Sasha's was ever-present, and Thomas' were yet to come, but he loved them.

Sasha was a good girl. She was polite and always did her duty when yeomen came or chores were required. As a younger girl, she had often challenged his teachings, asking 'why' more than her siblings did. She had stopped asking the last few years, but he suspected the questions remained.

Oh, that I could help you, my daughter. Ask me the questions that trouble your soul, and I will answer them and tame that beast within you.

Mrs. Neilson led another song, then read from the New Testament, a speech by Jesus on the importance of loving your enemy. Everyone knew why these readings were being done. Sasha was not the only member of their community to break their commandments. Even Alexander, decades ago, had suffered through being the target of a mass. But it was what was necessary for the community to guide a troubled soul towards a harmonious place.

As a third song ended, Mrs. Neilson stepped off the front table. Alexander stood and stepped on the bench to stand atop the table. His long legs allowed him to climb effortlessly. Mrs. Neilson had to hop down.

Alexander towered above the congregation, his height and the table working together so he could look down upon them all. He had a secret pride in the power he wielded when he stood in front of these people, though he believed it to be the Will of God.

'We are all, all of us, men. We are all born in His image, we follow the teachings of His prophets and His Son, and we die to live with Him eternally. But we are not Him, nor His Son. We are but men and women, who live with flaws to our character, and suffer the pains of sins those flaws bring to our lives. "Sin is a mark upon the soul, a blemish that God sees through any words or thoughts we erect around the deed." But a sin by itself is not a permanent scarring of our immortal being. No, my friends, it is a start, but it is not the end.

'Once a sin is done, it is annulled or validated through the actions of the sinner. When a sinner recognizes that he has sinned, when he prays to God for His forgiveness, and when he looks into his heart for the root cause of his sin, he can absolve himself of the sin. He will always carry it with him, in the lesson he has learned, but it will not bar his entry through the gates of heaven.

'Or he can ignore the sin. He can say to God 'I have not sinned.' But man does not tell God what to do. God tells man. If God says you have sinned, then you have sinned. And a man, who ignores God's commandments, takes the sin on his soul and multiplies it, adding new sins onto new sins until his soul is black.

'My friends, we do not live in an easy world. The world challenges us to prove our worth on a daily basis. We see armed men come to take what they will. We see a family starve despite hard work. We see men distracted by things that matter little in God's eyes.

'I beg you to recall three years ago. A sunny summer's day, no different from a hundred other summer days. But on this day, we all heard a drone, echoing through the forest. We asked ourselves, what could it be? We gathered, and then we saw. It was an aero-plane, a device built to travel through the air, adorned with the King's Emblem and colors. We all saw it. And for weeks, our children swept through town, arms outstretched, each claiming they would someday fly. They lost themselves to something that does not matter.

'Does that aero-plane change anything for us? Should we wish to fly above the earth, where only God should be found? Should we pray to be the men who built that contraption? I tell you, my friends; such men had no sooner finished that one device when someone demanded from them a better one. That is no life for a God-fearing man.

'We live simple lives, as God intended. We raise our children, grow our crops, and build our homes. We do this because it is the simple life that gives us the clarity to live the life God wants us to live. Even then, we are tempted and tested. It is no easy thing to live the life we live.

'This last week, two of my children faced such a test. We all know children can be aggressive in their games, and their aggression can turn to bullying. My son, Thomas, found himself the target of such a game. He faced this test by running. He did not fight. He hoped that by removing himself from the situation, the boys would lose their aggression. But the boys gave chase, their aggression overpowering their better judgment.

'My daughter, Sasha, saw this chase begin. She had her own test to face. She could ignore her brother's plight. She could go and get an adult to bring maturity to the children and end the conflict. But Sasha did not think, and with good intentions in her heart, she rushed into a fight. She blemished her soul to try and protect her younger brother. Good intentions, but a sin nonetheless.

'There was violence. There was blood spilt. The situation may have continued to deteriorate, had a barbarian from the north not attacked the children with firearms and demanded primal rights to my daughter. The children rightly fled this man.

'There is blame for many in this story. But there is redemption for one, today. Sasha knows what she did is wrong. She knows she erred. No matter what her intentions were, violence is never an appropriate response. She knows this, but she did not think before she acted, and she has sinned.

'Sasha has received the punishment of the family; she is restricted to bread and water for two weeks, and will have plenty of time with the Bible, so that God's words may reach into her soul.

'But our community is not based on the individual, or the family. As our founder, Saint Alvin of Albany, said in his Treatise, "We are a community before God; the mark on one soul marks us all, and the absolution of that mark is a quest for every member of the community." We all must help Sasha to receive the word of

God and atone for her sins. We are a community before God, and we are all responsible.'

The Alvanists all stood up. 'We are all a community before God,' they echoed. They faced Sasha as they spoke, and those close enough put their hands on Sasha's shoulders.

'We are all responsible for each other,' Alexander said. The community echoed his words:

'In God's light we live our lives together,

In God's word we hear peace and acceptance,

We live our lives as a beacon to Man,

Live that others can look to as an ideal,

We accept the lives of our members,

And bear responsibility for their souls accordingly,

In the name of God, His Son Jesus Christ, and the Love of Man, we pray for you.'

Alexander finished the prayer, then waited for the congregation to follow. 'Sasha, hear our love and feel our support. We will not give up on you, Sasha Evelyn Small. You are one of us.'

◆◆◆

Sasha felt the hands on her shoulders and heard the voices of the Alvanists in the town hall. She had been here before; often as the recipient of the Alvanists' support, a few times as one of those chanting.

She was expected to stay silent until the end, when she would respond in the expected words.

As her father finished the prayer, she began her response.

'I am an Alvanist, and a part of this community, before God,' she said.

31

The scroll base in her bodice seemed to burn.

'I am responsible to my friends and my family.'

The man in the forest smiled at me.

'In God's light I live with others. In God's word I hear peace and acceptance'

It was a good fight, he said.

'I live my life as a beacon to Man. I live that others will follow my ideal, as others are a beacon to me.'

You know right from wrong, and you're ready to fight for it. Even if you know you're going to lose.

'I accept the lives of my members, and accept responsibility for their souls as if they were my own.'

Life, Liberty and the Pursuit of Happiness.

'In the name of God, His Son Jesus Christ, and the Love of Man, I submit myself for atonement, to clean my soul of the sins that blacken it.'

She said the words. She said them with her father standing over the congregation. Her mother stood immediately to her right, her hand on Sasha's shoulder and a pleasant smile on her face. Michelle stood to her right, squeezing her hand. Thomas leaned in from the far side of their mother, holding Sasha's other hand. All of the congregation, fervently hoping that God's word would guide her towards a peaceful future.

Sasha felt her soul change. She thought it could be God, guiding her heart towards a future, but it was not a future in this hall. Sasha had often hoped for a revelation, something to make her feel at home.

Instead, she had a revelation that home was not here.

I am not an Alvanist. I do not belong here.

The words stilled her tongue as the Alvanists sang their last hymn.

What am I going to do?

Chapter 4

Penelope's Haven celebrated several holidays. The Lutherans and the Alvanists celebrated Christmas and Easter together, as one community, in the town hall, the only two times during the year when the celebrations were held jointly. The Lutherans celebrated the New Year, the Alvanists did not. By king's decree, three additional holidays - the King's Birthday, the Great Emperor's Birthday, and the Founding of the Kingdom of North Mississippi- were scattered throughout the year. Mayor Cartier organized brief celebrations on those days, but they were half-hearted.

Sasha did not care for most of those holidays. There were fine feasts on Christmas and Easter, but the ceremonies droned on. The king's holidays were never taken seriously by the inhabitants, and much to Sasha's chagrin, she had been born on the same day the kingdom had been founded. It was a distinction she could have lived without. She had always wanted to celebrate New Year's with the Lutherans, but her father has expressly forbade it, keeping watch on her all night to keep her from joining the festivities under the cover of darkness.

There was an additional holiday that came once a month. Sometimes it was early, sometimes it was late, and no one knew exactly when it would come. This March, it came on the Wednesday after Sasha's revelation in the town hall.

Sasha was hauling water from the nearby lake towards town. She led a small group of teenagers. It had not snowed recently, so the path was well worn as they handled their loads, a thankful blessing. They were almost home when one of the teens gasped at two horsemen who trotted up the road. They were not the green-jacketed yeomen from Walker County. They wore plain brown clothes, wide brimmed hats, and carried short carbines. Sasha spied them, and smiled, as did every other person who saw the pair ride up.

It was Caravan Day.

Penelope's Haven was not large enough to have a dedicated general store. Instead, the townsfolk purchased items from the Hollander Company Caravan, a large wagon train that meandered through the countryside from Duluth to Fargo and back. Hollander Caravans travelled the same route, so the teamsters and guards and accountants who rode the wagons were as friends to the peasants who purchased their wares. And as friends, they brought good will and laughter along with their goods. It was like a fair when a Hollander Caravan stopped in a town.

Mayor Cartier and Alexander Small would deal with the caravan captain, a genial man named Augustino Madero. They could not spend freely. Penelope's Haven saved only the portion of their harvest allotted to feed them for the next year. The rest was taken by the Tax Column, and once the County Assessor had tallied his totals, Penelope's Haven was given gold for the excess harvest they had grown. In a county as poor as Walker County, it was a meager amount of gold, and other than wine for the yeomen and some more feed, it was jealously guarded. Every tool that had to be replaced was one fewer coin for the future.

Sasha, rushing to get the water to her mother, saw the wagons coming down the road. A score of mounted rifles, certified by the king to carry weapons in escort of the Hollander Company's caravans, rode alongside massive wagons. Sasha had seen one get stuck in the mud several years ago; it took hours to unload everything, pull it free, then reload it. Teams of oxen and draft horses hauled the wagons. Dozens of people sat on the driver's bench and on the wagon sides, waving at the people coming in from fields and pens to welcome their friends.

Augustino Madero rode forward to meet with Alexander and Mayor Cartier. He waved to people as he passed them. He was well-dressed; not as colorful or ornate as the yeomen, but clean. He smiled. He was polite.

Behind him, on a smaller horse, trotted a pretty girl, fifteen years old. She had long, jet black hair, a wide smile, and tan skin like her father. She wore a dress with flower on it; it was dirty and worn, but prettier than any dress in Penelope's Haven. She tied her horse next to her father's, then turned to see Sasha standing nearby.

'Sasha Small,' Mariposa Madero said with a big smile, 'I do hope you have some trouble to tell me about.'

'I do, if you can bring one thing to lunch.'

'What's that?'

'A dictionary,' Sasha said.

Mariposa Madero was Sasha's only true friend. She was shorter than Sasha, with a carefree spirit, who treated everyone with the same smile and laugh. The Hollander family was not nobility, but they were among the richest families on the continent, and the laws protecting their caravans and employees, even Mariposa, were strict and final. She looked like Sasha imagined every young woman should look: free and unrestrained.

Sasha and Mariposa walked to Sasha's home. They always lunched in Sasha's alcove, watching the square through the window. It took some time to make the short travel. Other girls would say hello to Mariposa, who had inherited her father's pleasant nature and answered every call. The more adventurous boys would say hello as well, hoping to catch some of Mariposa's affection. Mariposa dismissed them politely, without offending anyone. Sasha saw Samuel Cartier stare at Mariposa with no small longing, but he refused to approach her while Sasha was in proximity.

Soon enough the pair were ensconced in Sasha's alcove, a lunch spread out before them. Mariposa always brought a fine lunch for them to share, much better than the meager meals Sasha had on a daily basis. The Hollander Corporation spent large amounts of money providing their caravan captains with supplies just for these occasions. Because it was spring, the rich bounties of the previous year were largely gone, leaving canned foods and salted pork, but still a feast by all accounts. Mariposa pulled the dictionary she had taken from her father's small private library and hidden in the basket.

'So,' Mariposa said, 'why a dictionary?'

Sasha closed the curtain, opened her bodice and pulled the scroll out. Mariposa took the scroll and read it. Sasha watched for her reaction.

Sasha was not sure why Mariposa had focused on Sasha as a friend in Penelope's Haven, but she was glad for it. Mariposa had traveled all over Minnesota, even down to the Royal Cities, where the great rivers merged and the king held court. Her whole family worked for the Hollander Corporation, and with her uncles she had sailed to the Archduchy of Sault Sainte Marie and rode the rails as far west as the Earldom of Bismarck. She could read fast and do her numbers better than most men. She often joked that if she had been born thirty years earlier, under the old Republic of Minnesota, she could have lived her life as a leader in the company; then again, she said, most women in those positions did not survive the Conquest.

Mariposa read the document quickly, and then looked at Sasha with wide eyes. 'Dios,' she said. 'Do you know what would happen if anyone found you with this?'

Sasha nodded and related the story of where it came from. She described the fight, and the man, and the questions the next day. Mariposa listened with rapt attention.

'It has been a busy week for you, hasn't it?' Mariposa asked with a smile.

'Do you know anything about this?' Sasha asked. 'Do you know what Great Britain is? Or the United States of America?'

Mariposa thought for a moment. 'I have never heard of Great Britain. The United States, I think that was one of the Empires from the Before Time.' She read the list of names at the bottom of the document.

Sasha saw that. 'You don't think the Virginia there is the same Virginia City east of us.'

Mariposa shook her head. 'No. I recognize some of those names. New York is a city several thousand miles east of us; the Carolinas are south of that, I think. There may be a Virginia out that way . . . .'

She trailed off. Her eyes narrowed in concentration as she looked out the window. Sasha let her think, turning her attention to the sandwich until Mariposa turned back.

'Sasha,' she said hesitantly, 'our company gets reports, from the Crown, about bandits and problems. We received one for Walker County a few weeks ago.'

Sasha gasped in surprise. Walker County? Nothing ever happened in Walker County. Even the last bandit company had moved through the county without much in the way of looting. 'Did you read what it said?'

'My father put it in the caravan lockbox, so yes,' Mariposa said with a smile. 'It seems that someone has been killing bandits and yeomen in your county, not twenty miles from here.'

Sasha was shocked. Twenty miles! Walker County was a square only fifty miles to a side. She had never heard anyone was killing yeomen. And she didn't even know a bandit company was in Walker County.

Sasha closed her mouth and felt anger rising. Her father did not believe in learning about the outside world. Knowing about the world made you want to change it; he would rather be ignorant and focus on the task at hand. Penelope's Haven received broadsheets, either from the caravan or the occasional rider, but rarely would Alexander let the Alvanists read any of them. Sasha stole them when she could, but it was never often enough to feel in touch with the world outside Penelope's Haven.

'There were bandits in Walker County,' Sasha said, her voice low with anger.

Mariposa nodded. 'What I heard, and read, is that a small company of maybe twenty bandits occupied a town east of Walker Estate for the winter. The yeomen learned of them, but figured they'd wait until spring, 'cause the bandits wouldn't have enough food to last through the winter and they'd be starving come the thaw. But New Year's Eve, during a small blizzard, with the bandits drunk and ravaging the town, someone killed most and left two alive, when morning came. One of them escaped to Walker

Estate. He told the Count his story, said it was soldiers who killed them, then was hanged as a bandit.

'Count Walker figured the bandit was too scared to tell the truth, that it was peasants and not soldiers. But armed peasants are a threat to the count, so he sent yeomen to round up the peasants and punish them. That was two months ago,' Mariposa leaned in, 'and he's lost almost twenty men.'

Sasha let the story sink in. 'The yeomen were here, after my encounter, they looked wary. How many yeomen does Count Walker have?'

'Less than fifty,' Mariposa said, 'much less now. We carried recruitment papers to offices in Duluth and Fargo, and sent more to Saint Cloud and the Royal Cities. Most likely, he's trying to get more.'

'Wow,' Sasha said.

'Anyway,' Mariposa waved her hand, 'I wonder if this man, who gave you this, was one of them.'

'A bandit?' Sasha asked.

'No,' Mariposa shook her head, 'a Mardurer.'

'A what?'

Mariposa frowned. 'I don't rightly know where it comes from,' she said, 'but I heard someone in Walker call them that. I think it's something the Count called them.' She shrugged, and said something in Spanish. 'Maybe he was a Mardurer.'

'I thought he was a Woodsman, from the north,' Sasha said, disappointed.

Mariposa smiled. 'No reason he can't be both. These Mardurers have been killing yeomen on the roads, using guns. They probably have a Woodsman or two amongst them.' She looked at Sasha. 'What are you thinking?'

Sasha paused before answering and peered around the edge of the curtain. The rest of the house looked empty, no sign of any other family members. Satisfied, she turned to Mariposa, and took a deep breath

'I'm not an Alvanist,' she said. She forced herself to speak slowly. 'I love my family, but I am not an Alvanist. I read these words, and I know I'm meant for something else. I don't know what, but it's not here. If this man was a Mardurer, then I guess I'm also a Mardurer. At least I mean to be.'

She looked at Mariposa, wondering what her friend was going to do. Mariposa thought for a moment before she responded.

'I can't really say I'm surprised,' she said. 'I always figured someday I'd be hiding you in one of the wagons, carting you off to one city or another wrapped in a rug. Are you just going to walk there?' she asked.

Sasha shrugged. 'I really haven't planned nothing. Other than the realization that I need to get out of this place.'

Mariposa bit off a response, thought, then said it anyway. 'You go with your father to Walker Town, right?'

Sasha nodded. Alexander Small was the town assessor, appointed by Mayor Cartier. Alexander never promoted the idea of government work, but was swayed by arguments of community need, and had looked at the duties as another challenge to accept. Mayor Cartier was freed from a job he did not want, and gave the villagers another man to grumble about. Sasha, in the absence of a home of her own to take care of, helped her father in the assessor duties. If anything, they let her work on her math. 'We're riding up to Walker next week, to meet with the county assessor.'

'Where do you stay?'

'The Shining Crown,' Sasha said. Of the two inns in Walker Town, the Shining Crown was the more respectable, and more quiet.

'Ever been to the Two Crossed Tools?'

Sasha scoffed. The Two Crossed Tools was the other inn, the less savory inn. Travelers spent the night there when they had no other option. It was, as Sasha understood it, a place where a small copper penny bought you enough room to lay down, once the nightly revelry of ending a workday was done. The farmers, fishermen and poorer tradesmen - who were unwelcome at the Shining Crown - spent their nights at the Two Crossed Tools.

'You really should,' Mariposa said. She giggled at Sasha's expression. 'Yes, I've been there. It isn't a horrible place, Sasha. The people are dirtier, yes, but so what?'

'I heard it was a den of sin,' Sasha said, 'whores and men of a vile nature.'

'And who told you that?'

Sasha frowned. 'My father,' she admitted.

'There are whores at the Shining Crown, and vile men too, but they look nicer. The Two Crossed Tools has its share of bad men as well, but there are some good people there, too. In fact, if you have a chance to go there, try to find the sergeant's Euchre game. Tell them the Butterfly sent you,' she smiled. 'I think you will enjoy the experience.'

Sasha considered that. Her father was friends with one of the tradesmen; they dined at the Shining Crown whenever they were in town, Sasha stuck between two older men who spoke on topics of little interest to a teenage girl. She was rarely out of her father's sight on those days, but maybe if she feigned sickness . . . .

Mariposa made a sad sound, and Sasha followed her gaze out the window. The caravan's crew was packing up. The caravan could make thirty miles on a good day, and today was a good, if cloudy, day. They could probably make it to Walker Town, which meant two more villages on the way, two more small celebrations, with food shared and news exchanged. The caravan would never leave a town on an empty stomach.

The pair made their way down the ladder. Mariposa stopped in the center of the Small residence.

'Sasha,' she whispered, 'I'm all for you leaving and making your own way in the world. I'd take you on our caravan if I could. But are you sure you want to leave? Life here isn't great, but it could be worse. And, who knows how you'd be accepted in the Mardurers. Perhaps you'd find them more interested in your tits than your talent.'

Sasha blushed at Mariposa's words. 'I can't stay here,' Sasha said. 'I've got to try something new.'

'Well, if you have to,' she said, leaning in closer, 'but if it doesn't work out, try to make your way to Duluth. Worse comes to worst, we'll take you in. Mother is at the main office most days, and she'll know what to do.'

Sasha nodded her thanks and followed Mariposa out the door. The townsfolk crowded around the wagons, waving goodbye as the crew mounted up. Mariposa embraced Sasha and climbed onto her horse.

'Good luck,' she said, following her father as he led the caravan north. The oxen bellowed, the wagons rumbled, and the caravan continued northward. Sasha watched them until her mother beckoned her.

Chapter 5

Sasha survived another Sunday Mass. She had behaved herself, and except for the prayer for her recovery that would be said every Mass until her punishment was lifted, she avoided having attention brought to herself.

Sasha was glad for that. It was almost a week since Mariposa and the caravan had left, and Sasha felt like a thief caught with her hand in the charity box. Ever since she had told Mariposa of her revelation, Penelope's Haven had not felt like home. It was no longer where she belonged. She still loved her family, and in truth she loved the town as well, but she did not want to be here anymore. She promised herself she would leave after she returned from Walker Town with her father.

Sasha busied herself preparing for her journey. She decided to prepare enough for a journey to Duluth, more than one hundred miles east. She could make it to Duluth in less than a week, but she was not sure how long she would spend looking for the Mardurers. Once she moved away from the highway, there was more than two thousand square miles of lakes, forests and villages to search. And that assumed the Mardurers were actually in Walker County. It could be some time before she found any sign of them.

Sasha planned to be on foot; a horse would require more food than Sasha was willing to carry, and she did not want the yeomen looking for a horse thief. Her boots were in disrepair, but so were most after the winter, and all of them were to be repaired over the next week. She had her blanket from her bed, a bit larger than she'd like, but it was still spring and it promised to be cold at night. She had a sweater as well.

Sasha had two dresses, one heavier for working in the fields, one nicer one for Sundays and special occasions. She preferred the field dress, with the leggings and thicker cloth, to the thinner Sunday dress, but wanted to take both with her, in case she had to go into a town she would not look like a vagrant. She planned on cutting off the field dress' skirt, adding the cloth to her legs as makeshift pants. She also wanted to remove the high collar, when the time came.

Sasha planned to steal from her family's home. She squirreled away what she could beforehand; a box of matches, a sewing kit, some candles. She made a note of where other items were, things she could not take before leaving; knives in the kitchen, a drinking cup, food.

Sasha was careful about planning food. Every family kept a supply of canned food and dried biscuits during the winter months. The biscuits were about to be ground up and fed to farm animals, so Sasha secreted away a stash of them. They were not good, but they were food. She knew where the cans were, and planned to take some of them.

Sasha debated taking several coins as well. While the town's gold was kept in Mayor Cartier's residence, most families has a small hoard of silver and copper pieces. They might be used to buy supplies from fellow townsfolk, purchase something from the caravan, or bribe yeomen not to take a daughter away. Abigail Small kept the family fortune in a false stone in the fireplace, a secret only the parents were supposed to know. Sasha had learned it by accidentally knocking the stone loose one day. There was not much, but only a few pennies might buy Sasha food if she needed it.

Sasha felt more confident about her decision as the plan took shape. For the first time in her life, things were going her way.

◆◆◆

The snow continued to disappear, helped not by spring sun but by spring showers. The mud had become calf deep in some places, and the rain had finally let up after four days. The clouds still blanketed the sky, but stopped drenching everyone who stepped outside.

The fields had not repaired themselves enough to let the goats out to eat themselves full, so Sasha was sent to fetch a bag of feed from the granary. She trudged back across the square, the heavy bag over her shoulder. She was rounding the statue when a figure stepped in front of her.

'I heard tell, you fancy yourself my wife,' Samuel Cartier said.

Sasha froze. Samuel stood in front of her, and she heard squelching sounds around her. Chuck Webster, the largest of her tormentors, stood behind her. David Dell, the smallest, now stood to her left.

'Samuel,' she said, but he interrupted her.

'I guess all those times you provoked me into hitting you, it was because you liked it!' he said. 'That's good, 'cause I liked it too. Maybe we are a good match.'

The other two chuckled. Sasha was good and trapped.

'Samuel,' she said, 'this ain't a conversation for public.'

Samuel glared as Sasha. 'The first lesson you need to learn: shut up! My woman ain't going to talk. She ain't got no need to. All she gotta do is make my food and get naked when I tell her to.' He leered at her, making a show of looking up and down her body, finally stopping on her chest. 'And you goin' to be naked a lot. No reasons to hide those tits.' Sasha heard his friends chuckle again.

'I'll not be your whore!' Sasha growled.

Samuel smiled. He had gotten the response from Sasha that he was looking for. 'You damn well will be. I'm the eldest son of the mayor, and I'll be the next one when Pa passes. And if I want to pass you off to my friends, you'll spread for them. And if I want to bring another woman into our bed,' he said, 'you'll enjoy it! My uncle wrote me from the Royal Cities, says for enough coin, he can get two girls to play with each other and work him over. My bitch might not be as pretty as a big city whore, but she damn well is going to be cheaper.'

Sasha felt angry. Not the anger she had felt before of a woman insulted, but of a woman who no longer believes such insults should be common place.

'So come on,' Samuel said, oblivious to Sasha's fury, 'there are a dozen places we can go, where you can lie down and learn your trade. Maybe all you ever needed was a good bedding.' The boys laughed again, and Sasha attacked.

She had to lose the feed bag. It was bulky and heavy and Sasha could not swing it like she might want to. Instead, she heaved it at David, who had been looking at Samuel and did not see the bag until it smashed into his face and toppled him over. That left Sasha with two standing bullies and no weapons.

Chuck behind Sasha tried to embrace her in a big hug. Sasha expected that. Chuck always tried to grapple her. Sasha escaped his grasp by charging Samuel, swinging her fist. Samuel raised his arms the avoided most of force of the blow, but Sasha lost her balance and tumbled into Samuel and both fell over.

Chuck hauled Sasha out of the mud, standing over Samuel. Sasha stomped her feet down on Samuel's body and pushed up; she and Chuck fell over again. Sasha scrambled to her feet and kicked at David, sending him sprawling over the feed bag. The three bullies were standing up; Sasha again stood with the statue at her back.

'I am not a whore,' she growled at Samuel. 'I am a woman, and my life is my own. If you try anything like that, I will cut your manhood off!'

The bullies all stared at Sasha. She had fought with them before, defended herself, but she had never threatened them. She stood, fists clenched, eyes narrowed at the three of them, head held high. This was not the conflicted girl they had fought with so many times. This was someone new, someone dangerous.

Samuel was not ready to give up. He took a few steps forward, his friends branching off to flank her. They were wary of her. She looked like she wanted to fight.

'If you're going to be my wife…,' Samuel stopped when Sasha laughed.

'Me? Your wife? You must be drunk. I'll not be your wife. You, Samuel Cartier, are a small, cowardly bastard, and you couldn't handle me. The only chance you have with me is by force.' She chuckled at the amazement in their face; she felt so free, throwing anger back at them instead of trying to be the voice of reason. 'So take your chance.'

The three boys paused for a second, and lunged. Sasha charged Samuel, splitting his lip with one punch, before the other two tackled her. The four of them ended in the mud, Samuel suddenly laughing, kneeling above her.

'Well, now, at last we . . . .'

A hand grabbed Samuel's collar and pulled him up, tossing him against the statue's rough base. A new figure stood over the fight. Chuck stood and punched; the figure gripped his wrist, pulled his punch around. He lost balance and fell to his knees; his arm now held in the newcomer's hands.

Sasha looked up at the newcomer. It was a woman, a little taller than Sasha. She had light brown hair, cut short like a man's would be. Her brown eyes swept over the scene, and Sasha saw that the right side of her face was burned, marring her skin. When the eyes stopped on Sasha, she had to gasp. There was no mercy in those eyes.

. . . *the rest would have killed them*, the man in the forest had said.

Sasha and the bullies stood up. Sasha was on guard; the others watched the strange woman.

'Let him go,' Samuel tried to command her. His voice cracked with nervousness.

'Who are you to give orders?' the woman asked. She had the oddest accent, one Sasha had never heard before, but her words were strong as iron.

'The mayor's son,' Samuel said.

46

The woman scoffed at Samuel's proclamation. 'And does the mayor of this tiny village allow his son to beat and rape its women.'

'She's not a woman, she's a girl,' Samuel said weakly.

'And that's better?' the woman asked. Samuel had no reply. 'Get your father.' No one moved. 'Now!' she yelled, and the two bullies ran off, leaving Sasha, and the woman, still holding Chuck in her grip. Sasha saw the woman's face. It looked like stone, with eyes like a wolf.

'You need to learn how to fight,' she said. 'Your punches are weak and your footing is poor.'

'You're the second person to tell me I need to learn to fight this month,' Sasha said. 'Both after saving me from a fight.'

'Bitches shouldn't fight,' Chuck growled. The woman twisted his arm and he grimaced in silence.

'Keep quiet in front of the crowd,' the woman growled in response. Sasha looked around.

The townsfolk of Penelope's Haven were beginning to assemble. Sasha wondered how many had watched the boys attack and now only came out that the fight was over. They kept a respectable distance. Some of them brought out farming implements. Teresa waved a Bible. Old Man Sanchez loaded his musket. When he clicked the hammer back, he looked at the woman, who smiled a dangerous smile back at him. He paled.

The Smalls came out. Abigail held Thomas' hands, hushing his protestations. Michelle looked on with sympathy. Alexander Small finally pushed his way through the crowd.

'Sasha! Come away! That woman is not of good character!'

Sasha did not move. 'This woman saved me from the bullies while the rest of the town did nothing. I'll not leave her.'

Alexander's protest was drowned out as Mayor Cartier pushed his way through the crowd, his son by his side. He looked at the woman with no small amount of distaste.

'Let him go,' he said, gesturing at the restrained bully.

'This boy is one of several who attacked an unarmed woman for unsavory reasons. I expect there will be punishment,' the woman growled. Several townsfolk closest to her inched away.

'That girl,' Mayor Cartier emphasized girl, 'is a known menace, who has provoked many fights with these boys. I will not punish them for her sins.'

'You have my word that she provoked nothing,' the woman said.

Mayor Cartier shook his head. 'The word of a traveling whore means little to me.'

The woman stared at the Mayor, then nodded. 'Fine,' she said, and with a twist she broke Chuck's arm. Even Sasha gasped at the sickening snap. Chuck started crying, still unable to move. Several men took steps forward, but the woman's gaze held them all at bay.

Mayor Cartier shuddered with rage. 'This is a peaceful town, we do not....'

The woman turned her back on him and looked at Sasha. Her face was still stone, and she ignored the threatening mayor and the crying boy.

'You will have to suffer because of this,' she said Sasha.

Sasha nodded. 'As I have before.'

'When you get sick of it,' the woman said in a low voice, 'head east.' Her voice got loud, interrupting the mayor. 'I apologize, young lady, for the injustice you are about to receive.' She turned, pulling Chuck up and pushing him towards Mayor Cartier and started walking. Everyone stood clear of her. Sasha watched her, outnumbered and alone, walk through the crowd of armed men and scared women without so much as a side glance. Several men detached themselves to make sure she left, following from a respectable distance.

Alexander Small marched up and grabbed Sasha's arm. 'Wait for me at home!' he hissed, pushing Sasha towards her mother.

Chuck was being taken away, and Samuel sneered at Sasha as she left.

'Alexander!' Mayor called out over the crowd. 'We need to speak about your daughter!'

◆◆◆

Sasha was escorted to her home by her mother and sister. Thomas danced around, calling out 'You're in trouble,' at Sasha until her mother told him to go outside. Michelle and Abigail stayed with Sasha in their house.

Michelle sat in one of the chairs, resting her big belly. Abigail stood at the doorway, a guardian. Sasha paced back and forth. She could not sit down. She was angry. She was angry at the bullies for attacking her. She was angry at Mayor Cartier for insulting her. And she was angry at her father for the speech he was about to give her.

'Sasha,' Abigail began, but Sasha whirled and cut her off.

'No! I will not marry that tiny little boy. He won't treat me with any respect. He'll beat me and whore me to his friends, and I'll not have it!'

Abigail was speechless at her daughter's anger. Sasha had never been belligerent after a fight. Once she cooled down, she always saw the error of her ways. But now, as she paced back and forth across their floor, Abigail actually worried her daughter would attack her husband when he came in.

'Sasha,' Michelle said, her voice calm, 'I know you're upset. But you have to calm down. You cannot keep yourself angry. You need to calm down.'

Sasha said nothing. She wanted to be angry at everyone, but she found she could not be angry at her mother or Michelle. Abigail tempered Alexander's lessons so her children could understand them. Michelle had always accepted Sasha's fighting as a part of her, and never made her feel guilty for it. Even Thomas was

49

exempt from her wrath; Thomas wanted to make their father happy, and did so by exemplifying Alexander as he thought he should. Sasha focused on her father.

'Sasha,' Abigail said again. 'Your father cares for you.'

Sasha said nothing again. She glanced at her mother, and at her sister. Both seemed nervous at Sasha's attitude. Sasha felt a little guilt at their nervousness. But most of all she was angry. She was still angry when her father came through the door.

Alexander closed the door and faced his daughter. Sasha was obviously riled up. Her head was high, her fists were clenched, and her eyes glared at her father as if he was now her enemy. It was enough to check Alexander as he approached his daughter.

'Sasha,' he said, 'Mayor Cartier has forbidden any marriage between you and Samuel.'

'Good,' Sasha scowled, 'I refuse to marry that little bastard.'

'Sasha!' Abigail exclaimed. Michelle turned red. Alexander took a deep breath.

'I do not know what has gotten into you, young woman, but you are heading towards a future without a husband or a family. You will be alone for the rest of your life! No man wants to be with a woman who will attack him on a whim.'

'What whim?' Sasha interrupted her father. 'I have never attacked anyone on a whim. I have defended Thomas, and I have defended myself, against the attacks of a bully! I have only ever fought when necessary! I am no monster, Father.'

'Fighting is a sin in and of itself, Sasha, and it will not be tolerated. It is against your faith!'

'I have a right to live my life as I see fit, without fear of rape or death!'

'Rights?' Alexander's voice raised for the first time, for Sasha had uttered a word that Alvanists did not revere. 'Rights are a manipulation, Sasha, used by unscrupulous men to trick others into campaigns for their own power. Your rights are important until they get into power, then they mean nothing. All you have is faith, to follow the Lord's word and live a simple life.'

'I do have rights, Father, and I will not surrender them to make life simpler for myself.'

Alexander stared at his daughter in horror. 'I do not know where you heard these falsehoods,' he said quietly, 'but they are just one more challenge for you to accept.'

'You are enough of a challenge,' Sasha spat, 'to overcome, not to accept.'

Alexander closed his eyes and took a deep breath. Sasha realized she was making him angry as well. She had never made him angry before. She would usually come into his presence, head bowed in guilt and eager to make amends. Now she threw the lifetime of his teachings back in his face. This was truly a grand challenge God was giving him.

'I would leave you here,' Alexander started, 'lock you in a room with a Bible and the whole community, to sing to your soul until God breaks down whatever walls exist and banishes these demons from your soul. But I cannot. Mayor Cartier has demanded I remove you from this town for some time. We are leaving tomorrow for Walker Town. Perhaps, removing you from this town, from your family and friends, and from the temptation to fight, will begin to reach you. But you will not eat until you begin to change, and unless I give you a task, you will read the Bible until God speaks to you!'

Alexander's anger was wearing through his normally stony countenance. Abigail looked frightened.

Sasha wanted to fight him, but she wanted to go to Walker Town, to speak with the men Mariposa had told her about. So she muttered surrender to her family and climbed to her alcove. She lay down, staring out the window. A short while later, someone climbed and put a Bible next to her feet, but she did not look to see who it was and she did not acknowledge it in anyway.

Instead, she felt the scroll in her bodice. *Patience*, she told herself.

Michael Bernabo

Patience.

Chapter 6

Alexander placed Michelle's bed at the base of Sasha's ladder, so Sasha could not sneak out. Sasha did not want to sneak out, but she was not going to tell her father that. Her silence was being accepted as silent contemplation, and she allowed him to continue thinking that.

Alexander had them up before dawn. Two of the town's horses were silently prepared, their saddles packed with simple food and a few canteens. Few people were stirring when they left, but one of them was Chuck's mother. She glared at the two of them as they passed the well. Alexander tipped his hat to her, but Sasha glared back. She was done feeling guilty for defending herself.

Alexander and Sasha had traveled this path before, so there was little need for speaking. The sun rose as the pair rode silently on, passing one town, then through the second. Hours passed and nothing passed between them. Their saddles were provisioned with water, bread and dried meat, which they ate as they wanted. Only the clink of their saddles and the rhythmic staccato of hooves broke the silence.

The townsfolk of the two towns between Penelope's Haven and Walker Town knew the two well enough to call out to the pair. Both Alexander and Sasha answered when necessary, but they shared neither a look nor a word between them.

Their pace was slow and steady, passing a few other riders, one or two wagons, and a small patrol of yeomen. Some vagabonds on their feet walked along the side of the road. Sasha hoped to see the scarred woman again, but few enough were women, and none of them wanted trouble from a mounted pair.

Sasha focused on the countryside, ignoring her father. She thought about how she would walk through the woods. She watched the men and women walking the roads, tried to remember how they moved and looked. When she left, she did not want to be caught easily. There were worse fates than being returned to her father. Yeomen were feared by women in towns and villages, where their families and fellow subjects could protect them. But young women who traveled alone, rare enough as they were, were more terrified, and every so often there would be a silent burial on the road of some young woman, captured, molested and disposed, her name unknown, her only mark on the world a blank wooden cross that would not survive the next rainfall.

The thought made Sasha angry, not only that she might become the victim of some insult or another, but that her father might not respond to any such insult. To him, everything in life was a challenge, not to be defeated but to be endured, in promise of greater reward in the next life. It would not surprise her that he would ignore such an insult to her. She prayed she would not have to find out for sure.

The horses were old and slow; Sasha felt she could walk faster than they were moving. But she enjoyed riding more than walking, and if she kept her attention away from her father, she could almost feel content.

Almost.

They reached Walker Town shortly before noon, having taken four hours to travel fifteen miles up the road.

Walker Town did not sit on the highway, but lay half a mile to the east, on an isthmus that jutted east into Leech lake then curved south, with Walker Lake to the southwest. The eastern approach to the town was fronted by a small stream that drained Walker Lake north into Leech Lake, cultivated by the inhabitants for years into a broad marshland, difficult to cross over except over two bridges on the north and south sides of the marsh. The southern approach was the private land of the count and his family.

The town was the largest in Walker County, almost a thousand men and women. Scores of buildings lined named streets, with elevated walkways and drainage ditches. Several buildings were two stories tall. Docks for fishing boats, cargo barges and a rarely used yacht, owned by the count, lay on the northern edge, though fishing was nothing more than a meager supplement for the count's table.

Standing above the town, but by no means dominating it, were three hills Count Walker had appropriated for his purposes. On the west-most hill was the Golden Crown, along with several townhomes for visiting nobles that had rarely been used. The easternmost, overlooking the lake, was the cathedral, built in the European style at the request of Countess Walker before her death. It was a beautiful building, Sasha had to admit, as grand as it was foreign.

The central hill, on the southern edge of town, was where Walker Estate lay. A large home with several out buildings, surrounded by a fortified wall that ringed the top of the hill. It was a castle in all but name, as counts were not allowed to build castles. Like the cathedral it was a pretty building, but the townspeople could not visit this one, and it stood as an example of the oppression they lived under, guarded by the yeomen who carried out that oppression. Sasha had never hated that building as much as she did riding into town that afternoon.

Sasha almost said something when they reached the bridge. Normally there was no guard, but today four armed yeomen stood on the western end. Like the yeomen who appeared in Penelope's Haven after the woodsman, they were nervous, one always keeping a watch towards the highway and the trees beyond. Alexander spoke for them, showing their papers identifying him as a town assessor. Sasha looked down at the yeomen, noticing that for once they looked at her as a threat and not a treat. Alexander sent her a glance, as if to lay the guilt of their presence on her. Sasha ignored him as best as she could.

Alexander led them to the stables of the Golden Crown Inn. The Inn was not just one large building, but several that surrounded a central garden. There was a stable, a large dining hall, sleeping apartments, luxurious townhomes, and servants' quarters. Alexander and Sasha always stayed in a small servants' room, a large closet with a single chest and one set of bunk beds, a room reserved for servants of the nobles and rich men who rarely graced Walker with their presence. It was an allowance from Count Walker to peasants in town on official business, to open the servants' quarters for their use.

55

As Alexander met with the host at the front desk, Sasha looked over the front hall. A large painting of King Xavier sat over the fireplace, large enough Sasha could see the ornate gold uniform he wore, the large jeweled rings and earrings, the sword in his hand, all contrasted with the darker skin of the man. Alexander's resistance to knowledge of the world beyond meant Sasha knew less about the king than she wanted to, but she knew he was from the south, from the Mississippi Empire. A lesser some of that dynasty who became king of North Mississippi when the Great Emperor crossed the ocean and conquered freedom.

Over the front desk was a painting of Vittorio Montessori, Count Walker. He was a thicker man, at least in painting, wearing his own uniform with his yellow and green colors. His hair looked thinner, and he frowned at the world. This man was also not of Minnesota; he had crossed the Ocean with the Empire's armies, and found employ in Minnesota as a reward for his service. Sasha could not remember where exactly he was from, only that he was also a younger son of a nobleman. She wondered for a second if he could be from this Great Britain the documents spoke of.

We are ruled by the tyrants of foreign lands, Sasha thought, and felt a chill.

Alexander had their room key. Sasha followed him around the dining hall towards the servants' quarters. The dining hall was a proper room, with chairs around small tables, instead of benches. A gramophone plaid in the corner, soft music Sasha enjoyed but did not recognize. Several people, merchants most likely, were having a late lunch. One woman, dressed in finery, saw Sasha and Alexander and pointedly turned away. Sasha wondered if she was reacting to their station as farmers or as Alvanists.

The servants' building was not a horrible place to be. The outside was adorned with the same facings as the rest of the inn's buildings, so it did not disrupt the scenery. Inside it was clean, if barren. The floors were hard wood, the walls painted a dull white, with candle holders instead of lanterns. Each room was barely enough for one pair of bunk beds and a single chest. Two candles and a box of matches sat on the window sill.

Alexander and Sasha brought little with them. Each had their Sunday clothes and the remainder of their travelling food. Alexander also brought a Bible and the assessor books. He handed the Bible to Sasha and pointed at the top bunk. Sasha climbed up and lay down to read. Alexander sat on his bunk, pouring through the ledgers.

They sat silently for hours, until the sunlight faded enough for Alexander to light a candle. She heard the bells on the cathedral chime; she counted them, realized it was quarter to eight.

Alexander stood. He paused, decided against speaking, and left the room. Sasha ignored his departure.

◆◆◆

Alexander stood outside the door, hoping to hear his daughter call out for him, but there was only silence. They had said nothing to each other all day, barely even traded glances. Abigail had said Sasha was a stubborn as Alexander, which would be a great strength for her once she accepted her faith. But until then, she was as the walls of Jericho.

Alexander walked down the hallway and down the stairs, out into the brisk night. March was ending, April nearly upon them. Hard work would begin soon, the weather would warm, and the sun would come out. Another year of toil, simple and rough, as it should be.

Alexander sat on one of the benches in the garden. Most of the guests would be indoors, with warm fires and blankets, but it was not cold enough to drive him in. A servant was already lighting the candles, but Alexander paid him no mind. He was deep in thought over his daughter's intransigence.

In a way, Sasha reminded him of himself at her age. He had gotten into a few scraps, always at the losing end. The fighting had never solved anything, and the anger had turned into acceptance through prayer and meditation, and the bullies had moved on to their own families and lives. He had stuck to his principals and refused service when the dying Republic had called men to its bloody banners, and lived through the bloodletting that followed. It had not been easy, but he stepped up and led Penelope's Haven through those dark times. More than forty men, including the old and young, left to defend their country; half did not come back, and some who did were disabled. Some yelled in their sleep, even to this day. In the chaos during the occupation, before the king fully took over the Republic, he made sacrifices to keep the town safe, but he had done it, guiding the people to the new order of the king.

The king chose his counts, men from the Mississippi territories, or acquired from the conquering armies, men loyal to the king and not the people. They chose their own retainers and mayors, and somehow Edgar Cartier had been chosen instead of Alexander Small. Not that Small cared; political power was anathema to an Alvanist. Alexander had never been a Citizen of the Republic, only a Subject, without voting rights or political representation. His leadership of Penelope's Haven had been incidental only, necessary to the situation.

Edgar became the mayor, lord of Penelope's Haven, and he lorded it indeed. Alexander survived that as well, just as he survived Mayor Cartier and a squad of yeomen raping his wife.

Mayor Cartier wanted everyone to understand who was in charge, and visited each family in turn. Alexander tried to explain that he accepted Cartier as mayor, but Cartier felt the lesson had to be learned. Sasha was not yet a year old, Michelle too young to understand, Charles old enough to be afraid. They were forced to watch. Abigail suffered through it, and in the end Mayor Cartier was satisfied his supremacy was accepted. Abigail recovered, though it was years before they received Thomas.

It was not that such things did not bother Alexander. He felt fear, and anger, but he let them go very quickly. It used to take hours; now he could do it in a few breaths. He needed to pass that on to Sasha. She was a pretty girl, and the longer she went without being calm enough for a husband to take her, the more likely she was going to be taken by yeomen, or Mayor Cartier's son and his friends. And if she was not calm enough to accept such an event, like her mother had so many years before, it could destroy her.

Alexander took another deep breath, and whispered a prayer for his daughter. The cathedral bells chimed again: eight o'clock. He stood and walked towards the town's street. Alexander had few friends in the world, but one of them lived in Walker Town, and he would have a nice dinner ready for Alexander, and some conversation to make up for the silence of the day.

♦♦♦

The rooms of the servants' quarters had locks that could be secured from the outside only, for those few travelers who traveled with slaves.

Alexander had not thought to ask for one of those. He assumed Sasha would remain in the room where he silently commanded her to stay. But at eight o'clock, Sasha slipped out of the room. She paused at the doorway to the courtyard, seeing her father leaving for his friend's house. She felt a pang of regret that she would miss a dinner with the Gifford family, for Mrs. Gifford was an excellent cook, but the children Sasha used to play with were no longer children. Annabelle would gossip and boast about the number of gentlemen who graced her presence, and the gifts they brought for her attention. Horace was a nice enough man, who seemed to entertain some idea of taking Sasha as his wife. Sasha was not sure if that was the case, but if it was, he at least was a proper gentleman about it.

Sasha walked the garden a few times, to give her father a head start. She watched some of the people in the dining hall, eating fine meals served by pretty girls in dresses. She wondered how many of the girls were whores, and how many patrons used their services. Oddly enough, Sasha realized she could not hate these girls. They were trying to make their way in the world the best they could. Who was she to judge, when she was trying to do the same?

Sasha finally left the garden after fifteen minutes, making her way into Walker Town. She kept along the road north to Fisherman's Way, towards the Inn of the Two Crossed Tools. Fisherman's Way was thinner than Noble Boulevard, as it did not have the central lane of trees. There were fewer lanterns. It smelled of rot.

Sasha walked along the road, coming to the inn. She was ignored by the few people on the street, except for one man who asked a price. She ignored him and continued on her way. The entrance to the inn faced a crossroads, with a shovel and a pitchfork swinging in the wind. The boards were faded, and the windows shuttered against the cold. The smell of tobacco and beer was strong. Several men and women sat on benches near the front, looking up at her as she approached, but saying nothing.

Sasha took a deep breath and walked through the door.

Chapter 7

The Inn of the Two Crossed Tools was originally a warehouse, and it still retained the spacious room. A second level had been added on to one end of the building, and the other half had a large chandelier. The air was thick with smoke. There was no front desk and dining area; instead there was a large counter, running one short side of the building, with a mountain of bottles and kegs behind it. Long benches lined the hall, filled with men and women. Serving girls moved back and forth from the bar to the kitchen to the tables. They were a mixed lot, with young, pretty girls slipping through the crowd alongside older women as large as barrels who pushed through like bulls. Everyone was talking, laughing, singing, and dirty. Sasha had never before been in a place like this. Her eyes watered, and she could not breathe from the new smells. She gulped as she imagined trying to push her way through.

'Oy!' someone grabbed her and pulled her aside. It was a large man, with a huge grey beard. He glared down at Sasha. 'If you came here to preach, Alice, then piss off!'

Sasha shook her head. 'I'm not here to preach!'

He did not believe her. 'You think I came out o' the oven this mornin'? We got enough preachers, waltzin' in here, nose in the air, demanding we stop our sinnin'. Well, we ain't got much to do but sin, and we ain't going to take kindly to you tryin' to change it!' He started to push her towards the door.

'I'm here for the sergeant's game,' she said.

The man stopped and turned around. He looked her up and down. 'What sergeant's game?'

'I was just told to ask for the sergeant's game,' Sasha said.

'Told by who?'

'Mariposa Madero,' Sasha said. 'From the Hollander caravan.'

His face softened. 'Ah, the butterfly. Why the sergeant's game?'

Sasha shrugged. 'I don't rightly know, sir. Just that she said I should come and ask about it.'

'Huh,' he said. Then he leaned in. 'Loosen your blouse,' he said.

Sasha turned red. 'What?'

'Most folks here don't like preachy types, especially Alvanists. And some of them are drunk enough to do something about it, and I ain't looking to clean up no fights tonight. You loosen your blouse and show off some flesh, most fellas won't notice your dress. Just, be polite when you push 'em off.'

Sasha nodded. She had not thought to wear anything other than her Alvanist clothes; she did not have anything else. She opened her blouse up, pushing the scroll down so it could not be seen. She felt a little freer without the restrictive collar around her neck, and a little cooler, but she was very much aware of how exposed she was. Most of the women she could see were as exposed, and they did not seem conscious of it at all.

The man chuckled, 'First time open, Alice?' he asked, then laughed as she turned red. 'No worries, love. You're good enough for a gander, and no man'll do more without your say so. Just say no the first time, and slap the second time, got it?' Sasha nodded. 'Good. Louisa!' A serving girl arrived. 'Take this young lass to the sergeant's game.'

'I already got a full load of ale, and you want me to babysit some street walker?'

'Bah, woman, she'll carry some o' that for ya, I reckon, if you ask polite.'

The woman grabbed Sasha and pulled her to the bar. 'Well, dearie, if you can haul two o' these across the floor, we'll be best friends for life.'

Sasha took two of the large steins, watching the woman. She realized this woman was only a few years older than she was. She was dirtier, and her dress accentuated her body, whereas Sasha's hid it, but she knew her job and she was doing it. Sasha wondered for a second if she whored at night, but decided it was not a question to ask.

Louisa led Sasha through the crowd. A quarter of Walker Town must be in the inn, Sasha thought, even more as they passed a large door leading out to a courtyard with more tables. The sounds was deafening, and the crowd looked immovable, but Louisa found a hole and dug through it. Sasha followed as quickly as she could. She was doing well until halfway, when a hand grabbed her arm.

'Hello, you're a new little bit, ain't ya,' said an older man. He was missing half his teeth, and most of his hair, and he leered at Sasha's blouse. 'Has someone claimed you, or are you free for Sweet James Ash.'

'I'm just visiting,' Sasha said, trying to get her arm out of his grip.

'Well, no worries,' he said, 'we don't need long, though it shames me to admit that, and you'll be back with your friends before you can say….'

Louisa materialized out of the crowd and kneed the man in the groin. He fell to the ground, unbalancing Sasha, who lost some of the drink on one of the steins.

'You watch yourself, Jim Ash, or Dan'll toss you out on your last tooth,' she said, then turned to Sasha. 'And you spill anymore of that drink, I'll force you to spend the night with Jim Ash here!'

Sasha hurried after her.

Louisa led her to a door in the back, one of several leading to smaller, private rooms, right up one with a strange mark chalked into it; three pointed stripes. Sasha recognized them as what the Yeomen-Sergeants wore on their sleeves.

Louisa paused outside the door and turned to Sasha. 'Now, when you put the ale down, set is in the middle of the table, and make sure to bend over real good, let them get a nice look at ya. They'll look, and they might make some comments, but words only, they won't touch. They're good folk, and they've earned it,' she winked as Sasha, and pushed the door open with her hip.

63

The room was filled with smoke from fireplace, candles and pipes. The table filled most of the room, where four men sat, chuckling at some jest. All of them were older, Sasha would guess in their fifties or sixties, much older than many men would live to be. They wore old clothes, clean but worn, and they were well groomed. They welcomed Louisa with a chorus, then drew strangely quiet when Sasha put down her mugs. She felt her dress shift, but stared at the table until she could stand up again.

'Who's the new girl?' one of the men said.

'Oh, no,' another exclaimed. He looked at Louisa. 'You're leaving us, aren't you? Leaving us for that drover! Oh, how we will miss your gentle presence.' He pulled her closer by the hips and tried to lay his head on her breast.

Louisa slapped his ear. 'No, I ain't leavin'. Dan told me to bring this one to you. I'll be back,' she said and hurried out the door.

The four men looked at Sasha. Sasha blushed and curtsied. One of the men clucked.

'Shut your mouth, Dell, she's young enough to be your granddaughter.'

'Yeah, but she ain't!'

'Quiet,' said a third, his voice sharp. He looked at Sasha. 'You are Mariposa's friend, aren't you?'

Sasha nodded. 'Yes, sir,' she said, 'Sasha Small.' She was nervous, in front of these men, and not only because she was uncomfortable with her blouse opened. The men, Sasha noticed, were scary looking men. One was missing an arm, another an eye. Their skin was tough and leathery, their hair was grey, and they did not slouch.

'Then sit down,' the third man said, gesturing to an empty chair, 'and don't call us 'sir'.' She sat down, looking around all of the men. They all looked back at her.

'Allow me to make introductions,' the third man said again, standing up. 'To your left is Sergeant Ray Dellwood, Second

Battalion, First Duluth Infantry. His eyes enjoy wandering, so if you begin to feel uncomfortable, just slap him upside the head.'

He gestured to the man with one arm. 'This is Sergeant-Chef Maurice Le Croix, formerly of the Seventh Battalion, Quebec Fusiliers. He doesn't speak much, but he does listen.'

'To your right,' he said, indicating the one eyed man, 'is First Sergeant David Wells, Second Iron Rangers. He's done things he can't tell anyone, and you shouldn't believe anything he does tell you.'

'And I am Sergeant Major Michael O'Rourke, Dawson Guards Regiment. I am the ranking NCO here, and I therefore welcome you to the Sergeants' Room.' He made a deep bow to Sasha. 'So tell me, how much of that did you understand?'

'I know that a sergeant is a rank, and that I should slap Dellwood if I feel uncomfortable,' she said, 'other than that I don't know most of what that means.'

The men chuckled. 'Mariposa says you're a bad Alvanist,' Wells said, 'says you get into fights.'

'I do,' Sasha admitted. 'The mayor's son makes a point of picking on my brother and me. I've had to fight them a number of times, and I used to feel guilty about it when I did. Now I can't understand why I have to be the victim and the villain in the same story.'

The men smiled, and Sasha felt some of her fear go away. A room full of men, none of them judging her for fighting. Instead, Wells pushed his ale towards her.

'Ever try alcohol before?'

Sasha shook her head and took the mug. It was a heavy taste, like oatmeal with too much water, but Sasha managed to swallow. She sighed.

'Want to try a pipe?' Dellwood offered. Sasha took it and puffed.

'She's turning green,' Le Croix said.

65

'I'm fine,' Sasha muttered, but she had to pause for a few seconds.

Louisa came back through the door and took one look at Sasha.

'What did you do?' she asked.

'Offered her some tobacco and ale,' Dellwood said.

Louisa reached over and slapped him upside the head. 'You drink strong ale, and that tobacco you smoke would stun a buffalo. You don't start a girl on that!' She leaned down to Sasha, 'I'll bring you some proper food and a water, and don't worry, these gentlemen'll pay for it.'

Louisa was gone, the door banging shut. The sergeants all chuckled.

'How did this game start?' Sasha managed to ask as her stomach settled.

Dellwood spoke, 'Prison!' he chuckled. 'We were all in the same camp together, when the Empire came and took out the Republic, and the Kingdoms, and everything else. You would have been, what, three?' he asked.

'I was born on Founding Day,' Sasha said, 'so the War happened before I was born.'

'That young?' Le Croix asked in surprise. His Quebec accent was thicker than any Sasha had heard before. He turned and looked at his fellows. 'We're too old.'

'Yes,' she replied. They all laughed. When they stopped, she continued. 'I don't know much about the Republic; my father did not speak much about it. I know he was a Subject of the Republic, not a Citizen. He always said being a Citizen required too much devotion that should be going towards God. I think he's happy everyone is a Subject now.'

The sergeants grumbled at that. Sasha felt embarrassed. Louisa returned with a leg of chicken and some vegetables, and a mug of water.

'So why did Mariposa send you to us?' O'Rourke asked.

Sasha looked at seven expecting eyes. 'I hoped you could tell me. All I did was tell her I realized I couldn't be an Alvanist, and that I had to go somewhere else. She told me I should talk to you. She didn't say why.'

The sergeants all looked at each other. Le Croix spoke up. 'Why are you a bad Alvanist? Why do you fight?'

Sasha told them the story of the dog. 'My father's message never made sense to me, no matter how much I tried to fix it,' she admitted. 'And I wanted to fix it.'

'Do you like fighting?' Le Croix asked.

'What the hell does that have to do with anything?' Wells asked. The two started arguing in another language.

'Gentlemen,' O'Rourke said, 'our guest does not speak Quebecois.'

'No,' Sasha said, trying to steer the conversation back on topic. 'I don't like fighting. I've been scared every time I've done it. But I fight when I feel I have to. And once I start fighting, when I'm actually doing it, I feel calm. I'm scared before, and I'm calm during.'

'Good,' Dellwood said. 'We've all seen combat, we've all felt that fear. And that's actual combat, Miss Small, not a brawl with bullies. With smoke and bullets and fire.'

'Fighting is fighting,' Wells said. 'If you feel calm when it starts, then you're on the right track.'

'For what?' Le Croix asked. 'What future does she have in fighting?'

'The Mardurers,' Sasha said.

The four men went quiet and looked at her.

'Do you even know what a Mardurer is?' Dellwood asked.

'I know they're fighting yeomen, which seems like a good start. I don't know what the word means,' Sasha admitted.

'It's a funny story, actually,' O'Rourke said. 'Our beloved count, as you may have heard, is not one of our own local Minnesotans. He isn't even some Mississippian, which at least an English speaking nation on our own continent. He's an Italian nobleman, a younger son of some duke, who stood to inherit nothing. As many young men who face such a prospect did, he joined the Imperial Commonwealth Army and marched across the globe.'

'The what?' Sasha asked. 'I thought he came from the Empire?'

The sergeants laughed. 'It's simpler to call them the Empire, as it sounds so dramatic,' O'Rourke said, changing topics. 'They call themselves the Imperial Commonwealth. Every nation belongs to the Commonwealth, which promotes peace between the nations, at the point of a gun.'

'How did he become a count here?' Sasha asked.

O'Rourke sighed at the second interruption. 'I'm getting there, hold on. See, the Imperial Commonwealth does have a leader: the Great Emperor Tiheam. He sent diplomats ahead, to all the kings and presidents, saying that he was coming and they should join him. Minnesota, and Iowa, and several others, said no, and they fought. Some, like the Kingdom of Quebec, said no, but Imperial Agents found those willing to betray their king for gold and land. King Jean-Mark III was assassinated, along with most of his family, and King Jean-Constance was crowned.' Le Croix cursed the name.

'What followed was the Commonwealth War, where most of our continent rose up and fought the Imperial Commonwealth and the Quebecois kingdom that joined them. Among them, was the Mississippi Empire.

'Emperor Sebastian VI of the Mississippi Empire and the House of Santiago-Locke had long coveted the rivers that flowed towards the capital of New Orleans. The Mississippi, the Missouri, and the Ohio. But against the Commonwealth we were allies. We all were. And we were holding our own, too. Then some naval battle occurs out in the ocean, and suddenly the Commonwealth controlled the seas.

'If he's going to keep talking, I'm going to order some whiskey,' Dellwood said.

'Emperor Sebastian sent out his ambassadors to the Commonwealth, asking for peace. The Great Emperor, he responded that since the Mississippi Empire had stood against him, some punishment must be made, but if the Empire helped him conquer Atlantic America, he could mitigate his punishment. So the Mississippian Empire silently prepared to stab an entire continent in the back.'

Sasha listened with rapt attention. She did not notice the glass in front of her being refilled with whiskey. She just drank it.

'The betrayal was accomplished with great surprise. His forces swept across the south, into Florida and to the Atlantic. A coup occurred in Michigan and removed the People's Republic from the war. Boston surrendered. Minnesota and Iowa fell later, crushed between Quebecois and Mississippi troops, with some help from the Commonwealth.

'Now, Emperor Sebastian had to learn what sort of punishment he might receive. And it came down from the Great Emperor that Sebastian would rule the Mississippi and its tributaries, but as an imperial margrave, charged with keeping the peace on behalf of the Commonwealth. The Mississippi Empire, including the occupied nations of Minnesota and Iowa, would be split into three nations, and spread amongst his heirs.

'Emperor Sebastian VI became Margrave Sebastian, Lord of the Mississippi Margravedom for the Imperial Commonwealth and Great Emperor Tiheam the Conqueror. Prince Xavier the Useless became King Xavier of North Mississippi. And generals of the conquerors became the nobles of the new Kings.

'Our own count was a General of Division in the Imperial Army, and not a very good one,' O'Rourke said.

Le Croix said something in Quebecois. 'My battalion fought with his division at Albany. He sent his troops in waves, only to the front. No maneuver. Many casualties. Bad general.'

'So the Great Emperor did not want him in his army, but he could not just dismiss him, so he gave him to King Xavier. Xavier needed counts, and generals, and flunkies. And the conquerors had them in spades.

'Now, come this latest new year, there is our General of Division Sir Vittorio Montessori, Knight of the Imperial Cross, Red Banner, now Count Walker, Colonel of Yeomanry for the poorest county in Minnesota - let's face it, not what he had in mind when he departed noble Italy for his own title - when he hears that someone has killed some of his yeomen. Then a week later, some more.

'Count Walker is angry. Now he makes a big speech, to yeomen and clerks, leaders and flunkies. He says that Walker County Yeomanry are not scared of such Mardurers, and they will not run.'

Sasha felt her head spinning, from pipe smoke and alcohol. 'So, it's a word from Italy?'

The men laughed. 'No,' Wells said, 'he tried to say marauders, or maybe murderers, but he doesn't speak English too well, and the name kind of stuck. These Mardurers haven't given themselves a name. They learned from the Range Riot.'

'What?' Sasha said. She took a deep drink of water to try and clear her head.

Dellwood started rooting through a backpack for something. The other three gaped at Sasha.

'Your father keeps you that much in the dark?' Le Croix asked.

Sasha nodded. 'I try to find out as much as I can. But most people know my father and respect his wishes. I know little.'

Dellwood sat up with a book in his hand. He thrust it as Sasha. 'Here!' he said, with no small amount of pride.

Sasha opened the book up. Louisa came back with a bottle of whiskey and several small glasses, a loaf of bread, and an admonishment to Sasha to drink slowly.

The book was not full of words, but of pictures. Paintings and drawing and photographs, newspaper articles and broadsheets, some of them looked to be older than she was. 'What is this?' she asked.

'Anything I can find about the Republic. We spent three years in camp, and a lot of stuff got burned by the Commonwealth Army, or the king's men when they came to power, but I found what I could.'

Sasha flipped through. She saw pictures of men in uniform, in fine suits. Some men had the same square chin and sharp eyes. She pointed. 'Who are they?'

'They're Dawsons. And some Imperians. The two families are mixed a little bit,' Dellwood said. 'I guess you don't know anything about them either.'

Sasha shook her head.

Wells put a small glass of whiskey in front of her. 'Drink that slowly,' he recommended.

'The Dawsons founded the Republic, way back when it was a loose collection of communities on the Iron Range. They were heavily involved in the government for the entire length of the Republic. The Imperians were the last governors from the Before Time, who survived in the Metropolitan Cities until unified into the Iron Republic, when they became as committed to the new nation as they were to the old. Both good families,' Dellwood said, his voice breaking. 'Most of them were eliminated in the fall of the republic.'

'Dawsons,' Sasha said, looking at O'Rourke, 'Dawson Guards?'

He nodded. 'Some of the more powerful families could raise their own battalions or regiments, and the Dawson Guards were one of the best.'

'Did they have something to do with this Range Riot?'

'Yeah, but it's getting past your bedtime,' Wells said. 'It's dark. Shouldn't little girls be in bed?'

Sasha bridled at Wells. She downed the glass of whiskey, grabbed the pipe from Dellwood, and sat back in her chair. The sergeants glanced at each other and chuckled.

'So,' Le Croix asked. 'What do you want to know?'

Chapter 8

Sasha was sick. Very sick. Her head spun, her stomach stormed, and her every move caused trouble. She was dimly aware of the world around her. She was in a nightgown, in a bed. Someone sat by her side, giving her bread and water, which she nibbled at. She slipped in and out of sleep. It was daylight when she could finally focus her eyes on the woman at the side of her bed. 'Mrs. Gifford?' she croaked.

'Good, you're still alive,' Mrs. Gifford offered a small smile. 'I had rather wondered if you might give up. You've been here half a day already.'

Sasha laid her head on the pillow; she could not hold it up. 'What…where am I?'

'Horace was coming home from a gambling event early this morning, and found some…gentlemen escorting you home. They kindly released you into his care and he brought you here.'

'Father?'

'We told him you took a fever coming back from the Cathedral.' Mrs. Gifford made a scowl. 'I have a hard enough time dealing with that man in a good mood, I did not want to see him going on and on about his daughter coming home smelling like a tavern harlot.' She leaned in to Sasha. 'You were not aggrieved in any way?'

'No,' Sasha said quietly.

'First night with drink?' Sasha nodded. 'And pipe?' she nodded again. 'Well, at least you were with a good crowd. Horace says the men who were walking you home were known as upstanding people, for ones who visit the Two Crossed Tools, at least.'

Sasha simply nodded. Something flashed in her mind.

'My clothes,' Sasha started. She was wearing a sleeping gown, not her usual clothes.

'Annabelle and I changed you. She's washing the smell of whiskey and tobacco out so your father will be none the wiser. Don't worry, Horace was not in the room, your virtue is still intact. Although,' Mrs. Gifford said, pulling the scroll from her pocket. Sasha went still, her eyes wide. 'Annabelle thinks this is an Alvanist custom, keeping verses of the Bible close to the heart. She was less interested in reading it then.' She leaned in. 'And I'm shocked that you would have something like this in your possession. I assume, considering where you hid it, your father does not know you have it.'

Sasha nodded. She wanted to reach for the scroll but she did not have the strength. 'I've had it only a little while, and it is dear to me.'

'It is dear, and dangerous, Sasha Small. I wonder if it might not be better if I burned it,' she turned to toss it into the small fireplace.

Sasha lurched at Mrs. Gifford, but her weakened state, and the blankets, tangled her up and she fell to the floor. Mrs. Gifford knelt beside her.

'Oh, dear, I wasn't going to burn it.' She helped lift Sasha back into bed. 'But I think it might be best if I did. This is not the sort of words an Alvanist should be reading, Sasha.'

'I'm not an Alvanist, Mrs. Gifford,' Sasha said. She looked up at the woman to see her reaction.

Mrs. Gifford looked at Sasha, then nodded. 'Okay,' she said. She put the scroll under Sasha's pillow. 'Well, that's all for tomorrow. For today, sleep.'

◆◆◆

Alexander put off their return to Penelope's Haven until the next day, a Sunday. He had packed the horses, settled his bills, and completed his business. Sasha was feeling well enough to ride. The

Gifford family gave them food for the ride home, and bid them farewell.

Alexander and Sasha did not speak at all until they were past Camperton.

'Do you think I'm the April Fool, Sasha?' Alexander asked.

Sasha frowned, then nodded. 'It's the first of April,' she said. It hurt less to say it out loud than to simply think it inside her head.

'And you think I am the April Fool,' he stated again. 'There are two priests at Walker Cathedral. Both of them were with Count Walker the other night. The count was worried about morale of the town, with the attacks in the eastern county, so he called community leaders together. They were not at the cathedral to speak with a young girl who was having a crisis of faith. Neither did I miss Annabelle and Horace staring intently at their shoes. You were out being sinful that night.'

'I was not sinful,' Sasha said in defiance. 'I spoke with people you've never let me speak to. I tried alcohol, I tried tobacco, and I suffered for it. But there was no sinning, Father. They did not touch me. They did not do force anything on me. I am still me.'

'And we must spend Sunday on the road, not in church,' Alexander sighed.

'Why did you never tell me about the Range Riot?' Sasha asked.

Alexander looked stunned. 'That was none of your business.'

'Really, Father?' Sasha asked with scorn. 'Not one hundred miles away, thousands fighting and dying.'

'The last gasp of a dying nation,' Alexander said.

'Men fighting for freedom!' Sasha cried. She stopped her horse and turned to her father. 'Those men were fighting for the right to decide their own lives!'

'And look what happened! Hundreds killed fighting; hundreds executed; thousands imprisoned. Fifteen thousand shipped south as slaves and replaced with southern farmers. More than thirty thousand men, women and children, killed or displaced. And you find that honorable? You find that admirable?'

'They died for something!'

'They died for nothing!' Alexander snapped. 'Nothing. Nothing has changed, except many who were here are dead, and many others will spend decades toiling under lash and chain. There is nothing, NOTHING, that can make up for such loss.'

Alexander realized he was yelling and took a deep breath to calm himself. 'We are meant to suffer in this world, Sasha. There is no one who does not suffer, from the lowest peasant to the highest of kings. What matters is how we carry ourselves with the weight of such suffering. It is in the next world that the peaceful are exalted and the wicked punished. That is why you must suffer, Sasha. I know you hate it; I hate it too. But it is part of life! And it cannot be avoided!'

Sasha did not respond. She was staring down the highway.

There was a column of yeomen making its way north on the highway. There were more of them than Sasha had ever seen before. Half a dozen mounted yeomen led the column, and another half dozen rode behind. Marching between was almost thirty men, some wearing the same green jackets with yellow facings as the mounted yeomen. But most wore a simple green jacket with a yellow sash tied from hip to shoulder. Sasha also noticed two horses carrying women, girls, really, about her age; two sharing one horse and another riding alone.

Sasha felt her stomach twist in fear as they drew closer. The girls hands were bound, and their eyes red from crying. And the men who marched in the column were not the clean yeomen she was used to. They were dirty and rough, and as Sasha got closer she saw them eyeing her with a particularly brutal lust. One of them said something in a language she did not recognize and they laughed. One younger man, cleaner than his compatriots, smiled meekly at Sasha. Yeoman-Lieutenant Marks, riding in the middle, called his column to a halt and raised a hand to stop Alexander and Sasha.

'Mr. Small,' Marks said. Alexander greeted him in kind. 'I have already spoken with Mayor Cartier, but I feel I should inform you that Count Walker is taking steps to curb the insurrection in eastern Walker County.'

'Is it so serious?' Alexander asked.

Marks nodded. 'More than half of our yeomanry has been killed or wounded, and the villains have killed or captured a number of our horses. These men,' he gestured to the brutes behind him, 'are going to round out our numbers and garrison some of the villages along the highway. Penelope's Haven has already been garrisoned, and Mayor Cartier will have words with you when you return.'

Alexander nodded. 'I understand. I am sorry events have turned so grave.'

'Be on the lookout for anyone who is aiding the insurrection. Penelope's Haven has seen one girl assaulted and one boy broken by transients, all while playing their childish games.' He glanced at Sasha, perhaps hoping to get a response.

Sasha was only half listening. She was acutely aware she was in danger. Not only were the walking brutes eyeing her, but the mounted yeomen had surrounded her and her father. This was no village where scores of eyes watched; this was remote and lonely.

'If you do know of anyone, inform us immediately,' Marks said. 'In addition, Count Walker is preparing for the future. He plans to build onto Walker Estate, and increase the patronage of nobles and aristocrats from outside the county. He has therefore asked that the towns along the highway each contribute one teenage girl for work with the domestic staff, to learn servants' work, for the day when Walker County can host guests of great status. It will be hard but rewarding work, and Mayor Cartier volunteered Sasha for the honor.'

Sasha's stomach sink as one of the yeomen grabbed her horse's reins. She felt hopeless. She looked at her father and knew the next words out of his mouth even as she prayed for him to say something different.

Alexander small closed his eyes. 'Sasha will serve.'

'Father!'

'Sasha,' Alexander said quietly, 'perhaps hard work in a structured environment will bring you to your senses. It will remove you from Samuel Cartier and the temptation to fight him. You will be looked after, you will learn skills, and your energy will be put towards a productive end. You will bear it, Sasha, and come out stronger for the challenge.'

Sasha looked at her father. Never had she felt so ashamed of him. There was no protest in his voice at all. His eyes were closed, his voice weak, and his shoulders slumped. He hated this, but he did nothing to fight back.

He was truly small.

'You bastard,' she whispered. Tears streamed down her face.

'Come, Sasha,' Yeoman-Lieutenant Marks said, 'please join young Miss Rachel here.'

Sasha was tied to the young blond girl who rode alone. Her pack was removed from the horse and its reins tied to Alexander's saddle. When Marks called the column to continue, her father finally looked at her.

'Sasha,' he said, 'I will send you your Bible.'

'And I will burn it,' she growled. They rode off.

The column moved slowly, the men on foot under no hurry to make their way north, and the mounted men in no mood to push them. Sasha was mounted behind Rachel, who cried silently to herself. Sasha wanted to hit her or tell her to shut up, but she knew she would not be able to stop once she started, and she had no intention of heading into Walker Town tied up even more so. Her head would be high, for as long as she could hold it. And when she could, she would run. That much she was certain of.

They had not traveled more than a quarter mile when Yeoman-Lieutenant Marks rode up next to Sasha.

'Your father is right, Sasha,' he said. 'You will benefit from this. It is hard work. You'll learn to clean to a degree far beyond what you're used to in the fields. You will learn to serve, and curtsy, and treat your betters with respect. And at night,' he chuckled, 'well, you should know that no respecting nobleman would invite guests to his estate if the domestics were not fully prepared to warm beds.'

Sasha felt Rachel shudder. She kept quiet and watched the road ahead.

'You'll learn quickly, I think. The best domestics become the count's favorite, and the favorites aren't touched by anyone else. Maybe even the son will take a liking to you, or one of the officers. Maybe I'll take a liking to you. If not, you'll find plenty of teachers willing to take you, and if you are so bad as to misbehave, well, then you get put in the barracks with the yeomen, and these brutes here don't leave their women unmarked.'

Sasha did not react until Marks grabbed her hair and pulled her back. The horses stopped and Sasha, pulled halfway off her the saddle, feared she was going to fall off. Rachel cried out and grasped the reins to keep from falling. Marks looked down on her, his face inches away.

'I think I'll take you first. You may be a scrapper in Penelope's Haven, but you try any of that crap in bed and I'll blacken your eyes for a month. Tonight, you'll be a good, docile girl. It might hurt for a bit, but then . . . .'

A clap echoed in the forest, and Sasha choked as her face was covered in blood.

Marks fell, pulling Sasha and Rachel off their horse. Sasha heard Marks gurgling and Rachel screaming for only a moment before the woods thundered and drowned out all other sound. The girls landed on top of the officer. Marks grasped at his throat, only to find it torn to shreds, pulses of blood coating the girls. Other yeomen fell off their horses, and rider-less mounts began to panic and run. Sasha held Rachel as the horses bolted. She looked down the road.

More than a dozen bodies lay sprawled across the road, some motionless, others crawling towards the forest. The boy who smiled at Sasha was grasping his bloody stomach and crying. The rest had spread into the forest. She had no idea where the other girls had gone, but they were not lying on the road. Sasha peered into the trees, trying to keep her head down. She saw smoke, and shapes moving from trunk to trunk, and flashes from guns.

Rachel started to panic, trying to free herself of the ropes. Sasha grabbed her. 'Stop it, they're too tight.'

'We can't stay here,' Rachel said, 'we shouldn't be here!' She started repeating herself, struggling against the ropes

'Right,' Sasha said. Marks had gone still, his eyes wide at the sky. Sasha saw a knife on his belt and pulled at it. Rachel was not cooperative, so Sasha had to drag the girl before she could reach the blade.

A voice broke through the din. 'Fire!' A volley of smoke and thunder poured out of the forest.

Sasha had the knife. Rachel was immobile and hysterical. Sasha worked on the rope connecting the two. If she could just split it they would be free.

A chorus of explosions rocked the ditch, each spraying mud and leaves into the air. They were immediately followed by a scream and a score of figures rushed from the trees, crossing the highway with bayonets fixed to their weapons, one woman leaping over Sasha and Rachel. Several bullets snapped through the air. Sasha could not see much else. Too much to see, too confusing to understand.

Sasha cut the rope between the two girls. Their hands were still tied, and Rachel continued to rock and repeat herself, so Sasha decided to cut her own bonds first. She concentrated on trying to get the blade around to cut at her wrists and did not notice the battle ending, or the figures approaching.

'Let me get that,' a man said. Sasha jumped in fright and turned, bringing the knife up against his throat. They both froze.

All she saw was him. He was a handsome man, with sandy blond hair and blue eyes. He did not seem frightened by the knife, but he went still as it pressed against him. Beneath the blade, on his lapel, she saw a black circle and a red cross, conspicuous against the drab green of his clothes. Several of those around her drew their guns on her but he raised his hand. They did not fire.

He spoke with a slight Quebecois accent. 'If you wish to kill me, mademoiselle, cut to the side of the neck. You'll cut an artery, and I'll be dead before anyone can help me. But,' he smiled, 'I kindly ask that you do not cut. Enough have died today.'

Sasha made no reply. Her heart was pounding, and her head seemed to be clouded by fear. She had been fine when there was a fight and she was being ignored, but now there was a man in front of her and a weapon in her hand. *Was he a threat? What did he intend?* She was just now noticing that the fighting had stopped, but what did that mean? Too many thoughts rolled around in her head.

The man must have recognized the look in her eyes. 'Breathe,' he said. 'Take a deep breath for me before you do something we'll both regret.'

His calm voice cut through the fog. Sasha took a deep breath. She felt a little better and her head started to clear.

'If you remove the blade from my neck,' the man said, 'I will cut your bonds. I mean you no harm, and I give you my word.'

Sasha nodded, took another breath, and handed him the knife.

'Sorry,' she said.

He smiled at her and cut the ropes around her wrists. Then he stepped over and cut Rachel's bonds. Sasha rubbed her wrists, and looked up when another figure stood over her.

It was the woman, the one from Penelope's Haven, with the scar on her face. She was not wearing a traveler's cloak, instead she wore the same drab green clothes the others were wearing. She had a black circle and an 'X' made by crossing a rifle with a sword on her lapel. She held a rifle, with a long bayonet attached. The bayonet had blood on it.

She looked down on Sasha. 'I am glad you did not kill him,' she said. Sasha simply nodded. The woman held down her hand and pulled Sasha up. 'What were you doing with the yeomen?'

'He,' she gestured at the dead lieutenant, 'said that Count Walker was selecting women from several towns to work as domestics in his estate. We were to be cleaners and whores,' she said.

'And hostages,' the woman said. 'If your town rebels, you are punished.' She looked past Sasha. 'Come with me,' she said. Sasha followed. Behind them, two people began to search the dead lieutenant.

There were dozens of men - and women, Sasha noted with no small delight - working around the battlefield. Some were searching bodies. Others were tending to the wounded. Some stood guard over the captured yeomen. One had a bulky camera and took a picture of the prisoners; one of them tried to look defiant, but the others looked scared. Sasha had never before seen a scared yeoman.

'You feel sorry for them?' the woman asked. Sasha nodded. 'Don't. Not one of them wouldn't rape you and kill you if they felt like it. We should execute the whole lot of them,' she said, loud enough for the prisoners to shiver under her stare.

'Lieutenant Colonel Snow,' a man said sternly as he emerged from the forest. He was a tall man, with soft brown eyes and light brown hair, maybe thirty years old. He wore a brown uniform, immaculate in its presentation, with two gold stars on his lapel. His eyes looked over the scene before him, and Sasha felt her mouth go dry. She recognized the square chin and the nose from the sergeant's pictures.

He was a Dawson.

He walked towards Snow, followed by a pair of guards in striped clothes. Everyone who was not guarding the prisoners stood tall and saluted.

'General Prince,' she said.

'Lieutenant Colonel Snow, we do not shoot prisoners.'

'With respect, General, these are not soldiers,' she said, gesturing at the prisoners, 'these are rapists and thieves. Parasites, sir, who live off the hard work of others and give nothing back.''

Prince stepped by Snow and looked at the prisoners. They wilted under his gaze. 'I agree, Lieutenant Colonel Snow.' He addressed them. 'You are rapists, thieves, and worse. Honest men and women starve, whilst you live on their harvest, take their daughters to your beds and kill any who oppose you. There are few here, now, who would not cut your throat if I allowed them to.

'But I won't give that order,' he said. 'I will not allow the men and women under my command to march down the path you follow. Instead, you will go back to Count Walker and tell him to leave while he still can. This county is no longer his. Tell him the Renaissance Army of Minnesota has taken it from him.'

General Prince turned from the prisoners. The Quebec man was standing nearby. They spoke for a minute. Prince turned back to the prisoners.

'Colonel Aristotle tells me two of the wounded will need to be carried. You will carry them north to Walker. Colonel Trumpeter!'

A short barrel of a man with a thick mustache, standing next to Aristotle, snapped to attention. 'Sir!'

'First Regiment will follow. Any yeoman who tried to desert or drop a wounded comrade will be shot.'

'Yes, sir!'

General Prince looked at the prisoners one last time, then walked away from them. Sasha watched him. She felt a strong attraction to this man. Not because he was handsome, though he was, but because of his confidence and his words. She for one did not think they deserved any leniency, but now that Prince has spoken, she felt that she was wrong to think so. Sasha wanted his attention, and his respect.

'Breathe,' a voice said, startling Sasha. Snow had a slim smile. 'You're not the first woman to blush at his presence, but he doesn't need another one fainting at the sight of him.'

Sasha turned red. 'I didn't, I mean,' she stopped. 'Sorry.'

'Don't be, and come with me.'

Sasha followed. 'You are Mardurers, right?'

Snow turned at the name. 'We are the Renaissance Army of Minnesota, or RAM, but will answer to the name Mardurers if you want.'

Sasha felt elation.

The Mardurers were stripping the dead. Weapons, belts, boots, canteens, backpacks, even coins and valuables were being sorted. The horses, those that lived, were being tended to. Sasha looked at the activity around her and realized there were more Mardurers than she had thought. There were at least sixty now, not including those who marched off with the prisoners. They wore dull colored clothing, mostly shades of green or brown. A few wore patterns of stripes or rough blotches. All were busy.

Snow led Sasha towards the pile of equipment. Several Mardurers stood around, taking inventory of the equipment. One of them looked up at the pair of them with annoyance. Snow approached one who stood with his back to her and touched his elbow.

'Good haul?' Snow asked. The other simply nodded.

Sasha took a deep breath. General Prince was walking towards them.

'Snow, impressive performance,' he said with a smile.

'You too, sir,' Snow said.

Prince looked at Sasha. 'You seemed to have picked up a tail,' he said.

Snow smiled. 'This is the girl I told you about, the fighter in Penelope's Haven.'

Prince smiled and bowed. 'Ah! Three bullies at once, I understand. You had cause to fight, I trust, Miss . . . .'

'Sasha Small, sir, and yes, uh, sir,' Sasha said. 'They tried to, uh, take certain liberties,' she stumbled into silence.

Prince grimaced. 'It seems to be a common story. Our children grow up emulating the yeomen who abuse their parents, because their parents look weak by comparison. I'm glad you, at least, are willing to defend yourself.'

'I have the right to life, liberty and the pursuit of happiness,' Sasha said without thinking.

Snow and Prince both looked at Sasha with surprise. Next to them, the officer Snow had spoken with turned and looked at her very intensely. He too wore two gold stars on his uniform, just as immaculate as Prince's. He had a closely trimmed beard, reddish in contrast with his black hair, and his eyes reminded her of her father's, cold and judging, trying to stare into her soul. She felt uncomfortable under his gaze, but she stared back at him.

He spoke. 'That is a very specific phrase, Miss Small, and I believe you do not come to it by accident.'

Sasha stared at the second general. She had heard many accents before: Mariposa's Spanish, the rapid Quebecois, even the calm Dakota. But she had never heard an accent like this before. Every word was clear and concise, but spoken no slower than any other.

Finally she shook her head and opened her bodice to pull the scroll case out. 'A man in the forest gave this to me, after another fight.' She handed it to Snow.

Snow looked the case over. 'It's Fox's,' she said with a smile.

'He did say he gave it to someone who had earned it,' Prince said. 'A woman who earns the respect of Fox or Snow is someone to be remembered; someone who earns the respect of both is to be recruited.' He looked at Snow with a smile.

Snow looked at Sasha, examining her. 'Do you want to go home?' she asked after a moment.

'No,' Sasha said immediately.

'Are you sure?' the Prince asked.

Sasha nodded. 'My mayor wants me a hostage in Walker Town, and his son wants me a whore at home. My father will not defend me; in fact he will return me to Walker on his own horse, explaining why it would be good for me to serve the Count. I have few options, and none of them I like. I need to make my own life. I want to fight with you,' she said to Snow, then looked back at Prince.

Prince smiled again. 'Excellent. Please stay here for a moment.' He gestured for Snow to follow him back towards some of the other officers. The other general whispered something to one of the sergeants nearby, then looked up at Sasha.

'How well did you understand what you read?'

'I got most of it, I think,' she said.

'Without context, much of its meaning would be lost,' he said, then lapsed into an embarrassed silence.

Sasha watched the work being done. She saw the second horse carrying the other two girls return, led by a Mardurer who had chased them down on his own horse. They joined Rachel on a log by the roadside, quietly watching the work around them. Sasha made no effort to join them.

A minute later, Snow took Sasha aside. 'Are you serious about coming with us? With me?'

Sasha nodded. 'Yes, I am.'

'Good, because . . . .'

She was interrupted.

'Sasha Evelyn Small!' an unwelcome voice called out. Alexander, riding his horse, with the second following behind, rode onto the battlefield. He looked in horror at the bodies lined up alongside the road, the blood stains, and the dozens of armed men and women standing around him. Several of the Mardurers looked up at him, their weapons in hand, but none made any threatening gestures. Only when Alexander approached the generals did they move, several of them stepping in between him and their commanders. Their weapons remained pointed away from the Alvanist, but were still ready.

'Sasha, come with me,' he said quietly but firmly, 'we need to leave.'

'No,' Sasha said.

Alexander did not react for a moment. 'Sasha, this is not a game. These are violent sinners; wicked men and women who will drag you down to hell.'

'So instead I should return home, to a mayor who wishes to whore me out and a weak father who will let him?' Sasha shook her head. 'No, Father. I have suffered the challenges of living in your house for long enough. Now I will make my own way in the world. Without you.'

'You cannot do this, Sasha,' Alexander said, 'you are not old enough.'

'How old does she have to be,' Snow said, 'before she can defend herself?'

'If she is prone to violence, then she is not old enough,' Alexander said. 'Violence is not an answer. Recall, I pray you, all of you, that in the garden of Gethsemane, when Simon Peter struck off the ear of Malchus, Jesus told him to sheath his sword, lest he die as he lived. Jesus knew the importance of peace over violence.'

'Then is would be wise to wonder why Simon Peter still had a sword after three years of ministry,' the second general said.

Alexander eyed him suspiciously. 'And who are you, to presume to tell a man of God what His son's words were? Have you read the Bible?'

The bearded general cocked his head. 'I have, and I recognize the many instances of genocide and slaughter that God allowed the Hebrews to inflict on their enemies.'

'Heathen Jews,' Alexander said, 'without the enlightened words of Jesus Christ.'

The general sighed. 'An uncivilized response from an ignorant peasant, who . . . .'

'General Caesar!' Prince interrupted. Caesar went silent but made no apologies, still staring up at Alexander. For the first time ever, Sasha saw her father lose a battle of wills and break the contest. Sasha felt no small admiration that someone who seemed to know the Bible as well as her father did would argue its implications and morals, and Caesar's standing grew in her mind.

Prince turned to Alexander. 'Mr. Small, your daughter wishes to come with us. She has made her request in her own free will, under no duress or persuasion, and I believe her to be old enough, and competent enough, to make her own choices.'

'She is an Alvanist!' Alexander cried.

'Father,' Sasha said calmly, 'I am no Alvanist. I cannot accept a world that demands I submit to any injustice another wants from me. I cannot go back. Give Mother, Michelle, and Thomas my love. But I am going with them.'

Alexander was stunned and silent. 'You have been corrupted,' he announced. 'I will pray for your rehabilitation. For all of you,' he said loudly, addressing all the Mardurers.

'As you will,' General Prince said, 'however, in the meantime, there are three other young ladies who should be returned to their families, and I note that you have room on your horses.'

Alexander looked at the captured horses, freed from the yeomen. 'I assume you are preparing to use those horses to do violence.'

'Most certainly,' Prince said with a sly smile. Some of the Mardurers chuckled.

Alexander frowned. 'Let me save these three girls, at least, from your doom.' He closed his eyes and began whispering prayers.

Snow took Sasha's arm and pulled her aside. 'This is not going to be easy, Sasha Small. I command the Third Field Regiment; we're a light formation. We live in the woods, fighting and running. And you are untrained for it. You will hate it at times. But if you choose to, you are welcome to come with us.'

Sasha looked at her father, eyes closed and ignoring the world around him. 'I understand, and I chose to come with you.'

Snow smiled. She turned towards Prince to find Caesar and a sergeant, holding a rifle and a backpack.

'Some supplies,' he said. 'Drawn from the captured pile. Enough to balance your presence in Third Regiment, and the rifle is the same caliber as the rest of the weapons.' He took the rifle and held it towards her. It was a large, heavy weapon, with a thick wooden stock. She worried how heavy it would feel after carrying it through the woods.

'Thank you, General,' she said earnestly. She realized Caesar must have assembled the equipment before she had agreed to go with Snow. *How had he known?*

'Third Regiment!' Snow called. Sasha put on her backpack and held her rifle and found herself surrounded by more than a dozen men and women, most of them her age. Snow looked at them, and at Sasha. 'Let's go,' she said, leading them into the woods.

General Prince saluted them. 'Good luck, Third Regiment,' he called after them. Others called their own words. Sasha refused to look back at the quiet man on the horse.

It was almost noon on the first of April, 2475, and Sasha Small was finally free.

Chapter 9

For Sasha, her first three days of freedom meant hiking. Snow marched parallel to the highway until just before Penelope's Haven, when they veered off and began marching through the forest. Sasha was no stranger to exertion, but the pace of the regiment and the amount of time they marched had her winded.

That night she exchanged her dress for a spare field clothes and her shoes for a Mardurer boot: legs wrapped in cloth to the knee, fitted in a leather sock, with a wooden sole fitted to her feet and tied with leather straps up to her knees. It was uncomfortable, but she was assured it was better than her farming shoes.

On their third day, Snow kept the regiment marching past their normal midday rest, ending the march about two o'clock in the afternoon. Snow looked about and decoded a series of symbols carved into the trunks of the trees. She smiled.

'We're here,' she announced to her regiment. 'Let's take a look, shall we?' and led them up an incline.

Here was, in Sasha's opinion, nothing much to look at. It was a gully, situated at the base of the hill, about twelve feet deep. It was surprisingly broad and long; a dozen Third Regiments could have stood in there comfortably. There were dried bushes and rocks strewn about, mixed with debris carried down the hill from years of rainfall and melting snow. The ground was still muddy in some places, and it smelled like several animals had recently died there.

'Well that looks about as inviting as a bobcat,' someone said.

'I know we didn't get to stop at midday,' Snow said to her unit, 'but we got a lot to do and not a lot of sun to do it. Officer Mary, there is a stream or river a few hundred yards east of here. Make sure we can drink it, then find us a bathing spot. Take Beth.'

Mary nodded and dropped her pack, pulling out one of many small kits she carried around, and handed over the rest to Sasha. 'Watch that for me, okay, Sasha?' she asked with a smile.

Sasha smiled back with a nod. Mary was the regimental surgeon and was a warrant officer, a specialist in her field. She seemed to have a number of other duties she did for the regiment, mostly having to do with assisting Snow. She was also an exceedingly polite and pleasant person.

'Captain Saber,' Snow said next, 'you, Corporal Winnie, and Gunner Jim, start mapping out a ring of foxholes, all around the camp. Make sure you have placements for Jim prepared ahead of time.'

Captain Saber was the regiment's other commissioned officer. He was a tall, older man who was older than Snow but subordinate to her. He nodded at her orders and gestured to the two others to follow him.

'I am going to take Sonja and Rick up to the top of the hill, get a lay of the land. Master Sergeant, clean up.'

Master Sergeant was the oldest man in the group. He did not have a code name like the officers did; instead he was simply addressed by his rank. Like Captain Saber he was an experienced soldier, who looked out of place amongst all the teenagers. He gestured, his hand in a circle over his head. It meant something to all the remaining Mardurers, who clustered around him. Sasha followed them.

'Third Regiment, it looks like we have a problem. We've got a bed, but it's full of crap! Let's clear out the debris and branches. Sergeant Esmeralda, once we get a spot cleared I want you to hack out a fire pit; we should have more than enough stones lying around. And if you happen to find a dead animal, feel free to carry it out of here and bury it. Let's get to work!'

There was a lot of debris, but eight men and women working without pause made a dent almost immediately. Every Mardurer carried a small hatchet or shovel, and soon the cluttered gully was clearing into a respectable campsite. Sergeant Esmeralda worked on a fire pit, digging a small hole surrounded by stones, and some of the Rifles were hauling a dead wolf out of the camp, when Master Sergeant tapped Sasha's shoulder and beckoned her to follow him.

91

Sasha followed him to one of the walls of the gully, underneath a tree. He pulled a bayonet from his belt and marked out a rough square in the side of the wall, then handed Sasha an axe and a shovel.

'Cut it one arm's depth into the hillside,' he said, 'and cut a trough into the bottom.'

'Do I get any help?' Sasha asked.

'Nope,' he said and walked away.

Sasha sighed and started hacking at the roots and rocks. She saw others members of the regiment at work, hacking and cutting and moving. She was not being picked on, and she expected she was being watched.

Except for Mary, most of the regiment was largely ignoring her. They were polite enough, but it was obvious they all knew each other, and she was an outsider. She had asked Mary what she should do. Mary had one bit of advice for her. 'Do what is asked, as best as you can, and don't complain.'

Sasha bit her lip and threw herself into the digging.

After an hour, Sasha stopped to shovel the pile of debris at her feet off to the side. The setting sun still lit the camp, the fire pit was done, and other groups were beginning to cut other alcoves into the sides of the gully. Mary approached Sasha with a long string of canteens.

'How are you doing?' she asked, handing over a canteen.

'My hands and arms hurt,' Sasha said, drinking some water. Mary inspected her hands. Sasha hissed when Mary poked her palm.

'I thought farmers were supposed to have tough hands,' Mary said.

'I'm not weak,' Sasha said curtly.

'I never said you were,' Mary responded. She handed over some of the canteens. 'Can you take these up to the top of the hill?

Colonel Snow has established an observation point and they need some water.'

'What about my hole?' Sasha asked.

'You finish it tomorrow,' Mary answered.

'But why?'

'Don't ask,' Mary said. 'Just take the water.'

Sasha took the canteens and started up the hill, grumbling. Her arms were sore and her hands ached because she had worked so hard to finish that hole before it got too dark, but that was impossible. So why had she been told to do it? Was it a test? Something to see how hard she would work when she had a reason to slack off? Or just some joke to play on the new girl?

She was almost to the top before a figure stepped out from behind a tree before her. It was Corporal Winnie, a young woman maybe a few years older than Sasha, who scowled at her. Sasha heard a sound behind her and turned to see Rifle Rick, a shorter man who had never said a word to her, standing behind her. Sasha looked back and forth between the two Mardurers.

Sasha sighed with the familiarity of the situation, and launched herself downhill at Rick, swinging the canteens up.

Rick deflected the canteens with his arm, but could not avoid Sasha. She knocked him downhill, rolling to get back on her feet before Winnie could catch up, and swung the canteens to try and catch Winnie. Winnie checked her advance long enough to avoid the canteens, stepped forward and punched Sasha hard in the face.

Sasha fell backwards, tripping over Rick. She dropped the canteens and rolled back to her feet, lunging back uphill at Winnie, throwing punches. Winnie was a better fighter than the bullies Sasha was used to, using her arms to protect her head against Sasha's wild blows. Sasha managed one decent hit to Winnie's stomach before Winnie sidestepped a punch and landed a harsh blow to the side of Sasha's head.

Rick was back on his feet, coming downhill. Sasha's arms were mush, and Winnie was too close, so Sasha dove at Rick's feet, tripping him up so he fell into Winnie. She pushed herself back up and jumped at Winnie, punching her in the face. But Rick was up and moving again and hit Sasha hard in the stomach, knocking the wind out of her. Winnie and Rick each grabbed one arm and forced Sasha into the ground, stomach down and head downhill. Sasha could not move with the two holding her down. She tried kicking out, but neither one of them close to where she could hit.

'Stop,' a voice said. Snow stood over the three of them. 'Let her up.' Winnie and Rick stood up. Rick held out his hand to Sasha and helped her off the ground. Winnie did nothing.

'Corporal Winnie?' Snow asked.

'She's weak,' Winnie growled. 'She has no strength, no endurance, and she can't take a hit to save her life.' Sasha started to respond, but Rick jostled her and she stayed quiet.

Snow turned to Rick. 'Able Rifle Rick?'

'She had good instincts,' Rick said. 'She needs to learn blocking, strength and endurance, but she's quick on her feet.'

'She can't fight for shit!' Winnie said sharply.

'Could you fight any better before you joined up, Corporal?' Rick asked pointedly.

'Enough!' Snow snapped. 'Corporal, take the canteens up to the observation post. You've got the night watch. Rick, you took a hard fall, check with Mary, get your head looked over. Sasha,' she said, 'you stay with me.'

Snow waited for Rick and Winnie to leave.

'Are you okay?'

'You told those two to attack me,' Sasha said heatedly. Snow nodded. 'Did you tell Master Sergeant to work me hard, too?'

'Yes,' Snow said unapologetically. 'The regiment cannot stand a weak link, Sasha, and you are untrained. I must test you, to find your strengths, to discover what training you need. It might have been better had you gone with General Prince.'

'I want to be with you, Colonel,' Sasha said.

'Then listen. We don't have the people or time to train you properly, Sasha, so we're going to train you as we go along. It's going to be difficult. Keep training, keep learning. Trust me, there will be enough to keep you busy.'

'Colonel,' Sasha asked, 'do you know what my role will be here?'

Snow looked at her levelly. 'We need fighters,' she said. 'And you do not seem like a woman to shrink from a fight.'

'Fighting bullies is much different than combat, Colonel.'

'It is at that,' Snow said. 'What are your thoughts?'

Sasha reflected for a moment. 'I don't know,' Sasha admitted. 'I've thought about it since the ambush, but I just don't know. I do know that I don't want to fail you, or the regiment.'

Snow nodded. 'Sasha, train to be a rifle. Train for combat. I would much rather you have the skills and not need them.'

'And if I don't want combat?' Sasha asked.

'Mary could use an assistant,' Snow said. 'I could use an aide. Trust me, Sasha, as the regiment grows, there will be positions for those who do not wish to fight. And you do not have to decide now.'

Sasha nodded. 'Okay, Colonel.'

'Good. Now get some food.'

Sasha walked back to the campfire. She joined the circle of Mardurers around the campfire. Mary had checked over Rick, and now handed Sasha a small bit of cooked meat and bread.

'How are you doing?' Mary asked.

'I'm fine,' she said. 'Just, hungry.'

She looked around the other Mardurers. There was some conversation, but nothing Sasha felt comfortable getting involved in. Mary was discussing food options with Sergeant Tomas. Rick and Beth were whispering something to each other. It was Grenadier Erick who finally caught her attention. Sasha slid over to him; if he noticed her, he ignored her. His was fully engaged in a book.

'What's that?'

'A book,' he said.

'I know that,' she said with a nervous chuckle, 'what kind of book?'

'A history book,' he said. He finally looked at her. 'I can't imagine an Alvanist knows much about history.'

Sasha shook her head. 'I know stories I've heard around town, but my father only allowed us Bibles to read. About the only education I've had is news pamphlets I scavenged, and the math I needed to help my father.'

Erick nodded. 'This is about the War of the Three Fools. One hundred years ago, the Mississippi Empire, the Kingdom of Quebec, and the People's Republic of Michigan went to war over the Great Lakes. Not only did none of them gain their objectives, they strengthened the countries between, including the Republic of Minnesota. The war lasted six years. It's not an easy book,' he said, handing it over to her, 'and if you need any help understanding it, let me know.'

'I will, thanks,' Sasha said.

'Just, be careful,' Erick said. 'We only have three books in the regiment, and one of them is a Bible.'

'And the third?' Sasha asked.

'Beth's book of bedtime stories,' Erick said with a smile.

'Don't forget my library,' Mary said as she sat down next to Sasha.

'True,' Erick said. 'If you want to learn about organs and field medicine.'

'Not a bad thing for a soldier to know,' Sasha said.

'True,' Beth said from across the fire. 'First time you get clipped in battle and those books will seem like the most important thing in the world.'

Sasha laughed with the rest of the regiment. She glanced through the book in her hand, opening the first few pages.

'Here's a hint,' Erick said. He flipped open to one of the earlier pages, one covered in small boxes with various marking inside. 'These are the icons that indicate military units on the maps. First thing you should do, memorize those. It'll help with the maps.'

'Thanks,' Sasha said, and started reading, still listening to the conversation around the fire. For the first time since she left her father's side, she started to feel comfortable.

Chapter 10

The regiment dug for two days straight. They dug alcoves for supplies, and sleeping dens that could fit two or three people at once. Snow was the only one who had her own den, dug before a large tree trunk that was cut down into a desk. Rifle pits were dug around the camp, and a large observation post was cut into the top of the hill. Some of the regiment knew how to put together simple wooden benches for the fire pit and Snow's Den. The observation post was covered and hidden. Mary even directed them on dredging the bathing pond so the regiment could immerse themselves by kneeling down.

Sasha thought she had never been so tired in her life, and then the third day began.

Master Sergeant woke Sasha up before dawn and had her running on a path that encircled the camp. Sasha had never run like that before, tiring before one lap of the half-mile trail. Master Sergeant slowed the run down to a moderate jog and explained pacing and breathing to her. She ran four times a week after that.

The Mardurers had no end of short physical exercises that they demanded from Sasha whenever it struck their fancy, and with no end of critique. She completed only seven push-ups her first time, but Captain Saber said only two of them counted. Sasha blushed the first time Gunner Jim held her ankles so she could do a sit-up. At least her embarrassment at flailing about learning to do a jumping jack was mollified; someone's loud and obnoxious comment about her form prompted Master Sergeant to get every Mardurer in earshot exercising in unison.

At lunch, Mary sat down pulled out a small book of symbols. She explained the ranks, chevrons and rockers, the simple circles and squares that the commissioned officers used, the triangles of the warrant officers. She showed the insignia of the branches, most of which Sasha had never heard of before. Only two of them were present in the Third Regiment, but Sasha was expected to know them all.

'Seems simple,' she said after some study.

'That's the beauty of it,' Mary said. 'It IS simple. No ornate uniforms or dress codes. If Colonel Snow walked around here wearing a curtain on her shoulders and a pumpkin on her head, but with the Colonel's circle on her dress, she is still properly identified.'

And there were rules. More rules than Sasha expected. There were a score of codes, a set of between five and ten rules that the Mardurers knew by heart. The Code for Conduct in Combat. The Code of Authority. The Code for Civility. The NCOs and Medic had their Creeds. Every day they went over one code or another. Sasha complained to Beth once that she did not like having so many rules. Beth glared at her.

'The yeomen don't have rules, so we do,' Beth scowled. 'It's the difference between soldiers and sinners.'

Sasha learned the weapons. Not shooting, because Third Regiment didn't have the ammunition for proper training, but she learned safety and maintenance. Sasha had seen guns before, carried by the yeomen and the caravan guards. She had little knowledge about them until Beth sat down and explained them to her.

The regiment carried ten rifles, and the large one Sasha had been given at the ambush Beth showed Sasha how to work them, 'Both are Tennessee Arms, Gulf Pattern, 30 caliber weapons,' she said, 'using the same bullet. What most of us carry are cavalry carbines, designed to be lighter, and for us, being light troops, it works. What you have is an infantry long rifle. Much heavier, longer range, but since you don't know how to shoot it, it doesn't matter. Just get used to the weight. Both have good stopping power; when you hit someone, they'll know it.'

Beth also taught Sasha about the other weapons that she was probably not going to be using for a while. There were Quebec MARQ Submachine guns that the regiment simply called automatics. Sonja, a sharpshooter, had a Verendrye long rifle that looked worn but cared for. She could shoot someone at a thousand yards, Beth said.

'Gunner Jim carries the LAMB,' Beth said.

'The what?' Sasha asked.

'Lansing Armament Manufacturing Bureau, Year 2441 Infantry Machine Gun. We call it the LAMB.' It was a long, heavy weapon, with a bipod below the barrel, and a magazine feed in the side. She realized why Jim, a big man with large arms, was the one who carried it.

Sasha received her first real instruction in the pistols. Sasha's palms sweated when she first held it in her hand. It was Snow's pistol, and after a day of digging at that. Snow did not say anything about it, just had Sasha squeezing the trigger over and over on an empty weapon until she could do so without the barrel dropping. Snow made her memorize the Four Rules of Weapons Safety, something she had to recite every time she held a weapon. Over and over again:

'Treat the weapon as if it is always loaded;

Do not put your finger on the trigger until you are ready to fire;

Always know what you are aiming at;

Always know what is around your target.'

She learned to fight: how to use her whole body to fuel a punch; how to deflect and block blows. The Mardurers knew what they were teaching. She watched them practice, sparring with each other almost every night. Some were quick, moving swiftly to land blows where they could. Others were slower but stronger, landing single devastating blows that could end a fight.

They did not let Sasha spar since she was not ready. Every night they had her go through exercises, keeping her footing, blocking, deflecting, and punching. It was much different than fighting the bullies in Penelope's Haven. She was preparing for combat. She could tell the difference.

Sasha learned how to be part of the unit. Master Sergeant led small squads through the woods, giving hand signals instead of talking. Sasha became part of these squads, learning to move as a soldier, drop when required, be silent when necessary. Sonja showed them all how to move through the woods quickly and quietly, and had to single Sasha out for lessons less often than some of the others.

Third Regiment was not just building a base; it had a purpose. While Sasha could not accompany Snow or Saber when they left on missions with portions of the regiment, she could work at the camp and free up those who could. She was delighted to learn that for the Mardurers, cooking and cleaning and sewing was not a chore restricted to women, and that some of the men were better at sewing and cooking than she was. The chores were shared by all except the officers and Master Sergeant.

'Rank has its privileges,' Mary said with a smile.

Colonel Snow took a squad and left for two days. The second night, Sasha stood watch, not sleeping until the morning. She was given a loaded weapon, and was kept awake with the other three watching, being awoken only twice. When Snow returned the next day, Sasha helped secure the goats and chickens they brought back.

'The family that had them needs them no longer,' Snow growled.

Sasha had time to read every day. Erick's book tested her reading skills, but she persevered. She was already learning the formations and terms, and almost everyone was willing to help her out. Her reading increased and her questions decreased as she continued.

Sasha was constantly tired, often sore and bruised, and fell asleep as soon as she was given the opportunity. And she was happy.

Except for one small obstacle.

◆◆◆

Sasha stretched as she woke. She had stood the first night watch the night before, and then had the den to herself for the rest of the night. It was nice when it was by herself. She shared the den with

101

Mary and Beth, and though it was supposed to be big enough for all three of them, Sasha was not convinced. It was crowded with two of them. Luckily, between sleeping outside and night watches, they had never attempted to shove all three of them into it, and Sasha did not look forward to the first time they tried.

She wanted to go back to sleep, but she heard a conversation happening outside her den, and there was probably work to be done somewhere. She pulled her jacket down from the shelf and slipped out of the den.

Beth and Sonja sat at the unlit fire pit, arguing.

'How can you possibly believe that?' Beth asked hotly, standing up suddenly.

Sonja looked up impassively. 'Why shouldn't I? It's simple.'

'It ignores the problem,' Beth replied. 'RifleMAN? Wagon MASTER? All of these names and titles that automatically assume anyone who can do it has to be a man!'

'That just gets to be ridiculous,' Sonja said. 'I think it should be neutral. Rifle, Wagon Leader,' she gestured to herself, 'Sharpshooter.'

'But it ignores the differences between men and women!'

'Who cares?' Sonja asked. 'Why is that important?'

'Because even a neutral name carries an assumption. If you hear the word Rifle, you think a man. If I'm called a Riflewoman, you can't think I'm a man.'

'Maybe, but I think Rifle sounds more dangerous.'

'A rifle is an inanimate object, Sonja,' Beth said.

'I know that, Beth! But it doesn't matter if the rifle is wielded by a man or a woman. The job is the same!'

'It does matter! How can we expect equality if the names we use don't represent every individual? You have to get past the expectations that anyone of importance is automatically a man. You do that by forcing people to realize that both men and women are fighting.'

'So what do we call Colonel Snow, then? She-Colonel?'

Sasha chuckled. The two women looked over at her.

'If you find this so funny, what do you think?' Beth asked.

Sasha shrugged. 'Colonel Snow uses the neutral, so I think I'll go with that.'

'Why? Because Colonel Snow does?' Sonja said with some disdain.

Sasha was confused. 'But I agree with you.'

'But not because you've thought about it,' Sonja said. 'Agree with me or disagree with me, but do it because you HAVE an opinion about it.'

Sasha frowned. 'Okay, I'll think about it. But right now, I'm thirsty.'

'Well, our canteens are low, and the goats need watering. Why don't you take them over to the watering hole and kill two birds with one stone?' Beth asked.

Sasha gathered up the empty canteens and strung them together, untied the two goats, and led them out to the watering hole.

The watering hole was a large pooling of water just above some rocks that made a small waterfall. The goats drank heartily while she filled a dozen canteens with water. She drank some herself, and gathered the ropes to lead the goats back to camp. She turned and stopped.

Corporal Winnie stood a few dozen paces away. She had a fighting look on her face.

Sasha swallowed. She had almost no contact with Winnie since the first night, and the few times their paths had crossed it had been formal, if chilled.

'What can I do for you, Corporal?'

'You can leave,' Winnie growled.

'No,' Sasha said.

'Yes,' Winnie said. 'I'll take the goats and the canteens. And you can run along home.'

'I am home,' Sasha said.

'NO!' Winnie took a few steps forward, startling the goats. 'This is NOT YOUR HOME!'

Sasha took a deep breath, looking at the corporal. She turned and tied the goats to a tree and set the canteens down. She stepped away from the animals, facing Winnie.

'Just tell me why,' Sasha said.

Winnie growled. 'You think this is fun, don't you. Getting away from daddy, pretending to be a soldier. But you're a pacifist! Once we get our boots on firing line, you'll have some attack of conscience, and we'll be left with a hole. And I will not let that happen! This regiment will not see combat with a weak link on the line.'

'I am not a weak link!'

'You've never fired a weapon.'

'That's NOT my fault,' Sasha said. 'I've never had the chance.'

Winnie scoffed, but Sasha noticed how long she paused before she said anything else.

'This is not a game, Small,' she said, her voice serious. 'We are going to kill yeomen, and we are going to lose people. This is a time for strong people, strong soldiers, not children who run around the forest pretending. You've played along, done what you were told, but you don't have any direction. You don't know what you want. And when we get into a fight, and you decide you don't want to be there, you'll cry and run.'

Sasha clenched her fists. 'I will remind you, Corporal, that I was in the middle of the yeomen when you ambushed them, and I kept my head then, when I was splattered with the Lieutenant's blood. And before that, I had plenty of fights with bullies.' She dropped back into a fighting stance. 'And now I have to fight one more.'

Winnie scowled and charged.

Sasha had learned a great deal in three weeks. She deflected Winnie's first punch and landed a blow on her nose. Winnie blinked the tears away furiously while she punched out in Sasha's direction. Sasha circled right and punched at Winnie's head again, connecting with her temple. Sasha then yelped in pain as Winnie turned and laid her out with a hard hook to the chin.

Sasha jumped up as quickly as she could, diving into Winnie, shoulder into Winnie's stomach, knocking the wind out of her and bowling her over. The two wrestled on the ground, flailing punches as each other. Winnie wrapped Sasha up and twisted around her, burying Sasha's face in the dirt. Sasha elbowed Winnie in the ear hard enough to stun her and rolled out of her grip. She scrambled to her feet and faced Winnie again.

Winnie was looking over Sasha's shoulder, her guard down. She gestured to Sasha to come over to her, eyes still focused over Sasha's shoulder. Sasha glanced behind her.

A man stood at a tree, watching the two women fighting, covered in the shade of the branches, rifle in his hands. Sasha backed away from him towards Winnie, standing next to the corporal.

'Oh,' he said, 'don't stop on my account.'

Winnie pulled Sasha to her side. The two women faced the man. 'Who are you?' she asked.

'I'm armed, and not tired from slapping a young girl around the forest.'

Winnie's fists clenched, and Sasha scowled at the man. 'You may get one of us, but the other will kill you just as dead, so if you're looking for trouble, you better be ready to pay for it.' Sasha nodded at Winnie's words, though she certainly hoped no one was going to die today.

The man chuckled and stepped out of the shade. He wore tan clothes, carried a woodsman's rifle, and had sergeant's stripes marked on his lapel, next to a small X.

'You're a kit?' Winnie asked.

'Chosen Rifle,' the man growled. 'A courier, from General Prince, bearing dispatches to Lieutenant Colonel Snow.' He looked at the two women. 'I don't suppose you know where she is.'

'I do,' Winnie said. 'Can you prove you're a courier?'

'To Lieutenant Colonel Snow, I can. To some silly girl in the middle of the forest? No.' He fingered the trigger of his rifle. 'So, do we fight? Or walk?'

'We walk,' Winnie said. 'Sasha, take the goats and lead. I'll grab the canteens and bring up the rear. And the kit,' the man scowled at her, 'takes the middle.'

♦♦♦

A few hours later, Sasha stood at Snow's Den. The stump that was her desk had piles of correspondence the courier had brought, but her eyes were focused on Sasha's bruised face. She glared at Sasha, her scar emphasizing the expression. Sasha felt no small amount of guilt as the silence continued.

Finally, Snow spoke. 'Corporal Winnie has a problem with you,' she said.

'She thinks I am a pacifist, ma'am,' Sasha said. She was standing at attention, or the best she could do.

'Does she?' Snow asked. Sasha thought she saw a smile.

'Yes, ma'am. She thinks that I'll have an attack of conscience and put the regiment in danger.'

'Do you think she's wrong?'

'I know she's wrong,' Sasha said.

Snow thought for a few seconds. 'Winnie is a non-commissioned officer; it is part of her duty to identify problems in the unit and deal with them, without involving commissioned or warrant officers unless necessary.' She rose and stood in front of

Sasha, looking her in the eyes. 'Do I need to get involved, Recruit Sasha?'

Sasha paused before answering. If anyone could get Winnie to back off, it would be Colonel Snow. And not having Winnie stalking her around the camp, avoiding any further fights, would make life easier.

'No, Colonel,' she said. She was surprised she said it.

'Why not?' Snow asked, her voice neutral.

'Corporal Winnie believes I am a weak link. No one can tell her otherwise. I have to prove her wrong. And when I beat every challenge she puts in my way, she'll have to admit I'm not a weak link. So no, ma'am, you do not have to get involved. This is my fight.'

Snow examined Sasha for a moment, and then nodded. 'Very well, Sasha. I won't get involved.' She beckoned to someone outside of Sasha's view; Sasha resisted the urge to look and see who it was.

'Ma'am,' Master Sergeant said.

'How is Recruit Sasha's training going?' Snow asked.

'Adequately, Colonel,' he said. 'As we discussed prior to leaving Walker County, we don't have the facilities or personnel to conduct an extensive training program on our own. We're doing the best we can, and we've got some issues to work through, but that is as much our fault as Recruit Sasha's.'

'Sasha is at fault, Master Sergeant?'

Master Sergeant paused for a moment. 'A poor choice of words, ma'am. What I mean is that any deficiencies on Sasha's part may be because of our own failures in training her, and not through any failures on her part.'

Sasha felt disappointed. She thought she had been doing well.

'Sasha, we're going to be getting busy in the next few months,' Snow said. 'The good news that we found a location not too far away that might be useful for target practice. The bad news that I can't guarantee you will have sufficient training when we do see combat. I told you once you'd have a chance to decline if you do not want to see combat. It sounds to me like you want to fight, and we certainly can use you, but I want to hear it from you. Do you want to fight?'

'Yes, Colonel. Put my boots on the line.' Sasha thought she sounded much more confident than she felt.

'You could do worse than follow in Corporal Winnie's footsteps,' Snow said with a small smile. 'Keep your head about you, Sasha. Chances are we'll see combat before you know it.'

Sasha nodded nervously. 'Yes, Colonel.'

Chapter 11

Jim grabbed the handle, braced his legs, and pulled the box from the collapsed supply cache. The green box was muddy and wet, but intact. He lifted it up to Sasha standing on the hill and picked his shovel up.

Sasha carried the box back to the tarp to spread it out on the ground. Master Sergeant worked a crowbar in and pulled off the top of the box. 'The inside is wet,' he growled, laying the box next to the first one pulled from the mudslide. A half dozen Mardurers were checking the bullets one at a time, then working them through the rifles. Sasha went back to carry a leather case of miscellaneous gear to the tarp.

The rain storm from the previous night had wreaked havoc on the camp. The supply cache had collapsed, the campsite was a small pond, and everyone was wet. The observation post was being bailed out. Now it was time to take stock and make repairs.

The tarp was covered with ammunition, weapons, tools, little bits that used to be secured in the caches. Half of the dried food was gone, clothes were hung up between trees to dry. Some of the regiment was drying their clothes, working in their shorts and underclothes. Sasha felt a little embarrassed, being one of those who worked in her wet clothes around those who had shed them, but no one said anything to her about it.

Sasha was checking the sewing supplies when Colonel Snow checked in with Master Sergeant.

'How does it look?'

'Could be worse,' he said. 'We've lost some of our reserve food, some of the smaller odds and ends, but the ammunition is still good, even if we have to clean quite of bit of it. But all in all, it could have been so much worse, ma'am. Just need to let things dry for now.'

'Good. Captain Saber noted that the roots over the caches are still intact; he thinks with some decent lumber and some tar we can make them better.'

'We'll need tar,' Master Sergeant said.

'Among other things,' Snow said quietly. Sasha tried to focus on her work, not stare up at the two and ask what they were talking about. She was the most junior member of the regiment, and it was not her business.

'Colonel?' Master Sergeant asked.

Snow must have gestured, because Master Sergeant nodded and followed her up the hill. Sasha continued to work. A few minutes later, Mary came by. 'Sasha, how goes it?'

'Nothing looks ruined,' Sasha said. The sewing supplies were held in a leather satchel that had kept most of the water out. The leather case unrolled, with the supplies all separated into pouches. Sasha had opened each pouch. 'I might leave some of the spools out to dry.'

'I'll take them over to the bandages,' Mary said. 'You lose anything?'

'No,' Sasha said. 'Not much to lose, and I protected what I have.'

'Good,' Mary said.

Snow appeared. 'Sasha, I need you to go with Master Sergeant.'

'Yes, ma'am,' Sasha said. 'May I ask what for?'

'We're going to test out some of the weapons, and I want you to at least know what the kick of a rifle feels like.'

Sasha smiled. 'Yes, ma'am!'

'Sasha,' Snow wanted. 'This is serious. Pay attention, and do not do anything stupid.'

Sasha nodded, blushing.

Master Sergeant stood at edge of the camp, with Beth and Jim. Beth handed Sasha a bag with six rifles in it. Jim carried his machine gun, Master Sergeant and Beth carried the regiment's two automatics.

'Let's go,' Master Sergeant said.

They marched through the woods, about a mile by Sasha's reckoning, when Sasha realized the terrain had changed. The trees were spread out, and the ground was heavy with crumbled rocks. She looked around at saw debris, moss covered and worn, of the remains of houses. Several of them.

One of the towns, from the Before Time.

They passed through the quiet remains for some time before they found their destination: a long, stone-walled building, half collapsed, but with one wall still standing. A long corridor had been cleared out inside.

'Rather large settlement,' Beth said.

'This all used to be farmland,' Master Sergeant said. 'After the fall, the trees reclaimed the land and the buildings.' He looked around. 'I've heard stories that there were men and women who purposefully planted trees, helping spread the trees faster than they normally would have. Some say those men and women became the Verendrye.'

'I wonder if Sonja knows that story,' Sasha mused.

'Ask her later,' Master Sergeant said. He unrolled a long cloth sheet, about four feet to a side. Painted inside was the rough black silhouette of a person. Red and gold details were added over organs and limbs with a gold star right over the heart. 'Beth, go hang this up at the other end.'

They organized their end of the range, laying a blanket on the ground and stacking the weapons on a metal table. Master Sergeant handed Sasha one of the rifles.

'Check this weapon.'

She removed the bolt and inspected it. She glanced down the barrel and pressed on the spring. 'Looks good, Master Sergeant,' she said, reassembling the rifle.

111

Master Sergeant handed her two small cloth and beeswax earplugs. 'Put these in, then lay down.' she did so, her heart beating quickly. Jim and Beth stood off to the sides, and Master Sergeant handed her one stripper clip of five bullets.

'Load your rifle.'

Sasha opened the bolt and fit the strip into the groves. The bullets stuck, so she wiggled the clip until it lined up and pushed the five bullets into the rifle's magazine. She closed the bolt.

I'm now holding a loaded gun.

'You know how to aim, so do that. Take your time and line up your sights. Get used to the weight of the rifle in your hands and against your shoulder. Notice how the sights rise and fall with your breathing.'

Sasha focused, listening to Master Sergeant and trying to follow his instructions. The earplugs amplified the sound of her heart, rapidly beating in anticipation. She had held unloaded rifles before, but a loaded one felt a hundred times heavier. She adjusted her sweaty hands, and felt as though her whole body was blushing.

'Take a deep breath and try to calm yourself,' Master Sergeant said. 'Now, find the safety with your finger and turn it off.'

Sasha did so and heard the click of the safety.

'Now squeeze on the trigger, slowly until it engages and....'

The rifle fired, surprising Sasha, bucking into her shoulder. Sasha held on, her shoulder smarting. Her nose was filled with the smell of gunpowder.

'Did I hit it?' she asked loudly. Her head still rung with the gunshot.

'Nope,' Beth said. 'High and right.'

Sasha frowned.

'Okay, you're shifting your hand when you fire, and that's changing the trajectory. Load the next bullet and try again.'

Sasha worked the bolt awkwardly, ejecting the spent round onto the blanket next to her, and got herself back into position. She aimed at the heart of the figure, considered her breathing, and fired. The target jumped.

'Still high and right, but on the cloth,' Beth said.

Sasha finished the last three bullets, still hitting the cloth but not the target. 'Wow,' she said.

'Difficult?'

'Yeah,' Sasha admitted, disappointed in herself. Whomever had killed Yeoman-Lieutenant Marks had passed a bullet within inches of her face. *How often had they practiced to be able to do that?* Sasha asked herself.

Someone guessed the look on her face. 'With time and practice, you'll get it,' Beth said. 'Not that we have a lot of either.'

'You're slow on the bolt,' Jim said.

'I'm unused to it, I'll get better,' Sasha replied.

'Beth, take the next one.'

Sasha picked up the spent bullets as Beth grabbed one of the rifles. She checked it and loaded it, and while standing, put five shots into the gold circle that represented the heart. She worked the bolt smoothly and steadily, working into a steady rhythm. Sasha marveled at her skill.

'How long did it take you to get that good?' she asked.

'About three thousand rounds,' Beth said.

And I've only got five.

Sasha fired one clip through the last four rifles, trying one clip standing and one clip kneeling. She hit the target once, a shot through the arm that probably would have taken the arm off in real life. Sasha grimaced at that.

'I'm not good,' she pouted.

'No, you're not,' Master Sergeant said. 'But you're not meant to be. You're just starting out and you have no prior experience.'

'How is any of that good?' she asked.

'It means you don't have anything you need to unlearn.'

Master Sergeant loaded one of the submachine guns next. 'Kneel, Sasha.' He handed her the weapon. 'Remember where the safety is?'

'Yeah,' she said, turning the gun to look. He smacked her shoulder.

'Keep the weapon pointed down range!'

'Yes, Master Sergeant,' she said loudly, blushing again. She felt around. 'There.'

'Okay. Try it.'

Sasha pulled the gun close, lined up the sights, and pulled the trigger. The weapon tore through the magazine, spraying bullets wildly down the range. Master Sergeant grabbed her to keep her from falling over and firing in the wrong direction.

'Jesus Christ, Sasha!' Beth said. 'Are you trying to kill us?'

'Let's not give her one of those,' Jim said, laughing.

The gun was empty. 'That was quick,' she said.

'Yep,' Master Sergeant said. 'And that's why we don't give you automatics.'

The three stood back as Master Sergeant loaded the second automatic and smoothly fired at the target, squeezing only long enough to emit a burst of three or four shots. He emptied the magazine and ejected it.

'How many rounds did it take him to get that good?' Sasha asked.

'A million?' Beth guessed.

Jim moved in with his larger machine gun. Sasha grinned and he shook his head.

'Nope! Not giving you the chance to kill us all. Stand back and try not to hurt yourself.'

Jim had to lie down for his gun, a long sturdy weapon with a bipod. The magazine extended out to the side. Beth leaned over.

'That's actually a light machine gun.'

'They get bigger?' Sasha asked. Jim chuckled.

Jim's gun did not just have a safety, it had a selector switch. Jim started with several single shots, hitting the target directly. Then with a click he fired in three round bursts. When the gun clicked empty he reloaded as quickly as he could, flicked the switch to the third setting, and ripped off the entire magazine in three seconds of gunfire. Sasha saw how Jim had to hold the weapon in place as it fired.

'So he's not just carrying that weapon because he's big,' she said to Beth. 'He has to be big enough to control the recoil.'

'Yeah,' Beth said. 'In single or burst, one of us could probably control it, but it would hurt.'

Their final round was the pistols. They moved up to thirty feet from the target. Sasha was surprised her first shot missed by as much as it did, but she found the pistol easier to control than the rifle and managed two shots into the gold circle by the end.

'Poor Target Tim,' Beth said. The silhouette was greatly affected by the training, with bullets dotting every part of the body. Sasha tried to ignore the number of holes well outside the silhouette.

They returned to camp and stored the weapons, dropping the spent rounds into a storage bag until they could get their hands on some gunpowder and reload them. A late lunch or early dinner was finishing, and the regiment ate.

Sasha looked over at Snow, waiting for her to finish her meal. Snow ate with Saber and Master Sergeant, discussing whatever it was they discussed. They were a stern-looking trio, she mused. The two men were bigger and older, obviously competent and dangerous. Snow was smaller and younger, but her facial burn and her demeanor made up for it. Sasha watched the two men bob their heads in deference to their colonel, and wondered how those two came to be under her command.

So much I don't know.

The two men stood and saluted their colonel. Saber went off by himself, but Master Sergeant looked around until he saw Sasha and approached her.

'Sasha. The colonel wants to see you.'

Sasha nodded and made her way to the Den. The hill hid the sun, so the camp was getting dark. It was still too wet to get the main fire going, but a small one was starting up on the hill. Sasha picked her way around the puddles to Snow, sitting at her den, watching the approach.

'Well done,' she said.

'Thank you, ma'am,' Sasha said. She saluted. 'You wanted to see me, Colonel?'

Snow nodded. Sasha sat on one of the logs, still damp from the rain.

'Master Sergeant says you actually hit the target,' Snow said.

'Yes. I'm not sure I'll be that much of a help in the first fight.'

'Assuming you're in the first fight,' Snow said.

Sasha winced, but nodded. 'Master Sergeant said the same thing. I hate hearing it, but I understand. I'm the newest member, and I can't expect to be at the head of everything. And the regiment is doing well training me as best they can. But I also know there's a lot of work to do, and there isn't always someone to show me how.'

'Yes,' Snow said. 'We always expected to train in new recruits in squads. Attaching one individual was unanticipated.'

'I'm sorry.'

'Don't be,' Snow said, smirking. 'It's not a complaint. We should have considered it. And I think our solution was pretty good, seeing how you are turning out. Which is why I'm making you a Rifle.'

Sasha's breath caught. 'Colonel, I don't know if that is.....'

Snow interrupted. 'I do. Normally, you'd finish all the exercises, get a whole ceremony, a presentation to the regiment, but I'm afraid we don't have time for the niceties. You are still in training, but I need you able to fulfill the duties of the regiment. Understood?'

'Yes, Colonel,' Sasha said.

Snow smiled. 'Good,' she said. She turned back to her bag, but Sasha did not leave. Snow looked back at her. 'Was there something else, Rifle Sasha?'

'I was wondering if there was anything I could do to catch up.'

'Catch up? How so?'

Sasha shrugged. 'I don't know. I'm learning the basics, the actions, but it's like there's this whole idea that I'm still getting used to. It kind of reminds me of....' She stopped.

'Go on,' Snow said.

Sasha sighed. 'Every so often we would get a visitor in the Alvanist services. Sometimes it was another village member, usually a traveler who wanted to know what the services were like. They would go through the motions, stand and sing with us, listen respectfully - usually - but they did not understand everything. My dad called it a nuance, the distinction of expression. My mom said they knew the words and the notes, but couldn't hear the song.'

Snow nodded. 'I understand what you mean.'

'Do you?' Sasha asked.

'Yes.' Snow leaned forward. 'I do have something that may help you, or it may confuse you. Either way, it is a treasure that needs to be protected, understood?'

Sasha nodded, her curiosity piqued.

Snow stood and pulled out a small leather satchel. It was the book bag, a specially lined case for the regimental books. It was waterproof and fireproof, and very important. She pulled from it a small, red book with gold lettering on it. She handed it to Sasha, who tried to read the lettering in the disappearing light.

'*The Art of War* by Sun…T-zu?'

'Sun Tzu,' Snow said. 'The original text is three thousand years old, and was written in a land that is on the other side of the world. General Caesar gave this to me when I asked him for a book to use as a guide for myself and fellow officers. He said it was a nice start, but not perfect. He said, "It is a book of morals that does not include the fables." Lessons without the stories. Caesar actually said that you really begin to understand the book when you begin to see everything it doesn't say.'

'What is it about?'

'Warfare. Strategy, tactics, marching, terrain. It should help you learn the song, and not just the notes.'

Sasha smiled. 'That would be good. And I promise to take care of it, ma'am.'

'One more thing,' Snow said. 'Beth and Erick have both expressed an interest in obtaining a Warrant and becoming officers of the Regiment. They have been looking through that book. You will need to share it with them, if they ask.'

'Thank you, Colonel,' Sasha said. She made her way back to the fire, hoping there was room close enough for reading light.

Chapter 12

Sasha reached the end of the encampment and peered out through the woods. It was just as empty as it had been ten minutes before.

She waited a minute, turned and walked back. The camp was empty; completely empty. Other than Rick, who was in the observation post, everyone else was gone. Colonel Snow was out meeting with some local leaders and Captain Saber sprung a surprise field march on the remaining Mardurers, leaving Sasha behind with a rifle and the goats.

Sasha walked back towards the fire pit and her books. She had both of them, *The Art of War* and *The War of the Three Fools*, open on the rock.

She turned to the history book and the Battle of Tilbury, when the Duc de Montreal's Armee de Saint Clair ran into Lieutenant General Simone's XI Corps and started the war. There was a nicely drawn map of the isthmus, with the battle lines drawn out in color, with hills and towns and roads clearly labeled. She could look at the map and know exactly where every regiment and command was at the start of the battle, and some of the opening maneuvers.

She flipped through Sun Tzu, trying to see the words of the warlord applied to the war in front of her. Some of the rules were easy to understand, such as controlling a large force through dividing their numbers. Others, Sasha had to stop and think about. She tried to look at the decisions the generals in the book made through her own eyes, using Sun Tzu as a guide, but some of their decisions completely baffled her, and the fact that some of them actually worked struck her as downright silly.

After a short time, Sasha closed the books and walked around the camp again. She stood on the rifle steps and peered through the woods, imagining yeomen stalking through the woods. *How would I fight if I was in charge?* she asked herself. She knew how Colonel Snow wanted them to fight if the yeomen found them; they practiced their positions every week, and Sasha did not think she could improve on them. But Sonja's words whispered in her ear, and she wondered if that was because she honestly could not improve, or if she was not trying too hard because she did not want to upstage Colonel Snow.

She continued her patrol, looking out the other direction, and spotted movement. She shouldered her rifle and aimed out into the forest, the safety still on. She followed the shape with her sights until it cleared a clump of birch trees.

Sasha dropped the rifle barrel and waved at Corporal Winnie. Winnie had been with Colonel Snow's group, and looked like she had been running for some time. Sasha felt her heart race as Winnie jogged up to her.

'Is everything okay, Corporal?' Sasha asked.

Winnie nodded. 'Just...fine.' She took a few deep breaths before continuing. 'Colonel Snow split the squad. Two rifles and six new recruits are about a mile behind me. The colonel should be back by tonight.' She looked at the empty campsite. 'Captain Saber?' she asked.

Sasha nodded. 'He does love his marches.'

Winnie sat down and drank from her canteen. Sasha looked around.

'Should I get out the shovels?'

'Shovels?' Winnie asked.

'Well, we had to dig our own sleeping dens when we arrived. I think it's only fair they do the same.'

'Yes,' Winnie said after a pause as her face reddened.

Sasha realized Winnie had not thought about what to do once the new recruits got here. She changed the subject. 'Are they bringing food?'

Winnie nodded. 'Not a lot, though.'

The digging tools were out and waiting when the newcomers arrived. Three men and three women, one swollen in pregnancy, escorted by two Rifles. They looked about the campsite, seeing the sleeping dens, goats and fire pit. Winnie walked up to them.

'Welcome to the campsite, recruits. First: everyone digs their own sleeping den. Rifle Sasha and I have marked out two new dens; one for the girls, and one for the boys. Just dig within the lines and you'll have a nice warm place to sleep, in case of rain. The Rifles around you can be asked for advice, but they will not assist you in building your dens. Any questions?' There was no response. 'Get to work.'

The recruits moved towards the tools as Winnie circled the rifles around her. 'It's getting on midday. Keep patrolling, answer any questions they have, and get some biscuits out. I'm going up to the OP for a bit.'

She turned to leave but Sasha spoke up. 'We should give the pregnant woman more than just a biscuit.'

'We're on low enough rations as it is,' Winnie said. 'She can suffer a light lunch.'

'Not with a baby she can't,' Sasha said, her voice sharp against Winnie's indifference.

'We should not waste food, not without Colonel Snow's approval,' Winnie said.

'Then she can have my biscuit, until Colonel Snow or Captain Saber arrives.'

Winnie looked like she might argue, but finally just shrugged. 'Fine.' She turned and walked up the hill towards the observation post. Sasha and the rest watched her walk off before continuing with their duties.

It was only a few minutes later when Rifle David made a whispered call and pulled Sasha's attention to the rifle step. Sasha walked over.

'Someone's coming,' he whispered.

Sasha and David looked out into the woods. Figures began to appear, developing into a column. They were dressed like Mardurers, and lead by a Verendrye woman who was not Sonja.

'Think they're friendly?' David asked.

'Yes,' Sasha said. But she wished Winnie would come down from the Observation Post.

'Where's Corporal Winnie?' David asked.

'Not here, and we are.' Sasha said, she grabbed a root and lifted herself up onto the hillside, holding her hand up to the squad. Their guide saw them and stopped the squad. She motioned them to stay and sprinted forward.

'Third Field Regiment?' she asked. Sasha nodded. 'Good. First Sergeant Ward, Chosen Rifle. I'm leading a column from Walker with reinforcements.' She looked at the lack of any insignia on Sasha or David. 'Who is in charge?'

'Best we have is a Corporal,' Sasha said. 'She's up at the observation post.'

'Well,' Ward grimaced. 'I'm afraid I've got an officer. Might want to prepare yourself,' she whispered as she waved the squad up.

There were ten newcomers, led by a tall, confident man with the two bars of a First Lieutenant. He strutted into camp, looking about for anyone who might outrank him. He looked at Ward.

'Where's the Officer of the Watch?' he asked.

'Corporal Winnie is in charge,' Sasha repeated. 'She's up at the Observation Post, should be back any second now.'

'Ah,' he said, looking at the men and women digging. 'What are they doing?'

'They're digging their sleeping dens,' Sasha said. The other Rifles, despite being her nominal superiors, were letting her do the talking. 'First thing everyone does.'

'Well, my men and women are tired, so I think you mean they're digging our sleeping dens,' he said, with a curt nod to make his point.

'No, sir. They're digging their own sleeping dens.'

Everyone went still as the lieutenant turned to look down on her. He was a very tall man - a very handsome man, the truth be told - but he looked at her with a very stern look. 'I am First Lieutenant Buck, a commissioned officer. You are a Riflewoman, not even a non-commissioned officer. Who are you to question me?'

'I may only be a Rifle, sir,' Sasha said, 'but I know what the chain of command is, and until Colonel Snow or Captain Saber tells me you are in my chain of command, I will not follow any order that contradicts a standing order from either of them.' She paused. 'Sir.'

Buck looked around and smiled. 'Ah, a Corporal,' he said as Winnie jogged up. Winnie looked at the new arrivals with bewilderments. 'Corporal, this Rifle here is refusing to obey an order. She says that all new members, even officers, dig their own sleeping dens.'

Winnie looked between Buck and Sasha. She swallowed and nodded. 'That is correct, Lieutenant. Everyone pitches in; no exceptions.'

Buck Scowled. He glared at Winnie, but she did not back down. Finally he sighed.

'Very well, Corporal,' he said through gritted teeth. 'Everyone digs. But rest assured, the Colonel will hear of this.'

With that he turned to his squad and issued orders. The squad dumped excess equipment in a pile near the fire pit - including, Sasha noted with no small delight, six extra rifles and several boxes of ammunition- and started measuring out their own dens. Winnie answered a few more questions Lieutenant Buck had; Sasha stayed on watch, away from the irate officer.

Captain Saber's group returned an hour later, carrying a deer that Sonja had killed. Sasha cringed as Buck, on the lookout for an officer to complain to, scampered over to Saber and spoke to him in hushed tones. She tried to ignore them and continued on her patrol.

A minute later Saber approached, gesturing for Winnie to join them.

'I understand there was a bit of an issue,' he said.

'With all due respect, Captain Saber, Lieutenant Buck does not have any authority in this regiment until you or Colonel Snow tell me he does,' Sasha said before Winnie could speak.

Winnie nodded. 'I agree, Captain. Some odd officer coming into the camp does not get to start taking over the regiment.'

Saber said nothing. 'I will have to let the Colonel know, since Lieutenant Buck will inform her if I don't.' He turned and paused. 'And good job getting the recruits to work with the dens, Corporal.'

'That was Rifle Sasha's idea, Captain,' Winnie said begrudgingly.

'Hm,' Saber said and turned away. Winnie said nothing and went back to overseeing the digging. Sasha continued her patrol, hoping that the Colonel would show her the same support Saber did. She worried for four more hours before Snow returned, so much so she could not concentrate on the books when she was finally relieved of her patrol.

Dinner was almost ready when she and Winnie were called to Snow's Den. Snow had already spoken with Captain Saber, and was looking through a small pile of letters that had been delivered. She barely looked up when the two young women stood before her.

'I wanted you to know that I support the actions you took today,' she said, opening one of the letters. 'But Lieutenant Buck is now in our chain of command. Captain Saber is going to work with him to get him used to how we do things around here. So we will all have to adjust.'

'Understood, ma'am,' Winnie said. Sasha nodded.

'Good, because I need both of you to start thinking.' She looked up. 'Someday, you may find yourself in a position where you have to take orders from an officer you do not know. Those orders may conflict with orders you are following from me, or an officer of Third Regiment. In those situations, you may feel compelled to follow the orders of the other officer and not the orders of ours. You need to think now, so when that happens, you can be prepared.'

'We won't disobey your orders, Colonel,' Sasha said immediately. Snow glanced at Winnie, who shifted uncomfortably.

'Corporal?'

Winnie cleared her throat. 'Field Regiments do not operate under the strict rules that Line Regiments do. Everyone in a field regiment, even the NCOs, are expected to exercise a high level of initiative. Any order can be ignored, dependent on the situation they find themselves in.'

'So think about that, Rifle Sasha,' Snow said. 'If the situation arises, and you haven't thought about it, then you will not be prepared for it when it does. Dismissed.'

Sasha and Winnie saluted and turned when Snow spoke up. 'Sasha, stay.'

Sasha stopped and turned. 'Yes, Colonel?'

'What are you doing with those books?'

Sasha looked down at her hand. She had *The War of the Three Fools* and *The Art of War* fitted in with each other. She had forgotten she even had them in her hand.

'Oh. I've been using the history book to learn the war book.'

'How so?' Snow asked. She did not sound angry, just curious.

'Well, I read the history book, and I look through the war book, and I find the lessons that can be learned from the battles. It really is helpful! I mean, look at this!' She opened the two books, laying them down on the stump in front of Snow, unable to hide her excitement. 'Sun Tzu writes: 'Now the general who wins a battle makes many calculations in his temple before the battle is fought. The general who loses a battle makes but few calculations beforehand. Thus do many calculations lead to victory, and few calculations to defeat.' Now, look at the opening campaign.

125

Marshal de Montreal led 35,000 men in a surprise attack. He expected he would get into Detroit without a problem, even though he had no real plans. He expected to react to the battle as it developed.

'But General Simone, he was always planning. He ran monthly drills, plans for one invasion or another. So when his cavalry found the Quebecois Army advancing, he did not have to issue great big detailed orders. He simply told his generals where the enemy was, what he wanted, and everyone acted like . . . like a dance! He was outnumbered more than two to one and he trashed the Quebecois Army. Their three month war turned into a six year embarrassment.'

She smiled at Snow, who was actually smiling back. 'That's very good, Sasha. Though, both those armies were conventional armies.'

'What do you mean?' Sasha asked.

'Conventional armies are those who fight in pitched battle. We're a light regiment, so the lessons won't translate as well.' She saw the look on Sasha's face. 'Oh, don't get me wrong, I'm impressed, Sasha, and I'm glad you are enjoying yourself. But I would prefer that you spend your time first looking at the campaigns of Colonel Caroline Sudeikis. Her campaigns are much more alike to what we are doing.'

'Her?' Sasha was surprised.

Snow smiled again. 'I don't want to spoil the surprise. Keep reading, Sasha. And if possible, don't ever stop.'

Chapter 13

Sasha heard something drop inside the den. Mary had been sleeping inside, and had a habit of stretching when she woke up, usually knocking something off the small shelf.

'Are you okay?' Sasha asked through the curtain.

'Yeah, just causing problems.' Mary poked her head out. Sasha was sitting outside the den, reading her two books in the growing light, as she did every morning. Mary looked around. 'Where is Riflewoman Beth?'

Sasha shrugged. 'I think she snuck off with Rifle Rick again.'

Mary retreated back into the den. 'If Riflewoman Beth is not careful, she's going to be Rifle-mother Beth.'

Sasha giggled. 'Can you imagine Beth as a mother?'

'If she doesn't want to be a mother, she should keep her legs shut,' Mary said. 'Besides, we've already got one pregnant woman here. We don't need two.'

Sasha mumbled an agreement. 'Master Sergeant is on his way.' Mary yelped as she fell over inside the den.

Master Sergeant walked up. 'Is Mary in there?' he asked.

'Right here,' Mary's head poked out of the den again.

'We need an inventory of medical supplies, immediately.'

'Right,' Mary said. 'One second.'

He looked at Sasha. 'Colonel Snow wants to see you now.'

'Uh, yes, Sergeant. Mary, can you put these back for me?'

'Yeah,' Mary said, taking the books through the curtain.

Sasha stood and made her way to Snow's Den. Harriet, the pregnant woman, was already preparing a morning meal of gruel and venison. Others were stumbling about, but most were still asleep.

Colonel Snow stood over her desk-stump, looking at the map. It was a canvas back onto which the regiment was slowly sewing their region, using colored thread for rivers, forests, lakes and villages. Sasha still did not know where they were; maps were not popular in her father's house, so she did not recognize the lakes that showed on the map.

'Colonel,' Sasha came to a halt and saluted. Beth and Erick stood by as well.

'Sasha, good morning. I'm posing a tactical challenge to Beth and Erick, and as you've been reading the books, I wanted to include you.'

'Yes, ma'am,' Sasha said. Neither Beth nor Erick looked unhappy to see her, to her relief.

'Good. Here is the situation. Third Regiment is here,' she put down a block on the location of their camp, which was not otherwise marked, 'except for one small squad of three Rifles here, under Corporal Winnie.' She placed a second small blue block near a river mouth on one of the lakes. She placed a small red block across the river from Corporal Winnie. 'The enemy force is a troop of bandits, between twelve and twenty strong, all mounted. They've been raiding in the east, stealing some foodstuffs, and are preparing to move west, towards the Dakotas.'

'I want you to tell me where they are going, and what, if anything, we should do about them.' With that, she turned and walked away.

Beth and Erick began studying the map, so Sasha did as well. The lakes were all to the east, the camp northwest of them. Sasha was not sure of the scale, but Winnie would not be too far away.

Sasha tried to recall Sun Tzu. Imagine the enemy: what are they after, what are they capable of? What are the objectives of the two forces? How are they different? Ideas came and flowed, considered and forgotten. She started to get a sense for what she was thinking, when Beth tugged at her elbow to get her attention; not only had Colonel Snow returned, but Captain Saber, Lieutenant Buck, and Master Sergeant were standing around the map.

'Comfortable, Rifle Sasha?' Snow asked. The others chuckled, and Sasha turned white.

'Sorry, Colonel, just thinking about the problem.'

'And the solution, I hope,' Captain Saber said. Sasha nodded, but Snow cut in before she could respond.

'Okay, you three, you've had several minutes to consider the problem. Tell me what you think. Grenadier Erick, you are senior, you start.'

'Ma'am, I don't know where they're going, but I don't think it matters. We know where they are. We should hit them right now, with everything we can spare. Take them out before they can move.'

'What if one escapes?' Buck asked. 'One survivor runs into a yeomen patrol and we're found.'

'We surround them,' Erick said, trying to sound confident. 'Bandits can't have more than a few automatic weapons; mostly they'll have shotguns and rifles, and I doubt they'd be trained.' He gestured at the map. 'If we strike at them from here, we can push them off their campsite and into the river; they'll be in the open and we can shoot them as they flee.'

The officers glanced at each other. 'Able Rifle Beth, your turn,' Snow said.

Beth cleared her throat. 'Ma'am, I don't think we should do anything. If they number at most twenty men, and the most we can bring to bear against them is 25, we won't have the advantage we'd want, even in an ambush. Besides, like Lieutenant Buck said, only one guy has to get away for us to be revealed. There's nothing of value to the west of us for many miles. Better we lay low and let them move on by.'

'Sensible,' Saber said. Beth blushed, but no one was under the impression she had just received a compliment.

'Rifle Sasha,' Snow asked.

Sasha thought for one more moment. Both Erick and Beth had good points, but she disagreed with them.

'Ma'am, I'd move the regiment towards the river,' she said, westward of the bandits' camp site. 'If the bandits head north, they'll run into the rest of the Mardurers; south or east, there's the yeomen. They're going to head west, and I think we need to hit them when they do.'

'Why the river?' Buck asked.

'They don't want to be tracked,' Sasha said. 'They can move up the river without leaving any trail. Same as Captain Saber has us do during out evacuation drills.'

'But why hit them at all?' Saber asked.

'Because we're trying to win the villagers over to our side, and villagers hate bandits, especially ones who have struck them already. We would want to . . . ,' Sasha paused.

'Yes?' Snow asked.

Sasha sighed. 'We would want to kill or capture all of them. We can't let any of them get out.' *And that means killing them all,* Sasha knew. 'An ambush where someone could decide to surrender is one where someone could decide to run.'

Snow looked at the three of them for a minute. 'None of you have proposed a plan that would not be worth following. That's good. In fact, Sasha, your plan is remarkably similar to the plan we're going to follow.'

Going to follow? Sasha shared a look of surprise with Beth and Erick.

'Captain Saber, I'll leave you here with Beth and two of the new recruits, in case the bandits head towards camp. Master Sergeant, ready everyone else for action. Combat packs only, gentlemen. We'll be back by nightfall.'

The officer saluted and turned. Snow looked at the three rifles. 'Dismissed,' she said.

The three saluted and left.

'Holy shit,' Beth said. Erick nodded.

Sasha was quiet.

◆◆◆

The forest was full of sounds, of birds and squirrels and wind. The regiment was quiet, barely daring to even breathe.

Colonel Snow's force lay in the forest, a circle of guns and sharpened bayonets facing outward. Snow, Saber, Master Sergeant and Mary sat in the middle. Sasha lay between Gunner Jim and one of the new recruits who looked like she was about to jump sky high. Sasha felt the same way.

Her heart raced. She had seen combat, yes, but only seen it. It happened, suddenly and violently, all around her, while she watched. There was no anticipation to deal with.

Sasha thought that the anticipation would kill her. Questions ran through her mind. *Will I kill someone today? Will I be killed? Would I run and cry? Am I the pacifist Winnie accuses me of being? Will Snow send me home if I fail her? Do I want to fight today? Colonel Snow is following my plan; how do feel I about that? If it does not go well, is that my fault?*

Sasha heard her father's voice, his sermons and speeches. She could almost feel him now, standing over her, warning her not to do anything. *Violence is wrong! Killing is the ultimate sin!*

These men are violent, Father. They kill, they steal, they rape and pillage.

That is their sin! Do not take that sin on your shoulders! God will punish them, and will punish you as well.

If the bandits are allowed to live, they will kill and steal and more, across how many villages and towns? I am protecting the innocent.

The only innocent in the world are those who care for their fellow man. ALL fellow man.

No, Father. Killing these men proves I am protecting my fellow man.

131

First Rifle Susan, the runner Winnie and Snow were using to communicate, ran up to the circle through the woods. She had already run more than six miles today, but she was by far the best runner, and looked up to the task. She was breathing hard, but still reported to the Colonel. Sasha could not hear everything, keeping her eyes outward as she heard movement behind her. She wanted to look, but she her job was to look outward. Master Sergeant was very clear on that: do your job, trust everyone else to do their job.

Master Sergeant began moving, tapping soldiers. The regiment shook out into three columns, Sonja leading the regiment with Snow right behind her. Sasha found herself on the right side of the formation, trying to keep fifteen feet away from everyone around her. The regiment moved quickly; the hours spent moving through the woods around camp, preparing for just this moment, showed as the regiment swiftly cut through the trees to their destination.

Snow had chosen a bend in the river, placing her regiment on the inside of the curve. She posted machine guns on the ends, Lieutenant Buck on the far end and Master Sergeant watching the incoming river. Sasha found herself in a rifle squad under Sergeant Tomas, with Rifle John and Rifle Rick, right on the line facing the kill zone, next to another rifle squad, putting eight rifles on the line. They spread themselves out five feet apart, finding fallen branches and rocks to hide behind, piling ammunition and grenades around them for easy access.

They waited.

Sasha could not see downstream; she was in the kill zone. At this spot, the river was about forty feet across, maybe three feet deep in the middle. There was a fallen tree on the far side, jutting out into the water.

She tried to imagine people crossing it, how she would aim her rifle, how far she might be able to throw a grenade. What would she do if the bandits assaulted their position? What if they ran? What if they took shelter behind the tree? What if?

Singing. Sasha heard the singing, coming from her right. She pulled her rifle in close, praying they would not see her and would scuttle right into the kill zone. 'Focus and breathe', she whispered to herself. Realizing she was saying it out loud, she forced herself quiet. *Focus and breathe.*

The singing stopped and devolved into boisterous conversation and laughter. She was able to make out individual words, and the first bandits came into view. All farmers, even Alvanists, feared bandits, who answered to no law. The stories told made them out as inhuman monsters. These looked like normal men, varied in size as any group of men would be. Their horses were no evil beasts, just normal horses bearing normal men. Moving very slowly. Sasha and the other Mardurers slowly raised their rifles to their shoulders and aimed.

As the bandits moved into the kill zone, one started singing a new song, followed quickly by the others.

'Blond haired girls, they are the best
      With bouncy tits upon their chest!
Red haired girls, they are divine,
      Their honey pot, it tastes like wine!
Dark-haired girls, they are so sweet,
      You paint the ceiling with their feet!
Girls with children, they still rock!
      Threaten their kids and they'll suck your . . . .'

Third Regiment opened fire.

Sasha aimed at a fat, gray bearded man who was just bellowing the words. He twisted as her bullet struck him in the arm. She worked the bolt as he twisted to bring his rifle around, but one of the sergeants knocked him off his horse with a burst from an automatic.

Half of the bandits were down in the first several seconds, but the survivors were responding. Several tried galloping away, drawing the majority of the fire from Third Regiment. None of them made it more than fifteen yards. Others were firing back; some had automatic weapons, and sprayed the woods where the Mardurers concealed themselves. One bullet clipped the rock next to Sasha's face; she flinched and rolled back. Taking a deep breath, she returned to firing position and fired again.

Erick's rifle grenade echoed through the woods, exploding between the last mounted bandits. Several horses dropped to the water, splashing in their death throws as their riders fell into the water. Sasha joined the rifles in shooting at them, hoping to finish them before they stood up.

Sasha rolled back to reload. The firing had died out when she was back into position. Bodies lay in the water, weighted to the bottom by their weapons and equipment. A half dozen horses lay dead or dying, the rest having run off to die or be found elsewhere.

'Now what?' Sasha yelled. Her ears were ringing.

'Wait for instructions,' Tomas said. 'Hold fast.' He too was all but yelling after the short but furious fire. Other voices called out, sergeants' and officers' commands, calming the regiment.

Sasha looked out over the river, ears ringing, heart pounding. *How do people do this for hours or days?*

Another burst of rifle fire from the woods, further in than expected. 'Call out targets!' Snow yelled. 'Know what you are shooting at!'

The forest quieted down again. Then a voice called out.

'Colonel Snow! It's Corporal Winnie!'

'Report, Corporal!'

'Ma'am, we crossed downstream. Intercepted a stray who made it into the forest. I'm not seeing any movement, Colonel!'

There was a pause. Sasha looked out over the bodies of the bandits. 'Rifle Squads!' Colonel Snow yelled, 'fix bayonets!' Sasha fumbled for the blade and snapped it to her rifle. 'Advance!'

The eight Mardurers rushed out of the woods, weapons out. Sasha weaved between the trees, with John and Rick on either side of her. The first bandit she came across lay slack, eyes lifeless and mouth open. She moved around him, moving on to the next.

Rick approached one who was face down. He grabbed the shoulder and pulled the man over, and the man grabbed back.

'Rick!' Sasha shouted a warning. It was too late. The bandit had a pistol in his free hand, and he fired it into Rick at point blank range.

Sasha was ten feet away. She brought her rifle up as Rick fell, firing a single shot that struck the bandit in his shoulder. She did not waste time reloading; she charged and stabbed with the bayonet, pinning him by the throat under water. He tried to raise his hand with the pistol but Sasha stepped down on it. The river water turned bright red.

'One round, every bandit, NOW!' Tomas called. The bandit had stopped moving. She released him and he started drifting away. She turned to Rick, slowly pulling himself towards the edge, the river around him a sickly red.

'MARY!' Sasha screamed, pulling Rick onto the shore. Mary and Master Sergeant dropped down beside her. Rick was blinking repeatedly, gasping for breath.

'Okay, Rick, hold on,' Mary said, She had her knife out, cutting his shirt away. There was a neat little hole in his chest, blood pumping out. Mary's face turned white.

'Okay, Rick,' she said, grabbing her kit. He grabbed her hand.

'Don't,' Rick gasped. 'Don't waste the bandages, Mary.'

Mary froze. 'Rick . . . .'

'I know . . . what a kill shot is . . . I was taught . . . to shoot to . . . kill.' He coughed. He glanced up as Colonel Snow stepped up. He looked up into her face. 'Colonel . . . tell Beth . . . .'

'I know,' Snow said. 'She knows too.'

Rick nodded and looked up into the sky. He tried to say something else, but coughed up blood and convulsed. Mary and Master Sergeant held his hands as his eyes relaxed.

Sasha looked down at Rick and felt a tear fall down her face. Others had stepped up around, watching their friend die. Several of them were crying. Sasha could not put together a thought. This wasn't supposed to happen. Not to them. They had done it right.

Snow stood up and looked around. 'Third! We have a job to do. I want everybody searched. Every tool, every weapon, and every bullet we can salvage! If you know how to butcher a horse, let's salvage some meat. If you get a live horse, keep it that way! Mary,' she said, in a quieter tone, 'let's make a stretcher.'

Master Sergeant and the sergeants started organizing the Mardurers, yelling to get their attention away from the body. 'Sasha! Get to work,' Tomas shouted.

There were sixteen bandits in all, bodies dragged to the shore. The youngest was maybe sixteen, the oldest gray haired and grandfatherly. The Mardurers stripped them of everything, even the belts and boots, nice leather gear that should not be wasted. These bandits favored shotguns and automatic carbines, with a number of pistols and grenades between them. The bandits were loaded with stolen goods from peasants: roasted chickens, wheels of cheese, slabs of bacon. Two horses were found and brought back, loaded with everything they could carry. Horse meat was cut out of the rest.

Third Regiment moved back towards camp in a sullen mood, Rick's body was carried by his friends in turns; someone suggested using a horse, but the idea was quickly dismissed. The Third Regiment decided it would carry their dead. They reached camp in the late afternoon. Beth ran out to meet them and came up short at the looks on their face. Sasha was at the rear of the column, but she could still hear her cry of anguish from all the way back.

The camp was a flurry of activity. Supplies were stored and the horses tethered. Within an hour, the bulk of the regiment moved out to a field a few hundred feet beyond the camp, a small, nondescript field that Snow had purposefully left undisturbed for just such an occasion.

The grave was already dug, six feet deep. Rick was bound up in a blanket, tied with rope. Beth stood over the grave, next to Colonel Snow, as the regiment filled in around the grave.

Using ropes, Rick's friends lowered him into the grave. The rest stood at attention as Mary read from the Bible. 'So it will be with the resurrection of the dead. The body that is sown is perishable, it is raised imperishable; it is sown in dishonor, it is raised in glory; it is sown in weakness, it is raised in power; it is sown a natural body, it is raised a spiritual body. If there is a natural body, there is also a spiritual body.'

'Lord,' Colonel Snow said, 'we bury Rifle Rick Olson, Combat Rifle, Third Minnesota Field Regiment, Renaissance Army of Minnesota. Rifle Rick came from a large family, a family where his older brothers were conscripted into the king's army, and his older sisters were forced into the noble's bed. He ran away from home, and fell in with the Mardurers, to fight for a better future.

'He was a good man, always ready to work hard. He did not complain, he did not gripe, he did whatever he could do to help those around him.

'We all knew this would happen. We knew there would be losses. Rick was the Rifle that went first, an honor one of us would have to accept. He was content with his choice; he died with a purpose. We will not miss him any less. We will remember that he was first. And we will honor his memory.'

'Third Regiment, for the Rifle that went first, a moment of silence.'

Sasha felt the first tear drop. She felt closer to the women of Third Regiment than the men, and she had never known Rick as well as she could have. She felt most sorry for Beth. Beth really liked Rick, and Beth was her den-mate. She could do nothing for Rick, but she could help Beth. She could . . . not understand what she was hearing.

Several Mardurers blinked and looked around. Master Sergeant was singing, a sad, mournful tune. It captivated the regiment, standing over the open grave. Everyone had tears in their eyes as Master Sergeant sang.

A dozen back out of four score,
Of the rest we'll hear no more,
Men who died, first in the Fore,
    The best Soldiers never come home,

They fought for flag and fife and drum,
They fought with fist and blade and gun,
They fought to the end and there they won,
    The best Soldiers never come home,
The fields grow and the trees spread,
Where once men fought and mud turned red,
It is our duty to remember the dead,
    The best Soldiers never come home,
And to our children we must tell,
Tales of those who fought and fell,
And hope they live and die so well,
    The best Soldiers never come home.

Master Sergeant's voice faded. Third Regiment stood silent and still.

'Dismissed,' Snow said in a small voice, and her regiment returned to camp.

Chapter 14

The next morning, Sasha woke up alone. Mary and Beth were both gone, and sunlight was brightly visible outside. She heard voices outside. She rolled out of her den, wearing the same clothes she had slept in.

Most of the regiment was gathered around the campfire, discussing something. Sasha could not see Mary or Beth with them. Buck was there, sitting outside the circle, whittling something but not partaking in the conversation. Sasha stretched and walked over. 'Morning,' she said. Several responses came at her. Someone handed her a canteen. 'What's going on?'

Sonja leaned in. 'There's some sort of meeting going on. Beth, Mary, Master Sergeant, Snow and Saber are at the bathing pool.'

'I think she's going to run,' someone said.

'I think you need to shut up!' Sonja growled.

'Who started it?' Sasha asked.

'Don't know. Buck there does, but he's not saying anything. I'm willing to bet it is about Beth.'

Sasha felt the sadness again, the hot coal in her chest that burned her heart, so hot she felt sick. She took some deep breaths and dried her eyes.

Harriet was finishing some simple biscuits, not much more than water and flour. Sonja and Sasha split one, neither having much of an appetite. The conversation turned towards the ambush, discussing each individual's actions.

'All the times I've fired that gun,' Jim said, 'never realized what it would do to a human being. The man shredded like he was nothing. Even killed his horse.'

'You okay with that?' Sasha asked.

'Yeah,' Jim shrugged. 'I mean, I'm not happy, but if we're fighting to win, we got to be willing to kill, you know?' A chorus of agreements. 'Besides, the fight was so confusing, I was reacting more than thinking. Wasn't really angry. Not like you.'

Sasha blinked. 'What?'

'That bandit, the one who shot Rick. You shot him, then stabbed him, all while screaming like a demon.'

'I was not!' Sasha exclaimed, but the regiment laughed.

'Sorry, Sasha, you were,' Sonja said. 'Loud and angry. Surprised the hell out of everyone.'

'That was you?' Winnie asked incredulously.

'It was,' Sonja said.

'I thought it was a bobcat,' Winnie said with a sly smile. The regiment laughed. Sasha blushed.

'I didn't realize,' Sasha said. 'Sorry.'

'Don't be,' Winnie said. 'Scream like that in battle you might just scare the enemy off.'

The regiment laughed. Their attention was so distracted that none of them saw Master Sergeant walk up to the circle.

'THIRD REGIMENT!' he bellowed, causing everyone at the camp to jump. Buck laughed. 'Formation at the Colonel's Den! NOW!'

That was unusual. Master Sergeant made sure everyone knew the basics of military drill, but other than saluting and attention, the regiment rarely used it. When Snow made an address, she usually had them sitting around the fire, or standing as she stood above them and spoke. Now, she stood in front of the Den. Saber and Mary stood by, along with . . . .

Sasha gasped.

Beth stood next to Mary, her head freshly shaven. Her eyes were still red, but she was no longer crying. Instead, she looked

140

fiercely resolute as she watched the regiment fall into the loose formation they had learned.

Snow waited for them to fall in and settle down. 'Third Regiment,' she began. 'Yesterday we won an important fight. Maybe not a grand fight in the great scheme of things, but an important one. It was our first test in combat as a regiment. For some of our new members, it was their first test as an individual in combat. And for all of us, it was our first test of loss.

'As Colonel of this regiment, I must say that I am very proud of you all. No one failed in their duties. No one shirked. No one ran. We succeeded in our objective. A good first outing. One that warrants some acknowledgements of personal success. Tomas, Winnie, Susan and Sasha, up front!'

Sasha blushed as she fell out, following the others up to stand before the regiment. She stood next to Winnie, wondering what Snow was up to.

'The four standing before us acted with great courage yesterday. Corporal Winnie, in locating the bandits, shadowing them, and cutting off their fleeing remnants. First Rifle Susan, in accomplishing great feats of running, and still being prepared for combat. Sergeant Tomas and Rifle Sasha, both reacted to a sudden threat quickly and with determination. For their actions, I am promoting each of them one rank.'

Sasha blushed again. She felt odd being congratulated on her actions the previous day. She was proud of what she'd done, for the most part, but she was not sure she deserved a promotion.

She may have been the only one who thought that way, since the regiment was cheering the four of them. She glanced out the corner of her eye at Winnie, who had also turned beet red.

She's a sergeant, now . . . Sasha realized with some concern.

Snow shook each of their hands and dismissed them back to the formation. She continued.

'But we must realize that this upsets our original timeline. While the population has little love for the count or his yeomen, it will be all but impossible for us to keep word from reaching the yeomen's attention. I expect that we will begin to see increased patrols, and perhaps some efforts of controlling the population or finding our location. So we need to be on our guard, and prepare accordingly.

'First of all, at her own request, Rifle Beth has been removed from combat duties. She will be acting at the Regiment's Assistant Training Officer, focusing on bringing any new recruits up to speed, training any militia we get to raise, as necessary to prepare forces for the upcoming campaigns.

'Second, we need to begin scouting and establishing secondary and subordinate bases. As such, a detachment will be leaving tomorrow morning for an extended mission. Captain Saber will be leading the mission, with Sergeant Esmerelda as his NCO. One gunner and three rifles will accompany him; he will contact those individuals before evening time. The mission is expected to last approximately three weeks.

'Third, we did recover from the bandits several items taken from the villages. We are going to return them. I will lead a detachment to return what we can, and to show the population that we are on their side. This mission should take two or three days. I'll be taking the bulk of the rest of the Regiment with me. Lieutenant Buck, with the trainees and the rest, will stay here.

'Regardless of which group you are going with, I want all weapons and gear cleaned and ready,' she looked up at the sky, judging the time, 'in three hours. Dismissed!'

♦♦♦

The regiment worked to clean all their weapons. Not a simple cleaning, but a full disassembly. Sasha had never done one before, so she sat with the other recruits as Tomas led them through the steps. It amazed Sasha that such a solid weapon could have so many parts, and yet every piece broke down again and again. She cleaned and coated and reassembled her rifle, finally hearing that telltale 'click' of a successful reassembly.

She was going to move on to the rest of her equipment when Winnie tapped her on her shoulder. 'Come with me,' she said.

'Yes, Sergeant,' Sasha said nervously and followed.

Winnie sat down next to a blanket, with the regiment's four submachine guns. 'We're going to give these a good cleaning,' she said.

'Okay.'

Winnie show Sasha how to disassemble the weapons. Much like the rifles, the number of parts was astounding. But soon enough, all the parts lay in a somewhat organized mess on the blanket. Sasha and Winnie went to work cleaning the individual pieces.

'I wanted to say,' Winnie finally spoke, 'that I am impressed with how you handled yourself yesterday.'

'Me too,' Sasha said. Winnie chuckled.

'What was going through your mind?' she asked.

Sasha paused before she replied. 'So many things. So many questions. What was going to happen? What was I going to do? Was I going to kill someone? Was I going to die?' She started cleaning again, pushing a long wire brush through the barrel. 'I imagined my father talking at me, trying to convince me to go home. The same old arguments. I think it might have actually helped me stay. It reminded me why I was here. Why I had to fight.'

Winnie nodded and accepted the brush from Sasha. 'I remember your father, from the ambush where we picked you up.'

'What did you think?'

'He seemed . . . petty,' Winnie said. 'Like someone who would close his eyes and sing to himself rather than face the men picking through his purse.'

143

'No, he'd watch them do it and congratulate himself on being a victim,' Sasha said sadly. They were silent for a few minutes before Winnie spoke.

'One of the drill sergeants back in Walker told me that the people who are best ready to handle a situation are those who ask themselves if they are ready, and that those who simply say 'I'm ready' without asking often have no idea what they were getting into.'

Sasha considered that. 'I guess that makes sense. Like how Snow runs us through training for all these scenarios. So we spend less time thinking about it when it actually happens.'

'Which is why you killed that bandit so quickly.'

Sasha paused. 'I still wasn't happy to do that.'

'Do you regret it?' Winnie asked.

Sasha saw that Winnie had stopped and was staring at her with great interest. 'No,' Sasha admitted. 'I'm not happy about it, but I know why I did it. He was a threat, and as a bandit, he wasn't a nice man. If he'd surrendered he'd be treated with respect, but he didn't. He killed Rick. And so I killed him.'

Winnie looked at her. 'Good,' she finally said. She led Sasha through reassembling the first weapons, then grabbed the next two. 'Sasha, Snow has asked me to prepare a squad of select fighters. A squad she can call on for important missions. I want you in the squad.'

'Who else is in it?' Sasha asked.

'As of right now, just me.'

'And I'm the first one you asked? Not long ago you wanted to beat me out of the regiment.'

'Yes,' Winnie said. 'But I'm not going to apologize for that. You were unproven. And it is my responsibility as an NCO to identify and correct weak links. As far as I'm concerned, I kept you from slacking in your training and responsibilities.'

Sasha looked at her, wondering if she was serious. Winnie smiled.

'That's not entirely true,' Sasha said.

'No, but it's not entirely untrue, is it?'

Sasha thought for a moment. 'No, I guess it isn't.'

'Look, Sasha, We don't have to like each other; we can even hate each other. But Snow made you a Rifle, and you've stepped up to the responsibility.'

'And that makes you want me in your squad?'

'That, and that yesterday, you killed the bandit who shot Rick. I asked around; when he fired, everyone else ducked, but you attacked. That's an aggressive spirit, and I respect that. I want you.'

'What would it mean for me?'

'Some extra combat training, a few times a week. How to handle a submachine gun, clear a structure. I know some things with a knife that you might find interesting.'

Sasha finished disassembling her gun. 'Okay,' she said, 'I'll be in your squad. But just so you know, I don't hate you. I respect you. I've been working so that you would respect me back.'

'Then you're doing a good job,' Winnie said with a smile. She was about to say something else when a shadow appeared. 'Colonel!'

Snow stood over them. 'How is this going?'

'Two down, two to go,' Winnie said. 'Sasha agreed to the squad.'

'Good,' Snow said. 'I want both of you ready to travel tomorrow. You're joining me as we tour the villages. Expect to be gone at least two nights.'

'Yes, ma'am,' Winnie said. Sasha nodded.

'Good,' Snow said. She looked at the two of them, sitting and speaking cordially. 'Good job, you two.'

145

'Thank you,' they both said, and went back to their guns.

Chapter 15

Snow led them out the next morning, their weapons and uniforms as clean as could be expected. The two horses were loaded with loot to be returned, each led by a Mardurer. Snow shook them out into formation and proceeded east before the sun was fully up.

Sasha's view of the world outside Penelope's Haven and Walker was limited. When she had traveled to Duluth, she had seen some of the villages, but her father mostly kept her busy with Bible passages and advice on the proper role of a woman in a marriage. And except for one day spent at a festival in the city center, most of her time had been stuck in the Alvanist community on the north side of town. She hated not seeing the world around her, but her father spent much effort to keep her blind. With the Third Regiment, she spent all of her time in the forest. She had seen their tapestry map of the county take shape, but it was not until now that she knew where she was.

Third Regiment was encamped in the northwestern corner of Brainerd County, southeast of Walker.

Brainerd County was a more prosperous county than Sasha was used to. Not by much, but Sasha saw differences immediately. The villages and towns were made up of small houses, most painted and cared for. The fields were expansive and well maintained, the crop looking strong in the early summer morning. Sasha saw animals that were fat and plentiful, more than enough for a town of the same size in Walker.

Snow had given them a chance to learn their position on the map. They were in an area full of lakes, dozens of them. There were a number of villages amongst the lakes, small communities of a hundred people at most. These villages were connected by a single road that wound through the lakes in one large loop. It was called the Whitefish Loop, after the largest of the lakes.

The road started and returned at Pelican Point, a community of almost two hundred. It was big enough to be a town, and as such, it had a mayor, not a headman. Snow told her regiment he was an important man, capable of influencing all of the villages in the area to come to their banner.

'It is important we make a good impression,' Snow said. 'Best behavior, all around.'

Third Regiment approached Pelican Point from the road, making sure the townsfolk could see them coming. Sasha was posted in the middle, so by the time she saw the actual people they had concentrated, watching the regiment come in. She had expected they would look more prosperous than what she was used to, that they would be as colorful and happy as Mariposa was, but she was disappointed. They wore the same dark clothing, with muddy faces and worn hair.

You can't escape it, Sasha thought. *The sadness.*

A man stepped forward, hand up to ask the regiment to halt. Snow made her way forward.

'Mayor Middlestedt,' Snow said with a slight bow.

Sasha immediately liked this man. He was just as muddy and tired looking as everyone else. His beard was messy, and his clothes worn. He was strong and his hands rough. A farmer and a mayor, a strong difference from Mayor Cartier.

'Colonel Snow,' he said. 'I am surprised to see you return so soon. And surprised to see you bearing the horses of those who raided us not a week ago.'

'Their former masters no longer had need of them.'

'Indeed?' Middlestedt asked and managed a smile. 'The yeomen came through, asked some questions, and left without so much as a promise that they would pursue the scum. How is it you came across them?'

'We found their camp,' Snow said. 'We anticipated their movements, awaited the right moment, and struck with great violence. The entire company, from boy to elder. It was a fast but furious fight, one that cost us one of our own.'

Middlestedt bowed his head and muttered a soft prayer. 'Those men,' he said, 'took our coin, stole many of our goods, and had their way with a dozen of our women. We are lucky that they did not kill, and that they could not find our children. I will shed no tears for them. I will ask: why are you here?'

'We have brought back what goods we could salvage from the horses we killed or captured. Several horses escaped, and some of the goods were damaged, but we brought back what we could. I return these goods to you.'

'Every village was raided,' Middlestedt said. 'How do you know we won't take more than what was lost?'

'I don't believe you to be that kind of man, Mayor Middlestedt.'

There was a pause as he considered her offer. Sasha saw that many of the villagers were watching intently. She herself could barely keep her attention on the crowd.

'You have a doctor?' Middlestedt finally asked.

'I do.'

'The bandits didn't hurt too many people too seriously, but the women they assaulted have suffered greatly. I would appreciate a visit to them.'

'Of course,' Snow said. She turned over her shoulder. 'Mary, take an appropriate guard and attend to the wounded.'

Appropriate guard. Sasha fumed at the fact that rape was so common place the regiment had to have a phrase to specify a woman-only detachment to deal with its survivors. She could tell from his stance that Jim was equally angry, and Winnie scowled darkly.

'Winnie, Sasha,' Mary said. The two fell out, and the three of them followed a guide towards one of the common buildings. The villagers parted as the three women walked through, eyes glancing at their faces and weapons. Sasha smiled at them, tried to look pleasant. Some smiled back. Some looked at them with fear. Most just looked tired, as if the regiment were nothing special to be acknowledged.

149

Passing one house, a small group of boys sat on the porch, ignoring the crowd and talking among themselves. When they saw the women walking by, one whispered a joke that all laughed at, their eyes followed the women like a predator's.

What was it Prince said? 'Our children grow up emulating the yeomen who abuse their parents, because their parents look weak by comparison.' Here are more children brought up to be bullies.

A group of older women watched them approach. Mary came to a stop and saluted them. 'Hello. I am Able Medical Officer Mary, Third Regiment's Surgeon. I was informed I could be of some assistance here.'

The women looked at her sternly. Some of them sported black eyes or bruised lips, but none of them looked particularly broken. They stood defiant. *Their children are inside*, Sasha realized.

One of them stepped forward, the eldest of the group, bowed with age and greyed with wisdom. 'Aye, some need help. Why should we trust you to offer it?'

'I am an officer of Third Regiment, which is now returning stolen goods. I completed six months of training to become a qualified field surgeon and medic. And I am a woman who hates to see others suffer.'

The woman did not look too impressed, but her retort was stilled by an audible groan from inside the house. 'Do you have experience dealing with rape?'

'All too much,' Mary said.

'Then come in,' she said sternly. 'But only you.'

'I understand. Sergeant Winnie, guard the door.'

'Yes, ma'am,' Winnie said. She nodded at Sasha and they moved to flank the doorway. The women and Mary disappeared inside.

It was odd to see Mary acting like an officer, but Sasha was forewarned. However casual and friendly the regiment was at home, in public they were a military unit. Mary, Sasha's friend and den-mate, did have a Warrant and was, in the somewhat confusing ranking system that the Mardurers used, superior to Lieutenant Buck in the chain of command. So in public, she was to be addresses as 'ma'am', and deserved a salute and respect.

The kids still laughed at their jokes, sideways glances aimed at Sasha and Winnie. Several families were returning home, holding treasured possessions regained from the bandits. Some smiled at the pair of women, some looked at them with distrust. Winnie was polite, and Sasha smiled at them. Every now and then a groan emanated from the room behind her, and Sasha felt a growing anger.

'Don't get angry,' Winnie said. 'Justice has been done.'

'Has it?' Sasha asked. 'Does that make those girls' suffering any easier?'

Winnie's response was cut off by a shout from the boys. 'Hey!' one of the older boys yelled. 'You know, the yeomen said if they find any of your Mardurers out here, they're going to capture all you girls and whore you around the villages. Give every man a chance to show you your place. And they'll only charge a penny.'

'They must charge by inch,' Winnie said. Sasha burst out a sharp laugh.

The boys had not expected a laugh. 'What was that, you blond tramp?'

Winnie slung her automatic over her shoulder. 'At ease, Sasha. We might be here a while.' Sasha rested the rifle butt on the ground, her hands on the muzzle.

'We're talking to you! Don't you know you have to respond? Or do only the dumb ones get a gun?'

The women were silent. Sasha focused on the people walking around, smiled at them when she caught their eyes. The boys seemed content to yell from their porch, showing a disturbingly large array of curse words. After several minutes, they scattered and ran, disappearing to the other side of the town.

That was odd, Sasha thought when another group approached. There were eight of them, men and women, looking to be Sasha's

151

age or older. Sasha stiffened at their approach, but they did not look angry or threatening. One, a tall blond man who towered over the girls, came to stop before them.

'I'm sorry,' Winnie said, 'but we cannot allow access at this time.'

'I don't want access, I want to talk to you,' he said. 'If we go with you, will we be safe?'

'Safe?' Sasha asked.

'Safe,' he repeated. 'I'm seventeen. I'm strong and healthy. Next tax column comes through, I'm sure to be conscripted. I don't want to go, I don't want to fight, and I got a baby on the way. If we go with you, will we be safe?'

'There is no place you can be completely safe,' Winnie said. 'You won't be conscripted. Your wife won't be harassed. But we can't guarantee that the yeomen won't cause problems, or that you won't get sick.'

'Why?' a young woman asked.

'Because life is chaos,' Winnie said.

'And you shouldn't believe anyone who promises such things,' Sasha said. 'You come with us, we will put you to work, with the goal of freeing the county, ending the conscription and rape and theft. But we can't guarantee safety.'

'We're at war,' Winnie said. 'War means danger.'

'You're at war,' one of the younger boys said. 'We're just in the way.'

'Was no one in this village raped by a yeomen prior to us coming here?' Winnie asked. Their silence gave their answer. 'The war was one sided before we got here; now it isn't.'

'I don't want to fight,' the tall one said. 'I don't like violence. I don't want it.'

'Not everyone needs to fight,' Winnie said.

'Not everyone should fight,' Sasha said.

'How many people have you killed?' the woman asked.

'Five,' Winnie said.

'Only one,' Sasha replied.

The small crowd shifted uncomfortably. Sasha understood. Anger and action were two entirely different frames of mind, and angry at home was more familiar than action in the unknown. She vaguely remembered feeling the same when the Mardurers rescued her on the highway.

The door opened behind them and Mary stepped out. Sasha and Winnie snapped to attention, surprising the villagers who looked up at her with wonder in their eyes. Mary looked at them all, cleaning her hands with a cloth.

'Hello,' she said. They all remained silent. 'I do hope you're not trying to get inside.'

'No, ma'am,' Winnie said. 'They are expressing an interest in the joining the regiment, but are warry of combat.'

'Sure,' Mary said. 'Not everyone is a fighter.'

'No, ma'am.'

'Are you an officer?' one of the girls asked.

'I have a Warrant. I am a specialist in the medical fields: sanitation, surgery, general hygiene.'

'Do you need help?'

'Always,' Mary said. 'If you come with us, there will be rules to follow, but we don't make people fight who don't want to. We could use a lot of help.'

'They've killed people,' someone said.

'Yes,' Mary said. 'They have.'

The crowd waited for her to say more, but Mary left it at that. Soon the crowd had to part as Snow and Mayor Middlestedt came through.

'Mary?' Snow asked.

'In private, Colonel,' Mary said. The three walked off to the side, leaving the crowd with Sasha and Winnie. They still looked undecided, and, after a few whispers, left.

Snow returned a few minutes later. 'Mary needs to stay here for the night. I want you two to stay with her. We're going to continue on to the villages. Meet back at camp when you're done.'

'Understood, Colonel,' Winnie said.

'Stay safe,' Snow said. They saluted and she left.

'One person on the door at all times,' Mary said solemnly.

Yes, ma'am,' Winnie said.

◆◆◆

Sasha and Winnie took turns, one hour on, one hour off. Winnie would nap on her time off; Sasha would read. Both stayed at the front door, in sight of the villagers.

The day was nice, with a cool breeze and just enough clouds to keep the sun from getting much light in. A few people stopped by to ask questions. The annoying boys would run by, yelling some insult or another, often to be chased off by an adult. Sasha and Winnie ignored them, purposefully keeping their weapons slung over their shoulder and their eyes moving.

'If the yeomen come, we grab Mary and run,' Winnie said.

'She might not like that.'

'She definitely won't like that. But that's what we're going to do.'

Lunch was trail mix and water. Mary came out and dozed for a few hours. Sasha read more. Winnie cleaned some of her equipment.

'You read too much,' she said late in the afternoon, as Sasha sat down and opened her book.

'I can't believe anyone can read too much,' Sasha mused.

'But is that going to help you be a better soldier?'

'It'll help me be a better person, so yes.'

Winnie's retort was cut off as Mayor Middlestedt walked up. Sasha shut her book and stood.

'How are things going?' he asked.

'Well, I believe,' Winnie said. 'I can ask for a status check, if you'd like.'

'Please do.'

Winnie ducked inside, returning with Mary a few moments later. She and the mayor discussed the work she had been doing. Sasha stood, her eyes watching the village, trying to ignore Mary's descriptions.

The yeomen were never this brutal, she thought. Their harassment was a constant reminder of the order they imposed on the villagers, but they rarely got violent. They kidnapped the occasional woman for Walker, yes, but that violence was always far away, another threat to be wary of. There were always stories of them being worse, but Sasha could not remember an actual time that it happened in Penelope's Haven.

I guess we got off pretty easy, she thought, then hated herself for that.

A lesser degree of evil is still evil.

She tuned back into Mary's conversation.

' . . . I can't leave just yet. But perhaps Rifle Sasha is willing.'

Sasha blinked at the three looking at her. She chided herself for not paying attention.

'I'm sorry, ma'am, what was that?'

Winnie hid her smile, but Mary did not. 'Mayor Middlestedt has requested one of us join his family for dinner. I am unable to leave at this moment, and Sergeant Winnie is rested enough to stand

155

watch for several hours, with her naps. I think you, Sasha, are the best choice.'

'That's kind of you to ask, ma'am, but . . . .'

'She wasn't asking, Rifle,' Winnie said.

Sasha blinked in surprise but resigned herself. She hefted her rifle. 'I'll be back,' she said, following the Mayor into the village. 'I'll bring you something if I can.'

'Please do,' Winnie said, taking her spot at the doorway again.

Chapter 16

The Middlestedt home was no bigger than the other houses of the village, with one large central room that served as the kitchen and family room, and two smaller bedrooms on either side. A three-bunk bed stood against one wall. The decorations of the room were nice, but by no means as rich as the Cartier's house had been. There was a nice desk, over which hung the obligatory painting of King Xavier, but the painting was a small thing that hung crookedly on the wall.

The mayor's family was waiting for them to return. And it was a large family. Four adults, including an elderly man who stared at Sasha from a rocking chair in the corner, and five children, ranging from a toddler to a girl maybe a year younger than Sasha. Mayor Middlestedt introduced them, Sasha repeating their names so she would remember them. Except for Kyle, a nephew, all of them seemed genuinely interested in her. Sasha recognized Kyle as one of the boys from the porch. He pointedly ignored her.

'Can I take your rifle?' Rachel, the mayor's wife, asked.

'I should put it someplace safe,' Sasha said. She looked around and saw the musket hanging on the wall. 'May I hang it with your weapon?' That was agreeable, and Sasha checked the safety on the weapon, before hanging it next to the town musket.

Sasha offered to help with dinner, but the women would have none of it, bustling through the kitchen while the men set the table. Sasha sat off to the side, listening to the young girls telling the stories of their dolls. The two boys were watching her from a doorway, whispering to each other.

'Dinner,' Rachel said, and the people collapsed into their places. Sasha found herself next to the Mayor and his eldest daughter, Bethany. The meal was a simple stew of chicken and potatoes, with mix of vegetables and a loaf of bread. The food was put on the table but not touched. The family held hands, Sasha awkwardly held the hands of her host and his daughter, and the mayor said a short grace, followed by crossing themselves in a way Sasha had never seen before.

Her difference was noticed. 'I take it you are not Catholic,' Rachel asked as she began filling bowls with stew.

'No, ma'am.'

'What are you, if I might ask?'

'I don't really know,' Sasha said.

'What, don't know your parents?' Kyle asked with an impish grin. Rachel shot him a look.

'No, I do,' Sasha said, trying not to rise to the unsaid accusation. 'But I don't follow their religion, and I don't know what else I might be, so I have to say that I don't know.'

'There's nothing wrong with not knowing,' Lorraine said. She was the Mayor's sister and Kyle's mother. 'Not every child follows in their parent's footsteps.'

'That is certainly true,' Sasha said.

'What would your parents say of you now?' Bethany asked. She looked at Sasha with intensity as she waited for her answer. She reminded Sasha of the group that questioned her and Winnie earlier, but she had not been with them.

'They would be glad I'm alive,' Sasha said, 'but they'd not be happy I was fighting.'

'Women shouldn't fight,' Kyle said.

'No one should fight,' Sasha said quickly. 'But we don't fight because we like it. We fight because we must.'

'Must?' Mayor Middlestedt repeated.

'Yes, must. I will not wait for my turn to be a victim at the hands of a yeoman. Nor should I watch others wait for their turn. I mean to fight against them, to end the harassment, the danger and death.' Sasha realized everyone had stopped eating and was looking at her sternly. She turned red.

'No government can exist without power over the people,' Mayor Middlestedt said. 'You are too young to remember the old Iron Republic of Minnesota, but for all its claims of democracy, so few had the vote that it was no different than the king and his nobles.'

Sasha nodded. 'That is true, I was not alive for that. But is it not also true that the sheriffs of the Republic would not take random women for their beds on a whim, nor steal the harvest or industry of their villages? For all the complaints of the Republic, it was never with the sheriffs, only the government.'

Mayor Middlestedt did not have a response to that. At the other end of the table, the grandfather, Richard, looked up from his bread. 'Those are not the words of a forest peasant,' she said.

'I read,' Sasha said.

'I saw,' Bethany said, smiling away the tension of the table. 'You read with a great intensity. I don't know that I've ever seen anyone so taken with a book before.'

'I have taken to it. I had little chance to read before I joined the Mardurers. Now, I have a few options, and I intend to read the most of them.'

'Why bother reading?' Kyle sneered. 'Strength is what matters, and no woman'll be stronger than the king!'

'Kyle!' Lorraine hissed. 'Sit down!'

Sasha responded. 'Strength enough to carry a rifle is strength enough to fight, to protect. A yeoman may be stronger, but I can kill him just as dead as he can me.'

'But you shouldn't!' Kyle said harshly.

'Why not?' Sasha asked.

'Because!' Kyle insisted.

'That's enough!' Lorraine said curtly. Her son glowered at Sasha. Sasha put down her utensils and folded her hands in front of her, staring at the boy.

Mayor Middlestedt cleared his throat. 'There isn't a father alive who doesn't want to see his daughter, his family, safe from the dangers of the world. But this isn't some fairy tale where the good triumph because they are good. You are a score of children, boys and girls, in the forest. Fifteen miles from here is the count, and he has more than a hundred armed yeomen, grown and accustomed to violence. And if they don't scare you, the railway connects directly to the Royal Cities and the garrisons. A battalion of soldiers could be here in less than a day, five hundred men, with weapons the likes of which you can barely imagine. And, if somehow you defeated the entire Royal Army, the Imperial Margrave has a million men in Nova Scotia. Aero-planes and machinery and artillery. The tools of war of a conquering people.'

The table sat quietly. Kyle silently smirked at Sasha, but Mayor Middlestedt had no joy in his face. Instead he looked like he has spat out an overly salted cut of meat and was enduring the foul taste left in his mouth.

'You are not wrong,' Sasha admitted. 'This is not a fairy tale. If it were, we might have those weapons that impress and cower populations with a mere whisper of their name. Instead, all we have are a large number of angry men and women, who have watched rape and theft and murder occur for too long, who are tired of the pain and misery.'

'You don't know . . . ,' Kyle said.

'Sometimes,' Sasha interrupted, 'you have to start with the fight in front of you, and deal with the next fight when it comes.'

'Some people would call that short-sighted,' Mayor Middlestedt said.

'I think it is better than looking so far down the road that you convince yourself not to fight,' Sasha responded. She was trying to keep herself calm. She wanted these people to be on her side, to join with the Mardurers, but she worried she was not up to the task.

'How do the Mardurers live in the forest?' one of the younger girls asked.

'We sleep on the ground, if the weather is kind enough, or in tents or small caves. We have enough food, though by no means are we feasting. We manage water and health easily enough. Mary is very good at hygiene.'

'A smart woman.' Kyle scoffed. Her mother slapped him on the back of his head.

'Mind your manners,' she said. Kyle scowled but said nothing.

'I apologize for my nephew,' Mayor Middlestedt said. 'The yeomen don't show much respect, and he has a mind to join them.'

'And then we'll drive you from the woods,' Kyle said with a smile.

The rest of the table went quiet. Sasha looked at the young boy, twelve or thirteen by the looks of him. He had the same look of arrogance on his face that Samuel Cartier had. It lacked the confidence of a yeoman, but had that youthful danger about it.

'What do you say to that?' Kyle finally asked.

Sasha picked up her fork and knife and cut into her meal again. 'I am amused you think there will be any yeomen left by the time you're old enough,' Sasha said before a bite of food.

Kyle turned white.

◆◆◆

The rest of dinner passed rather quietly, with more discussions of village and forest life. Sasha was amazed, but kept to herself, how different this village was from Penelope's Haven, a distance of only thirty or forty miles. Mayor Mayor Middlestedt might have known, but she could not ask. Where she was from was supposed to be a secret.

As dinner broke, Kyle disappeared. The women stood to clear the table, and Mayor Middlestedt excused himself properly. Sasha was making ready to leave when Richard, the grandfather, spoke.

'Young Sasha,' he said. 'Please come with me.'

Sasha looked around at the surprised faces of the family. 'Of course, sir.' she said, following him into one of the bedrooms.

Two beds filled most of the room, one a woman's bed with a large drawer bed underneath, the other a short, simple bed. The grandfather stood next to his bed, and for a moment Sasha wondered if he expected her to climb in.

'Why do you read?' he asked pointedly.

'To learn,' she said. 'To be better than I was.'

'But why read? Learning a skill makes you better than you were.'

'I am learning skills too,' Sasha said. 'But there's so much to know, so much to learn. So much that was cultivated, collected, imagined.'

'And lost,' he said. He sat down, his face somber. 'It is said that there used to be libraries that held thousands of volumes of books. So many books a library could sink if it wasn't built right. Books that covered every topic, every whim and nature, every imagined fiction or scientific fact. So much, lost.'

'I don't have a lot of books to choose from,' Sasha said. 'And nothing from the Before Time.' She wanted to tell him of Snow's book, but she had to keep that a secret. 'I don't know how likely it is to find a new book in the middle of the woods, but I'm keeping my eyes out.'

'Knowledge is a dangerous thing,' he said.

'I'll take the danger.'

He smiled, but he still looked sad. Finally he turned to his chest and opened it. He took out a smaller, leather chest, and opened that one. Sasha saw a number of leather wrapped items. As he lifted it out, Sasha realized they were books.

'I wanted to give this to you,' he said, handing her the item. She unwrapped it, finding a green covered book with black lettering on it.

'*A Concise History of the American Revolution*,' she read.

'That book is from the Before Time,' he said. 'Passed down through several generations. It is important, but I wanted you to have it. My son doesn't deserve it.'

'Why not?' Sasha asked calmly, still focusing on the book before her.

'Because he's betrayed you.'

Sasha looked up sharply.

'Count Brainerd has been worried about the Mardurers coming south,' he said. 'Word is he doesn't expect Count Walker to be able to handle an uprising of any sort, and that his neighbors will have to deal with that failure. He directed his men to prepare an outpost up in this district, something where he can base his men forward to patrol and protect the population.'

Sasha was listening. No one knew of any outpost.

'When was this order given?'

'Two months ago,' he said.

Sasha was worried now.

'When do the yeomen move in?'

'Two weeks ago. They're six miles away.'

'Well, six miles is a good bit. We're still far enough away that we can . . . .'

'My son sent them a message two hours ago. They're probably on their way here now.'

Sasha's stomach turned. 'Why?' she asked.

'He has four children,' he said. 'I'm sorry. I truly am.'

'Thank you,' she said, turning and opening the door. She walked quickly to her pack, stowing the book inside and throwing it over her shoulder. She picked up her rifle, the women looking on in surprise at her haste, grimacing when she worked the bolt and chambered a round in her rifle. Sasha looked around, but did not see the mayor anywhere. 'Thank you for dinner,' she quickly said as she ran into the night.

Most of the town was out, a surprise given how late it was. They were congregated in groups, behind houses, out of sight of Winnie. Sasha made a fast jog back, seeing Winnie still standing, unaware of anything amiss until she saw Sasha approaching.

'What's wrong?' she asked.

Sasha stepped close. 'The yeomen have an outpost, six miles away. Mayor Middlestedt sent them a message two hours ago.'

Winnie's face drained. 'Shit.' She unslung her weapon. 'Tell Mary.'

Sasha entered the building. Several beds and mattresses were set about, with women laying on each one. Some were sleeping, some awake. Mary and several of the older women sat around a table, drinking tea. Mary looked up when Sasha entered, her questioning face turning stern at Sasha's appearance.

'Ma'am,' Sasha said, 'it seems that Mayor Middlestedt has alerted the yeomen to our presence. We have to leave, now.'

'Are you sure?' Mary asked. Some of the women gasped at Sasha. One of them looked sternly at her.

'Yes, I'm sure,' Sasha said.

Mary started assembling her kit, leaving instructions for the care of the wounded. 'Go help Winnie,' she said.

The stern woman stepped forward and grabbed Mary's collar. 'No, you cannot leave. We need to turn you in, otherwise . . . .'

Mary twirled, hooking the woman's arm and twisting her around before pushing her back against the wall. For a moment, Mary looked as dangerous as Winnie or Snow ever did, and every women who had a minute earlier been comfortable with her stepped back.

'Help Winnie,' Mary said. 'I need to finish.'

Sasha nodded and went back out front.

Winnie still stood with her weapon out, but now she had a reason to be nervous. The men had emerged from the shadows and stood around, several carrying torches, others various farm instruments. One of them carried the town's musket, but kept the barrel pointed into the air. Winnie's barrel was pointed down, her finger along the guard, close to, but not on, the trigger. Mayor Middlestedt stood before the crowd, his face stern and unhappy.

'It is not personal,' he said to Winnie. 'I must protect my family. I must protect my village.'

'And so you will sacrifice us?' Winnie asked.

'I must do what I have to, to protect my family!' he said again. The crowd chorused, some louder than others.

'You have no right!' one of the other men called. 'To come in here, to dangle treason before us, promises you can't keep, to invite terror and destruction from the king's men! You are not from here! You risk nothing, hiding in the forest and picking fights when you want to and leaving us to face the wrath of those you hurt!'

More agreements, louder now. Some of the men gestured with their implements, the strength in numbers building the confidence within them. Beyond, Sasha could see women and children, those who came to watch but had not yet joined the crowd. The loud boys from the porch now stood at the edge of the crowd, their adolescent voices adding to the shouts. Sasha moved her finger and clicked the safety of her rifle off.

'You and your families are in danger regardless,' Winnie said. 'At least with us they'll have a better future!'

'Will they?' Middlestedt demanded. 'Sure, you might bloody the yeomen, but we asked her!' he gestured to Sasha. 'She has no idea how to defeat the Royal Army! What good will ending the yeomen do when the roads fill with soldiers; taking our grain, our livestock? The yeomen are a hundred men, and they take a girl every few months! A thousand will take one every day! No! I am mayor of this town, and I must protect my people from harm, no matter how it comes to us.'

165

'Put down the gun, missy!' Sasha heard Kyle call. 'Just give up.'

The crowd surged forward a few feet, and Winnie raised her gun to her shoulder.

The crowd went still as they looked at the weapon trained on them. Several women called for Winnie to stop, for her to not fire, but Sasha saw her finger was still off the trigger.

'Nothing comes without cost,' Winnie said. 'Right now, you are getting what you think is peace, and all you have to give up? Your toil, your goods, your children . . . and your respect. But that peace is dependent on the yeomen. Keeping them fat and happy while you live in the mud.' Some in the crowd disagreed but she shouted. 'Yes! IN THE MUD! Even if you don't wallow in it, even if you clean yourselves, you live there, in the mud with their boots on your head. You deserve better, your children deserve better. But you won't get it hoping the world gets better. There is no reason for those who have the power to share with those who do not.'

'Alive in the mud is better than dead underneath it!' someone called.

'Is it?' Winnie asked, her voice turned cold. She raised the gun fully and aimed it straight at Mayor Middlestedt.

'Sergeant,' Sasha said.

'Get Mary, get her out of there,' Winnie said.

'We can't just kill villagers,' Sasha said.

'It is my responsibility to protect Mary, and that I will do.'

The crowd shifted, some ready to charge, some anxious about Winnie and her weapon. They knew it was an automatic, they had seen yeomen carry them, and knew what it could do. Sasha kept her weapon down, but shifted her gaze towards the man with the musket. *If I must fight, I will kill you. I am sorry for that. I do not want to. But that is my mission.*

Sasha heard something behind her. Mary must be at the door, but she had not said anything. *Mary, if you have any ideas, now is the time.*

166

Something sailed over her head and landed between the crowd and the girls. Sasha saw something plop into the mud and sputter, a small fire began as purple smoke filled the air.

'Let's go!' Mary yelled.

'Run!' Winnie said and fired over the crowd's head. Men dropped into the mud as the bullets harmlessly flew over them. Sasha could not see the musket man anymore, nor the mayor, just smoke and people. She looked around, her weapon at her shoulder, when Mary grabbed her collar and pulled her back.

'I said move, Rifle!'

They ran. Winnie was in front, running down a path towards the trees, Mary just before Sasha. Behind them were shouts and yelling, and a single gunshot as the musket fired but hit nothing. In the growing darkness, the three were out of sight well before the trees.

They stopped at the tree line, taking position behind thick trunks, and saw the torches of the village behind them. The villagers milled about, walking around their town, but none took too many steps beyond the houses. They all gasped for breath, resting as they watched.

'What's that?' Mary asked.

Lights were moving up the roadway. These were not torches, but beams that extended out and moved fast up the road.

'Mounted yeomen,' Sasha said.

Winnie reloaded. 'We need to get into the forest. Do you know where the rest of the regiment went?'

Mary shook her head. 'No. We were just to meet back at the base. And that's where we need to go.'

The yeomen were in the town now.

'First we hide,' Winnie said. 'Let's go.'

Chapter 17

The night was long and fretful. The yeomen knew the terrain well enough to encircle and patrol, even at night. If it was not for the lanterns that gave away their positions, the three women might have gotten caught up by them. As it was, they spent their time behind trees, watching the yeomen methodically cut through the woods. They got frightfully close, so close Sasha was surprised they passed on by. Sasha could see their coats, the blue-gray with deep red fronting, the same black tricorns as Walker yeomen, the polished leather belts and weapons. They were a far cry from the loud and boisterous yeomen Sasha grew up with; they were silent, dangerous, professional, as Snow might say. Sasha hid as best she could, and watched them ride by.

They managed a little sleep, one always staying awake, watching the lanterns move about. It was well after midnight before the yeomen left, riding to some new location. The three took no chances, waiting patiently for the sun to rise. No speaking. Little movement. Sasha grew thirsty, felt the call of nature, heard her stomach growl, but did not move. Movement was death.

Morning started creeping over the trees. Three pairs of eyes looked about, watching for signs of danger. Several deer walked through the forest, birds sang their morning songs, but no other humans showed themselves. The three drank, stretched their muscles, and readied themselves for a day they had not expected.

'I did not hear any firing,' Winnie said. 'I can't believe Snow and the rest of the regiment would get taken without a fight.'

'Should we look for them?' Sasha asked.

'We don't know where they are,' Winnie said. 'All we do know is there are yeomen about, and we three can't take them all on ourselves.'

Mary spoke up. 'Snow told me that should anything happen, we were to rendezvous back at the base camp. We were not to search for or attempt to make contact with the rest of the regiment.'

'But we need to warn her!' Sasha said.

'The Colonel was very adamant. If we were to run into trouble, she wanted us to get out and get to a safe place. She did not want to have to worry about saving us from anything.'

'But . . . .'

'No,' Mary cut Sasha off. 'I know what you are going to say, but those were Snow's orders, and I agree with them. We're heading west. Eyes open, weapons ready. If we can avoid a fight I would prefer that to leaving a trail of bodies right to our camp. Do you have a problem with that, Rifle Sasha?'

Sasha hated it when Mary called her by her rank. She felt like she was being scolded, which, she had to admit, she was. She shook her head. 'No, ma'am.'

'Sergeant?'

'No problems here, ma'am,' Winnie said.

'Good. Let's move out.'

The three moved through the idyllic forest, the natural beauty marred by their heightened fear and fatigued minds. Several times they dropped to the dirt at some imagined threat, but no danger came their way. Their pace was so slow, Sasha feared she would still see their hiding place an hour after they left it.

They stopped at a stream to refill their canteens. 'Everyone okay?' Mary asked.

'Fine,' Sasha said. She was sore, tired, and her ego still smarted from earlier.

'Good to go,' Winnie said.

'Alright, I want to pick up the pace a bit. Try to get out of the area before . . . .'

Gunfire sounded in the distance. All three of them looked to the east, but the sound was miles away.

'Automatics,' Winnie said. 'Sounds like a pitched battle.'

'Snow has more than enough to worry about without having to add us to the mix,' Mary said. 'We need to keep moving.'

They moved away from the battle, the sounds dying away. Sasha ached to turn and find the battle, but dutifully followed her comrades. *Please let everything be okay*, she prayed. *Please let them all come back.*

The sun was fully up now, and a cool morning turned into a hot summer day. Sasha and Winnie took turns on point of their small squad, as Mary was not as experienced with land navigation. Nothing threatened them as they crossed fields and roads, through trees and underbrush. Sasha's shoulders and feet began to feel sore, the rifle heavy in her hands. She said nothing. *Winnie and I are finally getting along*, Sasha thought, turning her face away so Winnie could not see her wincing.

The trio stopped at another stream, taking a rest, still about six miles from camp. They drank, filled their canteens. Sasha wetted her sleeves and wiped her forehead and neck. She could not tell if she was hot or nervous. She did not know where anyone was. She did not know where the enemy was. She did not know anything. She hated not knowing anything.

'Get down!' Winnie hissed, jumping behind a tree. Mary and Sasha leapt for cover. Sasha held her breath.

A voice called out. 'Sergeant Winnie? Is that you?'

'It's Rifle Dave,' Mary said.

Winnie frowned and Sasha got nervous. Dave had gone with Saber's team, not Snow's.

'Sergeant? Please! We need help!'

'Rifle Dave!' Winnie called. 'Where is Captain Saber or Sergeant Esmerelda?'

'The Sergeant is dead!' Dave called. Sasha peaked around her trunk and saw Dave, less than a hundred yards away. 'The Captain is hurt! We need to get to Mary! Please!'

'You're not followed?' Winnie asked.

'No, I swear it!'

Winnie looked at Mary.

'Mary?'

'Let's go to them,' Mary said. 'They need our help.'

Winnie scowled, but nodded. The three of them moved forward.

Saber left with one sergeant, one gunner and three rifles. Now he lay on a makeshift stretcher, pale and white, surrounded by two rifles and a gunner who no longer had his machine gun. He was wrapped in a blanket, unconscious.

'What happened?' Winnie asked.

'We stopped by a farm house, someone Saber knew. I guess others knew he was friendly because the yeomen came down while we were there. They weren't expecting us, and we cut them up pretty good on the road, but they weren't done with us. Some of them got in behind us and stormed the house. Sergeant and Rifle Kim didn't get out. Neither did our friend. Saber took a bullet as we escaped.'

'Where's your gun?' Winnie asked Gunner Zack.

'Took a hit right on the breech. Could have fixed it with time, but Saber was adamant we leave, so I dropped it.'

Sasha looked down at the captain. Such a large man, confident and intelligent, reduced to the body before her. Mary was unwrapping his arm.

'He collapsed after a mile. We had to put together a stretcher to try and carry him home,' Dave said. He looked around. 'What happened to the rest of the regiment?'

'We stayed in Pelican Point to help some victims of the bandits,' Winnie said. 'Turns out the Mayor had warned the yeomen and they came for us. We just got out. The rest had continued on; I don't know what happened to them. We heard a battle, but beyond that....'

Mary hissed and everyone looked.

The bullet had passed through Saber's arm just above the elbow. The bone was shattered, bits mixed in with strands of muscle and tendons. A tourniquet was fixed above the wound, and the bandages had soaked up most of what remained. Mary bent in close to inspect, seeing how little was remaining between the forearm and the upper.

'I need to amputate,' Mary said. 'I need hot water.'

'We can get a fire going,' Winnie said, 'but I'm worried about being found.'

'Take every precaution,' Mary said. 'But I need to do this now, or he is likely going to die.'

Sasha watched, her stomach churning at the thought of what Mary was about to do. Mary turned to her.

'Sasha, I need a nurse.'

Sasha turned white. 'Okay,' she said nervously. 'What do I do?'

'What I tell you to, and nothing more.'

Sasha realized Mary was nervous. 'You've never done this before,' she said.

Mary shook her head. 'No, and out here, this can get bad. We don't have a lot of time, but I intend to be thorough.'

'But you do know what you're doing?' Sasha asked.

Mary glared at her. Sasha stopped talking.

♦♦♦

Winnie moved them to a small dell. They boiled water while Mary unrolled her surgery kit. Sasha had only ever seen her field medicine kit, with the scissors and tongs and small tools. This bigger kit had a series of knives and saws, several vials of liquid, needles, and various items Sasha did not recognize. It was a very vicious looking set of equipment.

Mary used a grease pencil to make a series of lines across Saber's arm. She injected something into his shoulder and fit a gag into his mouth. She paused, reciting something under her breath. Her worried eyes flitted over her tools.

Dear God, Sasha prayed, *please.*

Mary began.

She cut at the skin, following the lines to create a series of skin flaps. She cut into the muscle and softer tissues, still speaking to herself as she cut. Every so often she would put down the knife and pick up some clamps, one with needle and thread prepared, and sew at something inside. 'Clamp, pass through the vessel, tie off, pass around, tie off, pass around....'

Mary worked smoothly. Sasha tried to look anywhere but down.

'Sasha, I need you to brace his shoulder,' Mary said, adjusting Sasha's legs to the required positions. Sasha risked a glance and saw the bone, exposed, ending in a jagged point. The forearm was only attached by bits at the end.

Don't look,' Sasha thought. She shut her eyes when Mary reached for the saw.

She did not see the sawing, but suffered through hearing it, through feeling the arm shift under her. Saber remained unconscious. Mary continued until Sasha heard a sickening crack.

'Okay, Sasha I need your eyes. Wash your hands, quickly.'

Sasha did so, pouring water from the heated canteen over her hands. She ignored the lump of arm lying next to Mary.

'I need you to hold the flaps while I sew them,' Mary said. She held the flaps over the stump, looking like lips on some monstrous snake. Sasha held on.

Mary had needle and thread ready, and clean bandages and more hot water. She moved with more confidence now that she was past the difficult part. Sasha could no longer ignore the stump, holding the skin so Mary could sew. The skin felt odd in her fingers, cold and damp. She forced herself to keep her stomach calm, biting the inside of her cheek to distract herself. Mary worked thoroughly, refusing to rush the process, checking twice before sending the needle through. Mary had thoroughly taught everyone in the regiment on the importance of cleaning wounds, and she was taking no chances as she sewed. It seemed like an eternity before Mary began wrapping the arm in bandages.

'Okay, Sasha, you can let go.'

Sasha rolled back, away from the body, her stomach reeling. She grabbed for a canteen nearby, drinking the warm water to try and settle her stomach. After several swallows, she realized that was not going to help and doubled over, vomiting everything she had eaten since that morning onto the forest floor. She retched, having nothing left to throw up, and crawled away from the foul smelling liquid.

Someone put their hand on her and gave her a new canteen. 'Drink a little and wash out your mouth.'

Sasha nodded and rolled to sit down, pausing in surprise as she took the canteen from Snow's hand.

'Colonel?'

'Did not want to interrupt your surgery,' Snow said. 'How did it go?'

Sasha shook her head, unable to speak. She rinsed her mouth, then drank a small amount.

Mary finished with the bandages. She started to clean her hands and looked up at Snow. 'I've done the best I can for now.'

'Will he make it?'

'He's lost a lot of blood, and in the field there is always the chance of infection; I've cleaned the wound, tied off the arteries, installed a drain, everything I can to keep him alive. I'll do what I can once we get him back to base camp, but I can't say anything for certain.'

Sasha looked around. The rest of the regiment had joined them, including a half a dozen teenagers who sat nearby, having watched the surgery with wide eyes. None of them seemed injured.

'Any casualties on your end?' Mary asked.

'No. We got tipped off pretty early.' Snow frowned. Something was bothering her, Sasha thought, but she can't tell anyone about it.

'We need to get back to camp,' Mary said.

'Agreed. We will get moving in ten minutes. And then,' she grimaced, 'we hit back.'

Chapter 18

Snow sat at the Den, looking out at the regiment. The evening meal was sullen, quiet, without much banter. Mary was still tending to Saber. Beth had shown the new recruits around. Master Sergeant had run a cleaning drill for the weapons. But mostly, the regiment was recovering.

She looked down at the map and not for the first time, wished she was not the colonel.

It was not that she was afraid to fight. Violence had been a part of her life since she was thirteen, when a nobleman's anger destroyed her family and cast her to the streets, her face scarred. It was not long before she had been raped by some drunken longshoreman. A longshoreman whose throat she cut two days later.

She grew accustomed to violence in six years of survival. She'd robbed and murdered on a few occasions, sold herself on others. A few times she had tried to start a normal life, but there was always some fight she was pulled into. And with a prominent burn like hers, it was hard to not be noticed, or remembered.

Violence had brought her to the Renaissance Army of Minnesota. When she had discovered her only surviving relative, her sister, was in Duluth, a courtesan in a high-class brothel, she came to the city and saved her, only to be cornered in a warehouse. It was that fight that brought in the surprise help of man who had been nearby and overheard the commotion. A man who killed four others in quick succession and brought the sisters to a safe house. A man she now knew as Fox.

Their group did not have a name then, and there were no whispers that anything like this existed. All the sisters knew was this man killed to protect them and got them to a safe house. He got them food and new clothes, and introduced them to other members of their group. Men who, to the surprise of the sisters, did not demand sexual favors in return (though Snow would always smile when she remembered how red Caesar turned when he was offered).

Snow earned her keep with the RAM through violence, but now it was focused and directed. She conducted missions, some of which she was not proud of, all over the lakes. She rescued some people, hurt others. But the planning had been done by others; she was simply one of the ones who executed the plan.

When the Field Regiments were being formed, she had jumped at the chance to lead one. She wanted it: to prove she could plan a campaign, not just execute a battle plan. She had been so proud of herself when she got it.

And then?

And then the civilians did not respond with enthusiasm. And then you fought the bandits. And then the yeomen shot Saber. And then . . . and then . . . .

It was the responsibility that was beginning to get to Snow. The thinking and planning. Having dozens of men and women, some of whom still looked like children, waiting to fight at her command, for no other reason than someone said she was in charge.

What right do I have to order them? She wondered. *Prince is a natural at leadership. Caesar knows so much he has to have a higher office. Fox and Aristotle lead through example, with sheer skill. What do I have?*

A memory ran through her head. A man, older, standing a few inches taller than her, his fist shaking in her face, his red cheeks flapping as he yelled at her. 'You don't tell me how to fight a battle,' he screamed. 'I tell you. And you fucking listen!'

Colonel Senator. Snow had not thought of him for some time, and she scowled as she remembered that day. The man was one of the Old Guard, the last soldiers of the Minnesota Republic that survived to join the RAM. He was an experienced soldier and an officer, but he was stuck in his ways. During an ambush near Federal Dam, he made a simple mistake, an improper placement of a machine gun. Something she, as one of his subordinate officers, had fixed without letting him know. The ambush went off successfully, but when he found out she had moved it, he made an issue of it on front of the whole assembled force.

Snow remembered, and felt the anger burn away her worries. How dare he speak to her that way! She was Snow. The woman Prince chose for mission after mission because she led from the front and got the job done. The woman Caesar held out as an example to the first batch of militia officers from the liberated towns. The woman who had been a part of the RAM for longer than Senator had. How dare this archaic animal talk down to her over an insignificant change that was entirely within her power to enact. As if he would dare try to humiliate a male officer in such a public matter.

Snow took a breath to calm herself. Senator's attempt at public humiliation had been embarrassing, and Snow remembered wanting to attack him. But somehow, her silent endurance had enhanced her own reputation. She was shocked to discover from Aristotle that she was one of the more respected officers of the RAM. She could not understand why, but when it was announced to the Rifles that she was to command a new field regiment, more than sixty of them volunteered for duty under her command.

Remember that, she told herself. *They chose to be a part of Third Regiment. More volunteers than First and Second combined. They trust you as much as General Prince does. If they wanted to run, they could. But they're still here and that has to mean something!*

What do you have, you asked? You have the trust of the Generals, and the regiment. Now just trust yourself.

Snow looked at the map again, taking several moments to think through a number of ideas.

'Okay,' she finally said and waved to Master Sergeant. He made his way towards the Den.

'Ma'am,' he said.

'Master Sergeant, we find ourselves in a situation,' she said, gesturing for him to have a seat. 'We have, by my count, seventeen combatants trained in Walker, six partially trained volunteers, and five fresh recruits. Our opponent has a hundred yeomen, mounted and adequately trained, and apparently with the support of the population.'

'Are you counting Sasha in the partially trained?' Master Sergeant asked.

'Wouldn't you?'

Master Sergeant shrugged. 'She's hard to place, Colonel. Sure, she's got a few gaps in her training that the Walker-trained don't have, but she throws herself into what she does know with intensity. I reckon she'll be asking for a Warrant before too long.'

Snow felt a worry in her stomach about the warrant, but ignored it. 'We'll count her as trained,' she said. 'But we still have to decide what to do next. And some of that has to do with this camp.'

'Any idea where it might be?' he asked.

'Sasha was told it was six miles from Pelican Point. It's not on the roadway, so it can't be north or south, and we've patrolled the west, so it has to be east of the loop. Not much out that way; old summer cabins and plantations.'

'The old families who lived there lost much when the Republic fell,' Master Sergeant said. 'The new count evicted them for their actions. Rumor is he wanted to attract wealthy landlords, but has never been able to do so.'

'And now he's built something there.'

'Probably,' Snow said. 'We're in a tough spot, but I want to know what's out there. You and Beth need to get the new volunteers trained up. Focus on field-craft and rifle-work. We can get to the details later. Mary is busy with Captain Saber, and Winnie is going to be working her select squad roughly for a while.'

'That leaves us, Lieutenant Buck, and the rest of the Walker-trained.'

'Yes,' Snow faced the enormity of the task before her. 'If we hole up, they'll come for us.'

'Probably,' Master Sergeant said. 'These aren't the Walker Yeomanry. We pass them the initiative, they won't be stupid enough to pass it up.'

'Right. So the Walker-trained have two objectives: find this camp and keep the yeomen from concentrating.'

'And defending the base?'

Snow shrugged. 'Giving up the base is not out of the question. The Regiment is more important than the land. Review the Evacuation Drills. Make sure everyone is prepared to leave at a moment's notice.'

'And Captain Saber?'

'Have a stretcher ready,' Snow said. 'And if that won't work, Mary has her mercy pistol.'

'She won't like that.'

'No one would like that,' Snow said softly.

Master Sergeant nodded. 'Two objectives.'

'Right. I am going to take Sonja and two Rifles towards the camp, see if we can't find it and study it. Might take a few days, but I can send Sonja straight from there if necessary. I'll leave you here with a cadre, and send Buck out with the balance to patrol the villages and hit the yeomen.'

'Might be splitting the regiment too much,' Master Sergeant warned.

'Maybe, but we have too much to do.' Snow looked at the maps one last time. 'We weren't supposed to engage the yeomen until late fall. We're about four months too early for this.'

'This wasn't our fault, ma'am. General Prince was adamant that we help the peasants whenever we could. Mayor Middlestedt's betrayal was unfortunate, but beyond your control.'

'We almost lost Mary.'

'Not with Winnie and Sasha watching out for her. I know you'll hate to hear this, but we got off easy with the casualties we did take. And after how happy we were with the bandits, it may seem like we've hit a new low, but it is war. We'll bounce between both extremes enough times.'

'Did we really kill the bandits only three days ago?' Snow asked.

'Seems like a lifetime ago, doesn't it?' Master Sergeant smiled at his Colonel. 'That will happen a lot. You'll get used to it.'

Snow smiled back, then sighed. 'We're going to need help. The yeomen outnumber us three to one, and even with their normal duties across the county, they'll be able to bring a considerable number against us.'

'All part of a guerrilla campaign, Colonel. They'll have to split somewhere, so we wait for them to do so, then cut them apart.'

'You make it sound so simple,' Snow said.

'Simple in concept, difficult in execution. It's how wars are fought.' He saluted and left.

Snow watched him leave. 'Easy enough to say when you don't have to decide where to fight,' she whispered, then went back to staring at the map.

Chapter 19

Sasha stumbled into the camp. She went to her den, currently empty, and removed her pack, rifle, and belts. She just tossed them inside. She turned and sat down, back against the wall, removed a canteen, and poured it over her head. The water ran through her hair and under her clothes, washing away dirt and grime and heat. Her arms dropped lazily to her side and she just sat there.

Snow's orders had put the regiment into a high pace of training without much recovery from their experiences with the villages. There had been a service for Esmerelda and Kim, but without bodies it seemed even sadder than Rick's. Snow and Buck left that afternoon for their missions, leaving Mary in charge, with Master Sergeant actually running the camp. Captain Saber was unconscious, with Mary and Harriet attending to him.

Master Sergeant, Winnie, and Beth ran all the volunteers hard. Between physical exercises and field drills, they were being pushed at a quicker pace than Sasha had been. Their fatigue was obvious.

Sasha, for her part, seemed to bounce between the trainers and the trainees. She was used as a squad leader for many exercises, and was always willing to offer advice to the others on how to improve. But she was still running through the training with them, except for a few hours after lunch, when Winnie brought her squad together.

Winnie's special squad, which she called the First Squad, was a four-person team. The others she chose were men Sasha did not know too well before now.

First, Winnie had enlisted Corporal Jose, one of the trained rifles who came with Buck. Jose was a gentle man who Sasha always thought should be helping Mary. But Winnie knew him from their training in Walker, and considered him to be a particularly dangerous man. Sasha had not seen any danger from him, but he was dedicated and capable.

The other man was Rifle Samson, one of the newer volunteers. He was a large, muscular man about Sasha's age, who was passing every test Master Sergeant threw at him. He learned the lessons faster than anyone except maybe Sasha, and was quite the natural shot. While everyone else was training at shooting up to one hundred yards, Samson was training up to three hundred.

Snow's specific orders were to train in clearing and capturing houses. Some of the Walker-trained had some rudimentary training, but Winnie and Jose had more. They were not clear on where they learned it, but it was obvious they had gone through it together. Sasha and Samson were rushing to catch up.

Winnie and Sasha had searched the ruins near their firing range and found an appropriately large enough building for their purposes. It was big, enough for a score of people to sleep in, missing a roof but otherwise sturdy. Using rope and curtains, Winnie was able to build different layouts for their practices.

In addition, Winnie had assembled a number of targets made of two pieces of wood, one representing the faces and one the hands and body. She had about a dozen faces and a dozen hands. The bodies were the kinds of people they might run into: farmers, children, yeomen. The hands could be empty, holding a weapon, holding a farming tool. Winnie could switch them up, force her squad to consider the whole target and not just the head. Sasha had no idea why a grandmother would ever be holding a shotgun, but Winnie was adamant that they train this way.

They worked on clearing buildings, how to pass through doors and sweep through rooms. They had to yell *threat* as they were not allowed to fire their weapons during those exercises.

They did fire them at the firing range. Winnie had them practicing on tiny targets at close ranges, much different from the one hundred yard range Master Sergeant trained them at. Winnie would have them start with their backs to the targets, so they would turn, acquire, and fire quickly. She had them cycle through rifle, submachine gun and pistol. Sasha was okay with the pistol, but detested the lack of control with the automatic. She much preferred her rifle. At least the bandits had given them enough ammo to train with.

Winnie spent some time working on infiltration and climbing, but the other main focus of her training was on knife fighting. Watching Winnie and Jose sparring with each other was an amazing sight. The way they cut and blocked, danced about each other, it was obvious they both enjoyed the work and had practiced it often. Sasha and Samson were not nearly as good, but again, they'd only been at it for three days.

Where does the time go? She thought. Only three days since they returned from the villages. Only five since they buried Rick...or was it a full week? It was still early May, she was sure, just over a month since she left home.

I wonder what they're doing now. I wonder what they would do if I came to visit.

Sasha nodded off with that thought, to be shaken awake by Mary. The light had gone down some, and Mary was handing her a tin plate with some cooked chicken, a potato and a biscuit.

'Eat up,' she said. 'Doctor's orders.'

Sasha took the food. 'Not very hungry.'

'Well, that was the last chicken. Don't waste it.' Mary sat down next to her and picked at her own food. 'The villages were supposed to supply more food.'

'Guess that's not happening.'

'Not soon, at least.'

A pause. The whole camp was subdued, tired.

'How is Captain Saber?'

'He's got a fever,' Mary said. 'Not helping him wake up. His arm, at least, is not infected, but I'd like to have him up and about as soon as possible.'

'Right,' Sasha said. 'Can I ask a question?'

'Sure,' Mary said.

'Don't be mad.'

Mary frowned. 'Okay.'

'What happens if we fail? If the Mardurers, the Renaissance Army, whatever, fails to defeat the counts and king. If we have to run…what do we do?'

Mary was quiet for a minute. Sasha wondered if she had fallen asleep, but she spoke up. 'We've actually discussed this. Saber and Buck weren't happy about it, but Snow was set that we had a plan just in case. If we fail, anyone who wants to leave can leave. Snow will not force anyone to stay. Anyone who does stay, she will lead west into the Dakotas, set up with one of the city-states out there. The Dakota Plains aren't controlled like the kingdoms are, so we can disappear relatively easily in there.'

'I'm not really surprised Snow thought that through,' Sasha said. She realized she had eaten half her plate without noticing. 'I couldn't go home.'

'No?' Mary asked. 'Your father doesn't practice forgiveness?'

'He does, but forgiveness requires penance. He'd have me in Walker, suffering for my sins. And that's assuming Mayor Cartier doesn't have me arrested for banditry. Either way, I'd end up in Walker, a plaything for the yeomen.'

There was a rumble. Not gunfire, but thunder. The overcast clouds now looked dark and pregnant.

Mary wolfed down the last of her food. 'I'm going to stay with Saber for this. Try and get some sleep,' she said.

'I'll try,' Sasha said without much energy. 'Mary?'

Mary stopped and turned. 'Yeah?'

'Could you? Go home, I mean?'

'If I went home, my family would welcome me with open arms.'

'Where would you tell them you were?'

'They know where I am.'

'They do?' Sasha was surprised. Most Mardurers did not go into their backgrounds at all, but Sasha did know that most of them had left their families without any notice of where they were or what they were doing.

'They do, and if I went home, they would lie to protect me. I just...can't go home.' She smiled a sad smile and continue on her way.

The rain started a few minutes later, the heavy painful rain the skies had saved for weeks. Anyone who had been sitting around the campfire was driven into their dens in a hurry. The fire was dead within a minute. The ground turned muddy, then puddled, then became a small lake. Leaves and small branches fell off the trees to float around the camp like small boats.

Sasha was alone. Mary had Saber in a special den, and she had no idea where Beth was. She might have continued reading the American Revolution book, but she lacked light. She was tired, and lay back in her den, less than a foot above the water, to try and sleep. But her mind wandered.

She imagined going home. She did miss her mother and Michelle, and even Thomas, truth be told. She missed sleeping in homemade quilts next to her own little window overlooking Penelope's Haven. She missed fresh baked bread from an oven, not the pan fried hard tack. Her mother had a talent for making even simple meals taste wonderful: despite the Alvanist beliefs on the simplicity of food, Michelle had demanded an exception for her spices, and Alexander had lost that argument long ago.

Alexander...Father.... Sasha closed the curtain to her den, keeping out the increasingly strong splashing, but leaving some open for what little light could come inside.

Sasha had not given her father much thought recently. She used to imagine him scolding her for fighting, learning, wearing pants. Sometimes, like before the bandit ambush, she actually imagined a conversation, but mostly it had his eyes glaring at her and his array of small platitudes. Since the ambush, since Rick, she hadn't imagined him much. She had been too busy.

What would he say if I came home? She wondered. *Would he be happy to see me and glad that I was safe? Or would he be angry with me for leaving? I guess it depends on the manner of my return. Am I contrite? Or am I resolute? How much penitence is expected of me before I am one with the family again?*

Even if her father did accept her back, the Cartiers were another story. Sasha was not sure who she was more scared of, Samuel or his father. Mayor Cartier could turn her over to the yeomen for torture and punishment, or even punish her himself as the mayor of the town. It was rare, but as the mayor he did have the power to punish his townsfolk. If they did not submit, he could call in the yeomen. It was a threat rarely made, and it was a threat Sasha did not remember him ever carrying out.

Samuel, though. He had been harassing her for years, and if he saw a way to punish her for leaving, he'd take it. Worse, if he and his father were both involved....

Sasha pushed out the image of a public humiliation. *I can't go home.*

Where to, then? She could follow Snow west, into the Dakota Territories. The broad plains were not organized into kingdoms like the eastern regions were. Instead, a few cities existed amongst hundreds of thousands of square miles of land dotted by frontier farmers, tribes of freemen, and herds of wild animals. Sasha had heard stories, mostly from Mariposa, that life out west was freer than in the kingdoms, but rougher as well.

If not west, where to? She might be able to stay in Minnesota. She did not know if the yeomen knew her name or her likeness, so she might be able to find a life elsewhere. She could do farm work, or maybe go live in a city.

Maybe if I find Mariposa, I can work with her! Mariposa often told stories of the work the Hollander Corporation did around the Great Lakes, sailing and trading. Spending her life doing good work. Learning a proper trade. And maybe a....

The image that startled her was of herself, sitting in a rocking chair, reading a book while children played at her feet. Across from her, a man, undefined in her mind except for a sense of familiarity, rocked in another chair as he read. It was peaceful but unnerving.

In the six weeks since she left home, Sasha had never really thought about the future. She had been so busy being a part of the regiment she had not given a lot of thought to a year down the line, much less five or ten.

Is that something I want? A family?

Sasha thought about it. Like most country girls, the idea of a romantic marriage was the stuff of bedtime stories. They all dreamed about it, but the fact was there were not enough men within the area to make that a likely future. Most marriages were arranged by parents. The children had a little input, but in most cases simply accepted that their parents knew best.

Despite the problems that arose between herself and her suitors, Sasha had always expected that she eventually would marry and settle down. It did not matter if she wanted it or not, it was just going to happen, and it never filled her with any particular excitement to think about it. Her biggest concern had been who.

Christian Proctor was a pleasant enough man. He had not ignited any great attachment in her when they met for the first time, but he had come across as a good man to spend her life with. If that drunk had not tried for her necklace two days before the wedding, she might be content, if not happy, in Duluth, maybe even with a family. But her fighting made her undesirable to Christian's family, and that was that.

Horace Gifford had joked a few times about marrying her, but as far as Sasha knew he had never broached the subject with her father. She certainly never mentioned it. Horace was nice and pleasant, but his gambling had always struck Sasha as a troublesome habit. And besides, he lived in Walker Town itself, where the yeomen were a constant presence. Sasha did not like that idea at all.

That left Samuel Cartier. Marriage to him was a threat, and the only one she actively fought against. If it had gotten as far as marriage, she could not believe for a second that it would have been a happy one. She was happy events had destroyed any chance of that cursed union.

And now that she was with the regiment?

Now, she could chose who she married, or even if she wanted to be married at all. No one else in the regiment was married, and some of them were considerably older than she was, both men and women. Harriet, the pregnant woman who helped care for the camp, was about the closest to 'normal' of anyone in the regiment. Beth and Rick had been in a relationship, but Sasha was unsure of how serious it had become before Rick's death. If anyone else in the regiment was thinking about starting a family, it was not being discussed around the campfire.

For the first time, Sasha was asking herself if she even wanted children, or marriage. Being an adult woman without a husband and children was such a scandalous circumstance for a girl in the farmland that most were willing to accept their parents' arrangements. She remembered her pregnant sister, uncomfortable and awkward, and thought of the woman in Camperton who died in childbirth over the winter. If Sasha did not have children, she could do whatever she wanted. Certainly, she could keep fighting with the regiment.

As for needing a man, Sasha had never felt the need for one before. No one she knew from Penelope's Haven or any of the nearby villages held any interest for her. Neither did any of the men in the regiment, though she did like them better than the men in the villages.

Have I met anyone I'm interested in? She asked herself.

Unbidden, General Prince appeared in her mind. Strong, handsome, smart, confident. She remembered him denouncing the yeomen after she had been rescued. The way he greeted her. How he stood up to her father when he tried to take Sasha back. Sasha's breathing increased as she imagined Prince sitting in that chair from her daydream, reading a book. Playing with the children together. Living together, in a clean house full of books, without the danger of yeomen and bullies.

189

A peal of thunder crashed right overhead, and Sasha sat up, wondering if her den was going to collapse. After a minute she lay back down, seeing no weakness in the ceiling, and returned to her thoughts.

Someone like General Prince, she admitted to herself. *I could be interested in someone like him. Smart and respectful. Someone who makes my heart beat faster.*

A gust of wind blew the curtain aside and sprinkled her with water. The rain fell in torrents, and the sunlight was drowning in dark clouds.

Someone like him is not close to here and now, Sasha chided herself as she held the curtain closed. *If I don't need to answer this now, then I shouldn't worry about it. Focus on the regiment and the mission, not a future that's too far away to prepare for. What do you need to know now?*

Sasha started to recite the steps to dismantle and clean the LAMB gun. She had moved on to the automatics when she drifted off to sleep.

Chapter 20

The sloshing woke Sasha before the curtain was drawn back. Beth looked down with the morning sky brightening behind her.

'You slept all night?' she asked.

'I did,' Sasha stretched as best she could. 'Guess I needed it.'

'Guess so,' Beth said. 'Snow and Buck are back.'

'Both of them?' Sasha looked up at her bald friend. 'You don't sound like they're bearing good news.'

'They're not,' she said.

The camp still had several inches of water. Sasha joined the rest in wading across towards the hill, where the regiment was gathering. She did not bother strapping on the cloth and leather boots, as they were not waterproof, and it would have taken too long to do so. She saw others coming in bare feet, some of them wearing only a simple sleeping smock. A few of the men were shirtless, as it was turning into a hot day. The sight was less unnerving to her than it had been only a few weeks earlier.

What a sight we are; unbathed and half-dressed. Some rebellion we turned out to be.

Snow and the seniors were having a discussion near the Colonel's Den, leaving the regiment to congregate on the hill. Someone had a small fire burning, and she could see Harriet preparing coffee. Sonja sat there, looking dead tired. The first cup was poured and put in her hands.

'Now drink,' Winnie said, 'and tell us what happened.'

Sonja grimaced. 'Just talk softly for a minute.' She drank deeply, then looked around. She searched the assembled crowd until she saw Sasha. 'Sasha, when you were told of the camp, what did they say?'

'Grandpa Middlestedt? He said that the count had started building the camp when he first started hearing about the problems in Walker County. He wanted to be ready in case he had an uprising here, and that he wanted a forward position for his yeomen.'

Sonja nodded with a frown on her face.

'What's up, Sonja?' Winnie asked.

Sonja thought for a moment. 'That's wrong,' she finally said. 'That camp isn't something the Count built after hearing about Walker. That camp has been there for years. The guards had patrolled the perimeter so often there are tracks worn into the ground. Some of the buildings look pretty worn. That place is old.'

'What's it look like? Winnie asked.

'Like it could hold about two thousand people,' Sonja said, 'enclosed behind a double wall of barbed wire and what looks to be a minefield. The trees are cut back three hundred yards from the perimeter. There are guard towers on the fence, every hundred yards or so, standing about thirty feet tall, and built on top of concrete pillboxes.'

'Concrete!' Erick exclaimed. 'How thick?'

'I didn't get a chance to measure them,' Sonja said sarcastically, 'but I assume thick enough to protect against anything we could lug through the forest.'

'Great,' Winnie said.

'Attack at night?' Sasha suggested.

'They have electric lights,' Sonja said. The crowd went silent. 'Every other tower has a spotlight, and they turned them on every so often to scan the fields. The fences are have lights at every pole top, so the perimeter is lit, as are all the buildings. It's not great light, but sneaking around would not be easy.'

'How did the yeomen come up with something like that?' someone asked.

'They didn't,' Sonja said. 'There are some yeomen there, but most of the personnel are Inspectorate troops.'

The Mardurers who trained in Walker looked stunned. Everyone else, including Sasha, looked confused.

'What does that mean?' Sasha asked.

'The Inspectorate is one of the Departments of the Army,' Erick said. 'It means they're soldiers, with better training and equipment than we're used to.'

'So they're not yeomen,' Sasha said.

'Nope,' Sonja said. 'They're much better trained. They also don't seem to like the yeomen much. The two groups keep pretty separate, from what we saw.'

'How many?' Winnie asked.

'Forty or fifty? Enough to man the whole perimeter if necessary, but they wouldn't have much of a reserve.'

'Even with the yeomen?' Winnie asked.

Sonja shrugged. Sasha noticed that the Mardurers seemed more worried, and she understood why.

Yeomen were yeomen, trained to patrol and police the population. They could be poorly trained bullies like Walker or better trained troopers like Brainerd, but they were not combat soldiers. Master Sergeant had pointed that out a number of times.

Inspectorate troops were another matter. Even if Sasha had never heard of the term before, Erick had said they were part of the Royal Army, and fighting the Royal Army was something that was always discussed with a measure of seriousness. Everyone was worried about fighting the Army; the only point of argument between individuals was how many, if any, of the Minnesotans or Iowans or Omahanians might defect or desert rather than fight them. Even then, it was generally agreed that the king would only send the most loyal battalions against a local insurrection.

'What about you?' Sonja asked Sergeant Tomas, one of those who had followed Buck. 'Find anything?'

'Trouble,' he replied. 'The yeomen rounded up the families of those who left with us. Taking them to this camp, probably.'

'Did you see anyone go in?' Winnie asked Sonja.

Sonja shook her head. 'We must have just missed them.'

'How about the yeomen?' Sasha asked Tomas. 'Did you catch any?'

He shook his head. 'We found a couple of patrols but Buck didn't set up. Turns out they're patrolling in groups now. Squads, about a hundred yards apart as they go down the roads. Each squad had an extra horse carrying a crew served weapon of some sort.'

'If we hit one, the rest will maneuver and engage,' Winnie said. 'And Buck didn't attack?'

'We could have taken one group,' Tomas said, 'but not all of them. Not with the squad he had.'

'Snow could have,' Winnie said.

'I could have what?' Snow asked. She, Buck, and Master Sergeant were now standing slightly up the hill from the group. Sasha was not sure how long they had been listening, but a number of the Mardurers shuffled nervously.

'Could have attacked,' Winnie said.

'Anyone could have attacked,' Snow said. 'Buck didn't, and now we know our enemy is trying to adapt, and now our first strike will be devastating.'

'Yes, Colonel,' Winnie said, blushing slightly.

The regiment looked up at their colonel. Snow did not look as calm as she usually did, instead looking angry. Her regiment was responding to her anger, even if they did not know why.

'I take it you have all been informed,' Snow said. 'You know that there is a camp. You know it is big and well defended. You know it is being populated with locals. So, at least I can leave out that part of my speech.'

A couple of people chuckled.

'We haven't heard from Walker County in some time,' Snow said. 'Normally I'd send Sonja, but I feel I'm going to need her abilities here, so I'm sending Rifle Thames. Hopefully he'll return with good news.

'In the meantime, we've got some work to do. Beth is going to stay here with four of the newest volunteers and Captain Saber.'

'And the others?' Winnie asked.

'Volunteer Ruth is being assigned to Mary as an assistant medic; Volunteer Raoul will be aiding Gunner Jim. Everyone else is getting armed. The regiment is going hunting,' Snow said.

Winnie and Sasha gave each other a look.

'Count Brainerd has declared war on the population, and we're going to defend them. This is not just about furthering our cause. This is about defending the weak against the tyrannical. Yes, I hope the population joins with us. But even if they decide to leave the area, we are going to protect them.'

'What about the camp?' Erick asked.

'We're not equipped or trained to attack a fortified position like that,' Buck said.

'We're a field regiment,' Snow said. 'Ideally, we would cut it off and let it wither until it surrenders. But our first concern is to curtail the yeomen and their activities.'

'So we're hunting,' Winnie said.

'Sergeant, put together a squad of six, including yourself, to screen the regiment. Lieutenant Buck will take the gunners and grenadiers, and I'll command the rest. We move quickly, we find the enemy, and we cut them apart. Be prepared to leave in one hour.'

The regiment split apart, wading back towards their dens and the supplies.

'It's not going to be that easy,' Sasha said to Winnie.

'No,' Winnie replied with a nod. 'But we're not out here because it's easy, are we?'

'No,' Sasha agreed. 'We're not.'

Chapter 21

For four days, Third Regiment hunted.

It was not as easy as they hoped. The six villages of the Whitefish Loop were dotted around dozens of lakes. There were open fields, some farmed and some wild, spread out across the area. There were only a few places where the regiment might be able to conduct their ideal ambush, and the yeomen were taking care to avoid those spots.

Snow did not want to approach the villagers yet. She was worried they might follow Middlestedt's reasoning, and blame her for bringing this mess down on them. She wanted a victory first, to prove she had not abandoned them.

The regiment began to feel the strain. When marching they were slow, shuffling through the woods, eyes focused on putting one foot ahead of the other. When they made camp, without a fire for hot food or tea, everyone sat with slumped shoulders, their normal banter missing. Sasha read some, but she felt little enjoyment in it.

The officers were little better off. Buck tried to keep them smiling but soon succumbed to the quiet. Snow and Master Sergeant likewise were having a rough time getting the regiment up and moving. Snow in particular looking harried and nervous, as if she was losing confidence in her ability to complete her mission.

On the third day, Erick and Winnie got into a fist fight that almost caused a riot. Sasha had to pull Winnie off the grenadier. No one knew what was said between them, and neither admitted to Snow what was said. Snow admired their integrity as she restricted them to hard tack and water for three days.

No one ran, but it was obvious that things were not going well. Sasha remembered the conversation about the regiment escaping west to the Dakotas, but what if the regiment fell apart? What if the regiment fought itself to death?

And then the children came.

◆◆◆

Waking up from underneath dew-covered blankets was never a warm affair. Several of the regiment carried tea with them, but none were able to start fires as Snow had ordered no sign of their existence. Sasha had yet to develop much of a taste for what they carried, but anything that might put warmth in her bones would have been accepted. Instead, she took a stale biscuit from her pack and sat next to an exhausted Winnie.

'Sleep well?' Winnie asked. She had been on watch the night before and looked dead on her feet.

'No,' Sasha groaned. Her back protested every movement. She stretched a bit, hoping to get feeling back in her legs. 'I have watch tonight.'

'Best be rested for it,' Winnie said. She started to nod off, then snapped back awake.

'Why don't you sleep?'

'Not enough time,' Winnie said.

'No one would think less of you for sleeping when you can. I hear it's the mark of a true soldier to be able to sleep whenever and wherever they can.'

Winnie said nothing, as she had dropped to sleep again. Sasha continued eating her biscuit. Buck walked by.

'Sasha, want to fill up the canteens?'

'Sure,' she said.

'Great. Take Megan and Chris. Be quick; I don't know when Snow wants to take off.'

'Yes, sir.'

Sasha searched out the two newer Rifles, gathered the canteens, and led them down to a nearby creek. Every Mardurer was supposed to carry two, but the regiment had run out of canteens. A few of the volunteers had brought their own, the large circular ones that bounced around and made loud sloshing noises when they marched. Sasha much preferred the smaller ones that sat in pouches on the belt.

The three set about filling the canteens. The weight increased dramatically when water was added, and the three of them hoisted their heavy loads for the walk back up the hill to the camp. Chris stopped.

'Do you hear that?'

They all stopped to listen. Sasha strained her ears, listening to the forest. Then she heard it.

'Help!' someone called. It was distant, away from the regiment.

Sasha dropped the canteens, motioning for the others to do so as well, and unslung her rifle. She crossed the stream, the other two behind her. She turned and motioned for Megan to stay there, and led Chris up the opposite hill.

'Help, please, God!'

Sasha ran forward, moving swiftly and silently. Chris stumbled and followed behind her. Sasha reached a crest and looked over.

She saw a dead horse. Nearby lay another figure, a girl of maybe twelve. Sitting over her and crying was a younger girl, seven or eight. 'Help me!' she called again, between sobs.

Sasha was running down the hill. The girl turned with a start as Sasha skidded to a stop. 'HELP ME, PLEASE!' the girl cried, louder now that someone was there.

Sasha looked at the girl laying at her feet. She was wearing a sleeping gown drenched with blood. Her skin was cold and clammy. Sasha followed the stain of blood and found an open wound at her shoulder.

'Are you Mardurers?' the child asked. 'My brother is one of you. Samson. Samson the Mardurer. Please tell me you know him!'

'I know him,' Sasha said. Chris skidded to her side.

'We need to get her to Mary,' Sasha said. Chris picked up the wounded girl in his arms. Sasha picked up the younger. 'What's your name?'

'Anna . . . .' she sobbed into Sasha's shoulder.

'Anna, we're going to bring you to your brother. Hold on tight.'

Sasha ran back to camp. Anna was sobbing into her shoulder, hands clasped tightly around Sasha's neck. The wounded girl, cradled in Chris's arms, did not make a sound.

The picket barely gave her a glance, not realizing that she was running for a reason. The whole camp jumped up when Sasha broke the quiet, yelling for Mary and Samson.

Chris was right behind her, carrying the wounded girl. Mary was up and moving, her newly assigned assistant on her heels, pushing everyone else away from the girls. Samson was white-faced at the sight of his sisters, taking Anna from Sasha's arms.

'What happened to Becky?' he asked, but Anna just buried her head in his shoulder and cried.

'I'm going to need water,' Mary yelled.

'Sasha, the canteens?' Buck asked.

'I'll get them!' she ran back downhill, with Chris and another rifle right behind her. They joined Megan, grabbed the canteens, and returned up the hill. By the time they returned, the camp was quiet. Samson and Anna were crying together, and Mary was pulling a blanket over the Becky's head. Several of the Mardurers were weeping, some praying. Everyone was quiet.

Sasha, canteens in her hands, fell to her knees, and cried.

Snow finally moved over towards Samson. Sasha was close enough to see tears in her eyes.

'Samson, does your family observe any customs?'

'We have a plot,' Samson finally said, his voice thick from crying. 'Back home. It's where the family is buried. But we can't go back to bury her. The yeomen,' he stopped. 'They *shot* her.'

'We can bury her here,' Snow said. 'Protect her body until we can move it.' She glanced at Master Sergeant, who nodded and silently began assembling a burial detail. 'Samson, I need to know what happened.'

'I'll find out what I can,' Samson said, still holding his baby sister.

Sasha helped wrap the body in several blankets. She thought Becky looked amazingly serene, as if she had found peace in death. This girl was, according to her brother, eleven years old. Eleven, and she had been shot. She was only a kid.

A good one, Sasha thought to herself. *Brave enough to protect her sister, smart enough to get away.*

A sickening feeling washed over Sasha.

Like I would protect Thomas. What would Fox have seen in this girl? Would he see the same thing he saw in me?

She looked at Samson and Anna, still mourning in whispered conversation. She teared up again, and let them fall.

She was not the only one. Much of the regiment was sitting about, as they had been before, but instead of a quiet sadness, it was a quiet rage. They were supposed to stop this from happening. And they had failed.

Sasha realized that she did not know much about these people. Yes, she knew how they fought, but she did not know where they were from, why they came here. She wanted to ask them. *When you look at the body of a child, do you see a younger sibling you left behind? Is there a family praying for your return? Or are you alone?*

Sasha knew this was on purpose. Mardurers were not supposed to talk much about themselves. That way if one was captured, they could not reveal the families of the others. The officers used code names, Buck and Saber and Snow and Mary.

Other than names, she knew little of those who had not volunteered from within the county. Sasha was sure most of them were from Minnesota with the exception of Snow and Sonja. Most came from farming families. A few had mentioned siblings, but never names. 'Security through anonymity,' Beth had said once. Sasha never really understood that until now.

If I die here, my family cannot be prosecuted. They will be safe.

The grave was shallow, and a pile of stones was laid by to cover her with. The body was gently laid down. Mary read from the Bible, and several of the volunteers sang a song that Sasha had never heard before. She was too moved to remember it. Samson said a few words, and Anna simply said thank you to her older sister.

Sasha wept, still seeing Thomas.

When the last stone was placed, Snow spoke.

'Becky, age 11, was killed today. Except for her sister Anna, we might only be able to guess at what happened. But we know.

'The count has already incarcerated the families of those volunteers who joined us. He did allow, or at least his yeomen did allow, for the younger children to stay in the villages under the care of others. No longer.

'According to Anna, the yeomen swept in early this morning. They not only rounded up those left behind, but the headman and his family, and another, prosperous family of the town. All of them were given ten minutes to gather one pack of items and then were roped together. Anna said that they were warned that they might not get to rest until the next morning. I believe that the yeomen are going to hit all the towns, and imprison those who might influence the rest to our side.'

The regiment stirred. Less than half of them were from this county, but there was an anger from all of them.

'If Anna is remembering correctly, the yeomen plan to take the long route, through all the villages, before returning to their camp. Their last village will be Kimble. I mean to hit them before they get back to their camp, and free the prisoners. That means we're going to have to move fast and fight hard.'

'We're ready,' Winnie said. The regiment chorused in agreement.

'Good. Let's go.'

Chapter 22

Winnie's First Squad was screening the regiment, moving quickly south towards Kimble. Sasha kept her distance from everyone else, bounding forward with Winnie. They scrolled across the roads and streams. Snow stopped them for a brief rest, and then pushed them onward with a rush. The regiment did not complain; even Anna, being carried by her older brother, was quiet and focused.

Snow directed them towards Jenkins, one of the villages on the loop. It was built in the ruins of one of the towns from the Before Time, with hills of debris scattered about. The villagers were not out and about, and the regiment moved by not knowing if the yeomen had been through or not.

They turned east towards Kimble, passing the intersection that led south to Pelican Point.

Winnie was leading, Sasha about forty feet behind and on her left, closest to the road. Two other rifles were on Winnie's other side, and two more acting as a chain between Winnie and Snow. They moved from tree to tree, heading east. Sasha was crossing a small field within sight of Kimble when the first yeoman appeared less than a hundred yards away.

She dropped to the ground and observed. He was mounted, slowly patrolling the edge of Kimble. Behind him a few more milled about, with the squat houses of the village behind them. He gave no indication he saw Sasha, instead scanning the tree line. Sasha glanced out for any of her squad mates, but she could not see anyone. They had all gone to ground.

Great. I'm stuck in the open.

Several more mounted yeomen cantered out to the first's position until eight of them were assembled. Sasha watched them discuss something and then break up, two staying there and six heading westward towards the crossroads. Sasha watched, waiting for her chance to move.

When the six were out of sight, Sasha crawled forward. She angled away from the road, hoping to bump into Winnie and at least be with one person if a fight came on.

She found Winnie behind a thick oak tree, signaling back to the regiment with the broad arm gestures Sasha was still learning. She glanced down at Sasha, crawling up through the long grass.

'I thought they had you for a minute,' Winnie whispered.

'Me too,' Sasha said. Winnie was elevated slightly above the road, and Sasha could now see into the village itself. The people and yeomen were all concentrated in the center, with a few outriders patrolling the edge. The closest was about fifty yards away, eyes peering into the forest. Sasha swore she looked into his eyes twice but he never noticed her.

A wail from the village signaled the main body of yeomen was leaving. A column of people, about a hundred, dressed in the dull, dirty clothes of farmers, carried packs and shuffled as a group, tethered together by a long chain. Mounted and walking yeomen surrounded them, herding them down the road.

Sasha watched the procession, seeing men and women, the elderly and children, tied as if animals. She could hear children crying and the words of parents trying to calm their children as they marched into the unknown. Her hands tightened against the wooden stock of her rifle.

Winnie put her hand on Sasha's shoulder and gripped it so hard Sasha winced. Her sergeant was red with anger, fuming at the scene. 'Not again,' she said silently. 'Not this time.'

'What do we do?' Sasha asked.

'When the regiment ambushes, there is the possibility that yeomen will retreat back to the village. We're going to stop them.' Winnie looked back away from the road, where the other two rifles were supposed to be. She signaled to them, but Sasha was focused on the column and did not know if they answered.

'We can't let this happen,' Sasha said.

'The Colonel will know what to do,' Winnie said with confidence.

'I hope so.'

The regiment was not supposed to be more than five hundred yards back, so the column would not travel far before Snow would strike. Sasha peered after them, wondering if she might get a chance to see it.

One of the yeomen stopped and turned.

Sasha and Winnie shrunk and went still, wondering if they were spotted. The man waved and turned back at towards the village.

What was that? Sasha thought. She had a sinking feeling and looked back at the village.

There were still yeomen in the center.

'Oh, no,' Sasha said. She tugged at Winnie's shoulder. 'They're still in there!'

Winnie looked and cursed. 'That's not good. If they are in there and they heard the ambush, they'll . . . . .'

Sasha no longer heard Winnie; she was running towards the village. The field between her position and the village was half-grown grass, tall enough that she could crouch and make a good speed forward.

If they are in the village they will threaten the villagers remaining. At best, they'll use them as hostages. At worst, they will kill them. We can't let that happen. Not like Becky.

Sasha approached the first house, glancing about to see if anyone was watching. She did not see any guards.

Snow ambushed the column just as Sasha sprinted from the field to the corner of one of the little huts. The sounds of gunfire from the west sounded heavy, but a glance that direction only showed Winnie rushing to catch up.

'This is stupid,' Winnie said. 'Fix your bayonet.'

Sasha did so, hearing a deep THUMP from the middle of the village.

Winnie cursed. 'That is a mortar,' she said, gesturing for Sasha to follow. A loud explosion sounded from the attack. 'They must be blind firing.'

They found a pile of cut wood between two houses and peered over the top. Kimble was a collection of huts and small houses built in a circle. No villagers could be seen, but a number of yeomen bustled about. Five were clustered around a single mortar that looked to be no more than a steel tube on a heavy plate with two thin legs leaning on the ground. One yeomen dropped a bomb in and they all covered their ears as the weapon spat it back out in a high arc. Other yeomen were shuffling between their horses and some of the houses on the west side of the village.

'We need to end that,' Winnie said. The pair crouched behind the wood and aimed. 'Once we clear the mortar, shoot the horses,' she said.

Sasha nodded, her heart pounding in her ears. She drew a bead on one of the yeomen, clean shaven, well groomed, adjusting the dials on the mortar. She had killed before, yes, but that was a reaction to a threat. This was premeditated.

You are going to murder, her father's voice said weakly in her mind.

'Fire,' Winnie said.

Sasha's first shot struck one man in the chest; he shuddered and fell over. She worked the bolt and fired a second time at a yeoman scrambling for cover, missing. She steadied herself for her third and shot him in the back just before he reached a doorway; he fell inside, boots still in the mud. She fired her last three shots at the horses, killing two.

'Reload while we move, to the right,' Winnie said, pulling Sasha away from the woodpile. Already someone was shooting back, the wood splintering and jumping as bullets reached for the women.

'They're angry,' Winnie shouted. Sasha reloaded as she followed Winnie around the house, hearing impact of bullets. 'And now we're having a firefight in the middle of a fucking village!'

She's angry with me Sasha realized. She rushed across a separation, hearing a bullet streak by her head. 'Winnie . . . ' she said.

'Not now, Rifle!' Winnie snapped. She reached another corner and fired at someone. Sasha checked behind them but saw no one. 'I doubt that mortar was the only weapon they had. We need to find any others and take them out.'

Sasha nodded. They had circled around to the south and were continuing to the east of the village. The gunfire from the west was intermittent but noticeable, so Snow was involved in some sort of fight. Sasha doubted she and Winnie would get any help.

'Okay,' Winnie said. 'We're going to keep circling around to the right. Try not to draw attention to yourself. I want them looking for us and not focusing on the rest of the regiment. Once we start shooting, they'll know where we are.'

'Okay,' Sasha said.

Winnie led them around, darting between huts. Sasha risked a glace into the village square, saw the bodies and the weapons lying in the mud. She tried to guess how many yeomen might be left. *Five? Six? There were seven when we opened fire and four now lay dead. But there were more horses than yeomen. Did all of them have riders? What else might they be carrying?*

They were east of the square now. The rifle fire was down to an unsteady popping, but now there was a long staccato, one Sasha had never heard before. She glanced at Winnie with a quizzical look on her face.

Winnie frowned. 'That's a proper machine gun,' she whispered. The distance to the next building was large, about twenty feet or so, as they had reached the eastern roadway. 'We need to cross that,' Winnie said. She was not happy about it, and neither was Sasha. 'I'll cover you; run and don't stop until you get across. Then cover me.' Sasha nodded. 'Good luck. Go!'

Michael Bernabo

The mud was slippery and Sasha could not get up to full speed as she left cover and ran across the expanse of the road. When the first bullet buzzed by her she was so surprised that she slipped and fell. More bullets flew about her and for a moment, Sasha panicked. She froze in the mud, in full sight of enemy guns.

'KEEP MOVING!' Winnie yelled at her. She fired back at the yeomen, drawing some of the fire towards her. The wall coughed out handfuls of splinters and mud. 'MOVE, RIFLE!'

Sasha crawled quickly towards the far side of the road. She twisted when something hit her hips, and she cried, for she thought she was hit. *Please, no!* She reached the far side and searched her body for the wound. The mud coated her thoroughly, and she couldn't find the wound, until . . . .

'Ouch!' she pulled her hand back. She had a cut on the palm. She looked down at her hip and saw her canteen, a sharp tin rose where the bullet had passed through.

'My canteen,' she said with a sigh.

'You alright?' Winnie yelled.

'Fine,' Sasha said. She looked around and saw her rifle sitting in the mud, exposed to enemy fire and well out of reach. 'I lost my rifle.'

'I see,' Winnie called. She was still trading fire with the yeomen across the center. 'We can wait for the rest of the regiment!'

'No we can't!' Sasha called. 'We need to keep them off balance.'

'Where do you get that from?'

'From every bully I've ever fought,' she said. She drew her smaller knife, a small blade she had been using for Winnie's knife fighting instruction. *Three lessons is enough,* she hoped.

The machine gun sounded again and Sasha advanced despite Winnie's protest, coming to another break between buildings. Just as she reached it, a muzzle appeared around the corner.

For the second time in as many minutes, Sasha expected to die.

Sasha grabbed at the muzzel with her free hand, catching the yeomen off guard as she pulled the gun right out of his grasp, and slashed at his face with her knife. She connected, but her attention was focused on the gun, which had continued right out of her hands and onto the ground.

The yeoman was not distracted and grabbed Sasha by the collar. He swore as he turned and threw her against the wall, her head connecting with a hard thunk. Her knife was gone, and she went to her knees, eyes watering. *This is it*, she thought. *I wonder if my family will ever know.*

No blow came. She shook her head, clearing the confusion. The yeoman lay next to her, eyes wide and unfocused, a spreading red stain on his chest. She glanced about, saw Winnie standing in the middle of the road, working her bolt.

'Get over here, Rifle!' she scowled. Her weapon was pointing into the village center, and as Sasha started to stand, Winnie began yelling. 'Lay your weapons on the ground and raise your hands in the air. Do not try anything unkind!'

Sasha was with Winnie and picked up her rifle. The yeomen were stumbling out of the houses, some showing wounds, dropping their weapons and holding their hands up high. Winnie advanced. Sasha stepped beside her, weapon pointed at the men. Winnie ordered them into a line. They were bigger, mostly older, but had no fight in them.

We did it! Sasha thought.

The last few yeomen stumbled through doors. One of them was without pants, wearing only his jacket. Sasha grimaced at the absurdity, but Winnie went stone still.

'Sasha, watch them,' she said. She walked past the yeoman, who was pale white and shrunk beneath her gaze. She walked right by him and into the house.

Sasha grew cold as she realized what Winnie suspected. The yeoman made his way to the line, seven of them now, arms raised in the air.

Michael Bernabo

'Get on your knees,' Sasha said, trying to sound menacing. The men all knelt. Sasha looked around, hoping to see some support, but she was alone with the yeomen.

Winnie reappeared, red hot with anger. She walked towards the men at a fast pace.

'Sergeant?' Sasha asked, just before Winnie flipped her rifle and smashed the naked yeoman on the side his head with her rifle butt. The man collapsed, holding his ear.

'Sergeant! WINNIE!' Sasha screamed.

'You son of a bitch!' Winnie reversed her rifle again, bringing the bayonet-tipped muzzle down on the prostrate yeomen, and stopped.

Sasha had her own bayonet-tipped muzzle leveled Winnie's head.

'Stop, Sergeant,' she said, sternly.

'Back away, Rifle!'

'No. Mardurers do not murder prisoners.'

'Go in there!' Winnie growled. 'See the girl. Ten years, if that. See her ripped clothes. See her bruised flesh. See her slashed throat. Then tell me this thing deserves protection.'

'We do not murder,' Sasha said. 'The yeomen murder. We do not act like them. We are better than them. Back away!'

Winnie looked at Sasha with murder in her eyes. Sasha stared right back.

Please don't make me shoot you, Sasha wished. *See that in my eyes!*

Winnie broke eye contact as someone came up beside Sasha. It was Colonel Snow. She put a hand on both their shoulders.

'Stand down, ladies,' she said, calmly. Winnie took a deep breath and stood back, her rifle lowered. Sasha stepped back as well. A dozen Mardurers were in the center now, some watching the prisoners, the rest watching Snow. A number of villagers were emerging from their hiding places, mixing with the Mardurers.

'Good job,' Snow said. She looked over the yeomen. 'Master Sergeant! These here,' she gestured at the kneeling yeomen, 'are prisoners. This one here,' she gestured at the naked one, 'is under arrest for murder and rape. Get him dressed and keep him under close guard.'

Master Sergeant was not kind as he grabbed the man and roughly hauled him to his feet, pushing him towards the house he had come from. The villagers who had come out were beginning to yell, several of them crying. One flung a pot at the naked man, screaming a name through sobs.

'What will happen to him?' Sasha asked.

'He'll be tried and shot,' Snow said. Winnie turned with a huff and walked away. 'Let her go,' Snow said. 'We need to collect the weapons and the dead.' Snow started giving orders as Sasha mournfully watched Winnie storm away.

And we were getting along so well.

Chapter 23

The cart rolled up with another four bodies lying across the bed. Sasha and a villager named Sarah carried it to the table where she had been working, the wood already slick with blood.

Reminds me of a sheep slaughter, she thought.

The yeoman was missing most of his head, having caught a bullet behind his ear. Sasha could not distinguish his features, but he looked to have been on the older side, considering the grey hairs that had begun to filter through his scalp. His hands were rough, and he bulged a bit in the middle.

Sarah coughed. 'Can we get this over with, please?'

Sasha nodded and they started. First they stripped his boots off. He was not a large man, and they could be used by several members of the regiment. They took care not to damage the bindings, carefully picking the knots out.

Second was the coat. Stained by blood and mud, it would need considerable washing, but it was a good thick coat, warm for the summer but excellent for the winters. Sasha checked it for holes but found none.

'Think there was a hat?' Sarah asked.

'Probably not worth looking for,' Sasha mused.

This yeomen wore his belts underneath his coat, something some of the yeomen did in the summer, so they could ride with their coats unbuttoned. Sasha removed long magazines for a submachine gun *(So that's why someone took care to kill him first* Sasha thought to herself), a pair of long stick grenades, a knife, two canteens, and a pouch of coins.

Sarah patted down the coat, looking for anything sewn into linings or hidden in pockets. She found a few more coins and a set of small tools.

Sasha judged the shirt to be a loss as a whole. She began cutting off the unbloodied parts, putting them aside. After a good cleaning they could be useful as bandages.

'What about the pants?' Sarah asked.

'Too worn,' Sasha said. That was not entirely true, but she did not want to pull them off. If they were some nice leather riding pants, maybe, but these were the dull pants of a footman. Not worth the effort.

Sasha and Sarah carried the body to the next cart, to be taken out to the grave being dug by the prisoners out beyond the fields. When Sasha saw there were no new bodies to search, she washed her hands. Some blood had gotten on her clothes, which she tried to wash out with little success.

Guess I'll be bloody for a while.

A couple of the Mardurers were lounging about, resting after their turns at guard duty or body transport. Some food was provided by the village, a simple selection but better than the biscuits the regiment had been on. She sat down and ate. Mary came by and joined them.

'How are they?' Sasha asked.

'I don't know,' Mary said, solemnly. The success against the yeomen was marred by the casualties inflicted on the prisoner column. Five were killed outright and seven wounded. Children were among both the dead and injured. 'I've done all I can for now. We'll just have to see how it all comes together.'

'I got more bandages,' Sasha said. 'Cut up shirts, but a good wash and they should work.'

'I'll need them,' Mary sighed.

There was a burst of shouting from the mayor's building. Snow was in there with some of the prominent prisoners and Kimble's headman. They had a number of topics to cover, from their reaction to the count's round-up to the disposition of the yeoman under arrest. Sasha had no idea if they were making any progress.

Sonja came by. 'Got any apples?'

213

Someone tossed her one. 'Good shooting,' he said.

'Yeah,' Sasha agreed.

Sonja blushed and smiled. While Sasha and Winnie had been running behind the yeomen, keeping them distracted, Sonja was the one who protected the rest of the regiment from harm. The yeomen were able to set up one machine gun, and Snow was reticent to use Jim's LAMB or Erick's grenade launcher on the hut without knowing who else was inside. So Sonja, from six hundred yards, had killed the gunner with a solid shot right to the head. And then she shot the next one who took the position. And then the third. Not only had she kept the gunners from hurting the regiment, she demoralized the remaining yeomen. Some of the prisoners had given her dirty looks when she walked by them.

'I just did my job,' Sonja said.

'Six hundred yards?' Sasha asked. 'Three times? I thought the shooter who killed Yeoman-Lieutenant Marks while his head was next to mine was great, but you sure beat him out.'

'What makes you think that was a man?' Sonja asked with a smile.

The Mardurers laughed and Sasha's mouth dropped. 'That was you?'

'Yeah,' Sonja said. 'But if I knew who I'd be saving, maybe I should've shot a little closer to target. Saved us the headache.'

'Hey!' Sasha said as more laughter erupted.

'Come with me,' Sonja said with a smile. Sasha stepped up beside her. Sonja was unhinging the leather case she wore and pulled the lensed scope. 'Ever seen this up close before? You better say no, since I've never shown it to you and no one else is supposed to touch it but me.'

'No,' Sasha confirmed, 'but I am curious.'

'Good. Careful,' she said. They were at the edge of the village, facing west towards the ambush sight. 'Lieutenant Buck and a security squad are at that bend in the road. Can you see them?'

Sasha looked through the scope. The five hundred-some yards between them and the trees was reduced dramatically. She saw an individual walking out of the trees. 'It's Jim,' she said.

'What's he doing?' Sonja asked.

'He's peeing,' Sasha said.

Sonja grabbed the scope. 'Oh? How is he armed?' she peered intently through the scope.

'Sonja!' Sasha gasped. 'That's improper!'

Sonja slowly turned to Sasha, a grin spreading across her face. 'Improper? Why, Sasha Small, are you telling me you haven't once thought about sneaking off into the woods with one of our masculine . . . members?' she chuckled.

Sasha did not get the joke. 'No! Of course not! Why would anyone? It's improper!' she repeated.

'Like Beth and Rick?'

Sasha stopped. 'Well, I mean, they were a special case.'

'They weren't the only ones,' Sonja said, and winked at her.

Sasha felt shocked. 'You? But that's....'

'Improper?' Sonja laughed loudly. 'Guess there is still some Alvanist in you.'

Sasha turned red. 'What is that supposed to mean?'

'Well it's not an insult,' Sonja said.

'Isn't it? Alvanists are pacifists, and we're at war!'

'What does pacifism have to do with sex?' Sonja asked.

Sasha was bright crimson now. She glared at Sonja, who just beamed a smile at her.

'There's no reason to be upset, Sasha. Your parents taught you a lot of things you never thought about. You rejected the Alvanist pacifism, but you inherited their prudishness. That's not a bad thing. It's just who you are. And you can't ever be anyone other than yourself. Remember that.'

215

Sasha nodded. She wanted to talk about something else.

'Good,' Sonja said. She clapped Sasha on the arm and looked over her shoulder. 'Don't hurt her,' she said to someone behind Sasha.

'I'm senior,' Winnie said from behind Sasha. Sasha turned to see the sergeant sitting on a barrel, one of the yeomen's gun belts hanging off her shoulder.

'Congratulations,' Sonja said, stepping up to Winnie. 'Don't hurt her,' she repeated, face to face with the sergeant. Then she walked away, leaving the two alone.

Winnie looked at Sasha. Sasha stared back, fists ready. She did not want to fight Winnie, but if Winnie forced her to, she was ready.

Winnie reached into a pocket and pulled out a small wooden box. She pulled a thin cigar out, followed by a box of matches. Sasha watched as she lit the cigar, puffing a few time on it, before she reached over and offered the cigar to Sasha.

'I've heard that some of the Dakota share pipes to symbolize peace,' Winnie said.

Sasha reached for the cigar. She puffed, remembering for a moment the night in Walker Town. 'You want peace?' she asked.

Winnie nodded.

'Me too,' Sasha said.

Winnie looked at the ground. She actually looked embarrassed. 'You were right,' she finally said. 'You were right, and I was out of control. I don't like being out of control. And if you hadn't stopped me . . . .'

'A bad man would be dead,' Sasha returned the cigar.

'By murder,' Winnie said.

'From what I hear, he's going to be executed anyway.'

'Executed is one thing. It's formal; considerate. Killing in a fit of rage is murder,' Winnie said. 'The yeomen murder. That is one more reason we don't.'

Sasha agreed. They were quiet for a moment, then Sasha reached for the cigar. 'I'm sorry.'

'For what?'

'For disobeying your instructions. For rushing into the village.'

'Colonel Snow says that helped; the yeomen were so turned around, they couldn't figure out where the threats were.'

'Still, I'm sorry.'

Winnie smiled. 'You weren't thinking like a rifle,' she said.

'I'll try better,' Sasha promised.

Winnie actually laughed and looked at Sasha with a sly grin. Sasha had no idea what Winnie was so amused about, but she smiled back.

'If you don't want me in First Squad . . . .'

'Bah!' Winnie interrupted. 'You're chosen, don't worry about it.' She twisted the belt on her shoulder around and removed a pistol from the holster. Sasha started as Winnie ejected the magazine and locked the slide back, handing it to Sasha. 'This is a Fabrique Montreal Model 2354 Pistol, 10 millimeter, ten round magazine. One of the yeomen had it, plus a half-dozen magazines and two boxes of ammo. Not sure where he got it or why, but he won't be needing it anymore.'

Sasha checked the pistol, feeling the weight in her hand. It was a light gun, smaller than the pistols she had practiced on, but a good fit for her. 'Nice. A good trophy for you.'

'For you,' Winnie said, tossing the belt at Sasha.

Sasha blinked. 'I'm not an NCO or a Specialist,' Sasha said. They were supposed to have first choice of pistols.

'You're a part of the First Squad,' Winnie said. 'I talked about it with Colonel Snow. Ideally, if we were to assault a town like we did today, we'd do so with the automatics. But we couldn't today because we didn't have time, and while we did grab a bunch of automatics from the yeomen, we're probably going to need to give some of them to the villagers. So, Snow wants all of us to have our pistols. It'll be useful in close range, or if someone drops their rifle in the middle of a firefight.'

Sasha chuckled. 'Guess I'll have something else to point at your head next time,' she said, buckling the belt on.

Winnie was silent for a moment, her face taking a serious look.

'What is it?' Sasha asked.

'We got one more job to do,'

◆◆◆

Matters of minor discipline and punishment were handled by the village's headman or town's mayor. Major crimes required punishment by the County Magistrate, often the count or his appointee. But as the defendant was a yeoman, there was no chance of that, so the assembled fell back on the tradition of three headmen. The local headman, Mister Keyes, and two headmen arrested by the yeomen, Mister Reynolds and Mister Reyes, made up the tribunal. Master Sergeant acted as the bailiff, with the First Squad as his staff. There were a few other people allowed inside, including the victim's family, Mary, and a yeoman sergeant who looked at the accused with sorrow in his eyes. Other Mardurers guarded outside.

Sasha and Winnie stood between the headmen and the court, bayonets fixed to their rifles. Samson and Jose stood over the condemned, Yeoman Scott Davidson, a man in his thirties. His yeoman's jacket had no stripes of rank, and four stripes of service. He was a doughy man with a receding hairline and tiny little eyes. He looked never so much a danger, and if Sasha had not seen what she had seen, she might have believed this man was not capable of such horrors. He recognized the two women, and refused to look at Winnie directly.

Mister Reynolds led the proceedings. He was the oldest and the most forceful of the three, standing with the large Bible in his hand and thumping his chest.

'May God watch over these proceedings,' he said in a booming voice, 'and guide us to a tempered justice.'

Yeomen Davidson did not look well.

Sasha stood there for half an hour, trying to stay as still as Winnie. It was hard as the family recalled the attack on their daughter, Rain, age eleven. Sasha felt a rising anger at the violent nature of it. She could not see the headmen, but she hoped they were as angry as she was.

Mary was called as a witness, providing a detailed account of the wounds. She sounded cold and detached. Sasha had a hard time listening to the accounts, and could not understand how Mary could speak so dispassionately. She knew why, had been warned that Mary must be exact for the purposes of the trial, but it was still difficult to listen to.

Finally, Mister Reynolds spoke out. 'Yeomen Davidson, do you have anything to say in your defense?'

Yeoman Davidson looked around, eyes full of fear. 'I didn't mean anything,' he said. 'I just . . . lost myself to passion.'

'Lost yourself?' Reynolds asked quietly. 'Medical Officer Mary gave a full account of your 'passions', Yeoman Davidson. You did not lose yourself, sir, you let yourself go. So long as there were no consequences, you felt no restraint.'

Davidson looked over at the yeoman sergeant. 'Greg, I . . . .'

'I warned you, Scott,' the sergeant said quietly. 'I told you to ease off, but you didn't listen.'

'But Lieutenant Weathers . . . .'

'Is dead,' the sergeant grimaced. 'And you're in the hands of the people you hurt.'

The headmen left the room to deliberate and returned two minutes later.

'Yeoman Scott Davidson,' Mister Reynold's voice boomed from behind Sasha. 'It is the finding of this tribunal that you are guilty of the crime of assault on a child, of rape with a child, and the murder of a child. It is hereby decided that for your horrific crimes, you are sentenced to death. The execution of which, is to be carried out by the Third Field Regiment, Renaissance Army of Minnesota, by midnight tonight. And may God have mercy on your soul.'

The condemned man yelled out and fainted. Samson half-carried him out of the room with Jose. Mary escorted the family out. Master Sergeant stepped up to the two women. 'Stand guard at the front door. Only headmen or officers inside.'

Sasha followed Winnie out to the front. The village looked to be evacuating. The carts had been washed and were being loaded with supplies and a few belongings. Draft animals were harnessed, and smaller animals tied to the wagons.

'I wonder where they are going,' Sasha said.

'No idea,' Winnie sounded disinterested.

'Doesn't matter to you?'

'If they can get to a safe location, we won't have to protect them,' Winnie said. 'Until then, we're their guards.'

'You don't sound happy about that.'

Winnie shrugged. 'It ties us down, keeps us from moving freely.'

'Maybe Colonel Snow will give them the weapons we took from the yeomen,' Sasha said. 'They could probably use the heavier weapons better than we could.'

'Probably,' Winnie said. 'But we'll have to show them how to use them.'

'Beth can do that,' Sasha said. She did not continue. Winnie seemed to be in some sort of mood, and Sasha did not want to provoke her.

Snow began assembling the regiment in the town center. Lieutenant Buck and Colonel Snow both went into the house Sasha was guarding, making no notice of the two guards. Sasha wanted to ask questions, but she saw the looks on their faces were not ones of conversation.

You're only a Rifle, she thought to herself. *Winnie has more reason to ask.*

Master Sergeant emerged. 'Come with me,' he said. He called out for others and soon he had eight Mardurers. 'Unload your rifles.'

The eight of them stood in a line about thirty feet from a tree. Samson and Jose had tied Yeoman Davidson before them. He struggled, crying out for help. The yeomen prisoners stood by, as did a number of the villagers. The headmen stood as a group next to Snow.

'Yeoman Davidson,' Snow said, 'under the Code of Military Justice, Article 34, you have been found guilty of the Capital Crimes of Rape, Assault, and Murder. Under the authority of the CMJ, Article 55, having been lawfully found guilty, I will now carry out the sentence of execution. While I would prefer to hang you, Yeoman Davidson, we are under a rush, and I must resort to firing squad.'

'Squad, about, face!' Master Sergeant called, and the eight turned their backs on Davidson. 'Present arms for inspection.'

They held out their rifles, their bolts open revealing empty magazines. Master Sergeant took the first one, and turned his back to the squad. When he turned around, the bolt was closed.

'Five of you have real bullets,' he said. 'You will not know who fired the killing shots.' He did this for each rifle. Sasha could not tell if he given her a real bullet. 'The other three have blanks, with wax bullets that will not cause harm. Failure to fire on the order will result in severe discipline.' He finished the rifles and went back to a position before the eight. 'I know this isn't anything you want to do, but this is one of those unpleasant duties one must attend to.' He straightened. 'About, face!'

Davidson was now alone, crying and struggling against the bindings. A red cloth was pinned to his shirt and his eyes were covered with a blindfold. Master Sergeant moved to a side of the squad.

'Port, arms!' he called. The squad picked up their rifles from their sides and carried them across their chest.

'Ready!' The squad stepped forward with their left foot.

'Aim!' The rifles came up to the shoulder. Sasha sighted at the red cloth over Davidson's heart. She felt a moment of pity for the man, only a moment. Then she pushed pity under the image of the girl.

'Fire!'

Eight rifles barked.

Davidson convulsed as five bullets shredded his chest. He twitched a few times and went still. Master Sergeant approached and checked him for a pulse. Finding none, he hung a sign around his neck that read 'Rapist.' The body was left tied to the tree.

Snow said something to the yeomen and they turned to the east, to head towards their prison camp. The Mardurers and civilians started heading west.

Sasha marched next to Winnie. 'I didn't like that,' she said.

'No one did,' Winnie said. 'But we'll probably have to do something like that again.'

'Will that execution stop anyone from raping again?' she asked.

'Probably not.'

'Then why?'

Winnie shrugged. 'Because he deserved it.'

Sasha was unhappy as they marched behind the civilians. *I hope you're wrong, Winnie. I hope someone looks at that body and decides never to rape.*

Chapter 24

Sasha did not feel much better three days later when the regiment marched on Pelican Point.

It was not Snow's idea. Reynolds was a surprisingly passionate orator, and Sasha could hear his voice booming while the headmen debated. She was not able to hear the debate itself, much to her disappointment, but she knew the decision was made before he had finished his first speech. The headmen voted to accuse Middlestedt of betraying his oath, and officially requested that Snow provide security.

Buck and a cadre of the regiment was left to train the new militia company, about forty men and women who were willing to defend their villages against the yeomen. Snow gave them the machine guns and the mortar and what small arms could be spared, but not all of them were armed.

'At least we're not tied to them now,' Winnie said. Sasha chose not to point out that they still had to remain close enough to protect the villages, as Winnie was much happier now.

Snow took the rest of the regiment and escorted five headmen and several of prominent villagers. All of them looked very stern as they marched. The regiment looked just as stern.

They advanced with weapons in hand and bayonets attached. Snow marched in front with a number of her Rifles, including Sasha, Winnie and a number of the local volunteers. Master Sergeant and the remainder were to provide security around the village; Snow and her squad observe to watch the confrontation.

The townsfolk saw the column approaching. Anyone in the fields retreated back to the town, much as they did when yeomen approached. Sasha hated herself when they reacted like that.

Their arrival was not unexpected. The town square had a raised platform, on top of which now sat a large chair. Mayor Middlestedt sat in the chair, clean and dressed in fine clothes. He looked much like a nobleman, or what Sasha thought a nobleman would look like. His family stayed on their porch, watching.

Behind him, Middlestedt had assembled a dozen of his men, armed with farming implements and a pair of muskets. The rest of the villagers, the ones who didn't hide, stood to the sides, watching.

We could easily kill them, Sasha thought. *But he knows we won't.*

The headmen stepped forward to stand before Middlestedt's throne. The mayor sat upright, staring down at them as if in judgment.

'Gentlemen,' he said. 'What brings you here today?'

'We've come to discuss the matter of the arrests,' Reynolds said. There was no deference in his voice.

Middlestedt shrugged. 'That is of course unpleasant. But the count must keep order.'

'Order? Bad enough the count demands the arrest of families for the actions of their young men and women. But he did not need to order the arrest of anyone else. I have no children, I have no wife. The count is not even aware of my existence. And yet my arrest was ordered? If so, it was only because you pointed a finger at me, Robert.' Reynolds turned, addressing the crowd. 'I charge you, Robert Middlestedt, with betraying your position, and falsely accusing your opponents of capital crimes.'

'That is an accusation,' Middlestedt said. 'Not a charge. It cannot be a charge because nothing I have done is illegal.'

'You do not even deny it!' Reynolds shouted.

'Why should I?' Middlestedt looked down his nose at Reynolds. 'The count wants order. What has happened in Walker has shown that the loyalty of the king's subjects is fickle, and that there are those who would cultivate rebellion for their own cause. Much work must be done to bring the countryside back into line.'

'You know a lot of what the count wants,' Reynolds said. 'You sold your soul, didn't you? You got offered some nice new

225

position, some gold maybe? Then you pointed your finger at those you didn't like, those who resisted you, even if they opposed Snow when she first arrived.'

Middlestedt smiled. 'Robert Middlestedt, Esquire. Gentleman. Respected Landlord.'

'You sold your soul for a title.'

'I sold nothing!' Middlestedt stood. 'The count called and I answered. He believes that order brings prosperity. He wanted me to administer the lands, weed out the undesirables, and make the harvest productive.'

'And in return?'

'Safety. Income. Prestige.' Middlestedt looked very proud of himself.

'And how is the land to be bountiful if the men and women who work it are in some prison camp?'

'The workers were to be made up through other means,' Middlestedt said, suddenly looking nervous.

'So what does that mean, Robert Middlestedt, Esquire? Slaves? More families pulled from their farms and sent here in the hopes they'll be more respectful of the king?'

'It was either me or an outsider!' Middlestedt shouted. 'Would that be better, Master Reynolds? Some third son of a nobleman who doesn't care about us, who would reap what gold he could for as little work as he could get away with? If anything, I am a hard worker, and you know I would do everything in my power to see this land flourish.'

'Aye, you work hard, for whomever is in power.' Reynolds clicked his tongue. 'You were so proud to be a citizen of the Republic, weren't you? Always crowing about your vote, about your letters to the ministers. How many were returned? How much was ignored because we were but poor farmers?'

'I was, Master Reynolds. But the Republic fell. And it took our sons with it. And now we are under the governorship of a man close enough to listen when we speak. The count has but his own county to command, and we are not as lost in the shuffle as we were.'

'All governments require blood from men. This one adds the blood of virgins to the scale.'

Middlestedt nodded. 'Yes, but that would stop. The count will rein in his yeomen, bring peace and order back to us. This is a chance to make things better. Why can you not see that?'

'Because you started by hauling me off in chains!'

Middlestedt glared at Reynolds, who glared right back at him. Everyone's attention was focused on the debate occurring in the square, so none of them noticed the small squad who passed through Master Sergeant's security perimeter and joined the spectators.

'That was unfortunate,' Middlestedt said as he sat down. 'And perhaps that was the wrong decision. But I was in a rough position, Master Reynolds. These Mardurers, the Renaissance Army, the RAM, whatever you wish to call them, are pushing us to war. I felt it necessary to remove those who might support them.'

'Bullshit, Robert. Of all the headmen I was the only one who told her to go away. I all but tied up Tim Woyzchek's son to keep him home. But the count declared war on me anyway.'

'The count did not start this war,' Middlestedt turned his gaze on Snow. 'You did. You started this war. We were peaceful. We were happy. Then you invaded our county to spread your villainous beliefs.'

'Villainous beliefs?' Snow asked incredulously, speaking up from behind the headmen. 'That assault and theft and rape should not be commonplace? That everyone deserves dignity? That people deserve a say in their own government?'

'Why should people want that?' Middlestedt growled. 'Government is too important to let everyone have a say. A farmer does not understand politics. A farmer cannot know what is best for everyone. Best such things are left to the educated.'

'And if a farmer has no say,' Snow began, 'he is no different than a tool, to be abused and discarded.'

Middlestedt waved away her words. 'This is not Walker County, Colonel. We live in a county of law and order.'

'Law and order did not protect a young girl from assault and rape. Law and order did not protect you from the bandits.'

'I do not deny that you have done some service, Colonel, in eliminating the bandits, but it was not out of a good will. You had a purpose to your action. And as for the yeomen, they are punished when their deeds go too far.'

Reynolds snorted. 'Punished for going too far? Fined. Demoted. Branded. But still in the service of their lord.' He laughed. 'Too far? You fool.'

'There is a limit, even for yeomen. The yeoman who assaulted Rain will be punished. She was too young.'

'We shot him three days ago,' Snow said.

'And for killing a yeoman you will hang.'

'We tried and condemned him first,' Reynolds said.

'Then you will both hang.'

Reynolds was red, and Snow looked up at Middlestedt with fire in her eyes. The newcomers circled unnoticed, taking place on a shadowed porch to continue watching.

'Yeoman Davidson was branded,' Reynolds said for the crowd. 'Seventeen brands. Eight for theft, four for assault, four for rape, and one for murder. I asked him about the murder. Seems he took to a servant girl at an inn and forced her. She fought back and he bashed her head in. His punishment? The brand, and one month's wage fined, paid to the inn that employed her. Not her family.'

'No one is denying that Yeoman Davidson was scum, Master Reynolds, but he was protected scum. And protected scum still serves a purpose; they provide order. Brutal, but far preferable to chaos.'

Snow spoke. 'Brutal order is expected from men who suffer no consequences for insults.'

Middlestedt looked at Snow for a moment. Sasha wondered if he was preparing some insult against her, but he finally just shook his finger at her. 'You're not from around here. We've always known that, but I place you now. You're from the east, from the Erie territories. I'm right, aren't I? Ohio? Pennsylvania? Tell me, Colonel Snow, why you came to Minnesota. Was it to make trouble?'

'I came to Minnesota to find a new home,' Snow said. 'And I found it. Do not presume that I will lose nothing if this fails.'

Middlestedt shouted. 'What right do you have to come here and start a war?'

'Right?' Snow shouted back. 'What right do you have to demand everyone remains a victim so you can keep your station?'

'Everyone is a victim at some point in their lives, Colonel. Most have the good grace to accept it and move on.'

Reynolds snorted. 'Move on? How? How do they move on, Robert? Do they move on by hiding under as many layers of clothes as it takes for the yeomen to stop noticing, as our women learn to do? Do they move on by hoping to avoid conscription, or moving to a city to try and find work, as our men do? How many have we lost, Robert? How many don't come back. How many times have we buried a stranger on the side of the road and wondered if somewhere, a family was sending prayers that were already unanswered.'

Middlestedt closed his eyes and breathed deeply. 'This is the world we must survive in, Master Reynolds. It is not happy or bright, but it is what we have. The count is our Lord and Master and we must follow his guidance, regardless of the pain suffered.'

'He is putting our people into CAMPS!' Reynolds yelled.

'Because they are being misled. The Mardurers care no more for them than the Republic did. They are a new face on the Old

Guard. This will end no better than the Range Riot did. They'll bring back their precious Republic, or found something new.'

'The Mardurers do not want to bring back the Republic, Mayor Middlestedt,' Snow said. 'The name we call ourselves, the Renaissance Army, is not just a name we chose at random. We mean to end the Dark Age and bring about a new world.'

'Your army has a knack for making up words, Colonel,' Middlestedt mocked. 'Mardurer. Renaissance.'

Snow crossed her arms, obviously trying not to be provoked by the Mayor's childish antics. 'Mardurer was given to us by Count Walker; I don't much care for it, but it has stuck. And renaissance is a real word, Mayor Middlestedt.'

'It is now?' Middlestedt chuckled. Some of those behind him chuckled as well. 'Then, do tell, what is a renaissance?'

'It means rebirth!' One of the figures on the porch stepped forward, coming out of the shadows. 'Any period in which learning, art and culture are revived and renewed. It is most often used to describe the period of Europe about a thousand years ago, when interest in art and knowledge and science became commonplace and the world began to move forward out of a Dark Age.'

Sasha gaped, recognizing his voice even before she could see him. Winnie was likewise shocked and Snow, for all her anger just seconds before, looked at the speaker with wide eyes, her arms frozen halfway out of their crossed position. No one else recognized him, but they instinctively understood that this man was different. His tan uniform was immaculate, his face was confident, and two stars shone on his lapel.

'To rejuvenate the mind of society,' General Prince said, 'is so important to me, I made it part of my army's name, its core mission. Its purpose.'

Of all the assembled, Winnie gathered her wits first. 'Third Regiment, ATTENTION!'

The Mardurers assembled snapped straight. Snow turned and took a few steps before she stopped, saluting Prince. Some whispers blew through the crowd, while Middlestedt shakily stood from his throne.

'Your . . . army?' Middlestedt's voice cracked.

Prince turned his back on Middlestedt. 'Colonel Snow,' he said, smiling. 'I must say it was a hard time finding you.'

'General Prince, I didn't realize you would be looking. We hadn't heard anything from you in weeks.'

'Yes, well, things did get exciting. Count Walker,' he spoke louder, so everyone could hear him, 'assembled a sizable force of thugs and tried to terrorize the county into submission. His son displayed a surprising initiative in cavalry raids. He managed to kill many, burn towns, and cause trouble.'

'I'm surprised,' Snow said. 'He never seemed much of a threat before.'

'Remember General Caesar's First Rule,' Prince said.

'Never forget the enemy is also trying to win,' Snow replied.

Prince nodded. 'Correct. Giulio Montessori had never been tested, so there was no way to know what he could do. He might have made a great cavalry officer.'

'Might have?' Middlestedt asked.

Prince smiled a pleasant smile. 'Talent is one thing; experience another. Young Montessori was ahead of himself, and tried to do something grand and heroic. His grandiose gesture cut up his squadron.'

'He's dead?' Middlestedt asked. The crowd held its breath for an answer.

'No, he's alive. Lost a leg, but he's alive. He's in Walker, with his father and the rest of their yeomen. Besieged and cut off. Harmless, except to those still trapped inside.' He paused, gazing off into nothing for a second, before he turned back to Snow. 'In

231

any event, you are the only Field Regiment who has managed to stir up enough trouble to get my attention, so here I am.'

'Who are you?' Middlestedt asked.

'I am General Prince, Commanding General of the Renaissance Army of Minnesota. The man who destroyed the McGowan Bandit Company, who has taken Walker County away from Count Walker, and who is making life very difficult for the king.'

Middlestedt looked at him, studying the General closely. Prince looked up at him, but for all the difference that Middlestedt's riser gave him, Prince did not look smaller. Indeed, Sasha almost imagined he stood equally as tall as the Mayor.

'I don't see victory,' Middlestedt said. 'I see an army of women and children. Whatever you accomplished in Walker, I cannot see how you can expect the same thing elsewhere. How do you expect to win?'

'It's quite simple, really,' Prince said. 'We liberate a town from the yeomen. This is fairly easy, as yeomen are not trained for combat. Then we send in teachers. Teachers sow the seeds of the Renaissance, instructing the children. They tour the villages, as there are never enough of them, but they work hard. You'd be surprised how much some people want to learn, or what they're willing to learn about.'

'Of course, you are right,' Prince said before Middlestedt could respond. 'Not everyone wants to learn, and we don't force them. They usually let the children learn, since it keeps them busy for a time, and what parent doesn't want more for their children than for themselves. And I'll tell you, for some children, when they get that gleam in their eye, the spark of hunger for knowledge, it makes the whole thing worthwhile. They, Mayor Middlestedt, are the Renaissance. The future, hungering for knowledge. Even if they stay farmers, they'll have that hunger, and every once in a while we find a diamond in the rough.'

'The rough what?' Middlestedt asked.

A woman laughed on the porch. Sasha glanced over to see another figure in a tan uniform, a woman with long blond hair.

Around her was a squad of soldiers wearing striped uniforms and carrying black weapons. She immediately thought of the black carbines Winnie had spoken of a few times. Whomever they were, they were intimidating.

'Officer Bellona,' Prince cautioned.

The woman went silent. 'Sorry, General.'

Prince turned back to Middlestedt. 'It is a saying, Mayor Middlestedt. It conveys the notion that in anything ugly, there is going to be something beautiful. And among the people, no matter how downtrodden, how dirty or how ugly their existence is, there is still beauty and hope. With my teachers, I aim to find the diamonds, to find those who are called to a higher service than they were born to.'

'They're just farmers,' Middlestedt said. Several people behind Sasha muttered quietly at that remark.

'Say that again when your stomach is empty.'

'Not every farmer can be a lord!'

'No,' Prince admitted. 'There will always be farmers. It is a fine and noble profession, one that finds a curious amount of derision given how utterly crucial it is for civilized life. But not every farmer is meant to be a farmer. Some are poets; some are warriors, scientists, politicians. Some may even secure a position in a school of civil service, that they are forced to leave when fellow students conspire to expel them. Everyone should have the option of deciding their own fate.'

Middlestedt looked shocked. 'How did you...?'

'I always know my opponent, Mayor Robert Ezekiel Middlestedt.'

Middlestedt sunk back down into his chair, stunned at Prince's revelation.

'You had a chance,' Prince continued. 'You tried to take it. That is noble, as is coming back and making something of your life here. But why deny that to others?'

233

'They were all citizens,' Middlestedt said. 'Those that expelled me. Citizens of the Republic that cared little for the subjects they stepped on.'

'True,' Prince said. 'The Republic was deeply flawed, and more than a few people cheered its downfall. That is why I am not fighting to bring back the Republic.'

'Aren't you?' Middlestedt asked. 'I recognize your face, General Prince. You're a Dawson.'

The crowd gasped. Sasha glanced to see that Winnie was surprised by the news, but Snow was not. One of the General's guards started forward but Officer Bellona raised an arm and stopped him.

'The 'Royal Family' of Minnesota,' Middlestedt said. 'The Dawsons founded the Iron Republic when it was born in the mines of Mesabi. Not an administration came to power that didn't have a Dawson in the cabinet. You got rich, and fat. And when the Empire came, your family paid for it. Aye, more than they should have. An entire bloodline is a bit much, I think. You have my sympathies, General. What happened to your family was unfortunate.'

Prince was still for a moment before slowly turning on Middlestedt. Sasha could see his face, and his smile had completely vanished. He looked as stone.

'Unfortunate?' he asked. 'Unfortunate is a hail storm destroying your crops. Unfortunate is your milk cow dying. What happened to my family was familicide. The purposeful and deliberate extinguishment of an entire bloodline. Men, women, children. Massacred. The Dawsons, the Imperians, the Pierce-Montalbans. If the rumors are true, they suffered greatly before they died. If the rumors are not true, they still died.'

His voice was so cold, Sasha imagined Middlestedt's breath fogging in the summer air.

Prince turned, walking slowly in front of Middlestedt, inspecting the crowd. His eye swept over Sasha without stopping.

Why would he remember you? She asked herself.

'They did oppose the Great Emperor,' Middlestedt replied meekly.

'The Great Emperor had no business crossing the Atlantic.'

'No one could stop him!' Middlestedt spoke louder. 'Not Quebec, not Mississippi, no one. That is strength. And in the face of such strength, what can be do but suffer?'

Prince looked at Middlestedt as if he had grown two heads. 'We must suffer? That is not a new sentiment, Mayor. There is a quote, from many thousands of years ago. The Greek city-state of Athens demanded the surrender of the neutral island of Melos, citing their superior sea power and military forces. Melos refused, citing the injustice of such a demand. The Athenians position was one of political realism, stating "The Strong do what they can and the Weak suffer what they must." They took the city, executed all the men, and sold everyone else into slavery.'

Middlestedt looked shocked, and the crowd began to hum with whispers. Sasha knew why. Prince was discussing things from the Before Time, without any hesitation. *How would he know that?* Sasha wondered. *Where did Snow get a three thousand year old book on warfare? From the same place?*

'That being said, it is usually those in a position of power who make such comments. Those who suffer rarely accept it. I, for one, do not accept it. If a leader acts without the best interests of his people, he is a tyrant.'

'And what are you, General Prince? You're not a tyrant?' Middlestedt shouted. Some of the Mardurers stirred, but none moved. 'You attack the yeomen while hiding behind the farmers. You bring in your educators, without any regard for the wishes of the people you say you want to help. You shape our world, start this war, without asking us. You say we can be anything, but first we have to be your soldiers. Kill for you. For a promised future that might never come.'

'Some of what you say is true,' Prince said. Some of the crowd gasped. 'There is always an element of force to any leadership position. To believe in a vision that most others cannot see, you must be willing to push or pull other people into action. But I deny being a tyrant, Mayor Middlestedt. My army has never conscripted a single man or woman into their ranks. My educators have been asked to leave some villages, and have done so. I am leading this country back to something, not ordering it.'

'Your new government is still born on blood,' Middlestedt sneered.

'Rare is the revolution that does not spill blood.' Prince sighed. 'I detest it. I hate killing. I hate pain and misery. I've killed only once, and that was more than enough for me. I have others who are willing to fight on my behalf, and I appreciate what they do. If I could build this new world without spilling blood, I would gladly do so.'

'You kill the yeomen.'

'I do.'

'You kill to further your own cause.' Middlestedt had a thought and was building towards it.

'I do, that is true. But your next argument is invalid.'

'My what?' Middlestedt stopped and blinked.

'That I am a hypocrite. That the violence that I conduct, targeted at the yeomen, is not equal to the violence that of yeomen terrorizing a country side. Now, if I sent my soldiers to burn their homes down, rape and beat their families, then I would be a hypocrite.'

'The innocent are still killed by your fight, General. Half a dozen died when this one ambushed the yeomen.'

Snow stepped forward. 'It is true, we did execute an ambush that killed civilians.' She did not look defiant or happy about her admission.

'What did you learn?' Prince asked.

'I need to train up some dedicated sharpshooters,' Snow said, 'to avoid needlessly firing around innocents. I would also have dropped back, hit them from two sides instead of one. That way the far side couldn't use their prisoners for cover.'

'So what?' Middlestedt yelled. 'She says she learns a lesson, and for that she suffers no consequences?'

Prince turned and again stared at Middlestedt. 'The responsibility of the act is on her, Mayor Middlestedt. Every life taken, every action, is her burden to carry. She is a fighter, and a thinker, and a leader, and she is the colonel because she takes the responsibility of the regiment and the county seriously. She understand the ideals of the rule of law.'

'The king has laws, General.'

'Laws of whims, Mayor. Tomorrow, the king may wake up, take pen to paper, and write down that Mayor Robert Middlestedt of Pelican Point is found to be too uppity for a farmer and is to be executed immediately, and it would be law. The yeomen could ride in here, and if you tried to run or fight or argue, you would be breaking the law.'

'The King is stronger,' Middlestedt stammered.

'You keep saying that. By that reasoning, Mayor, I could assign a sergeant to follow you around, and on an order, shoot you, and it would be okay with you. But it is not okay, Mayor Middlestedt. That is not right.'

'Snow would shoot me on a whim,' Middlestedt said.

'If that were true, she would have hunted you down after you betrayed her. She did not. Instead, she defeated the yeomen, and came here to confront you.'

'She came in force!'

'At our request!' Reynolds stepped forward again. 'She did not want to come here. She was afraid of violence between us and you. But we asked her to, we forced the issue, because YOU, Robert Middlestedt, have lost touch with your people!'

'The count desires peace!' Middlestedt cried.

'The count will just have to desire peace elsewhere,' Prince said, walking up to stand right below Middlestedt. 'Walker County is mine. The count is reduced to his town, besieged, impotent. And now I come to Brainerd County, to take it as I did Walker. The count cannot stop me.'

'The count is not weak, General. The count will respond!'

Prince nodded. 'Yes, but not with enough force to stop me.'

'You cannot possibly think you can win!' Middlestedt was screaming now. 'Against the count? The king?'

Prince looked at Middlestedt, calm where they mayor was agitated. He turned and walked around the circle, looking at the assembled peasants. Sasha stiffened as he approached. Her heart quickened when he stopped in front of her and looked into her eyes.

Prince began speaking in a loud voice. '"We hold these truths to be self-evident, that all men,' and women, 'are created equal, that they are endowed by their Creator with certain unalienable Rights, that among these are Life, Liberty and the pursuit of Happiness."'

He stopped and looked at Sasha expectantly. She swallowed.

'"That to secure these rights,"' she began, trying to sound loud without yelling, '"Governments are instituted among Men," and women, "deriving their just powers from the consent of the governed That whenever any form of Government becomes destructive of these ends, it is the Right of the People to alter or to abolish it, and to institute new Government, laying its foundation on such principles and organizing its powers in such form, as to them shall seem most likely to affect their Safety and Happiness."'

Prince raised a hand and she stopped. 'Good job,' he said with a smile. Sasha blushed.

'Two months ago,' Prince said, turning on the Mayor, 'this woman was the daughter of a farmer, tied to a horse, being taken to Walker as a hostage, as a plaything, as a slave. Now she carries a rifle, fights for a cause, and quotes from memory a document that was centuries old before the Before Time fell. Tell me, Mayor

Middlestedt, how many yeomen can match that woman's determination?'

Middlestedt was silent. He looked at Sasha, recognizing perhaps for the first time the Rifle he had brought over for dinner not long ago.

'As I thought,' Prince said. He turned and looked out at the crowd, who looked back at him silently. 'We are in a Dark Age,' he said loudly, 'and I mean to end it early: with bullets, with books,' he turned to look at Sasha, 'and with a generation who hates the darkness as much as I do.'

Sasha blushed.

Prince turned his back to Middlestedt. 'Master Reynolds, if there is no more business, we must return to Arrowhead. I have an army assembling.' Reynolds nodded assent. 'Colonel Snow, shall we?'

The Mardurers assembled on the edge of town. Winnie took Sasha's elbow.

'That was impressive,' Winnie said. 'I doubt anyone else could have done that.'

'Not an example of me thinking like a Rifle, is it?' Sasha asked.

'No,' Winnie said with a smile. For once, Sasha did not worry about the meaning and smiled back, and the column continued marching towards Prince's army.

Chapter 25

Just outside of Pelican's Point, General Prince had collected enough horses to get everyone back to Arrowhead quickly, as long as most of them doubled up. Sasha paired up with Winnie sitting behind her, following the column north, a thundering squadron across the countryside.

The soldiers in the striped uniforms were called the Olympian Guard, Sasha learned. They were all older, experienced, equipped and assigned to guard General Prince. Most of them were men, Sasha saw, the youngest maybe thirty years old. And they looked at everyone, even Sasha, as a potential threat.

'They make me nervous,' Sasha said.

'Good. They're supposed to,' Winnie said. 'I heard about the trials they have to go through. Those there are some of the best-trained soldiers in this army, straight from the Old Guard.'

They were challenged by a guard just outside of Arrowhead, wearing the olive green that most of Third Regiment had started with. Sasha felt some annoyance that these Mardurers were respecting Prince more than Snow, but he was the superior officer.

But this is Snow's county, part of her thought. *He is a guest here.*

Beyond Arrowhead was one of those older plantations that had stood abandoned for years. The field was now cluttered with tents, organized into rows. Sasha looked out over the assembled forces as they approached: green and grey, khaki and olive, mixes and odds and ends. She did not know the significance of the uniforms, other than they were probably all different units. Including the pickets, there were probably at least three hundred men and women assembled.

They stopped in front of the plantation house, now guarded by the Olympians. Some Mardurers grabbed the horses and took them to a corral nearby. A dozen wagons were lined up against the tree line.

Prince said something to Snow and dismissed them. Snow led them to a part of the camp where Lieutenant Buck, with his squad and the Brainerd Militia, had set up several tents.

'Colonel!' Buck came to attention. 'They arrived a few hours after you left. Quite the sight, isn't it?'

'It is,' Snow agreed. Sasha thought her colonel looked almost nervous. 'Any of the Avalon Guard here?'

'No,' Buck said. Snow looked relieved. 'Some of the Artillery regiment, a training company, detachments from the Surgeons and the Quartermasters, plus a Provost troop. And a few units I can't identify.'

'No problems?'

'Not yet,' Buck said. His tone made Sasha think he was expecting trouble.

There was a coughing sound, just enough to get attention. A woman stood before them, with more than a dozen Mardurers behind her. She saluted, hesitantly. 'Lieutenant Colonel Snow?'

Snow stepped over, acknowledging her salute. 'Yes, Sergeant?'

The woman stepped forward with a letter in her hand. 'Ma'am, I come bearing a letter from Lieutenant Colonel Carpenter and co-signed by General Prince, recommending me for a Regimental Warrant as a Field Officer in Third Regiment.'

Snow took the letter and opened it. Sasha looked at the woman, a tall, lean blonde who looked nervous. She kept shifting her weight from one foot to another, and opened her mouth several times as if to say something, but closed it again.

'How old are you?' Snow asked.

'Seventeen, Colonel.'

'It says here that during a raid on Camperton, you took command of a training platoon and derailed the enemy forces, allowing time to evacuate the town. For which you got a Colonel's Star and a recommendation.' Snow looked at the woman with respect. 'I'm surprised you did not get a commission for that.'

'I wanted to get one,' the woman said, 'but I'm not good with letters. I couldn't pass the tests General Caesar gave.'

'General Caesar sure does enjoy his tests,' Snow said with a smile. She nodded. 'Very well, Field Officer Lynx. Welcome to Third Regiment. And these?'

'The new additions to Third Regiment, Colonel. One sergeant, two corporals, twelve rifles, one gunner, two grenadiers, plus a staff sergeant and a medical specialist.'

'Not a bad addition,' Buck said.

'That's more than we started with,' Winnie said.

'Lynx, this is Sergeant Winnie, one of our noncoms.'

Sasha felt a bit left out that she was not introduced, but shrugged it aside. *Still only a Rifle.*

'Winnie, we're heading back into the field tomorrow,' Snow said. 'The Quartermaster is going to drop off some canned goods, rations, and other supplies, so let's use up the flour we have left for some hard tack.'

Buck spoke up. 'The Q.M.'s got a field kitchen set up behind the house. They'll probably have some bacon fat we can add in for flavor.'

'Yes, ma'am,' Winnie said. She turned to Sasha, who nodded and began to follow.

'Sasha?' Snow asked.

Sasha turned. 'Yes, Colonel?'

'You brought your books, didn't you?'

'Yes, ma'am,' Sasha admitted.

'I'll need the *Art of War* back.'

'Yes, ma'am.'

Winnie and Sasha collected the flour the regiment had brought with them, with Sasha grabbing the book as well. She returned it to

Snow, who was having a discussion with Lynx, Buck, and the new sergeant. Then the two women began walking towards the house.

'Do you recognize any of these units?' Sasha asked.

'The olive green ones are one of the training companies, Wolf Company I think. The tan are Quartermaster troops: teamsters, cooks, armorers, and the like. The grey ones are artillery.'

'I didn't know we had artillery,' Sasha said.

'Heavy machine guns and heavy mortars,' Winnie said. 'No cannon or rockets or anything like that.'

'And those?' Sasha gestured nervously towards a pair sitting on horseback. A man and woman, dressed in a deep blue uniform with a gold plate handing from their necks. Their saddles had holsters for long guns, and each carried a club at their hip.

'Provost,' Winnie responded. 'They're like the yeomen for the Mardurers, but they're very professional.'

'They look like yeomen,' Sasha said. She felt nervous looking up at the pair, even if they were both smiling as they shared some joke.

'I'm not sure who did that,' Winnie said. 'I've heard lots of rumors, but none agree with each other. I think it's so that people, civilian and Mardurer, will automatically know their purpose is to keep order. Now where's that kitchen?'

There was indeed a kitchen behind the house. Two wagons were actually mobile stoves, made of metal and brick. Sasha had never seen anything like it. 'We could use some of those,' she whispered to Winnie.

'And be tied down to a giant wagon? No thanks.'

A master sergeant approached, a giant man with a bushy mustache. 'Welcome, my friends. Quarter Master Sergeant Harvey, here. Or should I say, Cooking Master Sergeant Harvey! HA!' He laughed at his own joke. Sasha smiled.

'Sergeant Winnie, Third Regiment. We were looking to turn this into some hard tack, maybe mix it with some fat for flavor.'

'Ug, hard tack. So unappetizing. But, we must do what we must do!' He turned and called out to some of his assistants, who soon were mixing the ingredients together. 'Not long, my dears!'

Sasha and Winnie sat back to watch the cooks do their jobs. They worked well without speaking much, efficiently, calmly. Others came up and spoke with Harvey, who greeted everyone with equal cheer and respect. It was hard to be serious around him.

'The stuff we do without,' Winnie said. 'One of the challenges of field units. We don't have the same logistical legs to stand on. On the other hand, those are legs the enemy can't break.'

'Sure,' Sasha agreed. 'But they have bacon.'

Winnie chuckled, but was cut off from responding.

'Ah, little Winnie has a playmate.'

Winnie snapped around and glared at the speaker. He was a tall, muscular man, one of those who wore olive pants but only a vest, showing off his muscular arms. His sergeant's rank was tattooed onto his arm, and from his belt hung a number of knives and axes. Behind him a tall, stick-thin woman loomed over, sneering at Winnie and Sasha. She had a huge, hooked nose and short cut hair. Winnie turned to face them, arms before her, ready to fight. Sasha stood behind her, surprised by the sudden conflict.

'Oliver,' she said in greeting.

'Sergeant's stripes, Winnie?' Oliver sneered. 'If your colonel were a man, I'd know how you got them, but I guess I'll just have to imagine how you got them with Colonel Snow.'

Sasha stared at Oliver with shock. Winnie looked up at the man and shook her head.

'Oh, Oliver. Four months now and still only a sergeant? Perhaps if you were good at your job, you'd have made Able Sergeant by now.'

Oliver turned red. 'I'm still senior, Sergeant Winnie.'

'And still a jackass,' Winnie said.

Oliver stepped forward and raised a fist. 'You've always had a big mouth, Winnie. And I've always been bigger than you.'

'And I'm an experienced veteran, Oliver, with three battles under my belt. I've killed a number of people. And I don't have time to mess with weak, small minded . . . .'

Oliver punched. Winnie stepped back and struck at Oliver's arm to deflect it.

The tall woman turned to face Sasha, but Sasha was already moving. Sasha drove full speed into the woman's middle, pushing her over and plunging into the dirt. She punched hard, but the woman recovered quickly and by the third punch Sasha found her arm wrapped up. The woman flipped around, twisting Sasha's arm and landing her own blow. Sasha pulled her arm out of the woman's grasp, her face throbbing. Someone grabbed her collar and pulled her up. She turned and punched, thinking it was the tall woman. She had only an incomplete image of a provost woman, in blue with the gold shield around her neck, already moving to wrap Sasha's arm. This time, Sasha could not break out, and she ended on the ground, face down, her arm twisted behind her painfully.

'STOP!' the woman yelled. Sasha stopped, and the provost eased up on her arm, still firmly pressing Sasha into the ground.

The woman Sasha had been fighting with was on the ground, a provost standing over her, rubbing his knuckles. Several other soldiers, cooks and those who had been waiting nearby, had pulled Winnie and Oliver apart, both looking bruised and bloodied. They still reached to get at each other, but too many held them apart now.

A figure stalked up. 'WHAT IN THE NAME OF THE HOLY FUCK IS GOING ON HERE?'

Sasha strained to look up at him. He was an older man, grey haired with a mustache, wearing a grey uniform with more red lace on it than any uniform Sasha had seen so far. A green aiguillette hung at his right shoulder, so she knew he was a quartermaster of some sort.

245

'On your feet!' he barked. Sasha was half-pulled to attention before the officer. She saw the warrant officer's triangle, with a circle after it.

A Command Warrant Officer, she thought. *Command Quartermaster?* Regardless, he was only a slight step below Snow on the Mardurer chain of command, the highest rank an officer could achieve with only a warrant.

'I asked a question, you four,' he growled.

'A soldiers' fight, Officer Stock,' Winnie said.

'Nothing worth noting, sir,' Oliver agreed.

'Really?' Stock asked. He did not look agreeable. 'Name and Regiments!'

'Sergeant Winnie, Third Minnesota Field Regiment.'

'Sergeant Oliver, Fourth Minnesota Field Regiment.'

Stock glanced back and Sasha and her opponent. 'I presume these two fought at your side?'

'Yes, sir!'

'Did anyone see what started this fight?'

If anyone did, no one spoke up. Finally Cooking Master Sergeant Harvey cleared his throat. 'Just a soldiers' fight, sir. Nothing to take note of.'

Stock did not look happy. 'Very well, Sergeant Harvey. A soldiers' fight then. No harm done? Nothing broken? Then I will limit myself to addressing your colonels when I meet with their commissaries.'

'Yes, sir!' the two sergeants saluted. Stock shook his head and stomped away.

Harvey spoke quickly. 'There, I just saved you from charges. Now stay away from each other, and if I have any more trouble out of either of you, your regiment only gets hard tack for dinner and your colonel will know why.'

Sasha took hold of Winnie's shoulder and pulled her away. 'That was close.'

'Shows what Stock knows,' Winnie growled. 'We don't have a commissary.'

◆◆◆

'Fourth Field Regiment?' Snow asked. The bruises had been impossible to disguise, even if the rumor mill hadn't reported that Winnie had killed a sergeant in an old lover's quarrel gone wrong.

'That's what he reported,' Winnie said. Sasha stood behind her, quietly paying attention.

'I wasn't aware a Fourth had been formed yet,' Snow frowned. 'Officer Lynx!'

'Ma'am!'

'Are you aware of a Fourth Field Regiment?'

'Yes, ma'am. Assembled two weeks ago, under Lieutenant Colonel Wild.'

'WILD?' Snow gasped. Everyone in earshot turned to stare at the normally calm woman turned red. She turned away from Winnie, speaking to herself.

'What are they thinking?' she asked herself. 'Why on earth would they give it to WILD?'

Sasha glanced over at Winnie, who shrugged. Lynx had turned bright red.

Master Sergeant was standing nearby. 'Wild is not a poor officer, Colonel.'

'Wild is not a poor *fighter*, Master Sergeant, and maybe a decent soldier. I still have no idea how he got a commission, much less a colonelcy.'

'General Caesar has always had a special spot for him,' Master Sergeant pointed out.

'The two tried to kill each other the first time they met, did you know that?' Snow said in disbelief. 'And now they're friends.'

Master Sergeant shrugged. 'Ma'am, it's not really your place to worry about the other regiments. Caesar and Prince have their own reasons, and you need to worry about your own Rifles.'

Snow nodded. 'Of course, Master Sergeant. And the next thing I have to worry about is a visit from Command Quartermaster Stock. We are lucky it was not Colonel Gold.'

'We are,' Master Sergeant agreed. He grimaced at whatever shared thought Snow had referenced.

'He threw the first punch?' Snow asked.

'Yes, ma'am,' Winnie said.

'Rifle Sasha?'

'He did, Colonel.'

'But you did fight, and that does require some punishment.' Snow looked at the two of them, and a gleam entered her eye. 'As punishment, you two must bring the remaining flour to the kitchen and have it baked into hard tack.'

Winnie and Sasha looked confused. 'We've already done that,' Sasha said.

'Well, how efficient of you,' Snow said with a smile. 'Dismissed.'

The two saluted and left. Winnie rubbed her hand. 'Ouch, he had a tough jaw.'

'It looked like it,' Sasha said. They walked back to their bags, sitting in a pile near their weapons. 'What was that fight about?'

Winnie shrugged. 'Oliver and I were in the same squad during training. The two of us were the best, but only one of us could be chosen to be sergeant. He cared about it more than I did, but I wasn't going to let him win. When he got selected, he tried to lord it over me and got upset when I didn't respond.'

'He got upset about you not being jealous?' Sasha asked incredulously.

'Yep. But then again, I got sent directly into Third Regiment, and he got stuck in the sergeant's class for another month.' Winnie bent down to her pack. 'Thanks for fighting with me.'

'Of course,' Sasha said with a smile.

Winnie retrieved something from her pack and stood. 'I want to go, try and find a few other people who might be here,' Winnie said. 'Want to come? You're pretty handy in a fight.'

'Mind if I stay and read?' Sasha asked.

Winnie laughed. 'You don't think like a Rifle,' she said again and left.

Sasha frowned as she pulled the book out. She knew she had not been through the same training, but she had been with the regiment for more than two months. *Why does Winnie keep saying that?*

Sasha found a tree stump and sat down, the light shining over her shoulder. She began reading and was soon lost in the words. She ignored people walking by, horses cantering, someone singing. She was only dimly aware of someone putting a plate of food next to her, picking up a log and dragging it over to sit across from her. The figure sat down, taking a bite of food before interrupting her.

'You are a surprisingly dedicated reader, Sasha Small. I am impressed.'

Sasha jumped and looked up at the man who spoke to her. Even sitting he was tall, with long black hair and a trimmed beard. His long woodsman's rifle slung over his back, and his lapel had two black squares and a black paw print. A man she had not seen since he rescued her from the bullies outside Penelope's Haven.

'Major Fox!' Sasha said in surprise. She smiled as he laughed.

'And now you know my name. At least, as far as this army is concerned. I've heard some word from Colonel Snow of how you have been progressing, but I wanted to see for myself. You are looking rather well, Rifle Sasha. Pants suit you.'

'Better than a wide skirt, at least,' Sasha said. 'I never got a chance to thank you, Major. You changed my life.'

'For the better I hope?'

'Of course, yes!' Sasha smiled. 'I've got friends, a place in this unit. I'm challenged, I grow, I read, and I train. I'm able to let my guard down without worrying about Samuel Cartier and his friends jumping out from behind a tree. It is a welcome change from home.'

'That's good,' Fox said.

Sasha nodded. 'Major,' she hesitated, 'can I ask you a question?'

'Of course.'

'Prince mentioned that part of his renaissance is sending teachers into villages to educate people. Do you know if that's true?'

'It is,' Fox said. 'It isn't an easy job. Illiteracy is common, and some people don't understand the importance of education. But we find enough people who take to the teachings well enough that it changes their lives. Those are good days.'

'Is there a teacher in Penelope's Haven?' Sasha asked hopefully.

A look crossed Fox's face, and Sasha felt her stomach tighten. 'I'm sorry, Sasha, I thought you knew. Penelope's Haven was burned by the yeomen. It's all ash now.'

Sasha gasped, looking for any sign of a joke from the man but saw nothing. 'The people?' she asked fearfully.

'Two families could not explain where their children were, so the yeomen executed the entire families, right down to the seven month old daughter. The rest were marched into Walker. As far as

I know, your father had dutifully reported that you had joined the Mardurers, and so the family was spared and are now hostages in Walker Town.'

Sasha realized a few tears had rolled down her cheeks and she wiped her eyes. 'At least they're still alive,' she said. 'What happens to Walker Town?'

'The town is under siege. We'll see what comes of it. I can't say more than that,' Fox said.

Sasha nodded. 'Right.' She stared up at some clouds, wondering if her family was staring at those same clouds right now.

'Tell me, Sasha,' Fox began. 'How did you find combat?'

Sasha blinked at the change of subject. 'What? Oh, combat.' She struggled to pull her thoughts back to the conversation. 'Scary,' she started. 'Master Sergeant keeps telling us we remember our training, especially since we've had so little of it, we have to make what we know count. When we ambushed those bandits, I was scared, and I was laying behind a log. Even when that bandit shot Rick, I was still scared, but I still killed him. And then at the village, when Winnie and I charged in, I was still scared, but I knew what I had to do, even if I expected to be hurt. I killed those yeomen, and looking back it is almost frightening how easy it was for me to do it.'

Fox gave her a half smile. 'You're a killer, Sasha Small.'

Sasha sat bolt upright. 'I am not!'

Fox actually laughed. 'That is not an insult, Sasha. Every army needs killers. Not everyone can be, nor should be, a killer, so you find the ones you have and put them in a unit and make that your killer unit. What do you think your First Squad is?'

Sasha still fumed. 'I am not a killer. Yeomen, they're killers.'

'Some of them are murders, and I would hope you know the difference,' Fox said. His tone took on a very serious edge to it. 'Pay attention, Rifle Sasha, because you must learn. Not everyone is a killer, and not every killer is a murderer. Many soldiers will kill but most of them will never take to it. Some of them will be troubled by their actions. Others, soldiers who can kill without being disturbed, are killers. They go into the hardest fights first, where you want people to fight without hesitation, where you need to win. They're often given higher praise and rewards because they carry more risk than others. But they fight for a cause, and if they do not enjoy the fight, they know they are good at it. Murderers kill for no cause, because they can or because they enjoy it. If you were a murderer, Sasha, you would have let Sergeant Winnie kill that yeoman in Kimble.'

'Winnie isn't a murderer!' Sasha said sharply.

'No, she isn't,' Fox said with a smile. 'And she had you to thank for that. But that incident emphasizes what Master Sergeant said to you. Your training is still very simple, and you need to keep up with it. Discipline is not easy to build, but it is very important, not just in combat but in life. Winnie almost forgot; luckily you were there to remind her.'

Sasha shook her head. 'I still don't like to be called a killer,' she said.

'Okay,' Fox said with a nod. 'I will remember that. On a better subject, what are you reading?'

'A book on the American Revolution,' Sasha said.

Fox's eye widened. 'Really? And where did you get that?' he asked.

'From Grandpa Middlestedt, before he warned us about the yeomen. I'm not very far into it, but I recognize some of the phrases. This is the war your document came from.'

'Yes,' Fox said with a smile.

Sasha started. 'Your scroll! It's back at our first camp. I didn't think to bring it with me.'

'No worries, Sasha. It is safe, and I can get it back the next time we cross paths. I'm more curious to know about your books. I am surprised you are spending time reading something as unfamiliar as this.'

'I am limited by circumstances,' Sasha said. 'I'm making my way through.'

'What has happened so far?'

'General Washington has besieged the British in Boston, and Colonel Knox is bringing down artillery from the captured forts.'

'So, fairly early,' Fox said.

'Right. I'm still trying to figure out if Washington is acting out Sun Tzu's highest form of generalship or its worst.'

Fox was silent for a moment, then looked up with a face of absolute astonishment. 'Sun Tzu?'

Sasha nodded. 'Snow has a copy of his book, *The Art of War*, and I've been reading it, comparing the lessons in there to the actions of the history books I've read. Sun Tzu said, "…the highest form of generalship is to baulk the enemy's plans…and the worst policy of all is to besiege walled cities." Now, at this point, Washington is outside Boston, keeping the British there and keeping them from doing anything. But the British aren't trying to do anything, so I don't know if it counts. And, Washington wants to attack Boston itself. True, he wants to because he's worried that his army is going to go home when their enlistments are up, not because he wants to get involved in an attack on a city, so I don't know if it counts.'

'Makes sense,' Fox said. He had a curious smile on his face now. 'Is this the only book you've done this exercise with?'

'No. I have a history of the *War of the Three Fools*. I've read through it several times.'

'Really? Fast and dedicated, eh?'

'I didn't start out that way,' Sasha admitted. 'There were so many words I had to learn. Luckily the Three Fools book included some appendices I could start with, learn names and organizations. When I found a concept I didn't understand, I had someone explain it to me thoroughly. After a while I didn't need any more explanations.'

253

Fox looked at her with admiration. 'May I use you for an indulgence?'

'What?' Sasha asked, confused.

Fox stood, handing her back her book. 'Come with me, please.'

'Where are we going?'

'There's someone else I want you to impress with your reading.'

'Okay,' Sasha said, uncertainly. 'The book?'

'Bring it,' he said.

Fox led her through the camp. No one paid much attention to them. The assembled army was mingling, talking laughing. Sasha spied Winnie sitting around an unlit fire with two men in dark blue uniforms and a woman in grey. Jim was at a wagon with several other gunners, looking over a weapon she did not recognize. Sonja was laughing at something one of the Chosen Rifles said to her.

A friendly army, for the most part. And I bet all of them can fight as well as we can.

Sasha followed Fox, and only when they were almost through the crowd did she notice they were approaching the plantation house, ringed by the general's guards.

'Oh, shit,' she said out loud.

'Yep,' Fox said with a smile.

Chapter 26

The Olympians saluted Fox but ignored Sasha. Sasha followed quickly on Fox's heels, feeling nervous about being here. They entered the house.

The front room of the house was a large entry hall. Stairs led up to a second level, but they had collapsed and sat in a pile to the side. Two open doorways, one on the far wall and one to the right, were draped in curtains, keeping them from seeing inside. An Olympian stood between the doorways and watched them enter.

In the middle of the room sat a desk. It looked old, probably left in the house years ago, but still sturdy. Sitting at it was the officer Sasha had seen at the Middlestedt debate, the blonde woman who laughed at Middlestedt's error. She looked up at their entry and stood.

'Major Fox,' she said courteously.

'Officer Bellona,' Fox replied.

Bellona glanced at Sasha, and Sasha looked back. Bellona was in her twenties, with dark skin and brown eyes. She was of unremarkable build and height. Her uniform was of the same style as General Prince's, tan and pristine, with a blue aiguillette on her shoulder. She looked confident, smart, and completely disinterested in Sasha.

'Matters of discipline are to be handled by unit commanders, Major Fox.'

Sasha turned red. Fox just laughed.

'This is not a discipline matter, Officer Bellona.'

'The General does not have time to meet every rifle in the army, Major.'

'The General has already met her,' Fox said.

Bellona looked at Sasha again. 'The farmer's daughter,' she said after a moment. 'You were the one today, with the mayor, who finished the Declaration quote.'

'I am,' Sasha replied.

If that changed Bellona's appreciation for her, it did not show. She sighed. 'Then what is the purpose of this visit?'

'To show off,' Fox said with a smile.

Bellona made a clucking sound like a chicken and sighed. 'One minute, major.' She turned and went through the curtains into the rooms beyond.

Fox looked at Sasha. 'Do forgive her, Sasha. Master Staff Officer Bellona is General Prince's aide-de-camp. She's very good at helping him run the army. That includes protecting his time from unnecessary interruptions.'

'Isn't this unnecessary?' Sasha asked.

'Depends on what the objective is,' Fox said.

The curtain parted. 'General Prince and Colonel Aristotle will see you now,' Bellona said. 'But please do not be too long.'

'Understood,' Fox said, stepping forward. Sasha followed on his heels, trying to ignore Bellona's harsh stare.

The large room that made up the majority of the bottom floor had been mostly cleared of debris, leaving an old couch, a small table, and a few chairs set before a fireplace. The large windows, long since broken, were covered with blankets or curtains, and a rear door leading out to the cooking wagons was guarded by another Olympian. The walls were stained and dirty, with a few spots showing where old pictures had hung until only a few hours ago.

Two figures stood as Fox led Sasha in. Prince she recognized right away. The other man took a moment.

'Good to see you again,' Colonel Aristotle said with a smile. It was much more relaxed than the smile he gave her on the road to Walker. 'Especially without a knife in your hand.'

'Yes, sorry, uh, Colonel,' Sasha said.

'Oh, yes,' Fox said. 'The woman who almost cut your throat when you tried to untie her bonds.' He looked at Sasha. 'You do make quite the first impression, don't you?'

Sasha was not sure how much more red with embarrassment she could get.

Prince waved off the other two. 'I did not get a chance to thank you, Sasha. I figured you had memorized the Declaration by now. Glad to see I was not wrong.'

'I'm glad I could help,' Sasha said. 'And after you took apart Mayor Middlestedt, I'm surprised you needed my help.'

'The mayor believed that I thought myself above him. He could choose to ignore my arguments on that basis. But a common rifle would be much harder for him to ignore.' Prince smiled, and Sasha found herself smiling back.

'So, Fox, tell me what brings you here,' Prince said.

Fox gestured to Sasha. 'I sought out Sasha to see how she was doing, and found her reading a most unusual book.'

Sasha held it out. Prince took it and opened to the title page. 'The American Revolution,' he said in surprise. 'Publishing date 2019. How fascinating.'

He passed the book to Aristotle. 'Where did this come from?' Aristotle asked.

'Mayor Middlestedt's father has a library. It's small, kept in special boxes, hidden away. He gave it to me.'

'Gave it?'

'Maybe he lent it,' Sasha said. 'I didn't think to ask, as we were soon running from yeomen. But I am treating it as best I can. I even have a leather wrapping I keep it in.'

'Tell them what you told me,' Fox said, 'about your difficulties with Washington at Boston.'

Sasha explained. 'I think the problem is Sun Tzu,' she said at the end. 'Colonel Snow warned me that his book was "the lessons without the stories". I think this is one of those times when his simplicity is working against me.'

Fox grinned. Prince looked at her with a mixture of surprise and admiration. Aristotle was mostly surprise. It was Aristotle who broke the silence and chuckled, saying something in Quebecois that drew a sharp look from Prince.

'Sit down, please,' Prince said, gesturing to the couches and chairs. Sasha took one of the chairs, sitting nervously as the officers all sat around her.

'You've read *The Art of War*?' Prince asked.

'Many times.'

'And you're applying the principals to the American Revolution. Did Snow tell you to do this?'

'No, sir.' Sasha explained to them about the first books she started with and why she started doing this.

'Ah,' Aristotle said. 'The War of the Three Fools. Not my country's finest war.'

'Nor its worst,' Prince said. 'So tell me, Rifle Sasha, who were the three fools?'

'King Jean-Louis III of Quebec, Emperor Santiago the Red of the Mississippi Empire, and President Theresa Gavigan of the People's Republic of Michigan,' Sasha repeated from memory. The names had come up often enough.

'Why would Sun Tzu call them fools?' Prince asked.

Sasha paused, then blushed. 'I'm sorry, General. I've thought about this before but never out loud.'

'Take your time,' Fox said.

'Start with one,' Aristotle suggested. 'Jean-Louis III. Why was he a fool?'

'He considered himself a military genius,' Sasha said, 'even though he never studied warfare in any detail. He thought too much of his own forces and too little of his enemies. He had a plan for defeating his enemies and held to it, even if the situation changed after he gave his orders.'

'And Sun Tzu says that's bad?'

Sasha nodded. 'Book Three, the three ways a ruler can bring misfortune to the army. "By commanding the army to advance or to retreat, being ignorant of the fact that it cannot obey." When the Armee de Saint Clair failed to break through the XI Corps, he should have changed his plans to account for the situation, but he didn't. The reserves that were supposed to have been sent to support General Simone were readily available to counter his other opening moves.'

'So far so good,' Aristotle said.

Sasha paused as a realization hit her. The three officers knew what she was talking about. She did not have to explain the map or the positions for the War of the Three Fools, they knew it. She did not have to explain Sun Tzu, they knew his words. They, who quoted ancient documents as casually as the Bible. For a moment, Sasha was speechless.

'And next?' Prince asked.

'President Gavigan of Michigan,' Sasha said hurriedly.

'Why?' Fox asked.

'In the words of Sun Tzu,' Aristotle added.

'Sun Tzu says "The good fighters of old first put themselves beyond the possibility of defeat, and then waited for an opportunity of defeating the enemy." The Quebecois invasion suffered greatly in the first two weeks. They pushed the Michigan troops back onto their fortifications but took huge losses to do so. The government was beginning to offer peace terms, when Gavigan decided to invade Ontario. Quebec suddenly found a new front, with terrain that suited their numbers. Gavigan had all but won, but she gave the Quebecois the opportunity to defeat her.'

"'There is no instance of a country having benefited from prolonged warfare,'" Prince quoted. 'Why did she do that?'

'I...uh,' Sasha mumbled. 'I'm afraid I don't know. I didn't understand that part too well, and since I was focusing on learning warfare, I only read through that chapter quickly, sir.'

Prince leaned forward. 'Gavigan reacted to internal political pressures. Her political opponents made much of her passive handling of the war. Especially since she was a woman.'

'She was powerful enough to lead a nation,' Aristotle said. 'A rather rare situation.'

'I understood that much,' Sasha growled. 'Why do people always assume a woman can't fight as well as a man?'

'Not everyone learns that lesson, and not everyone who learns it remembers it,' Fox said. 'Some people will always see a woman fighting as an oddity. They never see the strength of the whole.'

'At least we don't have political divisions here,' Sasha said.

The officers were silent, then chuckled at some shared thought.

'Do we?' Sasha asked.

'If you are unaware of them, Sasha, then please continue to be unaware of them,' Aristotle said, 'for as long as you can.'

'And Emperor Santiago the Red?' Prince asked.

'He didn't have to get involved,' Sasha said. 'He was separated from the Great Lakes by the cities of the Ohio Valley. Quebec occupied a few ports and some resources, but nothing close to his border. He used his influence to rile up the cities and created the United Cities of the Ohio Valley.'

'Why does Sun Tzu say that is bad?' Fox asked.

'Sun Tzu says "We cannot enter into alliances until we are acquainted with the designs of our neighbors." Santiago assumed that the UCOV would be loyal to him, and even demand annexation when the war was over. But he underestimated the people and their moods, and accidentally created a government that would oppose his empire for sixty years.'

'That doesn't make him a fool,' Aristotle said. 'The UCOV did keep the Quebecois from obtaining domination south of Erie. And that was his worry.'

'Right,' Sasha said. She turned red.

'Do you agree?' Fox asked.

'No,' Sasha replied.

'Why not?' Aristotle asked. He did not look upset at her.

Sasha took a deep breath. 'Well, Colonel, I don't think it matters if the UCOV did or did not do what he wanted them to. He started helping them expressly to get them hooked into his system, dependent on his depots and ultimately absorb them into his empire. He made no effort to guide them towards annexation, he just started giving them weapons and supplies. And when they refused to join him at the end, he invaded and lost, having learned nothing from watching the Quebecois Army fail to conquer them for four years. He was a fool.'

'*Tres bien*,' Aristotle said. 'Well put.'

'Do you agree?' Sasha asked.

'No, but I understand your point. Don't worry about agreement, Sasha. The free exchange of ideas doesn't require everyone to agree. It just requires everyone to respect each other.'

Sasha smiled and looked at her hands. She realized she was pulling on her thumbs and wondered if she had been doing that the whole time. She forced her hands to fold into her lap.

'How many times did you read the *War of the Three Fools* to get this much?' Prince asked.

'All the way through? Two or three times. I reread the chapters about Colonel Sudeikis maybe a dozen times. Colonel Snow recommended I do so. She said it would have the most bearing on what the regiment is trying to do.'

'Okay, Rifle Sasha, tell me about Colonel Sudeikis,' Prince said.

'Uh,' Sasha paused. 'Caroline Sudeikis was a staff officer from Cleveland, who argued against immediate surrender to the Quebecois. She set out with a few companies of volunteers and a handful of support from the city-states and won two guerilla wars against major empires.'

'What about the Michigan offensive towards Sandusky?' Fox asked.

'Defeated by General Krough's Army of the Wabash, helped by some of her veterans, but she wasn't present,' Sasha said.

'Do you like Sudeikis?'

'I do,' Sasha admitted. 'Not only is she a woman showing men who tell her she's wrong that she's right, but she acts almost exactly like what Sun Tzu says. She considers all her actions, calculating everything. She worked to defeat her enemy's plans, not their units. She got them reacting to her, how she wanted them to. But how did she know how to do that? Did she have *The Art of War*?'

Prince laughed. 'No. Some people just understand the basics of guerilla warfare. They don't need a primer, they just go out and fight the war they need to fight. They come from different backgrounds, countries, all across millennia. They have their own imprints on the concept of guerilla warfare, their own ways of interpreting and executing the same ideas. And all are equally important to know.'

'I would love to read about all of them,' Sasha said.

'Hopefully you'll get your chance,' Aristotle said.

There was a shift in the mood. Sasha wondered if she should say something, but Fox spoke up.

'We should let General Prince get back to rest,' he said, standing.

Sasha stood too. 'Sir, before I go, could I ask a question?'

'Is it about Walker Town?' Prince asked.

'No, sir. I know my family is in there, and I know you'll do what you can to end the siege peacefully, even though Sun Tzu says "if you lay siege to a town, you will exhaust your strength."'

'I know what Sun Tzu says, Rifle,' Prince said with a tired smile.

'Sorry. I wanted to know, do you hate the Mississippians?'

'The Mississippians?' Prince asked.

'Well, I know that it was the Empire that brought about the fall of the Republic and destroyed your family, but it was the Mississippians who led the way. And now one is on the throne. Many of the nobles are from the South. It makes me angry. I guess, when Middlestedt provoked you, I was surprised that you kept calm.'

Prince thought for a moment. 'No, Sasha. I don't hate them. Do you know the history of the Conquest, Sasha? It was, I think, before your time.'

'I was born on Coronation Day,' Sasha said. 'I am as old as the Kingdom. I know what I was told. That Minnesota fought against the wisdom of the Great Emperor and was conquered.'

'That's a rather simplistic version of what happened,' Prince said. 'Everyone was invited to join the Imperial Commonwealth, but no one wanted to. They even signed a treaty, formed the Lexington Organization to fight the Commonwealth. Quebec shifted when their new king took the throne, and that started the war. Mississippians and Minnesotans fought alongside each other for a year.'

'They did?' Sasha asked incredulously.

'Yes. But when the Commonwealth brought its weight to bear against the Organization, Emperor Santiago realized that they were going to lose. He defected, changed sides, to protect the empire his family had built for centuries. He didn't want them to be removed. He wanted his family's legacy to survive him, not die with him. His betrayal was brutal, yes, but I understand his reason.'

'Even if it cost Minnesota?'

263

'Minnesota tried to surrender,' Prince said softly. 'But they wanted conditions. And the Commonwealth demanded unconditional surrender. Maybe, if Minnesota had given up, they would not have been punished so. The Commonwealth does not punish unnecessarily. Minnesota might exist if the leaders had not thought to fight it out.'

'But your family?' Sasha asked.

Prince looked at Sasha gravely. 'My family died, Sasha, horribly. And I don't forgive those who killed them. But they did not do it as some personal slight. The Imperial Commonwealth, the Mississippi Empire, the Quebecois, even the Iron Republic, all grew out of the Dark Time. That's something a lot of people forget. What my family did in Mesabi, the Locke family did in the south, and the Chevaliers did in Quebec. Almost every power that exists was created out of those trying to end the violence and horror. They had their own ways to doing it, started their own traditions. Even the Great Emperor Tiheam; his forefathers carved out their kingdom as a stable throne surrounded by chaos. I can't hate them for ending that.'

'And we fight them?'

Prince nodded. 'As I told Mayor Middlestedt, there is always an element of force to leadership, be it political or military. But tyranny, true tyranny, should never be allowed. Think of it, Sasha. If the yeomen did not take what they wanted, if there was a rule of law that they abided by, would our banners have so many flocking to them?'

Sasha shook her head. 'No, I don't believe so, General.'

'So we fight them. A democracy is less prone to tyranny, Sasha, than an autocracy is. And after so long without the choice, the people of Minnesota will remember the importance.'

'But how will we defeat the Commonwealth?' Sasha asked.

'That's more than one question,' Aristotle interjected.

Fox laughed. 'And I should be getting Sasha back to her regiment. She's going to have a big day tomorrow.' He took Sasha's arm and guided her out the door.

'What's happening tomorrow?' Sasha asked as they exited the house.

'Tomorrow,' Fox said, his smile getting even wider, 'you get to meet Lieutenant Colonel Wild.'

Chapter 27

Sasha understood Fox's amusement the next morning.

Lieutenant Colonel Wild was a huge man. Not as tall as Fox, but wide and muscled. He dressed like a brigand, wearing a short-sleeved tunic that showed off his arms, unbuttoned and showing off his muscled chest, with a collection of scars and tattoos everywhere Sasha could see. He wore a wide-brimmed hat and clinched an unlit cigar in his lips. He carried a dozen knives and axes in his belt, and slung a bandoleer of shotgun shells over his shoulder. Next to him sat an animal - Sasha did not know if it was a wolf or a dog - that looked out over the meeting with bright blue eyes.

The Fourth Regiment sat behind him, including Oliver and the tall woman Sasha had fought. Most of them looked the same, with exposed arms and tattoos, and collections of knives and axes in their possession. The only one who did not was a small woman who dressed in an impeccable green uniform with the captain's insignia. Her name was Captain Tamarack, and she was Saber's counterpart in Fourth Regiment.

'Well, Colonel Snow,' Wild said, 'I'm just glad we got down here before y'all finished off those yeomen. Now if we can get them out from behind their walls, we can hunt them down.' His regiment chuckled.

'All the more reason for them not to come out of their walls,' Fox said. He was sitting opposite Wild, his Chosen Rifles behind him. They lacked a uniform, dressing instead in common, lighter colors that would blend into the forest well. They might not have looked like a unit at all if it were not for the long Verendrye rifles most of them carried.

'Then we force them out,' Wild said. 'Burn the walls down.'

'We will need those walls when the cities are ours,' Snow said. 'They'll protect the people while we take the war to the enemy.' Third Regiment sat behind her, large than both the other units by far.

'Hard to do if they're on the walls,' Wild pointed out. 'And walls can be rebuilt.'

'I have no desire to assault fortified villages,' Snow said loudly. 'Or villages, either. We keep the fight in the countryside as long as we can.'

'They've got horses,' Tamarack said. 'Going to be hard to keep up against those.'

'We have a couple of advantages,' Snow said, unrolling her map. 'We're in a lake-heavy area of the county, with only a few approaches to worry about. We know the yeomen are concentrated around their prison camp and Brainerd, and that we've given them a bloody nose to worry about.'

'If reports are true,' Fox said cautiously, 'he's getting more.'

'All the more reason to keep them off balance. By now, Middlestedt has informed Count Brainerd that Prince is here, and the count will be coming for him. Even if he does pull in volunteers from other counties, he won't have them ready for a few days, so we've got some time. Let's make the most of it.

'Our force is our three units, a smattering of volunteers from the militia who know the terrain, and Captain Lobo says we can grab a few of his heavy weapons trainees if we want to. So let's consider this carefully.

'Colonel Wild, I want you to focus on that camp,' she gestured at the black star. 'I want you to observe it, find patterns, count troops and weapons. I also want it isolated.'

'That'll put pressure on the prisoners,' Fox said.

'They'll be able to handle it,' Snow replied. 'Wild, I want Fourth Regiment to block any attempt to enter or leave that camp. If it's a patrol, ambush it. If it's a supply column, capture it. If its reinforcements, turn them back.'

'Sounds like a good fight,' Wild said with a grin. His regiment chuckled.

'I'll let you decide specifics once you get there, but I do have directive from General Prince. If the commander of the camp

267

wishes to surrender the camp, his garrison, or his prisoners, we are to accept it.'

Wild rolled his eyes. 'I would much prefer no quarter,' he growled.

'Wrong army for that,' Fox said coldly.

'If that happens,' Snow continued, 'you are to disarm everyone. Yeomen are to be escorted south and released. Any Inspectorate troops are to be detained until we can determine if any of them should be tried for war crimes. That last bit, according to Prince, is up for negotiation.'

'I'll dangle it in front of them, then graciously give it up to make them think they won something,' Wild said with a grin.

'What cannot be negotiated is that in such an event, the prisoners must be left to us,' Snow said.

'I gotcha, Snow,' Wild said. 'I'll take care of it.'

'Fox, I want you to do a survey of the wilderness, see which paths we should post a watch at, which ones we should check on regularly, and such. I want any ideas you have. We might be able to pull off more militia if we need to, but we need to know where to put them.'

'Will do,' Fox said.

'That leaves Third Regiment with the roads,' she gestured. Sasha was close enough she could see the map and the two roads Snow was talking about; one long one that twisted through a bunch of lakes, and one shorter, broader route that leads directly from Brainerd to Pelican Point.

'That eastern road is going to be tricky; it's long, narrow and we can move in anywhere along its length because of the lakes. Lieutenant Buck, that's going to be you. I want you to scout this road and find a dozen ambush sites. Plan them in advance, get people to know where they need to be. Hit them once, and don't use it again the next time. I'll do the same on the broadway. This here,' she indicated a small creek that flowed across both roads, 'is the southern limit. We don't go past that line.'

'What size force are we to engage?' Buck asked.

'If you can take it down, take it down,' Snow said. 'If it looks like a concerted push, harass and annoy, hit any specialists you see, but don't get involved in a sustained fight.'

'And Middlestedt?' Fox asked.

Sasha looked. Pelican Point was north of the line by a good mile.

'I'll detail a watch,' Snow said. 'If he wants to stay there, he can stay there. And if he wants to leave I won't stop him.' She looked at the officers. 'Anyone who wants to leave can leave. Don't stop them.'

Everyone nodded. Wild spoke up. 'What's our objective?'

'We want the yeomen blind about what goes on up here. Where we are, how strong, what types of units.'

'Anything else?' Fox asked.

'There is a small dell here,' Snow pointed to a spot near Kimble. 'That'll be the forward command post. I am going to leave Staff Sergeant Kemper there with a guard. Send messages there. The Quartermaster is going to be giving us some supplies; we'll store them there.'

'And if the yeomen come in force?' Fox asked.

'Fall back, send out runners.'

'Where will Prince and the Army be?' Wild asked.

'Not sure yet. Somewhere near here, probably.' Snow looked around. 'Any questions?'

Fox and Wild both shook their heads, looking intently at the map.

'Good, let's get going.'

The regiments began to stand. Winnie leaned over to Sasha. 'At least we're not tied down to Prince.'

Aren't we? Sasha asked. *Prince is picking a fight, and we'll want to be there.*

'Right,' was all she said despite her unease.

◆◆◆

They marched out after breakfast. Snow had secured a dozen militiamen, two medium machine guns and their crewmembers, and a significant amount of supplies. They filled their bags with canned food, wrapped vegetables, extra clothes and ammunition. Everyone's belts were full of canteens, pouches, grenades. Once they got to their new camp, they would store as much as they could and travel light.

They had ten miles to march before nightfall. It was hot but windy, and the clouds kept the sun from beating down on them directly. Thy used the road for the first six miles, cutting away before Kimble.

Snow found the new campsite and confirmed it was their new base before she sent off Fox, Wild and Buck. To the rest, she ordered, 'Dig in.'

The new camp was a depression in the forest, roughly oval shaped, about forty yards long and twenty yards at the widest part, that stood about four feet lower than the rest of the ground. A single tree stood in the center.

'I don't think we can do sleeping dens here,' Sonja said.

'Dig some holes for supplies,' Snow ordered. 'We'll string up some rope and cover with tarps, make a tent of it. Master Sergeant and Lynx will map out defensive positions; Staff Sergeant, please organize a fire pit.'

The work was done quickly. Sasha climbed into the trees to secure the ropes. Then the regiment and remaining Chosen Rifles went around the perimeter, discussing their placement in the event of an attack. It was nearly nightfall when Sasha could finally sit back and open up her books.

'What a surprise,' Winnie said. 'You're reading.'

'I like it,' Sasha said.

'You really don't think like a Rifle, do you?' Winnie asked pointedly.

Sasha frowned but did not respond. Staff Sergeant Kemper, it seemed, was something of a cook, and carried with him a decently sized pot that was soon suspended over a fire pit, filled with beans and pork.

'So he's a staff sergeant?' Sasha asked.

'Yep.'

'Not a combatant?'

'No,' Winnie shook her head. 'Nope, he's a specialist, like Gunner Jim or Sharpshooter Sonja.'

'Like a Warrant Officer versus a Commissioned Officer.'

'Kind of,' Winnie said.

Sasha looked at her book for a moment. 'What was training like in Walker?'

'Organized,' Winnie said. 'Surprisingly organized. The generals put most of their experienced sergeants in the drill companies, and they know how to get everyone moving. They ran us ragged, and made sure we knew we were growing. I think they had to shock us into realizing what we were capable of. Not just physically, but intellectually. They had many roles to fill and they needed to find the right people as quickly as possible.'

'And all of this during winter?'

Winnie nodded. 'We spent most of our time in crowded buildings going over hand signals and land navigations over and over again. We got into the field as often as we could, but it took a while before we could leave the buildings.'

Sasha thought about it. 'So I'm not so far behind everyone else?' she asked.

271

Winnie looked at her. 'I wouldn't think so,' she said. 'But I can't speak for Snow or anyone else.'

Sasha nodded. 'What do you think of Prince's plan?'

'It's a plan,' Winnie said. 'We'll do everything we can to make it succeed. Why, what do you think?'

Sasha shrugged. 'I think it's okay.'

'Just okay?' Winnie asked with a sly smile. 'Why just okay?'

Sasha thought for a moment before responding. 'It all depends on the count doing what Prince wants him to do.'

'The count knows that Prince is a Dawson; he'll have to do something about that.'

'And he's ignoring the camp,' Sasha said. 'What is it? Why is it there? How is that going to impact the count's thinking?'

'Don't you think Prince and the rest have thought about it?' Winnie said. 'I'm not saying you're wrong, but this low on the chain of command, we have the luxury of only worrying about what we can do to make it work.'

'I know,' Sasha said. 'And I agree. I just wish I knew what Prince's plan is.'

'So long as the count doesn't know what Prince's plan is, I'll be okay,' Winnie said. She paused. 'What would you do?' she asked.

'Me?' Sasha was surprised.

'Sure. What would you do if you were the general?'

Sasha mulled it over 'Right now, we have a more powerful force than usual, with the units General Prince brought down with him. But the count can reinforce as well, and he could call on help from the army. The longer we sit here, waiting, the larger a force the count can assemble.'

'So you'd pick a fight?' Winnie asked.

Sasha nodded. 'I'd go to the camp. Even if I couldn't attack it, I could threaten it, and if it really is that important, I think the count would have to respond.'

'You'd leave the villages uncovered,' Winnie pointed out.

'All the villagers who are on our side have assembled at Arrowhead. I'd leave them a decent force to bolster the militia, or even move them into the ruins we found so they couldn't be discovered. But we can't protect all the villages independently, and I think that if we went to the camp, we'd keep attention and pressure there.'

'What if we can't take the camp?'

'If the count isn't going to come out and fight us, I'd start putting pressure on him to stay at home. Get him worrying about where our main force is. If I can find a detachment of his that's small enough I'd hammer it hard.'

'And you might call down a bigger response.'

'Maybe so, but we already know how we'll fight that. Take to the forests and harass them. But that's too far in the future to worry too much about it. Right now, we have to deal with the count and his reinforcements, and that camp. And I think we need to hit it hard.'

Winnie nodded. 'That certainly is an aggressive spirit,' she said.

'But I'm thinking like a Rifle, am I?' Sasha asked. 'Someday I'll figure out what you mean by that.'

'I certainly hope so,' Winnie muttered.

Chapter 28

Two days later Sasha drew the late night watch. Lynx woke her around three in the morning, along with two other rifles, and led them out to their watch positions.

Sasha was unsure about Lynx. The young officer was timid and lacked confidence in herself, a complete contrast from the other officers Sasha had met. She was always asking the sergeants for their advice, and never contradicted them. Sasha did not want to find herself under Lynx's command when they got into a fight.

Snow agreed to her, she told herself, *so there must be something there. Even if I can't see it. You do trust Snow, don't you?*

Sasha started to patrol her short segment of the watch, waiting for the daylight.

The rider came in during that time between night and day, when the eyes have problems adjusting to the dawn. She heard him before she saw him, he appeared so close she almost shot him.

'Halt,' she said, firmly, stepping in front of the horse. Her rifle was out but pointed down, away from the rider.

'Are you the Mardurers?' the rider asked. He sounded like a scared twelve-year-old boy.

'Who are you?' Sasha asked curtly. She had been worried more about yeomen attacks than an unarmed kid riding through her line.

'My name is Tim,' he said. 'I'm looking for Colonel Snow. I have a message for her. The baker has too much dough.'

'That's your message?' Sasha asked in surprise.

The boy looked dismayed. 'I need to find her!' he cried. 'Please!'

'What's going on?' Lynx was there, along with at least one other rifle in the dark.

'I need to find Colonel Snow,' the boy said again, almost crying. 'The baker has too much dough!'

'Then he should trade it to the fisher,' Lynx said.

'Oh, thank God,' the boy said. 'I have a message....'

'Then bring it with me,' Lynx said. 'Carry on, Sasha.' She led the boy back towards the camp.

Lynx disappeared with the boy and Sasha was alone again. She look a position behind a tree and sat with her rifle out, wondering if there was a force behind the boy waiting to come in and attack. She saw nothing.

Half an hour later, two hours before she was supposed to be done, Winnie came out with a replacement Rifle and pulled Sasha off the line.

'You need to pack,' she said.

'What's going on? Is it about that boy?'

Winnie nodded. 'There must be a contact in Brainerd, waiting for the right time to send us a message. Had to send it. We're moving.'

'Where to?'

'The camp,' Winnie said.

Lynx was being left with a handful of rifles and one of the gunners. Two others were sent as runners, one to Staff Sergeant Kemper, one to Buck. Everyone else was packing their packs with two days of food and extra ammunition.

'Sonja,' Winnie said, waving down the sharpshooter. 'What's going on?'

'The yeomen are going for the camp,' Sonja said. 'They were supposed to be going for Prince, but they're going for the camp.'

'So the count thinks the camp is more important than General Prince?' Sasha asked.

'Maybe not,' Sonja said. She stepped in close, talking to Winnie, but Sasha could hear. 'The boy said that there were soldiers with the yeomen. Actual soldiers. It could be someone else is more worried about the camp.'

'How many?' Winnie asked. Sasha heard the nervousness in Winnie's voice, and looked at her sergeant. Winnie was pale, even in the morning light.

'He said more than a hundred, but less than two. Maybe a company,' Sonja shrugged. 'Enough that we'll have to worry about them.' She slipped by Winnie to finish assembling her kit.

Winnie looked like she was going to be sick.

'What's wrong?' Sasha asked. Winnie stumbled towards a tree and vomited at the base of it. No one seemed to notice but Sasha, who stepped around to shield her friend from the camp.

'Sergeant?' she asked.

Winnie took some deep breaths. 'I'm okay,' she said, softly. She finally stood up, staring off into the woods. Sasha was about to turn when she spoke.

'I'm from Mesabi,' Winnie said. 'My family got caught up in the Range Riot. My brothers even joined the fighting, despite my parent's protest. The riot thrashed the yeomen pretty good, but then the Army came up. And not one of those garrison battalions full of Minnesotans; it was a proper rifle battalion. Cut right through the rioters, Sasha, just right through….'

Winnie stopped, sickened by some memory. 'James was killed in the fighting. Quick and proper. Thomas was wounded, and got carried into our village just before the army occupied it. We all surrendered, knew it was no good fighting. Hoped there would be leniency, like we'd heard about to the east.

'There wasn't, Sasha. We got told we were being displaced, and packed up our stuff. Thomas was with the wounded, and the captain in charge of the village didn't want to waste time moving wounded, so he hung all of them in the town square before he marched us out.' Winnie started crying. 'I watched the army hang my older brother, with my parents crying over my shoulders.'

Winnie took a few deep breaths to steady herself.

Finally Sasha asked, 'How did you escape?'

'Luck,' Winnie said. She washed out her mouth with water from her canteen. 'We were in a makeshift camp near the railway and there was a hole in the fence big enough for the children to get through. My parents told me to go, to survive, whatever else happened. I didn't want to leave them, but I did.'

Winnie sniffed. 'I don't know how but I ended up in Virginia as a house worker. I told them I had been an orphan my whole life, but I don't think they believed me. They just didn't care enough to find out.'

Winnie stared at Sasha with that hard look on her face. 'If the Royal Army sent a company, it's going to be a loyal company. They're not going to defect. This is going to be a hard fight. And if we lose, they're going to roll over all those villages and bring pain and misery.'

'Then I guess we can't lose,' Sasha said. She looked at Winnie with a bit of a smile. 'Am I thinking like a Rifle?'

'No,' Winnie said and began walking towards camp, 'but you're thinking right'.

Sasha frowned and followed her.

◆◆◆

The regiment moved quickly. It was less than ten miles directly to the camp, but the lakes and terrain stretched that to almost twelve. The boy had said the enemy was moving out before dawn. That put the regiment about two hours behind.

When will the yeomen get there? The Army? Sasha thought. *What will Wild do?*

They stopped for a short break after three hours of marching, refilling their canteens and eating a few biscuits. The conversation was dulled by their efforts, enough that all of them could hear the gunfire.

277

'How far are we?' Snow asked.

Master Sergeant cocked his head, listening with an expert ear. 'Two miles. Doesn't sound like too rough of a firefight.'

'Yet,' Snow said.

They all but ran the last two miles, approaching the camp from the northwest. They halted at the edge of the clearing, Snow pulling out her field glasses to take a look, and Sasha caught her first glimpse of the camp.

She was more than three hundred yards away, but still it looked impressive, with thirty foot towers standing over broad pillboxes. The fences were twenty feet tall, with barbed wire at the base and the top. Sasha could see two such fences, ringing the entire perimeter. She saw figures within the fence and on the towers, but she could not see details. The field around was cleared for about three hundred yards. Several trunks of trees still dotted the landscape towards the edge of the clearing.

'Wow,' Sasha said.

'I sure hope we don't have to attack that,' Winnie said.

There was the sound of gunfire from across the field, several hundred yards away. Sasha listened, hearing a constant but weak sounding exchange.

'That's not a heavy battle,' Snow said. 'Master Sergeant, we're going to swing around the southern perimeter, try to keep ourselves away from the edge. I'm hoping that's Fourth Regiment trying to keep the road closed, so stay alert.'

They dropped their bags west of the prison camp and started circling south in a rough box formation. Whoever built the camp must has purposefully leveled the area around it, as the regiment was moving across a series of small hills, shallow and broad, much different from the flat ground that surrounded the camp. The trees were fairly well spaced, not many thick enough to hide behind. Sasha did not like the idea of having a fight here.

They approached the road, seeing a number of horses tethered up on their side of the road. A large number, about thirty or so, guarded by a handful of yeomen. The Mardurers went to ground, trying to find space behind logs and trunks. No one had noticed them yet.

Sasha was between Winnie and a new girl whose name Sasha could not remember, about seventy yards from the yeomen. She saw several of them caring for the horses, glancing nervously at the gunfire coming from further east. *The yeomen must have pushed Wild off the road*, Sasha thought. *They pushed him off, but they haven't let him go.* A number of bags had been placed in a row nearby, with a couple of yeomen standing over them.

One of the yeomen over a pack stood up. He was not wearing yeomen's colors, just some general travelling clothes. He stepped to the next pack and starting fiddling with it. Sasha watched, curiosity rising. Then the pack moved, raising a bandaged arm, and the man unrolled a leather pouch that looked a lot like the pouch Mary carried.

'A doctor,' she whispered.

'Try not to kill him,' Winnie whispered back. 'Unless you have to.'

'Why would I have to?' Sasha asked harshly.

Winnie didn't answer. Snow had crawled over and was whispering something to her. Sasha looked back to see the man working on the wounded yeoman. *I hope you stay safe, sir. Even if you're working with the yeomen.*

Snow started to crawl again when someone shouted from the roadway and fired in her direction. The bullet snapped overhead, and imbedded itself in a tree behind them.

The Mardurers fired back. Only a dozen of them could see yeomen to shoot at, with the rest waiting for their turn. Sasha aimed at one in a red jacket darting between trees and fired, but she missed. Someone else did a better job, and a yeoman in an orange coat fell over limply.

With their presence known, Snow and Master Sergeant were no longer being quiet, yelling commands for the Mardurers to shift in battle. Sasha also realized that Snow had forgotten to divide the regiment into squads, so she did not know who she was supposed to report to. She looked over at Winnie, whose grimace showed she had the same thought as Sasha.

'I'm sticking with you,' Sasha said, working the bolt of her rifle.

'Good,' Winnie said. She fired at the road.

Snow yelled. 'First Squad, advance on the road.'

'Is that us?' Sasha asked.

'It is now!' Winnie said. 'Cover me!'

Winnie jumped up and rushed forward. Sasha and a number of others fired at the yeomen, working their bolts rapidly without really aiming. Winnie dropped behind a tree ten yards ahead. She turned back and yelled 'Advance!' before firing her automatic at the yeomen. Sasha rushed up, trying to avoid a straight line as much as possible.

This wasn't something we trained a lot on, she thought. *Advancing under fire. We'll need to work on that.*

Sasha reloaded. One of the gunners had come with them, and he was firing in bursts. Master Sergeant was somewhere to the right, yelling the regiment into some sort of line to flank the yeomen, but Sasha could not tell if he was being successful. She was too busy trying to shoot at the enemy in front of her. Everyone, Mardurer and yeomen, was aware that that there was a limited amount of cover, and was spending as much time behind it as they could, only firing when they felt safe. Sasha tried to line up a shot on one yeomen, but another fired at her, not hitting her but forcing her to duck back. It seemed that everyone was firing rather blindly, rather than spend too much time in the open. Winnie rushed forward again, drawing more fire, but made it to the next tree.

Sasha glanced around the trunk, seeing the man still working on the wounded. He ignored the gunfire.

Sasha fired at a yeomen behind a tree, missing both.

There was a slapping sound and the girl to Sasha's right fell limply back, her blond hair now dark red. Sasha still could not remember the girl's name, even as she yelled for Mary.

The yeomen were having the worst of it, Sasha realized, as Winnie kept leading her line forward and the yeomen were pushing back. Sasha made a point of advancing towards the doctor; she did not want to see him hurt.

The yeomen were retreating now, rather quickly, south down the road. The man remained, not looking up as Sasha reached the tree near him. Six wounded men, five yeomen and one member of Fourth Regiment, lay in a row. He was busy removing a bullet from a yeoman's arm.

'If you wish to kill these men, you will have to kill me as well,' he said without looking up.

'Mardurers don't kill prisoners,' Sasha said. The horses had panicked and ran off, leaving her clear view down the road, seeing the fleeing yeomen.

'I've been told otherwise.'

'You were told wrong,' Sasha said. She looked back towards the camp. The figures she previously saw had disappeared. She saw movement in the towers and maybe in the pillboxes, but nothing for certain.

Snow was nearby, pulling her regiment forward. A voice called out from the far side of the road.

'Snow! Is that you?'

Wild!' Snow yelled. Sasha glanced across and saw the large man advancing.

'I sure hoped that was you falling on the enemy's back,' Wild said. He had a broad grin, and an axe in his hand that looked rather bloody. 'Never expected the yeomen to get so aggressive.'

'They've got a Rifle Company coming up behind them,' Snow said.

'Truly?' Wild whistled. 'What battalion?'

'No idea. Not even sure it's a company. But it's probably Army, and they're coming here,' Snow said. Mary appeared by her side.

'Rifle Cynthia is dead, Rifle Rice is wounded.'

Snow grimaced, and even Wild bowed his head for a moment.

'Mary, help these wounded,' Snow said. 'Winnie, take First Squad and scout south; I want to know where the yeomen are and where that rifle company is. NOW!'

They moved south, with a similar number from Fourth Regiment on the other side of the road. They had not gone more than a quarter of a mile when they made contact with the yeomen. The Mardurers ducked into cover, trading a few shots.

'Guess we found them,' Winnie said. 'Sasha, get over to the right, I want you watching the far side.'

Sasha nodded and sprinted past the others. The woods were not thick, and she could see the yeomen about a hundred yards away, spread out through the woods. Sasha did not fire; she had only used four of her clips, but she didn't trust herself to hit anyone accurately at that range.

Not everyone felt that way. Some of the yeomen continued to fire ineffectually. Sasha wondered if they thought they were keeping the Mardurers from advancing. One of the rifles with Fourth Regiment would fire, but the rest of the line sat and watched.

Sasha observed the yeomen. Their various colored coats did not lend themselves to concealment in the woods. They seemed to have taken up a position of depth; while they could have spread out and overlapped the skirmish line, no one was giving any orders.

Is that on purpose? Or are they confused?

A few of the yeomen were running about, carrying messages or supplies to the rest of the line. Sasha did not recognize most of the colors. A bullet snapped overhead, but she barely flinched.

Another figure moved forward. Sasha's first thought was that his jacket was a rather dull color for a yeoman, and he lacked the giant hats the yeomen tended to wear. Then she saw the weapon he was carrying: a long rifle, the type carried by footmen, not a horsemen's carbine.

They're here.

She glanced over at Rifle Sampson. 'Pass along to Sergeant Winnie. The soldiers are here.'

More soldiers were arriving now, displacing the yeomen. They were doing what the yeomen should have, extending out into a broad line that could overlap the small line of Mardurers watching them. Sasha felt her stomach tighten as she saw how many of them there were.

Finally the word came back. 'On the whistle, run.'

Sasha nodded. She tensed, waiting for something to happen.

Winnie's whistle blasted and Sasha sprang up to run, darting between trees. Two rifles followed her.

Behind her, Sasha heard Winnie fire on the soldiers.

Chapter 29

'God damn it, Winnie!' Sasha shouted. She turned behind one of the trees and fired a shot back. 'Come on, Sergeant!' she bellowed.

The soldiers were firing back now. The bullets were snapping close by, fast and furious. Winnie finally came running up as Sasha fired again.

'Keep moving, Rifle!' Winnie scowled.

'Right next to you!' Sasha yelled.

Sasha ran alongside her for another bit, turning with her pistol in hand and firing several shots south. She could see the soldiers were advancing, some moving and some firing. She swore she saw a bullet fly by her head.

Winnie was firing again, as was Jose. Sasha was hunched as she ran, pistol in one hand and rifle in the other. Part of her mind was surprised she had not been hit yet; she ignored it and kept running.

Where was the rest of the regiment?

She turned, shoving the pistol in her holster, and fired her rifle again. She fired three times, working the bolt as quickly as she could.

Jose was hit in the back as he passed her, falling with a grunt. His face twisted in pain as he tried to rise.

'I got you,' Sasha called, grabbing his arm. A bullet cut down a branch above her.

Is this where I die? she thought. *Will my family ever know?*

Why do you always ask that?

Ten steps ahead, hidden behind a log, Gunner Jim opened up with his machine gun. The whole regiment, whose line Sasha was now in the middle of, began firing at the soldiers. Sasha twisted around a tree, looking back to see a number of soldiers lying on the ground, and more hiding behind trees.

'Jose is hurt!' Sasha said to the nearest figure. It was Snow.

'Take him to Mary, at the road side.'

Sasha helped Jose towards the road. A body - *Cynthia*, Sasha reminded herself - lay covered in a tarp. The wounded lay as best they could behind the bodies of two of the horses. Mary, her aides and the doctor were working on them. Someone had laid a white flag with a red cross on a ramrod and stuck it in one of the horses.

'Mary!' Sasha said, calling for her friend. 'Jose is hit!'

Mary and the man brought him over. Sasha kept low. She could see several soldiers about two hundred yards down the road, manning what looked like a rather large machine gun.

'They're not shooting at us,' Mary said. She was cutting open Jose's shirt.

'They will if they have to,' the man warned. 'This boy's lucky,' he pulled the bullet out. 'Must have cut through a branch on its way in. It got stopped by the scapula. '

'We will clean and close,' Mary said. The man did not argue with her. She looked up at Sasha.

'Get going, Sasha.'

'What about you?'

'I'm staying here,' Mary said.

'What if we have to fall back?'

'I'm staying here,' Mary repeated. The man looked at her with something that looked like respect, then went back to his work. Mary glanced at her aides. 'Go with Sasha,' she said. The aides nodded and followed.

Sasha ran back towards Winnie. She could not understand what was happening. The sound of the battle filled the forest, and a cloud had darkened the already dusky battleground. A bullet tore past her and she skidded to a halt behind a tree.

Suddenly, Master Sergeant was beside her. 'On the whistle, retreat to the baggage.'

285

'We can't leave!' Sasha said, but he was gone. Sasha glanced over towards Mary, calmly working as another Mardurer was dragged over to her. *We can't do this.*

The whistle blew. The Mardurers started to run. Sasha wanted to stay, but the whistle blew again and she turned.

Good luck, Mary.

♦♦♦

Mary focused on the work. Not only because it was important to save the man, but because focusing kept her from thinking about the trouble she was in.

Doctor Miller, the yeomen's medic, was helping her, as was Field Medic Second Class Ruiz, from the Rifle Company. Miller was already impressed with her knowledge and skill, and Ruiz was following the doctor's example, letting Mary try to save the arm of Private First Class Sycamore.

Most of the work was done, and now Mary was sewing up the wound. Ruiz was assisting and Miller preparing the bandages.

'As long as he's in the field,' she said absently, 'there's a chance of infection.'

'We've got an ambulance in the back,' Ruiz said. He looked over at their makeshift hospital. Six wounded yeomen, seven soldiers, and two Mardurers. A number of others had been patched up and sent back to their units. 'We might need to use some of the supply wagons to make up the difference.'

'Or we can just cut their throats,' one of the yeomen lieutenants standing nearby growled. The two wounded Mardurers stiffened at his words. 'Have fun with the ladies, first, then....'

'Quiet your tongue or I'll remove it from you,' a voice said. Mary noticed Ruiz and Miller both stand, but she was busy finishing the arm. A pair of boots stepped near her, and the man lowered himself to inspect her work. 'That looks like a fine job, miss.'

Mary glance up. The man was a young, handsome man, with a pencil thin mustache. The two gold bars of an army captain pinned at his lapel. He smiled at Mary. 'Thank you for taking care of my men,' he said.

'I'll thank her,' the yeomen lieutenant said. 'Tie her up in a tent and....'

'First Sergeant, if Yeoman-Lieutenant Tracer says one more word, put a bullet in his head,' the captain snapped. The first sergeant drew his pistol, and the yeoman went silent.

'I'm Captain Terrance Lewis,' he said to Mary. 'B Company, Fourth Rochester Rifle Battalion.'

'Able Medical Officer Mary, Regimental Surgeon, Third Field Regiment,' Mary said. 'Hold the bandage here.'

He complied, allowing her to finish the wrapping. Finally, they both stood, Captain Lewis standing over her. He smiled. 'You have good hands, and you worked to save the life of someone trying to kill your friends.'

Mary shrugged. 'My teacher was very strict about that. "Anyone who comes onto your table is your patient first." He would be very disappointed if I let someone die because of their uniform. So would my colonel.'

'Even the enemy?'

'Especially the enemy,' Mary said.

Lewis smiled and glanced over at his First Sergeant. 'What's the butcher's bill, Mack?'

'Six dead, seventeen wounded enough to require attention,' Mack said.

'Twenty-three,' Lewis said. 'Only First and Second Platoons deployed?'

'Yes, sir.'

Lewis sighed and looked at Mary. 'Word spreading around the Army is that this is a minor nuisance of a rebellion; that the yeomen are pathetic enough for it to succeed; and the Army is going to bail them out. But I sent 76 men out and almost a third of them were killed or wounded. That goes beyond a minor nuisance.'

'That means a fight, sir,' Mack said.

Lewis looked at Mary. 'Unless you can help me convince your Colonel to surrender?'

Mary shook her head. 'Neither Colonel Snow nor Colonel Wild will surrender,' she said. 'I doubt many in their regiments will, either. They know what to expect.'

'And the Dawson? This General Prince?'

'If you were a Dawson, would you surrender, Captain?' Mary asked.

Lewis actually chuckled. 'No, I guess I wouldn't.'

'I must protest!' Yeoman-Lieutenant Tracer said. First Sergeant Mack started raising his pistol but Lewis raised his hand and the gun stopped.

'Protest carefully, Tracer,' Lewis said.

'This is an operation under the direction of Count Brainerd. Your company is here at his invitation. As such, any prisoners taken are to be turned over to the yeomen for questioning and punishment.' He leered at Mary. Mary started blankly back at him.

'Her regiments chased off your yeomen,' Lewis said. 'My company spilled blood recovering your wounded. Until I decide, they are my prisoners, and under my protection. First Sergeant, see to it.'

'And in the meantime?' Tracer said. He was red with anger.

'In the meantime, I intend to complete our mission.' He turned to walk down towards the upcoming wagons.

Tracer watched him for several steps before he screamed. 'THEY'RE NOT REGIMENTS!'

Everyone paused as Captain Lewis stopped. He turned and walked over to Tracer, his pace calm and his face cool. He had two inches on the yeoman, and looked down at him.

'Aren't they?' he asked.

Tracer refused to back down. 'You said so yourself, they're the size of platoons. Not big enough to be regiments.'

'Are you going to lecture me on military formations, Yeoman-Lieutenant?' Lewis asked. Tracer said nothing, fuming in silence. 'If you had kept your head during the battle, you would have seen what I saw. They fought, responded to orders, moved tactically. They retreated because they chose to, not because we scared them into running. And if they want to call themselves a regiment, I believe they have earned the right to do so.' He looked Tracer up and down. 'Who are you to say they can't?'

Tracer glared up at the captain. 'These scum don't deserve your respect. They're rebels.'

'And why are they rebels, Captain? The King's Law forbids rape, and yet the yeomen are famous for it. The King's Law forbids murder, assault, theft...and yet the yeomen get away with it.' Lewis seemed to have grown a foot, so small did Tracer look now. 'It is the yeomen who brought this on themselves, with their depravities and their excesses. If they followed their own rules, this Dawson would not have found the support he needed to build an army in the middle of a kingdom. Instead, your men lack the integrity to do their jobs correctly, so now I have to put my men in danger to clean up your mess.'

Tracer scowled. 'They need to know their place!' he screamed. 'You son of a.....'

'Mack!'

The first sergeant shot Tracer in the head. Several drops splattered over Lewis' face, but he didn't flinch.

Mary was at the yeoman's side quickly, checking the wound. Tracer was still breathing, but it was obvious it from the damage that he was not long for this world. She looked up at Lewis and shook her head.

Lewis looked around at the men watching. 'If charges are ever brought against me for this, I expect every man to tell the truth,' he said, and turned to walk away.

Mary wasted one last look at the lieutenant and went back to her wounded.

Chapter 30

'Twenty minutes,' Prince growled. 'Twenty god-damned minutes.'

Prince, Snow and a number of other officers were assembled to the west of the camp, watching the rifle company and their group of wagons enter the gates through large field glasses. Sasha and Winnie were among those posted on guard closest to the camp and the road, and were in earshot of the officers.

'We couldn't hold out,' Snow said. 'We expended a lot of ammunition, and the rifle company was about to outflank us and pin us to the field.'

'And those machine guns would have made short work of you out there,' another officer said. Sasha didn't recognize the voice, and could not look back at them to check. The Olympians were watching, and she did not want them to think poorly of her regiment.

'I don't fault you, Snow,' Prince said. 'You and Wild did what you could, and we were moving as fast as we could. I don't believe anyone could have done anything differently; we were never going to catch them in the open.'

'I didn't expect them to go for the prison camp,' Bellona said. 'I thought General Prince was far more tempting a target to go after.'

'Well, now they got Prince to come after them,' Wild said. He spat. 'And they're digging rifle pits behinds barbed wire.'

'Not ideal,' Bellona said.

'There's Mary,' Snow said. Sasha glanced at the camp but without field glasses she could not see much beyond the increased activity.

'Still at the hospital?' Prince asked.

'Yes. Which is guarded by soldiers, not yeomen or inspectorate troopers.'

'Telling,' Prince said. 'Still don't know which regiment?'

'No,' Bellona said. 'We didn't find any bodies to check their patches, and it was too confusing for the Third or Fourth to make any identification. But that's definitely a rifle company. 147 men, ten light and six medium machine guns, four field mortars. They took some hits during their skirmish, but I doubt they lost more than ten percent of their effective strength.'

They were quiet for a bit. Sasha kept her eyes on the forest, trying to find an approaching threat and not think about the conversation behind her.

'Okay,' Prince said. 'So they left one platoon on security in the forest, dug in with some reinforcements, say about fifty men total. The balance, plus yeomen and inspectorate, are fortifying the camp. About, two hundred, Major Bellona?'

'Two hundred easy, maybe closer to two hundred and fifty.'

'Across three hundred yards of fields, concrete pillboxes, towers, mines, and barbed wire.' Snow said.

'Officer Badger, can your heavy mortars destroy those pillboxes?'

The unknown officer spoke. 'Possibly. Not that we have any heavy cracking shells. Lots of H.E. and Smoke, so I could probably blind them for you, but I would not suggest relying on my mortars killing them.'

Officer Badger, Sasha remembered the name from Arrowhead. *Able Artillery Officer, commanded the composite battery Prince brought down.* Another warrant officer.

Prince was quiet. 'Officer Bellona, I want all commanding officers to meet at my tent in thirty minutes.'

Sasha wondered how many more commanding officer there were, but said nothing. The officers and the Olympians left.

'I'd love to be in on that conversation,' Sasha said to Winnie.

'Why? What could you add to it?' Winnie asked.

'I don't know,' Sasha responded. She looked out through the woods. Nothing moved. Most of the soldiers Prince brought with him were encamped on the far side of the moderately sized hill, where the camp could not see them. The enemy was staying near their camp and the road. Sasha was partly bored in her post, partly excited.

'Whatever happens, we're going to fight like crazy,' Winnie said. 'They just tell us where.'

'You don't want a say in it?'

'"Ours is not to reason why / ours is but to do or die,"' Winnie chanted.

'What was that?' Sasha asked. 'A prayer?'

'Something I heard once. It's some piece of wisdom handed down from sergeants for centuries. Officers plan and think about what to do. Soldiers and sergeants worry about execution. Someone will make a decision, we just have to carry it out.'

'Oh,' Sasha said. That made sense, but something about it did not sit well with her.

'It's important to know,' Winnie stopped. 'What's that?'

Two figures were coming through the woods now. They were obviously from the rifle company, one carrying a white flag on a pole. Sasha and Winnie took a bead but did not fire.

'Halt!' Winnie called. The pair stopped. 'Who are you?'

'We wish to parlay with Lieutenant Colonel Snow,' one of the men called. He had to be an officer, Sasha thought. He wasn't wearing the same soldier's belts as the other one.

'Stay there,' Winnie replied. She turned and looked, nodding at someone Sasha could not see. 'Get Colonel Snow.'

Sasha kept her eyes on the men. Neither of them made any threatening moves, waiting patiently. Sasha scanned the forest behind them, but saw nothing out of the ordinary. No men followed them.

White flag means talk, she reminded herself. She had almost forgotten.

'Don't shoot,' Winnie said as if reading her mind.

Snow finally arrived, inspecting the flagbearer with the field glasses. None of the other officers had returned. *Didn't want to risk being found out*, Sasha thought.

Snow handed the glasses and her weapon to Winnie. 'Sasha, come with me.' She began walking towards the white flag, Sasha scurrying to catch up. She heard Winnie curse behind her as they went to meet the enemy.

The man actually smiled, not a friendly smile but a smile nonetheless. He saluted. 'Lieutenant Colonel Snow, Third Field Regiment, I presume.'

Snow saluted in return. 'Indeed. And you are?'

'Captain Lewis, Company B, Fourth Rochester Rifle Battalion,' Lewis smiled. He was a Minnesotan, Sasha noted with surprise. She'd heard that Minnesotan officers were rare in the battalions that might be used to fight in Minnesota.

'By your words, it sounds like you've come quite a long way to fight, Colonel,' Lewis said, echoing Sasha's own thoughts.

'Much further than Saint Cloud, Captain,' Snow responded.

Lewis chuckled. 'You know your enemy,' he said.

'Fourth Rochester Rifle Battalion, Second Brigade, 5th Division, III Corps, Northern Mississippi Field Army,' Snow said.

'Did you memorize the whole army list?' Lewis asked in surprise.

'Just the units that might be sent to fight civilians in the middle of Minnesota. III Corps made a name for itself on the Range Riot, much better than any of the other corps. Much more likely we'd see them than someone who might defect.'

Lewis nodded. 'Good idea, Colonel. You seem prepared. General Prince must chose his colonels well. Tell me, is he watching?'

'Watching?' Snow asked, feigning disinterest. Sasha felt her heart quicken.

'We were told Prince was at Arrowhead, which is less than a day's march. Unless you're an idiot, and I truly believe you are not, you sent word to him and he's undoubtedly on his way, if he hasn't arrived already.' Lewis stopped and glanced up at the Mardurer position. 'Perhaps he considers this to be a trap? A flag of truce to lure out the General and kill him. Some might consider that a fair trade off, but I do not, I assure you.'

'You think you are different?' Snow asked. 'You're here to fight us.'

'Actually, that is not our mission,' Lewis said. 'Our mission was to come to this place and remove certain individuals to a new location. I had hoped we would not have to fight, but we did. I have no intention of taking the war to the civilians.'

'A whole company to move a handful of people?' Snow asked.

Lewis smiled. 'General Prince has made no great show of his forces; indeed, he seems to go out of his way to keep us blind as to his true strength. The numbers debated around the halls in Saint Cloud, how many men – excuse me, soldiers – must he have to take over Walker. Some put his army at ten thousand men. Never mind how one would feed such an army....' Lewis trailed off, then shrugged. 'A company was sufficient to get us to the prison. At some cost, and a few more prisoners to add to the mix.'

'Mary,' Snow said.

'Quite a remarkable young woman,' Lewis said. He glanced over at Sasha. Sasha realized he was not mocking them at all. 'Doctor Miller is already planning his stories to his colleagues about the woman doctor of the forest. It might even save her from the noose, in the end.'

'She is unharmed?' Sasha blurted out. The two officers looked at her and she blushed. 'I'm sorry, ma'am. Sir.'

'Your doctor and two wounded Mardurers are in the prison hospital, under guard and unharmed. The yeomen are itching to get at them, as they don't take kindly to rebels who ambush them. The inspectorate wants to hang them from the gates, as the inspectorate doesn't take kindly to anyone. Luckily, they surrendered to me, and so I get to decide their fates.' He looked at Snow. 'The two combatants fought well, and Mary is a very special woman. I do not want to see them wasted on a noose.'

'I'm surprised to hear a Royal Army officer say that,' Snow said.

'After seeing these yeomen, I have the utmost sympathy for your cause, as doomed as it may be. I can only hope that better minds will reform the yeomen system to the betterment of law and order. But I have my duty, Colonel, and I must carry it out.'

'And I have mine,' Snow said.

'But do they clash?' Lewis asked. He continued before Snow could respond. 'I called you here to propose a course of action. My company will leave with the prisoners we were expected to leave with. In exchange for an uneventful march, I will return to you Mary and the two wounded Mardurers I have in my custody.'

'You would give up prisoners?' Snow asked. She looked as if she did not truly believe the offer being made. Sasha had a hard time believing it, as much as she wanted to.

'I have the utmost respect for them, but my superiors, likely, will not,' Lewis said, and his face took a dark tone. 'Some of them want to make examples of people such as Mary. I do not agree.'

'And in exchange, we let you go.'

'Keep the yeomen, take the camp if you want,' Lewis shrugged.

'I'm not sure I can agree to that,' Snow said.

'Because of General Prince?' Lewis asked.

'Because of the villagers being held in the camp,' Snow said. 'Release them, and I will accept your terms on behalf of General Prince.'

'They are not mine to release,' Lewis said. 'They are in the custody of the Inspectorate.'

He wants to release them, Sasha thought to herself. She was sure of it.

'Nevertheless,' Snow said, 'we had no interest in this camp until Count Brainerd started putting villagers in there. They must be freed.'

'Major Dodd might take issue with that,' Lewis said. 'He thinks they're the only reason you aren't storming the camp. He thinks his camp is the entire target of your campaign down here.'

'We didn't even know it was there,' Sasha said. Snow snapped around and glared. Sasha turned red. 'I'm sorry, Colonel, I didn't....'

'Be. Quiet,' Snow growled. Sasha nodded in silence.

Lewis watched the exchange, then looked at Snow. 'That's not entirely true, is it, Colonel?'

Snow composed herself. 'We knew the county received regular payments from the Royal Treasury, for unspecified purposes.' She shrugged. 'It was a minor piece of information, Captain, not one to plan an entire campaign around'

'True,' Lewis said. 'But, unfortunately, the villagers are out of my control, and Major Dodd will not agree to that.'

'Then we have little else to say,' Snow said.

'I guess so,' Lewis said. He looked disappointed. 'I did not come here for a fight, Colonel, but I will fight if I have to.'

'We all will, Captain.'

Lewis nodded, then saluted. 'Very well, Colonel. If you change your mind, you know where to find me.'

'I do, Captain. Good luck.'

Lewis nodded and turned with his soldier in tow. Snow looked at Sasha, who imagined she was still beet red.

'Colonel....'

'There are times when you must be silent, Sasha, and that was one of them.'

'I'm sorry,' Sasha said. 'I didn't mean to.....' She fell silent, unable to find the words. They stood in silence for a moment. 'He wanted to let them go,' she said.

'He did,' Snow agreed. 'But is wasn't up to him. He's got his own rules and orders to work under, same as us.'

'So what now?'

'Now I report to General Prince and find out if I screwed up.'

'Why? Because letting the company go reduces the defenders of the camp?'

Snow looked at Sasha, and her anger turned to surprise. 'Yes,' she said. 'That's exactly it.'

'So what do we do?' Sasha asked.

'General Prince is in command here,' Snow said, and Sasha heard frustration in her voice. 'He'll decide.'

It bugs her, Sasha thought. *All the work to bring the county over and Prince is here to finish it. She feels like it's her failure that brought him here.*

'Once this is over, will General Prince leave?'

Snow looked at Sasha and a bit of that anger returned. 'Don't worry about that, Sasha. Worry about what you're going to do if and when we have to fight Captain Lewis.'

'Yes, ma'am,' Sasha said. She started to say something else but stopped.

'What is it, Sasha?' Snow asked.

'Captain Lewis, Colonel. He didn't seem like a bad man.'

'No,' Snow agreed, leading her back to the lines. 'It's easy to think of the enemy as evil, to remember the worst of them and assume that is all of them. But some of them are good people who follow a different banner.'

They got back to the line, Sasha to her place and Snow to report to General Prince. Winnie was waiting. 'When you go to sleep tonight,' she said, 'keep your combat gear nearby.'

'Think someone is going to try something at night?'

'I think they could, I think we could,' Winnie shrugged. 'Better safe than sorry.'

Okay,' Sasha said. 'Also, you are right. I need to think like a Rifle. I interrupted the Colonel down there, and I shouldn't have done that.'

'No, you shouldn't have,' Winnie said.

'So I'll start trying to think less.'

Sasha lay down and resumed her watch. She didn't see Winnie open her mouth, choose not to speak, or shake her head in frustration.

Chapter 31

Sasha snapped awake when a hand clamped down on her mouth. It was deep night, and Sasha could barely make out a person leaning over her. 'It's me,' Winnie said before Sasha could squirm. 'I was right. Get your gear on, quickly and quietly.'

The regiment's camp site was quietly buzzing with movement. They were over a rise from the camp, out of sight, but the only light was a pair of candles being passed around so they could tie their boots on. Very little was being whispered between them. The movement began to slow as they finished putting their equipment on.

We really didn't practice this, Sasha thought. Master Sergeant had run a few drills at night, but only in small groups. And never combat drills.

A figure was slowly making its way around the regiment. It was Master Sergeant. 'Good to go?' he would ask, getting a yes response. He disappeared and Sasha waited, not knowing who was next to her. *Was this for an attack?* She wondered. She was not even sure what time it was. Past midnight, she guessed.

The figure in front of her turned and tapped her on the shoulder. 'Follow the person in front of you, pass it on.' It was Sonja. Sasha turned and repeated it to the person behind her; Gunner Jim.

They started moving slowly. Sasha thought they were heading south, but she was not entirely sure. They were not making good time, wherever they were going.

They came to a stop and knelt down. Another unit was slowly making their way in the opposite direction on the same path. They came to a stop and knelt. One of them reached over and tapped Sasha on the shoulder.

'Who're you?' he whispered.

'Rifle Sasha, Third Field Regiment. You?'

'Pioneer Jones, Pioneer Company. Looks like we're heading in opposite directions.'

'Yeah,' Sasha agreed. Someone hushed them and they stopped speaking. Soon a voice whispered for the pioneers to stand.

'Good luck, Rifle Sasha,' he said, and was gone. Third Regiment started again shortly after.

Sasha could not see the camp, even though she was pretty sure it was in view. *They must have turned off their lights*, she thought.

Third Regiment moved south in the darkness. Someone had marked the trees with a white paint or chalk, and they followed the path. Sasha tried to count her steps, but the first time she bumped into Sonja she lost count.

The darkness was unnerving. She could not see. She tried to listen but the sounds of the regiment trying to be quiet interfered. She had to concentrate on staying in formation, following Sonja through the night. They bumped into each other, into the person in front, into Jim behind, all while whispering corrections. If Sonja hissed a warning about a tree branch she was too loud; if she did not Sasha invariably ran into it. She heard the sounds of someone tripping and falling, cursing at their clumsiness. Even if she had been able to count her steps, she was not moving at her normal pace. She could have taken a thousand steps and only been three hundred yards from where she started.

After an hour of marching they turned to their left. *East*, Sasha thought. The ground leveled out a bit, and the pace picked up. She sensed it was getting a little lighter. Dawn? No, they were reaching the road, and the trees had thinned out just enough that the moonlight was growing.

She heard whispering. The figure before her, now one of the new Rifles, turned and whispered. 'Winnie, Jim, Sonja, Sasha, Gregory, Samson, up front, pass it along.' Sasha repeated the phrase and moved up front, passing the rest of the regiment.

Snow was waiting at the edge of the road. The requested Mardurers assembled around her.

'Okay, ladies and gentlemen. You are the road squad. Up there,' she pointed north, 'is the Rifle Platoon standing watch over the roadway, approximately one mile away. The regiment is going to advance north until we make contact. Our mission it to tie them up, keep them from reacting to anything else happening on the field. With me so far?'

They nodded in the darkness.

'I'll take that silence as a yes,' Snow said. 'Winnie, you've got the road. Jim's here to give you support. Supposedly, Fourth Regiment is on the far side, so be careful. I'd like to avoid any friendly fire.'

'Right,' Winnie said.

'About half a mile, between us and the platoon, is a small creek bed, mostly dry right now. Once you get there, pause. The regiment will realign and continue north more cautiously.'

'What happens if we make contact?' Winnie asked.

'It you find their pickets without being fired upon, stand by. If you do get in a firefight, stay at a safe distance and keep them occupied. We need to catch and hold their attention, not assault their position.'

'We're not really experienced in night fights, Colonel,' Sasha said.

'I know,' Snow said. 'I've got some flares for the grenadiers, and the rifle company probably brought some for their infantry mortars, if not for the heavier mortars that may or may not be in the camp.'

'Remember when we were just guerilla fighters?' Sonja asked.

'Hey!' Snow snapped. Everyone went quiet. 'I know this isn't want we trained for, this isn't what we are supposed to be doing, this isn't what we want to be doing. But this is the job we've got to do. The people we are supposed to protect, some of your family members, are in that prison, and we need to rescue them. We're light troops, guerilla fighters, so we're going to find the enemy outside the walls and keep them there.'

'And the enemy inside the walls?' Jim asked.

'We have Pioneers, we have Marines, and we have the Artillery Battery with their heavy machine guns and heavy mortars, and Wolf Company for numbers. General Prince has a plan.'

'And our part it to find and hold that platoon,' Winnie said.

'Right,' Snow said. 'Wait for my signal, then advance. And remember, hold at the creek.'

'Yes, ma'am,' Winnie said. 'Sasha, you've got your rifle?'

'Yes, sergeant.'

'Gregory and Samson, what are you carrying?'

'Rifle,' Samson said.

'Automatic,' Gregory said.

'Okay. Sasha, team with me, front and right. Gregory with Sonja, front and left. Samson and Jim, follow behind a few yards. Stay on your toes, keep your eyes open, and don't lose track of the rest of us.'

Sasha nodded. She knew no one could see her, but she did not want to say anything.

'We've all had some night training,' Winnie pointed out. 'We know the short whistles Master Sergeant taught us. We'll just have to improvise the rest. How're we set for grenades? Supplies?'

The Quartermaster's column had supplied them pretty well, with a pair of grenades each. All of them had pistols, a full load of ammunition, and at least one knife. *I wonder what we'll actually use*, Sasha thought. They also each carried a small single use first aid kit, and Sasha cringed.

We don't have Mary. She had only met the new medic, Dominic, in passing, and did not know what to think about him. Except that he was not a warrant officer, and nowhere near Mary's level of expertise.

Sasha thought she heard a soft whistle. Sonja repeated it, a full-fledged bird call. Sasha simply repeated a single whistle herself, and started moving forward.

The road offered a break in the trees, allowing some illumination into the forest. Still, Sasha could barely see the trees she was walking around, much less the people to her left or right, whom she thought were Sonja and Winnie.

Several times someone whistled a stop. Then they started again. Sasha was getting better and seeing the trees coming out of the night, but it was still slow moving. Every once in a while she would get a glimpse of someone in the corner of her eye, hear a twig snap, or duck under a branch.

How far have we gone? How far do we have to go?

Sasha focused on her movement. After a while, she stopped to look around but could not see anyone, nor hear any movement. She paused, but nothing revealed itself. She had no idea if she had gone too far or not far enough, but she did remember the creek bed. She decided to press on.

The creek appeared a few minutes later. Sasha dropped into it, finding it dry as she had been told. But empty of people as well.

I got ahead, she fumed. *I didn't realize I was so far ahead.*

She turned, still hidden below the lip of the creek, when she heard movement. Someone else jumped into the creek further away from the road, and she froze. *Do I whistle? Ask? It should be Winnie, but . . . .*

'Damnit,' a voice said softly. It was a man's voice, an older voice, one she did not recognize.

'Shut up, private,' another voice said.

Sasha remained frozen. The Mardurers didn't use the rank of private; the Royal Army did.

'Yes, sergeant.'

'Stay here,' the second voice said. 'And stay awake. We're right behind you.' Sasha saw some movement and heard footsteps heading north.

They're advancing, Sasha realized with a shiver. The figure, barely visible, crouched in the creek bed, not twenty feet away, and she was stuck in an unhelpful position. She was laying on the incline of the creek bed, her rifle in her left hand, under her body. She was slightly twisted, looking over her right shoulder at the soldier. She did have her pistol, but she did not like the idea of firing over her shoulder. It was, in her mind, her best option, so she started moving her hand towards the holster. The flap was secured by a leather string, which she loosened. She hoped he would not hear or see her.

Maybe I can take him prisoner, she thought. *Hold him until the regiment gets here? But how long would that be? And what if the Rifle Company got there first?* She had the holster open and was sliding the pistol out. *And if we're engaging the whole company, not just a single platoon, we'll need everyone on the line. We couldn't spare one rifle to watch a prisoner.*

The man crept around the creek bed, coming closer to Sasha. He was looking south, watching for a threat he did not realize was so close. He stopped and tensed up and Sasha froze. He peered into the darkness and started to raise his rifle, slowly, as if he was not sure if he saw something.

Sasha realized he must have. He saw the regiment coming. He was going to fire. And in a moment, Sasha had a flash of realization.

The creek bed was a good position to defend. It was not exposed like the forest was, allowing for cover from incoming fire. It was the prime position, and she had to make sure her regiment got it.

'Sorry,' she whispered. She never knew if the soldier heard her, because she fired two shots into his head. The muzzle flash ruined her night vision, but she saw blood flying. She turned the pistol north.

Someone yelled from the north, 'God damn it, Private!'

She fired again. She could not see anything, and doubted she had the range to hit anyone, but she was not trying to kill now. She was trying to make noise. She pistol locked on empty and she dropped it by her side, raising her rifle.

'THIRD REGIMENT!' she yelled, trying to imitate a sergeant's voice. 'FORM ON THE CREEK!' She fired her rifle, and again. Someone fired back, a muzzle flash in the darkness. She aimed even as the bullet whistled over her head. 'FORM UP!' she yelled again and fired at the darkness. The soldiers started firing back in earnest.

A burst from behind her. Winnie, running and firing wildly. 'Sasha, what the hell . . . .'

'They're here,' Sasha said.

'No shit!' Winnie said.

'We need to hold this bed,' Sasha yelled.

Sonja was up, then Jim. Others filling in on the left. A smattering of fire to the right: Fourth Regiment, finding their own position in the creek bed to the east, across the road.

'It could just be a patrol, Rifle!' Winnie yelled.

Sasha's response was cut short by the sound of tearing cloth. Above, a series of bright flares erupted.

The grenade flares the grenadiers are carrying, Sasha thought.

The light filtered through the branches, and Sasha felt both vindicated and scared. The light revealed the rifle company, waves of soldiers, much more than both Field Regiments had brought to the creek bed. They were advancing cautiously. On the road, she saw a number of wagons, one of which looked to carry a large machine gun that was being trained on them. A voice called out, 'Forward!' ordering the men to attack.

'Oh, shit,' Winnie said. 'Sasha, I wish you had been wrong.'

Sasha reloaded her rifle. 'Me, too.'

Chapter 32

General Prince saw the flares ignite above the forest. They were much further south than expected, and much sooner than anticipated. It was quickly followed by the thunder of rifles and the chatter of automatics.

'That's no skirmish,' Bellona said.

'They must be breaking out,' Prince muttered with a curse. It made sense. Captain Lewis had told Snow that his mission was to evacuate certain prisoners. There was no reason for him to wait in the prison and just give the Mardurers time to besiege them within its walls, and under the cover of darkness was the perfect time for him to do so.

'They might need help,' Bellona said.

'How long to re-deploy?' Prince asked.

'Less than a mile directly, but two miles to detour, at night without proper guides, about an hour for the whole force. The assault units, the Pioneers and Marines, they'd be able to get there quicker, but that's only a third of them.' Bellona shook her head. 'The Field Regiments are outnumbered two to one, assuming the whole Rifle Company is heading south. I don't believe they can hold on long enough for the whole assault force to redeploy. Not without incredible losses, anyway.'

Prince looked at the dying flares, just above the tree line now. Flashes of gunfire lit the forest from below. A furious fight was forming.

I forgot the enemy is also trying to win, Prince chided himself. *And now those regiments will pay the price.*

'Sergeant Walters,' Prince said. 'Go to Captain Lobo, inform him he may begin his assault at his discretion.' The staff sergeant saluted and disappeared. Prince looked at Bellona, who shrugged in the darkness.

'Field regiments aren't meant to hold line,' he said. 'We're going to need to rebuild them before they can continue their missions.'

Bellona thought for a moment. 'Don't jump to conclusions, General. We don't know how many casualties they'll take. Maybe they'll get off without too much pain.'

'Don't count my casualties before they're dead?' Prince asked.

Bellona nodded. 'Grim, but true, General.'

Grim indeed, Prince thought.

◆◆◆

The field regiments, the Third to the west of the road and the Fourth to the east, had seized the creek bed. The soldiers attacked by the flare light, trying to push the Mardurers out of the creek bed before they could establish a planned defense.

It was a close, brutal firefight.

Sasha was no longer thinking about anything. Thinking would take too long, and in the furious night fight that was breaking out on the roadway, there was no time to waste. Even aiming was a luxury. All she could do was fire as fast as she could, reload, and repeat. The whole line of Mardurers was doing the same, pouring fire into the advancing soldiers.

The soldiers fought back, knowing the importance of the creek bed. Those closest died quickly, but bought their fellows time to organize a rough line thirty yards from the Mardurers. The soldiers were firing back, branches and bark exploded from trunks. The occasional explosion erupted, sending shrapnel and dirt across the battlefield.

'Keep firing!' Winnie bellowed over the noise. 'Don't leave the creek bed. The bed is safe!'

A mortar round exploded nearby, dropping dirt all over them

'Safe, huh?' Jim snapped.

'Stay here and fire!' Winnie yelled.

Master Sergeant was adding his own voice further away from the road, and others were yelling from Fourth Regiment. The army sergeants were yelling their own troops forward.

It's a wonder anyone can think in this.

Sasha tried to aim, but the movement, shifting light from the flares and muzzle bursts, and the sound of bullets coming too close for comfort proved to be too distracting. She heard Winnie and focused on her words, letting her body move automatically while her mind tried to make sense of the chaos around her.

The machine gun she had noticed on the road, mounted on the lead wagon, opened fire. The deep staccato sounded a dread warning before the trees began shuddering and exploding. Branches pelted the Mardurers, followed by the loud crashing of a tree falling. Sasha ducked back, hugging the protection of the creek until the fire stopped.

For a moment, the sudden silence confused her. She slowly peeked over the bank and into the forest, but she could not see anything. The bright lights still played with her eyes, and all she saw was blackness.

'Check ammo!' Snow yelled out. Sasha pinched her ammo pouches on her belt; two were empty, three full, and one had one remaining. Ten clips of ammunition, plus what was in her rifle. Less than seventy rounds. Three magazines for her pistol, which she remembered she had dropped. She found it easily enough, laying on the ground nearby. She worked the slide to make sure it would not jam. She also had her knife and two grenades.

Winnie's voice called out. 'Medic!'

Dominic's voice called out. 'I got wounded over here, how bad is it?'

'Pretty fucking bad! Sasha, get over here!'

Sasha crawled down the creek bed to Winnie. One of the mortar bombs had exploded nearby and wounded Jim. Winnie worked on bandaging his leg in the darkness.

'Does it hurt here?' she asked.

'Yeah,' Jim said, weakly.

'Okay, Jim, I've got you,' Winnie noticed Sasha. 'If that's you, Sasha, get on Jim's gun. I don't want to face an attack without it.'

Sasha moved to Jim's gun and took her place, maneuvering the large weapon into place and staring into the darkness. She was about to ask Winnie about Jim when the flare ignited overhead.

It was a red flare, which gave the battleground a sanguine glow. Branches and trees crossed the ground, cut down by the weight of fire between the forces. One tree had fallen across the road, blocking the wagons from being able to continue south, the gun now pointed straight up as the gunner reloaded from the safety of his wagon bed. And strewn about the forest floor were the casualties.

Sasha saw dozens of men, and not all were dead. One man sat against the trunk of a tree, tying a tourniquet to his leg. Another had taken hold of a log and was trying to drag himself back to safety. Several moans and faint cries for help or water were whispered into the night. And many were simply still, with no more life in them.

Sasha stared at the horror with wide eyes until the flare died down and the darkness gratefully consumed the sight.

Sasha tried to comprehend what she had seen. It was not the first time on a battlefield, seeing the casualties and destruction, hearing the cries of the wounded and smelling the gunpowder. But this sight had unnerved her. Maybe it was the hours of sleep she was missing. Maybe it was the red glow. Or maybe it was the knowledge that the battle was not over yet. Sasha struggled to focus her mind.

We can't lose this, her words to Winnie echoed in her mind. *This isn't over.*

A rumble from the north snapped her mind to the matter at hand, but there was no attack coming at her.

It was from further north. Prince was assaulting the camp.

◆◆◆

The Inspectorate troopers were part of the army, but were not combat soldiers. They were pulled from the conscription pools for their physical size, bullying demeanor, or marked sadism, aspects that served the Inspectorate well in prison camps and interrogation rooms. They were trained in riot control and interrogation techniques. Many of them looked forward to joining county yeomanry and the easy life such positions brought, once their terms were up.

They were not trained for the battle they faced that night.

Artillery Officer Badger had meticulously calculated the trajectories for his mortar bombs, and on the signal from Captain Lobo, began lobbing them in pairs at each pillbox on the north side. One high explosive round to scare the occupants, and one smoke round to blind them. They then began a slow but steady bombardment, to keep the defenders inside, while his heavy machine guns chewed up the watch towers and their occupants.

The first wave rushed from the tree line. Made up of Engineer Officer Hammer's Pioneer Company and First Lieutenant Mars' Marine Company, they were a particularly well-trained group of Mardurers. They rushed two hundred yards into the field surrounding the camp, quickly and quietly, avoiding detection as they pulled a sled across the cleared ground. Most of the troops stopped and dropped to the ground while Hammer and her team pushed the sled another twenty yards closer. Hammer sited the weapon and secured it to the ground, before falling back with her squad, a long thin cord trailing behind her to the weapon.

Hammer twisted the detonator, and the device fired. Three rockets flew out, up and over the wire and the mine field, trailing a

311

thick cord behind them. The rockets landed just inside the camp, with small parachutes keeping the cord strung out behind them. For a second the cords lay draped over the wire and mines, as if forgotten, before they exploded. Wires snapped and mines detonated, and a thirty foot hole in the camp's defenses lay open.

Mars led his Marines in, engaging the yeomen and troopers who were slowly reacting to the sudden attack from the north. Hammer and her pioneers followed, carrying the large explosive projectors they had brought with them. The closest pillboxes were hammered by three-pound warheads designed to penetrate armor. Both collapsed.

Wolf Company was close behind, flooding the base with Mardurers. One man tripped and fell on a mine, killing himself and wounding two others. The yeomen and troopers dug into their tenuous positions, running for the buildings and pillboxes furthest from the breech. Several of troopers took position in the prisoners' barracks, and shot some of the prisoners to keep them from fighting back.

Prince's forces were committed to fighting for the camp. For the time being, the field regiments were on their own.

Chapter 33

The soldiers attacked again. They had advanced to within fifty yards of the creek bed and were keeping up a steady fire, pinning the defenders down.

Sasha put the LAMB gun to her shoulder and fired. The gun burped a three round burst and stopped.

'What the hell?' she asked.

'Burst fire!' Winnie yelled at her. 'Don't change it. Breathe, and fire. Slow and steady.'

'Slow and steady,' Sasha began repeating.

The night was beginning to lighten enough to see the trees around her, but not enough to see the soldiers. She saw muzzle flashes, and tracers from the few automatic weapons deployed in their line. Grenades and mortars dropped their explosives throughout the forest, and Sasha had no idea if they were having any effect at all. Of course, Sasha had no idea if she was having any effect. She was firing, breathing, firing, and reloading.

'They've got to be moving to flank us!' Sonja yelled.

'Which side? Ours or the Fourth's?' Sasha asked.

'No idea!' Sonja yelled. 'But we can't sustain this for too much longer. Winnie! What do you think?'

Winnie did not respond. She looked over her shoulder.

Jim was laying there, unmoving. Sasha did not know if he was dead or not. Winnie was not there at all.

'Where the fuck is she?' Sonja asked. 'Did she run?'

'Winnie wouldn't run!' Sasha yelled back.

'Well, then where is she?'

Sasha reloaded, not having an answer. She still heard Master Sergeant yelling, keeping the regiment in the fight. She heard another voice across the road, yelling to keep Fourth Regiment in

313

line. The bullets and gunfire drowned out any ability to think, and Sasha felt a deep sense of doom. *I have no idea what's going to happen*, she thought. *No idea.*

The heavy machine gun opened fire again, the deep hammering reverberating through the forest. Sasha instinctively ducked at the sound. But the bullets did not come towards the creek bed. She looked over the lip and saw the large red tracers flashing westward, into the soldiers.

'Oh my God,' Sasha said. 'Winnie took their gun!'

'Fuck!' Sonja snarled. 'She's exposed and surrounded once they get to her, she's dead!'

Sasha thought for a moment. The army company had to clear the field regiments out of the creek bed so they could move the wagons south. They had established a base of fire to keep the regiments in place while they moved to flank and destroy them. Pulling out was not an option.

Winnie used the fallen trees to approach the wagons and took the first gun. And the wagons were the objective, not preventing the army company's escape. The wagons, and the prisoners inside them. Including Mary.

'We need to take the wagons,' Sasha said. She grabbed the satchel of ammunition for the LAMB gun and moved to the short bridge that crossed the creek. 'ADVANCE ON THE WAGONS!' she bellowed and rushed forward.

The fallen trees had indeed protected Winnie from being seen as she advanced, and now protected Sasha as she rushed forward. The branches reaching upward kept her out of sight of the soldiers, now reacting to the sudden threat of the gun.

Sasha followed a tree trunk up to the wagon, stopping on the eastern side of the road. One of the horses had been killed by the fall, and the other shot to keep it from bolting. Looking further down the road, Sasha could see the other wagons, pulled back from the firing. Beyond that, in the distance, a watch tower burned, bright flames dancing into the sky.

She saw movement, a group of figures emerging from the trees twenty yards in front of her and taking position next to the second wagon, where Winnie would not be able to see them. The army company was responding

Sasha spread the bipod, resting the legs on the tree in front of her, and aimed at the figures. She quickly fired a burst, striking the lead soldier dead on. She fired again, forcing the soldiers back into the cover of the trees.

Sasha felt movement beside her and someone standing behind the branches, firing over her head. She glanced and saw someone with the naked arms of Fourth Regiment. Someone fired to her left; Sonja, having come up behind her.

'Guess we're attacking, huh?' Sonja asked. The sound of gunfire followed; the regiments, it seemed, were advancing behind her.

'We have to keep advancing,' Sasha said. 'We need to capture the wagons, and meet up with the troops at camp!'

'You think the general captured it?' Sonja asked.

Sasha glanced at the burning tower. 'I think so.' She dropped the satchel and the LAMB. 'This is too heavy for me.'

'I got it,' another gunner came up. It was the tall woman Sasha had fought at the kitchens. She grabbed the ammo. 'I'll cover you!'

Sasha nodded, checking her rifle and fixing the bayonet. She checked her belt, the pistol and the knife and the grenades still in their place. Her heart raced and her breathing was heavy, and a worry in her stomach made her glad she had not eaten anything recently. And for all her fear, she realized, she had no interest in running away. This was her fight, their fight, and she was in it until the end.

'Ready?' she yelled.

'Fucking go already!' the woman yelled, already firing.

Sasha jumped over the log, keeping the wagon close to her left as she approached the gap between wagons. The next wagon was fifteen yards away, the horses dead. She took deep breath and sprinted across.

She was almost across when the covering fire slowed, and a man jumped out of the trees. He had been waiting for a lull in the fire and was rushing to the same spot she was, in cover from Winnie at her gun. He was so focused on listening for his chance he didn't notice Sasha until she was feet from him, bayonet leveled. His right arm was back in a throwing position, unready to defend himself.

Sasha speared him right in the stomach, putting her weight behind the blow. 'Gah!' he exclaimed at the impact. Something fell from his throwing hand as he grasped at the rifle imbedded in his torso, and Sasha had a moment to realize what it was.

'GRENADE!' she yelled before it exploded. The body of the soldier jumped and slammed Sasha against the side of the wagon, his head smashing into her head. She fell, stunned, to the roadway.

Everything was wrong. She could not hear. She could see, but could not focus. She would reach for something but forget what it was and reach for something else. Part of her mind knew she was in trouble, but she could not understand why or what to do about it.

Someone grabbed her collar and pulled her back. She looked up, seeing a person without comprehending what she saw. There was a snapping sound, but she could not find it. She was surrounded by shadows and echoes.

She felt a touch on her chin lifting her head up, and then water pouring over her face. For a moment the shock replaced the disorientation, and then her focus came back.

'Stop,' she sputtered.

'Good, you're alive.' It was Winnie. She had pulled Sasha back next to the dead horses and poured the contents of her canteen out on Sasha's head. 'You're bleeding like a stuck pig.'

As Sasha's senses came back into focus, the pain in her head erupted. The back of her head throbbed, and her lip stung. She touched her lip and pulled back her hand, feeling the warm blood on her fingers.

'Oh, dear,' she said.

Winnie laughed. 'Indeed. Are you up?'

'I don't have my rifle,' Sasha said. She stood, still feeling a little woozy. 'What's going on?'

'Fourth Regiment is pressing forward to the east. Third Regiment is pulling back to the road; it looks like the flanking attack was coming from the west and Snow is pulling out ahead of it. We're trying to secure the wagons.'

'Right,' Sasha said. She saw her rifle and tried to pick it up but fell to her knees. 'And the camp?'

'Still on fire,' Winnie said. 'No sign of any of our people, but if that fight turned into a real hard one I can't imagine we'll get much help from them.'

Sasha sat back against the wheel of the wagon, slowly checking her weapon. 'We should keep moving forward,' she said.

'You can barely stand,' Winnie said.

Several figures ran by, two stopping at the same wagon Sasha was leaning again. Sonja and Erick slid to a stop.

'What happened to her?' Sonja asked.

'Too close to a grenade,' Winnie said.

'I'm fine,' Sasha said. She had worked the bolt back and checked that her rifle was loaded. 'Mary could be in one of the wagons. We should go find her.'

'Can't,' Erick said. 'Hear that?'

Sasha listened. She had not realized that the gunfire had moved further north, or had stopped further south. In fact it was beginning to slow.

'I think they're about to attack,' Winnie said.

'Makes sense,' Erick said. 'They want the wagons, and we pushed them all to one side of the road.'

'They've taken some hurt,' Sonja said. 'They've got to have less than a hundred effectives now. They'll probably try to flank us.'

'They don't have time,' Sasha said. 'They know the camp has fallen and they can't be sure Prince isn't heading south right now. They've got to hit us now.' She was still leaning against the wagon wheel, but her eyes had cleared up.

'Keep your eyes open!' Master Sergeant yelled. He was past them, further north up the wagon train. Sasha did not remember seeing him pass her.

'At least Master Sergeant's still alive,' Erick said.

'Nothing'll kill him,' Sonja laughed. She had positioned herself at the front end of the wagon, laying her ammunition and grenades on the driver's step. Winnie was behind the dead horses. Erick was setting up next to Sasha.

'You've got the corner?' he asked her.

'Yes,' she said. She had the two grenades and the ammunition. She realized the blade for her bayonet had snapped off. 'You?'

'I can fire over the wagon,' he said. His rifle still had the grenade attachment. 'Two flares, a smoke, and four fragmentation,' he said.

Sasha shook her head again, trying to clear the last shreds of confusion out of it. 'Hey, Winnie?'

'Yeah?'

'What happened to Jim?' she asked.

There was a heavy pause. 'He bled out,' she said. 'Couldn't stop it. Mary might have, but in the dark, I had the bandage in the wrong place.'

'Oh,' Sasha said. She looked back out into the forest. *I should feel sad*, she thought. *Jim was nice. He was a good gunner, a decent man. Why do I feel numb? Is it the head wound? Will I feel sad when this is all over?*

Someone ran over from the next wagon. It was Master Sergeant. 'You're the southern wagon, ladies. Can you hold?'

'Unless they flank,' Winnie said.

'We're evacuating the wagons,' he said. 'Erick, on the command of 'light', fire a flare. Shoot at what you can. When you hear the horn, fall back to the east, approximately two hundred yards.'

'Any word from the camp?' Sonja asked.

'Don't worry about the camp! Light and horn, got it?'

'Yes, Master Sergeant,' Sasha said. He disappeared.

'Too bad that gun ran out of ammo,' Sonja said.

'Yeah,' Winnie agreed.

A voice called out, 'Light!' A half a dozen grenade launchers launched their flares.

Sasha peered out into the forest to see what the illumination revealed. The soldiers were advancing, fifty yards, and now scrambling for cover.

'FIRE!'

Sasha could see better in the flare light, and shot one soldier carrying an automatic. A second shot missed. The soldiers were in cover and firing back. Sasha was very much aware that the wagon wheels were not as solid as a tree trunk.

'We should start pulling back,' Erick said.

'Not until the horn!' Winnie called.

A bullet snapped by Sasha's head. 'Better be soon!'

'Just keep firing!'

Sasha went through another clip before the horn sounded. 'Go!' Winnie called, firing at the soldiers as the other three retreated twenty yards into the forest, turning to cover Winnie as she pulled back. It was a practiced maneuver, one Master Sergeant had drilled them in. Leap frogging backwards, into the darkness. 'Go,' one would yell, the others running to the next position.

It was on the third turn that the soldiers reached the wagons. Sasha had targets to shoot at; she and Sonja, side by side, watched the soldiers duck for cover as the pair fired quickly and inaccurately. They were not moving past the wagons, just taking cover at their side.

'Go!' Winnie called. Sonja turned to run. Sasha hesitated just a moment to fire one last shot, seeing a soldier duck out of cover and aim in their direction. She turned to run, seeing Sonja before her in the darkness. She heard the shot, felt the bullet pass by her head, and saw Sonja shudder with a sickening thunk. Sonja fell, her legs in the air as she toppled.

Sasha went to her knees. 'Sonja!' she called. Sonja's eyes were blank and unfocused. 'Sonja,' Sasha whispered.

The forest shook with a loud thunder, then another. Sasha looked at the wagon train to see the soldiers scrambling as a third explosion demolished a wagon, sending wood and boxes a hundred feet into the air.

'Heavy mortars,' Erick said, suddenly at her side. 'From the camp.'

Winnie was at their side now. 'That was the plan,' she said. 'They knew the soldiers would attack the wagons. We bought them time to aim.' She reached down and felt Sonja's neck.

'She's gone,' Sasha said quietly.

'Yes,' Winnie confirmed. There was gunfire to the west, but none of it was coming towards them. 'I think Prince is flanking them now. It's over.'

Sasha looked down at Sonja. She thought about Jim, and the soldiers she had killed, and wept.

Chapter 34

Sasha looked around the pillbox. It was cramped, with a low ceiling that even Sasha had to duck to stand in. The walls were wooden planks and the floor was packed dirt. The machine gun that had been emplaced here, long since removed, stood on a tall mount that left imprints in the floor before each of the firing ports. The ports themselves were eight inches tall and two feet wide, and revealed the walls to be four inches of wood with two inches of concrete on the outside.

'Pathetic,' Winnie said. 'The Pioneers' breeching rockets could penetrate a foot of concrete. You saw what they did to those two they hit?'

'I saw,' Sasha said. Those boxes had collapsed and the wood had burned, taking the towers above them down as well. The pillboxes that had been such an important obstacle to taking the camp had proven to be woefully inadequate to defending it. Third Regiment might have done it themselves.

'According to the Inspectorate troopers, the concrete was brought up from Saint Cloud in these slabs and put in place. Not poured here.'

'Must have been terribly cold in winter,' Sasha said. 'What a horrible place to be.'

'True,' Winnie said. 'Give me the forest and my legs over a concrete coffin anytime.'

Sasha shuddered at the word coffin. Her response was cut off as Mary came through the doorway. She looked exhausted, her clothes stained with dried blood. She sat down on a bend next to the doorway and leaned back, a canteen in her hand.

'Oh, lord,' she said.

'You okay?' Sasha asked.

'Tired,' Mary said. 'Twelve hours of triage and surgery and care. Even with the company medics and the prison staff and

321

Doctor Miller, and Colonel Aristotle with his field hospital, there's so much to do.' She took a sip from her canteen. 'Hot tea,' she said. 'Soothing.'

'How many did we lose?' Sasha asked.

'Too many, on both sides.' Mary groaned. 'Explosives do a wondrous job in devastating the human body. I almost prefer knife and bullet wounds.' She almost looked like she was asleep, except for the canteen.

'Any word on the prisoners?' Winnie asked.

'Three of them were killed when the troopers and yeomen opened fire on the camp,' Mary said. 'We saved the rest, but I think a few more might die. They've been in captivity for more than a decade, most of them, and they've suffered for it.'

'Was there a Dawson among them?' Sasha asked.

Mary looked at both of them, then shook her head.

'Damn,' Sasha whispered. She'd hoped that General Prince could find a family member, someone who survived the ever-growing horror stories of what happened to the Dawson blood line.

Mary changed the subject. 'The Quartermasters are tearing down everything they can, but they're using the kitchen for a hot meal. I'm hungry, and I could use the company.'

'Sure,' Sasha said.

'I'm going to take a nap,' Winnie said. 'But save me something warm.'

◆◆◆

The camp was bustling with activity. The Quartermasters were stripping everything they could, even the barbed wire off the fence posts. The Provost had secured some of prisoners in a few of the buildings, or were watching the rest dig the graves. The Olympians guarded the General's Headquarters in the former Camp

Commander's cabin. The newly freed prisoners, at least those who could stand, watched the camp being disassembled, eating freshly made food. The Royal yellow-and-green flag has been replaced with Prince's blue and white.

'Anything we're not taking is getting torched,' Mary said. 'If they can't disassemble the pillboxes, the Pioneers are going to blow them.'

'Makes sense,' Sasha said. She tried not to look at the field of freshly dug graves. Prince had ordered a grave for each soldier and Mardurer killed in battle, a show of respect he had said. Only the defenders who had shot the prisoners were to be dropped in a mass grave.

Like those bandits, Sasha remembered, laying on the edge of the broad river. No markers, no graves, just exposed to be reclaimed by the forest. *And it was only...how long ago was it?*

The camp's kitchen smelled of bacon. The benches, where the prisoners had usually eaten, were half-full of Mardurers eating over their short breaks. Third and Fourth Regiments had been stood down after their night battle, and their members were mostly sleeping or resting, but a few were at the kitchen. Among them, Sasha saw Sergeant Oliver, who returned his dishes and was now walking towards them.

Let him walk by without a fight, Sasha prayed.

Oliver saw the women approaching and stopped, his eyes fixated on Mary. He stiffened. 'Ma'am,' he said, 'I wanted to thank you for what you did for Rifle Arti. I thought she was dead for sure when I saw that wound.'

'It was a bad wound,' Mary admitted. 'But you guys got it packed pretty well. She'll keep the leg, but it'll be a while before she's running with the Pack again.'

'Oh, she'll probably surprise you,' Oliver said with a smile. He saluted. 'Thank you, Officer Mary.'

Mary smiled and nodded, which was enough for Oliver. His eyes turned towards Sasha. Sasha tensed...

...and Oliver touched the brim of his hat. 'Ma'am,' he said.

Sasha was stunned as Oliver started to move past. 'I'm not an officer, Sergeant!' she said quickly.

'Really? Could have fooled me with your yelling last night.'

'I wasn't yelling,' Sasha said.

'Like a bobcat,' Mary said with a slim smile. 'When you charged. Even I heard you, and I was locked in a wagon.'

'Fine, maybe I was, but before that, I wasn't yelling like an officer.'

'Yes, you were,' Oliver said.

'I wasn't thinking!' Sasha exclaimed. 'I just attacked to help a friend.'

'Some might call that initiative,' Oliver said. 'Like how you single-handedly assaulted an entire village of yeomen with an emplaced machine gun.'

'First of all, Winnie was following me. Second of all, I didn't assault the machine gun. Neither of us got close to it. We just kept the yeomen off balance. Sonja killed the gunners.' She winced at the name of her dead friend.

'I know what happened, Rifle Sasha,' Oliver said. 'And I stand by my statements.'

'I am not an officer!' Sasha repeated.

'Why is that?' Oliver asked.

'Because I can't be one.'

'Why not?'

Sasha opened her mouth but couldn't think of anything to say. She looked at Mary, who shrugged.

'Well,' Sasha said, 'because I'm not right for it. I'm too much of a civilian. Ask Winnie, she'd agree. She always says I'm not thinking like a Rifle.'

'Not thinking like a...,' Oliver began, then stopped and laughed. Sasha frowned.

'I'm sorry,' he finally said. 'I just...I forgot you didn't go through Carpenter's training program.' He looked at Mary. 'Didn't anyone tell her?'

'Winnie wanted her to figure it out herself,' Mary said.

Sasha looked at Mary, and back at Oliver. 'Figure out what?' she asked, her voice low and angry.

'Carpenter has this speech he gives,' Oliver said, 'when the recruits are first assembled. He wants to know how we think. Most of the first period of training is about figuring out who goes where. It's how Mary got tapped to be a medical officer, while I got tapped to be a sergeant. She thinks like a doctor; I think like an NCO.'

'I always thought she meant I was thinking like a civilian,' Sasha said.

'Aye, the first time, she probably did mean that. But she doesn't anymore. Winnie is saying you're not a Rifle, but she's not saying you're a civilian,' Oliver said. 'She's trying to tell you you're an officer.'

'No she's not!' Sasha snapped. 'How would you know?'

'We're both sergeants,' Oliver said. 'We both see you the same way. Willing to fight. Willing to jump up and take the initiative. Willing to force the battle one direction or another. If you don't believe me, ask her,' Oliver said.

'Fine, I will!' Sasha shouted. 'And after she laughs in my face, the two of us will come and knock some sense into you!'

Oliver chuckled. 'Promises, promises.'

◆◆◆

Sasha paced the same pillbox, unable to sit still. It seemed like an eternity before Winnie entered the small room. She looked at Sasha with exhausted eyes, waiting for Sasha to begin.

'Tell me it's not true,' Sasha said.

'I'd hoped you would have figured it out for yourself,' Winnie said. She sat down on one of the benches. 'I had hoped you would understand why.'

'I can't be an officer!' Sasha shouted.

'Why not?' Winnie asked.

Sasha started to speak but nothing came to mind. 'I'm not smart enough,' she finally blurted out.

'The Scholar of Third Regiment?' Winnie asked. She unscrewed a canteen and the smell of tea filled the pillbox. 'You've read more than enough in the last few weeks to make up for the rest of us.'

'That doesn't make me smart enough to be an officer.'

'Sure it does,' Winnie said after a gulp. 'I've seen Snow's *Art of War* book. You know what I did when I couldn't understand something? I put it down. You sat there with two books and went back and forth until you understood what he was trying to say.'

'But....'

'But what?' Winnie said with a stern voice. Sasha's mouth snapped shut. Winnie stood, imposing even in the small confined of the pillbox, and raised four fingers. 'Four pillars,' she said, 'four core values for an officer:

'One, intelligence. You read, you think, you talk. When Prince spoke to you during the confrontation with Middlestedt you answered correctly. Word for word, if what I've heard it true.

'Two, competence. You fight as well as we can expect from someone who didn't go through the training companies. You keep your head under fire. You get how to influence a battle.

'Three, morality. You kill during battle but when it's all over you know to stop. You even held a gun at my head to keep me from executing a man so guilty of a crime his own sergeant refused to defend him at this trial. Then stepped up and took part in his firing squad without complaint.

'Four, physical ability. You're in fit and fighting shape, no doubt about it. What else do you need?'

Sasha sat down and shook her head. 'I can't be,' she said. 'Not like Snow, or Saber, or Buck.'

'Why not?' Winnie asked.

Sasha 'Why do people keep asking me that?'

'Because you won't ask yourself,' Winnie shrugged. 'I've heard that story you've told, about your father and the dog. "Why is a dog able to defend itself but I can't", right? Well I ask you, Sasha: why is Snow able to be an office but you aren't? Why is Buck? Saber? Lynx? Why are you content to remain a Rifle?'

'There's nothing wrong with being a Rifle,' Sasha said.

'True. But not everyone can be a colonel.' Winnie sat back down. 'Your father limited your options for you. Now you're limiting your own. You are better than you were with your father, true. But you're confusing 'being better' with 'being your best.' You've broken the limits your father set, and I want you to break the limits you've set for yourself. You could be an officer, a great one, I believe. A worthy successor to Colonel Snow!'

Winnie realized she was yelling, and took a moment to calm herself. Sasha started at her, hearing the confidence behind her voice. The same voice that once told her she did not belong in the regiment, now telling her she could lead it.

Winnie looked out the pillbox's window. 'If you don't want to be an officer, you shouldn't be one.' She paused, and turned to look Sasha in the eyes. 'But, Sasha Small, I swear to all that is holy that if you don't think about this, if you don't seriously consider this, I will never forgive you.'

Sasha returned Winnie's stare and felt the sincerity of her words. She finally looked away, blushing. 'I thought you were my friend.'

'I am. And as your friend, you need to think about this. I'm also your sergeant, and as your sergeant, you need to think about this.'

'Why?' Sasha asked. 'Why is this so important to you?'

'One of the roles of an NCO is to identify weaknesses and take care of them before they create problems, to make the regiment the best is can be. And if you are not an officer, then this regiment is not the best it can be.' She took another sip of tea. 'And if we're not the best, how can we expect to win?'

Chapter 35

The Field Hospital stabilized the last of the wounded and moved them out of the camp. The Quartermasters took everything, even disassembling some of the structures for nails and wood. A few buildings remained, and were to be burned. The Pioneers were unable to break down the pillboxes, so they prepared them for demolition.

The camp now stripped, the units turned to burying the dead. Third Regiment lost four, including Jim and Sonja. Sasha helped lower Sonja into the grave, wrapped in her blanket, and shoveled the dirt over her friend, crying the whole time. One by one, each unit lowering and covering their own dead, the rest watching respectfully. Even the rifle company soldiers stood at attention, waiting their turn to bury their own.

Finally the remaining units were drawn up. Prince stood with the Third Regiment, Olympians, Pioneers and the Artillery Regiment, standing in formation. Across from them stood the disarmed rifle company, Inspectorate troopers and the yeomen. Between them were the Provost.

Five men, three of them Inspectorate troopers and two of them yeomen, had attacked the prisoners as the camp fell and were charged with murder. Four of them were found guilty and sentenced to death. All the assembled watched as the four men were hung from the archway between the Inspectorate field and the prison proper. Sasha hated watching it, hearing some of the protests even from the opposite side of the assembly.

I will never enjoy an execution, she thought. *May I never partake in one again.*

The Mardurers were not keeping their prisoners: they did not have the resources. Instead, the prisoners were stripped of every useful item and sent south. The soldiers who could march were allowed to keep their boots, in recognition of the honorable actions in the camp. The yeomen and inspectorate troops marched barefoot.

Captain Lewis led the column, as Major Dodd had shot himself when the camp fell. In contrast to the yeomen and inspectorate troops who brought up the rear of the column, his soldiers marched in formation. Lewis saluted Prince as his column headed south.

Those are real soldiers, Sasha thought to herself. *If I ever surrender a command, let me have the same respect as Captain Lewis.*

Sasha silently chuckled and shook her head as she realized what she had just thought to herself.

Fourth Regiment followed the prisoners south. The Pioneers blew the remaining pillboxes and fired the last buildings. The towers fell, replaced by columns of smoke. Only the archway with the four men was left standing.

Prince pulled his army north, back to Arrowhead. It was a relatively easy march, using the roads, though Sasha felt a bit exposed not being surrounded by trees. She was not the only one, and soon the two field regiments were moving through the woods alongside the column.

The camp was just as it had been left, the tents still up. Orders flowed quickly; the militia would take over the picket, and the assembled units would have the night off. The Quartermasters prepared a meal, some alcohol flowed, instruments were produced, and soon the camp was a place of merriment.

Sasha spent the evening speaking with the various units at the camp. The marines and pioneers, the rifles and provost, quartermasters and doctors and nurses. A celebration of surviving a battle and winning.

Sasha was shocked to discover she had a reputation. Two of them, actually, even if she was not necessarily named, and that the reputation mentioned was often dependent on the individual's unit. The marines and pioneers marveled at the Bobcat, who attacked the enemy relentlessly while screaming. The quartermasters and clerks spoke of the Scholar, the soldier of Third Regiment who always had four books on hand and read three languages.

Sasha quickly stopped identifying herself as either of them.

The only people missing were the officers, ensconced in the plantation house, surrounded by the Olympians. Several times Sasha found herself close by, staring at the house, wondering about what was happening inside. Snow was in there. Lynx and Buck. Prince, Bellona, Aristotle, Fox, Wild, Stock. The officers she did not know or could not name.

Could I join them? She asked herself.

Lynx is an officer, and she has trouble reading. I am a fighter; even Fox said so.

Fox said I was a killer.

But not a murderer. I stopped killing when the battle stopped. I controlled myself. I could lead others.

Her father's voice began. *It is bad enough you fight, Sasha Evelyn Small. Would you now dare to elevate yourself above others!*

Erick clasped Sasha on the shoulder, holding a bottle. 'Have a drink, Rifle Sasha. It is well-earned!' he smiled.

Sasha nodded, taking the bottle. 'To victory?'

'To victory, and my Warrant!' he said.

She smiled and drank. Her throat burned. 'I didn't know you were getting one.'

'Neither did I, until ten minutes ago,' he said. 'We're getting the bulk of the trainees from Wolf Company. Saber may be removed back north to recover, which leaves us with almost a hundred Rifles and the militia. The militia will elect an officer or two for their command; Snow, Buck, and Lynx will form their own companies, with the Rifles and Gunners. I'm getting the grenadiers and two of the machine guns we took out of the prison pillboxes.'

'What about Beth?' Sasha asked. Beth had also been working for a warrant with the regiment.

'She's going to be a full sergeant as soon as we get back to camp,' Erick said, 'running the training regime. Snow said that if Beth keeps at it, she'll have a warrant by the end of the year.'

331

Sasha smiled and took another drink. Erick took the bottle back and disappeared into the crowd, leaving Sasha with her thoughts.

Elevate myself above others? She thought to herself. *How? None of the officers in Third Regiment stayed out of a fight; Saber was wounded in battle and Lynx won her warrant in combat. Erick certainly doesn't lack for courage. And neither do I.*

But do I want to be one?

Sasha pondered that. Could she make decisions? Would people follow her?

They already have, she thought. *But is that enough?*

I'm not ready to be an officer, she thought. *Not yet. But I have control over my life now. I wanted to be part of the regiment. I am. What do I want to do now? Winnie wants me to break my own limitations. What goal do I want to set for myself?*

The door to the house opened and Snow stepped out. She started making her way towards the hospital. Sasha watched her, then began to follow.

The doctors had treated and released everyone they could, but there were a few wounded who required attention. Two large tents had been erected for their recovery. Sasha followed Snow towards the tents and watched as she went inside.

Ten minutes later, Snow and Aristotle emerged, having some conversation. Sasha stood in the path until they approached close enough to recognize her.

'Rifle Sasha,' Aristotle said. 'Having a good night?'

'I am, Colonel Aristotle,' Sasha replied. 'But I was hoping to speak with Colonel Snow about something.'

Aristotle glanced at Snow, who nodded. 'I will be at the house,' he said and continued walking.

Snow was looking at Sasha with a curious look. 'Something on your mind, Rifle?'

Sasha was not sure where to begin. 'Erick says we're getting most of the trainees from Wolf Company,' she started. 'And he's getting a warrant.'

'Both true,' Snow said. 'We've kicked up a hornet's nest and we'll need to be prepared. And if you're worried about your place in the regiment, don't be. You'll be a First Rifle, if not a Corporal, within a week.'

'I'm not worried about that,' Sasha said. 'I'm willing to serve where you want me.'

'Then what's with the nervous face?' Snow asked.

Sasha took a deep breath. 'I wanted to put my name forward as a candidate for the next warrant.'

Snow looked at her and said nothing for a full minute. 'You want to be an officer?' she asked slowly.

'I think so,' Sasha said. 'At least, I want to try. Maybe I'm not cut out to be an officer, maybe I am. Winnie and Oliver and Mary seem to think so.'

'What do you think?' Snow asked.

Sasha sighed and looked towards the campfires.

'I think I joined this regiment to get away from a life that was intolerable, and for the first time found someplace I belong. I made friends, who trust me to fight alongside them. I read books I never knew existed, developed skills I never thought I could learn. I became a much better person that I would have been back home.'

Then Sasha turned back to Snow. 'But, Colonel, I think I became lazy. I was so glad to be breaking those false limitations I haven't spent any time trying to find my real ones. I think,' Sasha began, and stopped, trying to sort out the thoughts racing around her head.

'I remember,' she finally continued, 'during the debate with Mayor Middlestedt, General Prince said something about Giullio Montessori. That he had never been tested, so he never knew what he might become. So he got ahead of himself and got a lot of his people killed. I don't want to be that. I want to test myself, to know what I might become. Maybe I am meant to be an officer, like Winnie says. Maybe I'm not, but, Colonel, I need to find out.'

She looked at Snow. 'At least, if you'll let me try.'

It was dark, but for a moment Sasha thought she saw Snow grimace. But only for a moment.

'Beth and Erick both expressed an interest in a warrant when they were in Walker for training,' Snow said. 'They've worked for a while towards this.'

'I know,' Sasha said. 'I'm willing to work to catch up.'

Snow nodded. 'I'm sure you will.' She looked at Sasha fiercely. 'But I promise you, Sasha: I will not go easy on you. If you want to be an officer, I will make you the best one I can.'

'Thank you, Colonel,' Sasha said. She wanted to smile, but kept herself serious.

'Tomorrow morning Third Regiment is moving back south. We're getting back to our main mission. Tomorrow evening, come find me and I will discuss with you what you should be prepared for.'

'Yes, Colonel,' Sasha saluted. Snow returned it, and Sasha turned, heading back to camp, her face breaking out in the smile she was no longer trying to hide.

I've got to find Winnie. If anyone can prepare me, she can.

Chapter 36

Shit.

Snow watched Sasha leave and felt a sense of disappointment in herself. She knew this was coming, even before word of Winnie's prompting reached her ears. She had hoped that by the time it occurred, she could have had a solution to her dilemma, but nothing had come to her yet.

Shit.

Snow turned and continued back up the path to the house. The Olympians remained at their posts, acknowledging the colonel but otherwise directing their attention outward. She entered the front door to find Officer Bellona.

'Colonel Snow. You can go on in,' Bellona leaned forward. 'It's First Circle only, right now,' she whispered.

Snow nodded and entered the main room. Most of the other officers had gone, leaving three. Those who had been a part of the Renaissance Army since before it had a name.

'Come, sit,' Prince said. He was sitting next to the fireplace, warming a pot on the small fire. Aristotle was uncorking a bottle of wine. Wild was unwrapping a selection of cigars. 'Celebrate a victory.'

'Of course,' Snow said. She sat down on the extra chair. 'Need help with that bottle, Andre?'

Aristotle frowned and said something terse in Quebecois. Prince smiled.

Wild handed out the cigars and leaned over to ignite a small stick in the fire. 'Quite the difference a year makes,' he said, puffing his cigar to life. 'From sleeping under the docks of Duluth to the forests of Walker.'

'We're in Brainerd,' Prince said.

335

'Ya' know what I mean!' Wild growled. 'Who knows what next year will bring! What heights y'all might go to.'

Aristotle managed to get the bottle open. 'We don't have cups.'

'Bah!' Wild said. 'We don't need cups. We're all but family here.'

Prince chuckled, the others following suit. Snow smiled. It was good to watch him unwind. General Prince may lead a rebellion, but Ethan Dawson was only a man. Smart, capable, charismatic, but a still only a man.

Snow became aware that everyone was looking at her. 'What is it, Jeremiah?'

Wild chuckled and handed her the lit stick. 'Andre was wondering why your Bobcat waylaid you on the road,' he said, laying back on his couch and putting his feet on the armrest.

'Sasha?' Snow asked, lighting her cigar. Aristotle nodded. 'She wanted to put her name forward for a regimental warrant.'

'Excellent,' Prince said. He took the wine bottle from Aristotle. 'I was pleasantly surprised by her words in the town, and her actions on the road. She would make a fine officer. You'd do well to train her as one.'

Snow tested her cigar, and took a deep breath. 'No, Ethan, I would not do well.'

The three looked at her. She glanced nervously at Prince.

'Go ahead, Amanda,' he said. 'Say your piece.'

Snow sighed and sat back, staring up at the cigar smoke clouding the air above her. 'I would not do well. To train Sasha for a regimental warrant, I would do adequately. And she would come out an adequate field officer. And she would serve this regiment to the best of her abilities, as she has been since we pulled her out of that ambush. And she would be adequate.'

Snow sat forward, resting her elbows on her knees. 'But, Ethan, she deserves more than adequate. I can teach her to be a field officer, hone her skills as a fighter, but I cannot shape her mind.

That will dull. And I've watched her. I gave her *The Art of War* to learn the basics of field warfare, and she went off and memorized the entirety of the Three Fools! She lectured me on its lessons. And do you know who she reminded me of?'

'Marcus,' Prince said.

'She is *le petite Caesar*,' Aristotle said. 'I had that thought as well.'

'When?' Snow asked.

'Fox brought her in here a few days ago,' Prince said. 'We had a discussion about the *Art of War*, the Three Fools, and the American Revolution.'

'A discussion?' Snow asked. 'Why did I not hear about this?'

'It wasn't an official meeting,' Prince said.

'I think Fox was showing off how far she's come,' Aristotle said.

'And she can go further,' Snow said.

'I agree,' Aristotle said.

'Andre,' Prince cautioned, but Aristotle shook his head.

'No, Ethan. She can.' He leaned back, looking at Prince levelly. 'And once more, you know it. And you know she's not the only one. How many young men and women have we met who have the spark of being the greatest of their generation, and we're struggling to find qualified officers. You wanted to find those who are "called to a higher purpose". She's one of them. Sasha Small is called.'

'The diamond in the rough,' Wild said.

'You too, Jeremiah?' Prince sighed.

Wild shrugged. 'Hate me if ya' will, but ya' can't expect to find future generals 'n' leaders who will meet all of the requirements a renaissance needs without training them.' He sat up and stretched. 'We need to begin forging them, now, out o' the best steel we got to forge with.'

Prince looked at the three of them. 'Outnumbered.'

337

'And wrong,' Snow said.

'Perhaps. What do you want from me?'

'Revisit the Templars,' Snow said. Andre barked a sharp laugh. Prince simply grimaced.

'Last time we spoke of the Templars, you said you disliked the idea. "What could an officer learn in a classroom she couldn't learn on the field?" you said.'

'And I was wrong,' Snow said. She held her hands out to Prince. 'I admit it. I didn't expect to find someone who spends every spare moment with their nose in a book. But now I have one, and I cannot convince myself for even a moment that I can do what Caesar would do with her.'

Prince looked levelly at her. She knew he was thinking.

'Even if you don't want to commit to the Templars,' Snow said. 'Give her to Marcus. Assign her to Caesar's staff. Even if he's resistant, you know him: she won't be there an hour before he's recommending books to her.'

Prince sighed. 'Amanda, when I return to Avalon, Marcus is going to put forth another proposal for the Templars.'

'He is?' Snow said, suddenly hopeful.

'Yes. He's revised his idea for months. Updating it for changes in resources, personnel, facilities.' Prince sat forward. 'I believe his latest plan is an autumn to spring project. September to May. Nine months.'

'I can count, sir.' Snow said with a smile.

'Can you part with her for that long?'

'Absolutely.'

Prince sat back, looking at Snow evenly.

Aristotle chuckled. 'So, General Prince,' he said, 'how many is that now?'

'How many what?' Wild asked.

'How many of your officers have formally requested the Templar Project? Colonel Snow. Captain Thunder. Commander Faro. Colonel Trumpeter. Brigadier Lily.'

'I know the list, Andre,' Prince said. He reached for the wine bottle and took a drink, lost in thought. Finally he called out. 'Officer Bellona?'

His aide-de-camp appeared a moment later, 'Sir?'

'When you were going through your apprenticeship with General Caesar, you spent some time going over the Templar Project, did you not?'

'Yes, General,' Bellona replied. 'General Caesar and Brigadier Lily considered the training Officer Saxon and I received to be a test of what was expected in the Templars.'

'Was it just the four of you?'

'No, General. Colonel Carpenter, Lieutenant Colonel Cicero, Major Archimedes; every officer was approached and interviewed at some point.'

'And do you support the Templar Project?' Prince asked.

Bellona thought for a moment. 'Yes, General, I do.'

'Do you remember Rifle Sasha from the other night?' he asked.

'Yes, and I think she would make an excellent Templar, General,' Bellona said without hesitation.

'How would you know?' Wild asked.

'I was impressed that she spoke up when General Prince prompted her at Pelican Point,' Bellona said. 'And I know General Prince was impressed with her after that late night discussion Fox brought her in for. And I, for one, am not easily impressed, sir.'

Prince smiled. 'Well, then, if only to change the topic of conversation, let's proceed under the assumption that Sasha Small is about to find herself thrown into a whole new realm of education. Before Third Regiment leaves in the morning, I want Snow to have some challenges for Sasha.'

'I have some notes for Colonel Snow I could put together,' Bellona said. 'Even if the Templars do not take off, Rifle Sasha will be well-prepared.' She turned and left the room.

'Good.' Prince looked back at the three colonels sitting down. He raised the wine bottle.

'Andre, Jeremiah, and Amanda. To the next Renaissance, and the world it will bear.'

'Hear, hear,' Wild said.

Aristotle lifted his glass. 'To the Renaissance, and those it will help.'

'To the Renaissance,' Snow said, 'and to those who hear the Renaissance calling.'

About the Author

Michael Bernabo has been creative his entire life, writing and illustrating a fantasy picture book in kindergarten, and a sixty-page epic science fiction story in middle school.

Renaissance Calling is Michael's first published book.

Michael currently lives in Minnesota, where he spends much of his time writing.

www.MichaelBernabo.com

Made in the USA
Middletown, DE
22 August 2017